THE LIBRARY OF HOLOCAUST TESTIMONIES

My Own Vineyard

To Deby
best best wishes and compliment

Miriam Akavia
ראה גם

13.4.08

The Library of Holocaust Testimonies

Editors: Antony Polonsky, Sir Martin Gilbert CBE, Aubrey Newman,
Raphael F. Scharf, Ben Helfgott MBE

Under the auspices of the Yad Vashem Committee of the Board of
Deputies of British Jews and the Centre for Holocaust Studies,
University of Leicester

My Own Vineyard

A Jewish Family in Krakow Between the Wars

MIRIAM AKAVIA

Translated from the Hebrew by Richard Flanz
Edited by Rafael F. Scharf

VALLENTINE MITCHELL
LONDON • PORTLAND, OR

First published in 2006 in Great Britain by
VALLENTINE MITCHELL
Suite 314, Premier House
112-114 Station Road
Edgware, Middlesex HA8 7BJ

and in the United States of America by
VALLENTINE MITCHELL
c/o ISBS, 920 NE 58th Avenue, Suite 300
Portland, Oregon 97213-3786

Website: www.vmbooks.com

British Library Cataloguing in Publication Data

A catalogue record has been applied for

ISBN 0 85303 519 9
ISBN 978 0 85303 519 0
ISSN 1363 3759

Library of Congress Cataloging-in-Publication Data

A catalogue record has been applied for

Originally published in Hebrew by Dvir Publishers

Printed in Great Britain by Biddles Ltd, King's Lynn, Norfolk

Contents

Foreword

Krakow! No city in Poland conjures up such deep feelings of history as does its ancient and great capital. Many of the grandest and also the gloomiest episodes in the millennium-long history of Poland were played out against the backdrop of the Wawel Castle and in view of the Vistula River. It is Krakow that is both the cradle and treasury of Polish culture. The city's university, founded by Queen Jadwiga and named for her husband, the Lithuanian Duke Jagiello, in 1348, is one of Europe's oldest seats of learning and the greatest sanctuary of Polish arts and science.

Unlike Warsaw, which was almost ravaged beyond recognition in the Second World War, the streets and spires of Krakow were hardly damaged, and its streets still radiate tradition and history. Its citizens go about their business secure in the knowledge that they are living in the most resplendent and most historic city in Poland, indeed, in one of the most impressive of all in Central Europe.

But another Krakow has gone forever – never to be resurrected. Unlike the fabled Atlantis, the material evidence of its existence is not far to seek. It is the world of Jewish Krakow – for 700 years a hothouse of Jewish creativity and spirituality. Here still stand some of the oldest synagogues in Poland and the graves of some of the greatest sages ever produced by the Jewish people. They are surrounded by dwellings that thousands of Jews once called home.

The 60,000 Jews living in Krakow in 1939 constituted 25 per cent of the total population of the city. They lived alongside Poles, but apart from them. Despite their fervent Jewish identity, in part accentuated by the antipathy of many of their neighbours, they eagerly imbibed Polish culture and immeasurably enriched it. In Krakow, unlike Warsaw or Lodz, Hassidic Jews speaking flawless Polish (as well as Yiddish) were a common feature of the landscape.

Although mainly concentrated in the Jewish district of Kazimierz (named after the great Polish king Kazimierz), on streets named after biblical heroes, Jews lived and worked in all parts of the city, and the *Hejnal Mariacki* that resonated from a trumpeter atop the tower of St Mary's Church on the Market Square stirred in them the same emotions it did in their non-Jewish townsmen.

Miriam Akavia was born and raised in inter-war Krakow and was witness to both its lights and shadows. She experienced first hand the creeping rise of anti-Semitism, and is one of a dwindling handful of survivors of the long black night that descended on the Jews of Krakow when the German hordes occupied their beloved city.

Others have compiled documentation on the destruction of Jewish Krakow, but it was Miriam who shared the evocative saga of a single family. One hesitates to say 'typical' – for that word does not do justice to the many thousands of families, each special in their own way, that were snuffed out in the unparalleled frenzy of murderous hate called the Holocaust. But certainly her compelling narrative, spanning several generations, provides unique insight into the lives of her forebears, family and friends. A gifted writer, Miriam tells her story with the touching sensitivity and perception that only one who lived through it could. Her words are passionate, at times nostalgic, but not bitter. Miriam's book is a soulful tribute to the tens of thousands of Jews, rich and poor, educated and simple, spiritual and secular, who met an end more horrible than we can imagine.

Among Miriam's neighbours in her home on Lobzowska Street were my great-uncle Benjamin Hirsz Bilgoraj – brother of my grandfather – his wife, Hencia, and their two teenage daughters, Lucia and Fela, who actually appear in the story. I never knew any of these close relatives – they were murdered in the Shoah, together with the other Jews of Krakow. I am, therefore, especially grateful to Miriam for introducing me to my own family.

May *My Own Vineyard* keep alive their memory, and that of all the Jews of Krakow, and may those memories be a blessing.

Laurence Weinbaum
Jerusalem, 2006

The Library of Holocaust Testimonies

Ten years have passed since Frank Cass launched his Library of Holocaust Testimonies. It was greatly to his credit that this was done, and even more remarkable that it has continued and flourished. The memoirs of each survivor throw new light and cast new perspectives on the fate of the Jews of Europe during the Holocaust. No voice is too small or humble to be heard, no story so familiar that it fails to tell the reader something new, something hitherto unnoticed, something previously unknown.

Each new memoir adds to our knowledge not only of the Holocaust, but also of many aspects of the human condition that are universal and timeless: the power of evil and the courage of the oppressed; the cruelty of the bystanders and the heroism of those who sought to help, despite the risks; the part played by family and community; the question of who knew what and when; the responsibility of the wider world for the destructive behaviour of tyrants and their henchmen.

Fifty memoirs are already in print in the Library of Holocaust Testimonies, and several more are being published each year. In this way anyone interested in the Holocaust will be able to draw upon a rich seam of eyewitness accounts. They can also use another Vallentine Mitchell publication, the multi-volume *Holocaust Memoir Digest*, edited by Esther Goldberg, to explore the contents of survivor memoirs in a way that makes them particularly accessible to teachers and students alike.

Sir Martin Gilbert
London, April 2005

Preface

This is the story of a single family, and, in a sense, of an entire minority population. It tells not of famous people but of ordinary people, as were most of the Jews who lived in Krakow before the Second World War.

The tale of the Jews of Krakow is similar to that of Jews who lived in other parts of Poland, yet not in every way. The life of Jews in Krakow was different to that of those who lived in the capital, Warsaw, and of course very different from that lived by Jews in other cities, towns and villages.

The characters described in this book live their lives in a complex, mixed and changing reality, facing large problems and small: the temptation to assimilate, religion and secular life, Zionism, earning a livelihood, raising children, death.

History, memory and imagination are interwoven in this narrative. With regard to the historical background, I am indebted to Dr Shlomo Netzer of Tel Aviv University and to Mrs Pnina Meislish of Bar Ilan University for reading the manuscript and commenting on it.

My memories were the 'raw material' on which I based the plot and the characters. When my loved ones were taken to be exterminated I was very young, and my childhood memories would not have sufficed had it not been for the help of those relatives of mine who survived: my uncle Moshe Plessner, my sister Leah Shinar, and my relatives in the Carmel family at Kibbutz Beit-Zera. To all these I extend my thanks.

In making connections between historical facts and memories, I have used my imagination.

Miriam Akavia
January 2006

PART I

Parents as Children
(1909–19)

1 A Death in the Family

The children stood huddled together around the big cooking-stove in the kitchen of the apartment in Paulinska Street. On the other side of the door their mother lay in bed. Their father and the doctor were in the room with her. This time the doctor had stayed longer than usual, and the children sensed that the situation was very bad. She had been lying there like this for weeks, barely eating, and fading away before their eyes.

During the last few days their father hadn't left her bedside. He had stopped attending to business, coming home from synagogue in the mornings as soon as the service was over, to sit there for hours on end, his calm, strong hand holding her thin frail one.

The children had become quiet, walking on tiptoe, speaking in gestures like deaf-mutes, so as not to disturb. Through the half-open door they could see their mother's hand resting in their father's. They saw how sometimes the mother's pain grew so bad that she would put a pillow over her mouth to stifle her scream.

The children believed in their father's power. The touch of his hand would surely radiate life and healing into her. He would share his health with her, give her some of his, give her powers which would help her to get well ...

The door of the room opened. The children tensed, ready do anything their father might tell them to. He turned to Mattel, the eldest girl, and asked her to place a wet towel on their mother's forehead. She moved off at once. Her sisters also wanted to do something; they each took a step forward, their eyes on their father's face. No need, he said to them wordlessly. There's nothing to be done.

Mattel, whom everyone except Father called Mania, was

quick, nimble, and very organized. She was already beside her mother's bed, holding two towels, one wet, the other dry. She placed the wet towel on her mother's feverish forehead, and the dry one on top of it. Her mother looked at her with gratitude and love, but immediately closed her eyes. The pain increased. She moaned and whispered something. Mania put her ear to her mouth.

'Look after the children, Maniusia,' the sick mother whispered. 'They're so little, my poor children ... And your father ... Oh, my God ...'

Mania caressed her mother's frail hand and stifled her tears. 'Everything will be all right, Mother. Rest. Sleep. Don't worry about us ...'

In the meantime, the father paid the doctor his fee, received a prescription for a sedative, and accompanied him to the door. There they exchanged some words. The father's bearded face looked very worried, almost desperate, even though his behavior was restrained. The doctor looked worried too.

'You put your hope in me, but there's little I can do,' he said candidly.

'We're willing to pay double ... I'll give all I have ...' said the father.

The doctor shook his head, as if to say: all the money in the world won't help.

He packed his small medical bag and went, leaving the father and the eight huddled children aware that he would not be able to delay the inevitable.

When the doctor had gone the father went up to the middle son, Hesiek, and sent him to get the medicine. The boy took the prescription and darted off. He returned from his errand very quickly. Mania was still sitting by the mother's bed. The father and Menashe, the eldest son, were preparing themselves for the *Mincha*[1] prayer.

Hesiek came into the kitchen. His four sisters and little Haim looked up at him as he advanced towards them. The two 'big' girls looked at him suspiciously, but Hela, Mania and Haim rushed to him.

4

'See what I've brought!' Hesiek whispered.

'Raisins and almonds!' Little Hela's mouth watered, and happiness spread over her face.

Haimke stood beside her, all anticipation, his eyes raised to his brother, who stood about four heads taller than himself. Hesiek brought out the bag, emptied his pockets of the few nuts that had spilled out, and corrected his sister.

'Nuts and almonds. All toasted, hot and very fresh. There weren't any raisins at the stall by the toasting-stove. Only chestnuts, but I didn't have enough money ...'

'What ideas he's got, this fellow!' Rozia muttered through her teeth, looking at him contemptuously. 'Mother's dying, and he's thinking about chestnuts. And how is it, my adored brother, that you don't have money?'

'Money doesn't grow on trees,' he said curtly.

'What do you mean, really?' Rozia scoffed.

'I've got no money left,' the boy said, ignoring his sister's comment. 'Don't worry, I'll get more ...' he added.

Meanwhile the little ones had wasted no time filling their mouths with nuts and almonds. The pile was getting smaller. Sala, the second of the bigger girls, came up to the little ones and said, 'Leave me some.' The little ones gave her some from their portions. Haim divided his diminished portion in two. 'I'll keep some for later,' he said. Rozia, who had calmed down in the meantime, turned to him. 'What do you mean you'll keep some for later? Give me some. Aren't I to have any?'

Haim was disappointed. Why had he divided up his portion? They could have given Rozia some out of the common pile. But what could he say to her?

'Here,' he said, as if he didn't mind at all giving her the 'smaller half'. Hesiek beamed, rubbing his hands together with pleasure. Then he went into his mother's room with the medicine.

He hurried reverently to her bedside and stood still. She lay there quietly, young and beautiful. She smiled weakly at him. Suddenly, he felt tears rising, and a lump in his throat. He so wanted her to stay, not to go, not to leave them. There were so many things he still wanted to hear her say. Or at least a word, just one word, some blessing he could store in his heart for ever.

But she was already far away. Her smile was frozen on her face, and Hesiek knew that she couldn't see him any more. Mania took the medicine from him. The brother and sister exchanged glances.

Just then their father returned from prayers to his vigil by the bedside. They went to the next room.

Early in the morning the father sent off for the doctor. When he arrived, there was nothing for him to do but to certify her death. The children made themselves scarce, so as not to be noticed by their father. In a whisper, but firmly, Mania oversaw the daily chores – the making of the beds, the dressing. She demanded that they all wash themselves properly and brush their hair, taking into her hands the command of the house and the care of the children.

The next day they buried their mother in the old cemetery in Krakow, near Plaszow, and the father recited *Kaddish*[2] over the open grave. The girls remained at home, because it was not customary in Krakow for women to go to the cemetery.

The apartment filled up with relatives and neighbors, who came with condolences for the mourners. All of them held back tears at the sight of the young orphans, who were all clean and neatly dressed, quiet and restrained. They stood in a group around their big sister Mania.

Mania's face displayed serenity, a serenity such as that reflected in the faces of pious *tzaddikim*.[3]

An atmosphere of bereavement enveloped the home. Though they did not understand what the future held for them, the children felt a sense of helplessness. Even the apartment suddenly became too cramped. They found themselves bumping into each other, even though they tried to keep out of each other's way. There were three spacious rooms and a kitchen, itself as large as a spacious room. Another two little rooms were not for the family's use: one was intended for a maid, and the other was a storeroom.

One of the three large rooms was the parent's bedroom. Now, after their mother's death, only their father went in there. The door which led into it, which had also been locked in the past, had not yet been opened.

Another room, the largest, served as a dining room. A large table stood in the middle, with ten chairs around it. In this room there was one single bed, and a narrow *chaise-longue*, upholstered with light brown velvet. These two sleeping places served the three boys. Some nights Menashe, the eldest, and Haim, the youngest, slept together in the bed, and Hesiek would arrange himself on the narrow *chaise-longue*. Other nights Menashe would take the *chaise-longue* first, leaving Hesiek with no alternative but to get into Haim's bed, which was already warm from the little boy's body. Sometimes Menashe and Hesiek would quarrel over the right to sleep on the *chaise-longue*, and it was difficult to tell if sleeping alone on that narrow bed was a prize or a punishment for them.

'Hershel, tonight you sleep on the *chaise-longue*. I'll sleep in the bed with Haim,' Menashe said one evening. He was a reserved boy, who rarely spoke; his features were delicate, and he had blue eyes.

'No, no,' said Hesiek, who also had blue eyes. 'It's your place, Menashe. I know you prefer to sleep alone, and I really don't mind...'

'A great treat, to sleep alone on that narrow thing,' Menashe said, and slipped under the blanket into Haim's bed, taking care not to touch his little brother or to pull the blanket off him. And Hesiek didn't know if Menashe really preferred to sleep in the bed with Haim, or if he was pretending, and giving up the *chaise-longue* to him. Either way, Hesiek was happy to have the opportunity of sleeping alone.

In the third room, the five girls slept in three beds. Mania with little Hania, side by side; Sala with Hela, one girl's head by the other's feet; and Rozia alone on a folding bed. That night, the first after their mother's death, each of the girls lay sunk in her own thoughts. Mania felt a need to be close to someone, and she hugged her little sister, who, shivering and curled up, pressed herself to her. Mania caressed the little child's soft hair, and whispered into her ear.

7

'Don't worry, Hannale. I'll look after you. You'll have everything you need ...'

'But I won't have a mother any more,' the little one mumbled. 'I'll always be an orphan. When people see me, they'll think "Poor orphan girl!" And I so wanted Mother to get better and go on living with us! And I wanted Father not to be so serious and worried, and everybody to be happy ...'

'Hush, hush,' Mania, 16 years old, tried to soothe her. 'Everything will be all right, you'll see. I'll take charge of things. I'll take care of the shopping and the washing. Roh'cze the cook will go on cooking for us ...' 'But she always cooks the same thing, soup with noodles, and noodles with soup ...' The little girl's voice shook with suppressed sobbing. 'Hush now, Haniusia.' She tried to calm her again. 'I'll make sure Roh'cze changes the menu. Everything will be all right, you'll see.' 'But you're still just a girl yourself. That's what all the aunts say. You still have to go to school too ...' Hania was speaking slowly now, on the verge of sleep. 'Sleep now, sleep,' Mania whispered gently. 'God will help us.' And to herself she silently repeated the *Sh'ma*[4] prayer.

In the other bed Sala and Hela had not said much to each other this evening.

'Take some more of the blanket, Heluniu,' whispered Sala. 'You're not covered at all.'

'Yes, I am,' said Hela, and fell silent again. A few minutes later she spoke again. 'What'll happen to us now?' There was no answer. 'You hear me, Sala?' 'Yes, my dear.'

'Do you think I'll ever be able to travel abroad? To London, Paris, Vienna? To wear fine clothes? And visit galleries, and museums?' 'Why are you asking such questions today? We're in mourning now. Mother left us only today ...' Sala said, and immediately felt remorse: had she hurt her 13-year-old sister's feelings? She decided to speak again. 'Let's hope you will be able to travel abroad when you're big. And that you'll be able to wear fine clothes ...' 'I'll learn a lot of languages,' Hela said dreamily. 'Of course you will.' 'And I will visit lots of interesting places ...' 'Can't you two be quiet?' Rozia's voice came from the folding-bed. 'Chattering away and not letting a person sleep!'

Sala and Hela stopped talking. But Rozia, instead of going to sleep, sat up in bed, clasped her knees in her arms, and started talking herself.

'What kind of a life did our mother have? I say she had a miserable life ...'

Sala and Hela froze. Little Hania had fallen asleep in the meantime. 'Mother never complained,' Mania said quietly. 'She never complained?' Rozia scoffed. 'In this house we have a tendency to be martyrs. Well, I don't want to be one. Our mother got married at 18, without knowing our father before that, and then she gave birth almost every year. I don't want that kind of life. No, thank you! I'll learn a profession, I'll earn my own living and I won't be dependent on anyone. Nobody's going to tell me what to do. I'd rather not marry than be a submissive wife, who's resigned to everything, and whose only rights are to bear children and to fulfill her husband's demands ...'

Rozia's words filled the air like arrows looking for targets. Her strong tone found its way to the hearts of her sisters. All of them sat up in bed without saying a word. Hela thought that Rozia was right but didn't dare to say anything. Deep in her heart she too dreamed of a prince on a white horse who would come and ask for her hand and whose love she would return. But the thought of what Father would say troubled her.

'You don't know what life's like yet,' said Sala. 'None of us do. Father keeps us so sheltered ...' 'Girls,' said Mania forcefully. 'Please be quiet. Rozia, you complained they weren't letting you sleep, and now you're disturbing Hania. Have pity on her. It's time to sleep.'

Sala and Hela slipped under their blanket again. Rozia took a deep breath, and then slowly exhaled, in a loud and prolonged moan. Then she curled up under her blanket and did not speak any more. Sala and Hela both changed their positions and their bed creaked faintly. Long shadows fell on the walls, swaying gently to the rhythm of Hania's regular breathing. A thin beam of light penetrated through the crack in the door.

'Good night, girls.' Mania's voice seemed to have come

from distant worlds. 'Good night, Maniusia,' they replied one after the other.

In the dining room the old argument repeated itself. 'Tonight I'll sleep on the *chaise-longue*,' said Menashe. 'But last night you said you prefer to sleep in the bed with Haim. I'll sleep on the *chaise-longue*, I really don't mind.' Hesiek was confused, because he still didn't know what his brother really preferred.

'Don't you know that I like to sleep by myself?' 'So why did you say yesterday that you can't sleep on that narrow *chaise-longue*, because you feel cramped there?' 'Yesterday was yesterday and today's today,' Menashe replied, in a Hassidic sing-song. 'You're making fun of me!' Hesiek complained. 'God forbid!' said Menashe. 'How can I make fun of you when you make fun of everybody?' 'I make fun?' Hesiek asked, getting carefully into the bed so as not to wake Haim.

'Let's sleep now. Father wants us up early tomorrow. We have to get up at five in the morning.'

Menashe lay down on the *chaise-longue*. 'I have to leave home quickly,' he thought. 'Find a way to make a living, maybe a good wife, become independent. Not enough room for me here.'

Hesiek thought of the heavy burden his father had to bear now. 'I must help him as quickly as possible … the girls … featherbrains, they don't understand a thing. I'll help in earning a living. Tomorrow I'll speak to Father.'

It was quiet in the house. One after the other the children fell asleep. In the third room their father sat beside his work bench. The bed in which for 15 years he had found pleasure and warmth was empty now, cold and frightening.

*   *   *

Moshe Weinfeld had come to Krakow from a place beyond the Carpathian Mountains. Where he came from everyone spoke Hungarian, and the Jews also spoke Yiddish. He was 18 when he set out with his brother for a new place in which to settle. Their parents had died when they were younger, during a grave epidemic.

He had heard about the Krakow community long before. It was one of the oldest Jewish communities in eastern Europe, dating back to the fourteenth century. It had known many bad periods; the Jews being a scapegoat in times of crisis in the lands where they settled. Poland itself had known crises, and foreign invasions. The invaders, whether Tatars or Swedes, Russians or Prussians, always found their way first to the Jewish quarter and killed indiscriminately. Only after this did they seek their victims in other quarters. When the invaders retreated, the Jews were accused of treason, and a wild Polish mob would assault the depleted Jewish quarter, to loot, plunder and murder what the invaders had left. The authorities and the police generally arrived too late to enforce order.

The Jews of Krakow had always had difficulties with their livelihood, because of the heavy taxes the authorities imposed on them, especially on the kosher slaughtering, and also because of the community tax. Sources of livelihood were few, limited to the few branches of manufacture and commerce that were allowed by law, such as land-leasing, work in wine factories and taverns. Here too, difficulties were piled upon difficulties; there was, for example, the prohibition against the employment of non-Jews in Jewish businesses. No wonder, therefore, that entire families converted to Christianity in order to improve their economic situation and their social standing. The gentile society was willing to stop degrading the Jews on condition that the Jews adapted to the Polish society within which they lived. Hence the danger of assimilation was great, and the leaders of the community struggled against it constantly.

Krakow, which had been the historic capital of Poland, was famous for its rabbis and sages. Among them were the famous Ram'a (Rabbi Moshe Iserlis) in the fifteenth century, one of the great pronouncers on the precepts, compiler of the *Mapah* to the *Shulhan Arukh*, the authoritative codification of Jewish observances. Of him, as of the Ramba'm (Rabbi Moses Maimonides), it was said 'From Moshe to Moshe there has not risen one like unto Moshe ...' Jewish Krakow had also been blessed with many scholars of the wisdom of Israel, and with authors who wrote both in Hebrew and in other languages, with famous doctors who brought healing to gentiles too, with lawyers and advisers who helped in the administration of matters of state and in the courts of the kings.

Many of Krakow's non-Jewish inhabitants worked in the sciences and the arts, which gave the whole city a unique character. In previous centuries the kings of Poland had lived there, in the magnificent Wawel Palace, and there their tombs remained even after the capital moved to Warsaw. The beautiful palace, on the banks of the Vistula, contains the treasures of the Polish kings, a memorial of days gone by, tales of heroism, history and folklore.

The kings of Poland took the Jews under their protection, and as a sign of gratitude the Jews served them faithfully and put their brains at their service, especially in financial matters. The history of the Jews is essentially linked to King Kazimierz, who reigned in Poland in the seventeenth century. King Kazimierz had been angry at the Jews of Poznan and Krakow for having, so it seemed, shown too much friendship to the Swedish conquerors, and had even threatened them with harsh decrees. But afterwards this king showed great humanity towards the Jews. He understood that it was impossible to expect of them a higher degree of patriotism than that of the Polish nobles, who had themselves flocked to the side of the Swedish conquerors. The Jewish community had suffered heavy pogroms during the Swedish conquest, and the good king sympathized with their troubles. In 1665 he published a writ of rights for the Jews of Krakow, to help them to survive and to take part in commerce.

The Jewish quarter in Krakow, 'Kazimierz', was named after this king. Only Jews lived in Kazimierz; the only Christians in the quarter were the house-watchmen.

The two brothers crossed the Carpathian Mountains, making most of their way on foot. At one stage of their travels, the elder brother separated from the younger and settled down in a mountain village in Slovakia.

Moshe continued until he reached Galicia. The city of Krakow attracted him with its beauty, its history and its

Jewish community. But it was not easy for a penniless Jewish youngster to make his way in the city.

He had come to Poland bearing letters of recommendation from famous scholars in the city of his birth. On arrival, he went to the village of Chszanow, which adjoined Krakow. Here, on seeing the recommendations he carried, the Jews directed him to Reb Leibush, a known hassid and a man of great wealth, who managed extensive timber concerns throughout the country. Reb Leibush, who always wore the traditional Jewish black *capota*,[5] and had a beard and sidecurls, bought and sold entire villages and forests, and supplied building timber to the authorities, institutions and private individuals. This man took young Moshe into his employ, and found in him a good and loyal assistant. The matchmaker too did a fine job, matching him with the daughter of one of the established, wealthy and highly esteemed families in Krakow.

The bride's name was Rela Carmel. One may well ask, where did Galician Jews in former centuries come by the name Carmel? The threads of logic lead, of course, to the range of mountains in the land of the fathers. A different interpretation, which connects the name to the 'Carmelites' and to the possible migrations of forced converts from Spain through France to Galicia,was not acceptable to the members of the Carmel family in Krakow.

Rela and Moshe set up their home in Kazimierz, in the apartment house in Paulinska Street. The young woman was a good housewife, and endowed the home with an atmosphere of happiness, warmth and calm; a constant sanctuary from the troubles of working life.

The children came into the world one after the other. Rela, the mother, began to weaken under the burden of housework and looking after the children, and the burden of earning a livelihood borne by Moshe was no lighter. Nevertheless, her husband enabled her to employ a Jewish housemaid and cook, and himself tried to make things easier for her as much as he could.

Moshe would rise early and wash his body in ice-cold water, even when the temperature reached 20 degrees below zero. By this he intended to clean his body, but also to purify his soul from any evils or sins he had committed, even unknowingly, against God or other humans. He never pitied himself, never ate to satiety, loved cleanliness and order, flowers and nature.

What he demanded of himself he also demanded of his children. He inspected their ears and their fingernails, and insisted on neat dress and appearance.

As the children grew, the problems increased. The girls grew like princesses, or the daughters of nobles. Mania, the eldest, was the only one who knew Yiddish. The others all spoke Polish even when their father spoke to them in Yiddish.

New winds were blowing in from Western Europe. Krakow at the time was under the rule of the Austrian Habsburg monarchy, and the Jews liked the old Kaiser. The girls, in particular, were taken up in the spirit of the time; they were well versed in the history of the Western nations, in the literature that called for emancipation and freedom, and were willing to lend a hand to these changes.

Now, with the death of his wife Rela, Moshe was profoundly worried. The burden of caring for eight little children was more than one man could bear. From now on, he alone had the responsibility for their livelihood, their health, their upbringing and education, and he had to keep them safe from the evil influences that lurked on all sides.

During the *shiv'a*, the seven days of mourning, many people had visited the apartment, among them uncles and aunts, and their sons and daughters. The front door of the apartment had remained half open all the time, and the visitors came and went without ringing or knocking, and without saying 'hello' or 'goodbye' on arrival or departure.

Menashe and Hesiek sat with their father in his room, reciting prayers and learning chapters of Talmud, for the elevation of the soul of the departed. The men among the visitors would join them, and from time to time a *minyan*[6] was formed, and three times a day *Kaddish* was said.

The four bigger girls, Mania, Rozia, Sala and Hela, sat in the dining room and spoke with the women who had come to condole them. Little Haim and Hania wandered, bored, among the rooms, looking about them, and finally settled in the kitchen. Here a gay fire burned in the stove, slowly consuming the firewood and charcoal that Roh'cze the cook kept adding. Here it was warm and pleasant. Roh'cze stood bent over a basin of water, washing the endless glasses and plates that kept arriving from the dining room.

Haim and Hania felt relaxed here and started running around the kitchen table.

'Get out of here,' Roh'cze scolded, without straightening her back.

'We won't, we won't,' Hania teased her. 'It's our kitchen, not yours …'

'I'll get a stick and chase you out …' Roh'cze wiped her hands on her apron.

'Who's scared of you?' Hania retorted cheekily.

Roh'cze was a heavily-built woman, with large, callused hands. No one knew anything about her past, apart from the fact that disasters had dogged her since her childhood. She could not read or write, and had neither mother nor father. Her body was covered with scars and various 'souvenirs' of what other people had done to her. Sala and Hela knew something about these 'souvenirs', but refused to talk about what they knew.

Her soul, though unhappy, was good. Instead of chasing them out as she had threatened, she put a plate in front of them, with remains of cake on it.

'Good Roh'cze, good Roh'cze!' Haim felt a need to give the miserable woman some pleasure.

'Are you here?' Mania came into the kitchen, followed by Aunt Matilda, their late mother's sister, who had arrived from Berlin. The three already in the kitchen fell silent.

'Say goodbye nicely to Auntie,' said Mania. 'She's going back to Berlin soon.'

Aunt Matilda approached the children. She was tall and slender, dressed in the best of Berlin fashion, which suited her fine figure.

Earlier, in the dining room, she had told the women seated

there how difficult and how moving it was for her to return to the world of her childhood, which she had left so many years before. Krakow now looked to her like a provincial town, she said, and could not be compared with Berlin, the third largest city in Europe. How small and narrow the streets of Krakow were compared to the long broad streets of Berlin. And the Jews of Berlin were completely different to the Jews here, who, she added, looked so strange to her, even ridiculous … as if they lived on a different planet. Isolated, differentiated, uninvolved in their environment.

'And how is it in Berlin?' the others asked her. 'A Jew is a Jew wherever he is, isn't he?'

'Oh, no,' said Aunt Matilda, and explained that the Jews of Berlin were completely different to the Jews of Galicia.

At the same time it was evident that Aunt Matilda felt herself a stranger in Berlin, a foreigner among the Berliners.

'Maybe because I miss my family,' she said. 'I so wanted my sister Rela to visit me in Berlin once. She didn't have time. She was always busy with the children, giving birth, and what for? To bring eight children into the world and to leave them? What's going to become of them? Life is full of difficulties, and these orphans will be helpless, like little leaves forcibly separated from the mother branch.' She wiped tears from her face.

'Is Auntie going back to Berlin?' Hania dared to ask, as they stood in the kitchen beside the door.

'Yes, my dear, right after the *shiv'a*.' Aunt Matilda's eyes were moist. 'When you grow up, come and visit us in Berlin.'

She bent down to kiss Hania and then Haim. The boy wound his arms around her neck. He must have got confused. She was so like his mother.

Sala thrust her head into the kitchen. 'Aunt Rohele Kovner has come!' she announced.

Some of the children stayed with Aunt Matilda and others went to greet Aunt Rohele.

'And where's Aunt Idess?' everyone asked Rohele, for they were used to seeing the two aunts together.

'Sick with the 'flu,' said Aunt Rohele Kovner. 'Idess apolo-

16

gizes and sends her condolences.'

Aunt Rohele came from the city of Kovno in Lithuania. This was why everyone called her Aunt Rohele Kovner.

On her head Aunt Rohele wore an impressive wig, platinum blonde in color, its plentifuls curls held together with pins. In appearance she was completely different to Aunt Matilda. She spoke fluent Yiddish and often told of her birthplace, Kovno, where there was a large concentration of religious Jews, many *yeshivot*,[7] newspapers in Yiddish – in fact a vibrant Jewish world. In contrast to Aunt Matilda, Aunt Rohele thought that Krakow was a large and progressive city. The Jews of Krakow, Aunt Rohele said decisively, were assimilationists compared with the Jews of Kovno, who were much more deeply rooted in their Judaism.

From the moment Aunt Rohele came into the room, she became the center of attention. Bubbling over with news, she spoke in a somewhat hoarse voice about politics and business. She had a sharp mind and a quick tongue, and everyone, including the men, respected her. From time to time she got up and peered into the room where the men were now starting to gather for a *minyan*.

In the meantime the doorbell rang, and in the doorway appeared Bronka. Bronka came into the room and Hania leaped up and ran to her, hugging her happily.

'I'm glad you came!' said Hania. Bronka curtsied to all the aunts, slightly raising her blue finely-pleated skirt.

The two girls found themselves a quiet place by the open window. They stood there, their backs to the room, looking out. Hania's black hair with its 'pony-tail' and Bronka's fair hair with its 'ear-locks' made of plaits rolled up into 'snails' over her ears, blended into a single mass, half black, half golden.

Under the window in the narrow street walked bearded Jews in black *capotas* and younger men, their sidecurls swaying. The street was noisy, active and colorful.

'Look there,' said Hania to her friend. 'Do you know that only a few streets away from here there's a different world? Look, even from here we can see the golden domes of the churches and the turrets of the ancient fortresses.'

The calming peal of a church bell came from that direction. A gentle breeze caressed the faces of the children at the window.

'Yes,' said Bronka. 'I know. I've been there, and I've seen it. I saw the Wawel Palace of the Kings, on the banks of the Vistula. It's very close to here. I also know the big market square, the Sukiennica,[8] and Florian's Gate.'

In the room where the men were, the evening prayer had concluded, and Hesiek came into the dining room. His sidecurls were nicely tucked away behind his ears and the ends of his fringes showed beneath his shirt. He glanced at the girls looking out of the window. Then he came up to them quietly and spoke to his sister.

'Hannale, the hem of your dress is undone.'

The girls turned their heads at once, sharply. Hania, ashamed and anxious, looked for the tear in the hem.

'Relax, Hannale, there's nothing wrong with your dress,' said Hesiek. 'I just wanted to see your friend's face.'

'You're crazy!' Hania said, angry.

Bronka blushed to the roots of her hair, and lowered her big blue eyes to stare at the floor.

'Do you want five stones?'[9] Hesiek tried to appease them.

'Go to hell, you and your stones!' Hania muttered angrily.

Hesiek turned to go.

'All right, give us them,' Hania whispered.

A glee flashed in his eyes. Happily, he gave them the stones and left the room.

Saying nothing, the girls sat down on the strip of carpet under the window and started playing. Hesiek went back to his place in his father's room.

During the *shiv'a* when the dining room was always full of people, Menashe and Hesiek slept in their father's room, and little Haim slept in the girl's room.

Hesiek had not spoken with his father yet about his wishes to help in earning a living. The seven days of mourning were not suitable for such conversation. He was full of ideas and energy to do something, eager to start working, and he counted the days.

2 Bronka

Bronka was her parents' eldest child, and she had three brothers. They lived in Kazimierz in Zisser House in Krakowska Street. Zisser House was a well-known building with a large enclosed courtyard inside four blocks of houses which belonged to a wealthy Jew by the name of Zisser.

In the same house at street level, her parents had a shop where they sold knitting requirements and embroidery threads, and in another street – Rabbi Maisels Street – they had a large storeroom, where they kept their stock of wool and other merchandise.

Bronka's father, Reb Aharon Plessner, was a handsome man, who had gained a reputation as a brilliant scholar highly versed in the Talmud. He absorbed himself wholly in his studies and his reading, and even wrote in the holy tongue. The business was run by her mother, Sheva, née Freilich; her time was taken up in business and his was taken up in the torah. The three little brothers had no one to turn to for anything except 'big' Bronka. She helped them dress and undress, took them walking around the 'Planty' gardens, which encircled the city, or to the Atlantic Cinema when there was a comedy with the funny pair Flip and Flap, or with the even funnier Pat and Pataszon.

Bronka's mother was beautiful and elegant, and lived beyond the norms accepted in those days. The world of a good woman then, even in non-Jewish circles, which were thought to be more advanced, consisted of *Küche, Kirche, Kinder* (kitchen, church, children) – in short, the three Ks, with the first place going to the *Küche*.

Sheva didn't like the kitchen nor their cramped apartment, which was always in a mess and where the children ran about noisily, often quarreling with each other and crying.

She had given birth in pain and suffering, with each birth her body was torn afresh, and she often felt that she would never again be the strong healthy woman she had once been. When her first son Wowek, a bright and alert infant, started walking, venturing even, into the long corridor outside their apartment, he still looked for his mother whenever he felt hungry, pressing himself to her delicate body, pinching her with all his might and crying piteously, not appeased until she brought out her breast.

And so, while she was still suckling her first child, she didn't notice at first that a new life was growing within her. Everything repeated itself: the sickness, the dizziness, hard months of pregnancy, and the birth tearing her body apart. And when it all began again for the fourth time, all in the space of six years, she bore her fate with only partial reconciliation.

Fortunately for her, she had borne healthy, good-looking children she could be proud of, and her eldest daughter, Bronka, was a great help to her from her fourth or fifth year on.

The father, Aharon, would leave the house in the mornings to go to synagogue for the morning prayers. Religious worship and matters of livelihood filled his world. She remained at home, with no one to turn to for advice. The children's beds reeked with the sharp stench of urine and they would come back dirty from the yard, their noses dripping and their fingernails filthy.

Laundry for such a family involved such hard work: in the single faucet in the kitchen there ran only cold water. Water had to be boiled on the cooking stove, then transferred into a huge wooden tub, which stood on two stools in the middle of the kitchen. Then all the sheets, blanket-covers, towels, underwear and socks had to be soaped and scrubbed, the water changed, the whole wash rinsed, wrung, and carried up to the attic to dry. The kitchen was hot as a Turkish Bath, and outside it was freezing cold. The woman who came to help with the laundry demanded food three times a day, and the children were ill most of the time.

In the meantime, Reb Aharon had acquired the shop downstairs, and Sheva began going down there more frequently. *Heder* was a good solution for the busy parents, and the three sons started going there from the age of three. Bronka was the only one who went to a 'real' school: She entered the First Grade in the Austrian girls' school.

Sheva proved her ability in the shop which, due to her initiative, became an unfailing source of income.

When Bronka started going to school and the boys to *heder*, most of the tension was concentrated in the mornings. Reb Aharon would get up first, dress himself meticulously, and leave for the synagogue. The others crowded around the only sink, in the kitchen, to wet the tips of their fingers and the corners of their eyes in ice-cold water, and then get dressed, the older ones helping the younger ones. To brush their teeth, each would receive half a glass of lukewarm water. Bronka felt it very important to be clean and tidy when she went to school, so as not to give anyone an excuse to call her 'Dirty Jewess'.

'I can't tie my shoelace,'wailed Szajek.

Bronka immediately stopped what she was doing and tied the lace for him.

'I've lost a button off my shirt,' cried little Muniusz. 'My shirt's open, they'll laugh at me ...'

'Put your *tzitzioth* over your shirt, and no one will notice,' said Bronka, solving the problem for him. The oblong cloth with a hole for the head and the ritual fringes at its corners would indeed cover the shirt-front.

Wowek, who had already acquired a reputation as an 'absent-minded professor', was looking for his *siddur*, the prayer-book that also provided texts for study in the heder.

'Who took my *siddur*? Has anyone seen it? Help me look for it! Bronka, help me ...'

'Get off my back, please,' Bronka pleaded, while looking feverishly for the *siddur*. 'It's already late, and I still have to get ready for school.'

It was like that every morning. Sheva would make a hot drink for everyone, in the kitchen. They would all grab a slice of bread with something on it, whatever was available, and go off. Sheva hurried to the shop, where buyers were already waiting for her, and, afterwards, her assistants. The apartment remained as it was left, with everything upside-down, clean and dirty clothes tossed together in corners, while in the kitchen the unwashed dishes piled up.

Then help came, from Sheva's stepmother – whom the children simply called 'Grandmother' – and her daughter Fela. The two women tried to be in the apartment during the noon hours, to receive the children when they came home from their studies. Fela was disgusted by the neglect in her elder sister's home, and was very critical of her. Each time she came into her sister's home and the sharp smell of ammonia struck her nostrils once more, she would hiss between her teeth: 'What an apartment! How can anyone live like this?'

And then, after a string of oaths, she would roll up her sleeves and start work. Her mother busied herself in the kitchen, cooking a meal for the family.

Bronka liked school. It was a tri-national school for girls: the administration was Austrian, the teachers were Polish, and the pupils Jewish. In class, Bronka forgot all about the difficulties at home, and about her brothers, and concentrated her attention on the Polish teacher, Pani Zegartowska. The authorities had made the study of German compulsory, but the language in which everything was taught was Polish, and Pani Zegartowska knew how to introduce into her lessons a large dose of patriotic feeling for conquered Poland, which was then divided up among three powers. The Jewish girls were infected by their teacher's enthusiasm, and eagerly learned the songs in which Polish poets called for freedom and independence: 'Arise, Poland, break your chains ...'

Every morning in class they would sing the Austrian national anthem, and after that, since the daring song by the famous Polish poetess Maria Konopnicka had been banned, Pani Zegartowska taught them another song, nominally a religious one:

God, who hast preserved Poland for generations on end,
In heroic resplendence and glorious blaze –
Thou, who from so many disasters hast protected our land,
Upon Thy altar a prayer we raise:

Lord of the world, hear our plea
Give us back Poland, give us back our liberty!

The last line – 'Give us back Poland, give us back our liberty!'
– was sung with the strongest stress. Bronka's clear voice
could be heard distinctly, and one could sense that she identified with the words. Pani Zegartowska decided that Bronka's
musical talents should be developed.

'Ask one of your parents to come to me and I'll explain that
it's worthwhile to make it for you to study music and voice
development.'

Bronka was delighted, but only for a moment. On further
thought she knew very well that her parents wouldn't let her
study music. Her busy mother wouldn't find the time or have
any interest in hearing the teacher's suggestion, and her father
– how could he come here, among so many women and girls,
a religious Jew like him? It was hopeless, all hopeless.

Bronka was grateful to her beloved teacher, but felt a
shame which she couldn't understand. Coming home, as
soon as she entered the stairwell, the enticing smell of the
midday meal reached her. Grandmother was standing in the
kitchen cooking delicacies, while her daughter Fela was busy
in the room folding the children's clothes. The brusque young
woman greeted the girl with a tart compliment: 'Here's our
beautiful princess!'

Bronka didn't respond, and tried to banish unpleasant
thoughts. She breathed in deeply, savoring the smell of the food.

'That smells good!' she said, and rubbed her empty
stomach.

'Hungry, are you? Did you eat breakfast today?' asked Fela.

Bronka was ravenous and the smell of the food made her
mouth water, but she restrained herself.

'Yes, I had something,' she said, and immediately felt she'd
made a mistake. What she should have said was 'Of course, I
had a good breakfast', for Fela jumped at anything.

'You had something. That's good too. It's very nice of your
mother to at least give you something to eat. And who made
the beds today?'

'Mother did, and I helped her,' Bronka replied, and blushed.

'That's not true!' Fela argued. 'When I arrived the beds weren't made. That's the truth. Her majesty your mother didn't have time to do them. Because she had to get all dressed up to go down to the shop in all her splendor.'

It was very unpleasant to hear such things said about Mother, even if there was some truth in them. Bronka understood Fela's feelings, but also understood her mother.

'So maybe today only we didn't have the time, the little ones nagged us so. Doesn't Mother work hard in the shop?'

Fela said nothing, but her silence was meaningful, as if to say: 'It's best if I don't answer you.'

Bronka went to the kitchen.

'Grandmother, how do you cook?' – and, without waiting for an answer – 'is there something I can lick?'

'You want everything: to know how to cook, and to lick.'

'And to study music too,' Bronka added. This was a good chance, she thought, But Grandmother ignored the comment.

'Here, take this and lick it,' she said, giving her a bowl with the remains of chocolate cream in it. 'Do it before your brothers get back from the *heder*. There isn't enough for everyone.'

The boys came home and the apartment filled with noise.

'Get out of here!' scolded Fela, who was ironing the collar of Bronka's school uniform.

'Get out, go and wash your hands!'

'Wash your hands, food's ready!' Grandmother called from the kitchen. Of course, on the way to the sink they knocked over a chair, threw some pillows, pulled the tablecloth, and quarreled with each other.

'Stop it!' Bronka placed herself between them and tried to bring them to order. 'I'll send you straight back to the *heder*! I want quiet!'

'He started it!' wailed Szajek.

'It's not true, he started,' Wowek insisted.

'Wash your hands, I said,' came Grandmother's gruff voice from the kitchen. 'The food's ready.'

When they were in the kitchen and their good grandmother had got them under control with the aid of a plate of soup, Fela said to Bronka: 'Here's your collar. Look after it till tomorrow. I just barely saved it from these little devils' hands.'

Bronka went up to her, her eyes expressing gratitude. 'If you're tired, Fela, I can take over. I already know how to iron.' She took the little iron, with the burning coals inside it, and made long movements forwards and backwards with it, creating a breeze. Through the tiny openings in the sides of the iron one could see the coals sizzling, raising little tongues of flame.

'Is there anything else to iron? The iron's still hot, look!'

'That iron! How hard I worked to get it hot! That's how it is with these irons.'

'Pity.'

'Why a pity? Nothing's a pity. Don't cry over spilt milk. It doesn't help. Come, I'll comb your hair; I'll plait it into braids and roll it into curls over your ears. The styling will last you till tomorrow.'

'Fela, you're so good, all my class will envy me tomorrow! And I was afraid to ask you, afraid you'd say: "Don't bother me, get your mother to comb you hair!"'

'Be quiet now. Enough. And if you don't want to be quiet, sing something nice.'

Bronka sat down on the chair and started singing, and Fela, armed with a comb and brush, stood over her and worked on her gentle silken hair.

In the kitchen the little ones finished their portions, while philosophizing noisily with Grandmother.

In the afternoon Bronka went down to the shop. Coils of wool in all colors filled the shelves along the walls. Under the glass counter there were shining embroidery threads, 'Molina' and 'D.M.C.', printed trimmings and other sewing articles. Mother stood behind the counter. She was a handsome woman, well-dressed, and held her head proudly under her blonde wig, which was designed according to the latest fashion. By the cash box sat her father, also impressive in appearance, with a large velveteen skullcap over his high broad brow. They didn't notice her enter; they were busy with their work. Bronka longed for some attention from her parents. If only Mother would ask: 'How was it at school? What did you learn? What did the teacher say?' Because then Bronka would have an opportunity to tell everything. But there was no chance: Mother wouldn't ask, and Father certainly wouldn't. He was meticulous and severe, and was not pleased at all that Bronka was going to that school. It would have been better had she gone to Beit Yaakov, like the other girls in Kazimierz. He did not allow Bronka to take exercise lessons, in which girls had to wear pants. As for music – why on earth music?

'Believe me, Breindl my daughter,' he had said to her once. 'All you need is a good rich husband, and of course a little luck.'

'But Father, I'm only 12,' Bronka had protested, disappointed with her father's attitude, but not daring to argue. So what was the point in talking to Father again? He hadn't changed his mind. More than five minutes had passed since she entered the shop, and they still hadn't noticed her. Other people came in, and received their attention: they asked questions and got replies. Mother was so polite to them, so patient, and Father received money so carefully, gave change, packed parcels, said 'come again'.

When the shop emptied for a moment, Bronka went up to the counter and stood close to her mother.

'Broniu.' Happiness and pride lit up her mother's face. Bronka pressed herself to her, gave herself to the embrace, sinking her head between her mother's soft breasts. A pleasant fragrance came from Mother's dress, and Bronka was happy. But these good moments were brief.

'Who's at home with the boys?' her mother asked in concern.

'They're on their own. I just came down for a little while.'

'They shouldn't forget to pray *mincha-maariv*,'[1] her father reminded her.

Customers came into the shop. Father climbed onto a ladder, brought down some parcels of wool, and Mother didn't notice her any longer. Next to the shop was a bakery, which belonged to a Jew by the name of Beigel. They baked bread, rolls and cakes, especially yeast cakes filled with cheese or cocoa. A good smell came from there. The last time she had been in the shop, her father had given her a few *groszy* to buy herself a cake. This time she wouldn't ask. She didn't want them to think that that was why she had come.

'I'm going,' she said.

Her father didn't hear, and her mother, busy measuring a knitted sleeve for a customer, said: 'When you have vacation from school, come here and help.'

The days of the *shiv'a* were over, and once more Hania waited for Bronka by the gate of her house, and the two of them walked to school together. During the first days after the *shiv'a* Hania was quiet, and a cloud of nervousness covered her brown eyes. Nor did Bronka speak much. They came out of Paulinska Street, into noisy Krakowska Street. Only Jews were to be seen in the streets, all in traditional garb, skullcaps with black hats over them, and black *kapotas* tied with a belt.

'My aunt from Berlin says we're living in a ghetto here,' said Hania, finally breaking the silence.

'A ghetto?'

'Yes, a ghetto without a wall. She said that in Berlin everything's quite different. Jews mix with Germans, and that makes the Germans angry.'

They were both silent for a long spell.

'Are Jews different from other people?' asked Bronka.

'It seems so. I don't know. I don't feel different in any way', said Hania.

'How can you know if you're different or not if you don't know other people?'

'I do know other people!'

'Who?'

'Pani Zegartowska.'

'She's not an example.'

In the meantime they had come out of Krakowska Street and had crossed Ditlowska Street. Here the human scenery changed. Traditional Jews were still to be seen in the street, but not in such density, and there were other people to be seen too. A short distance from here began the Planty, the avenue of broad gardens, a promenade with benches under chestnut trees, with playgrounds and artificial ponds, which surrounded the entire city. And on the other side, very close to here, ran the Vistula, which separated Krakow and Kazimierz from the suburbs of Podgorza. From here one could see the Wawel Castle and the wall of its fortifications built on the hillside. Not far from here was their school.

Their classmates greeted them with the news that Pani Zegartowska was sick. At first there was a lot of noise in the classroom, but after some time the headmistress came in, followed by Sala, one of Hania's sisters. At once there was silence in the room. The headmistress said a few words in German, and they understood that today Sala would replace their teacher. The headmistress left.

'Good morning, girls,' Sala greeted the class.

'Good morning, teacher,' they replied in chorus.

'I'm not a teacher. I'm just a pupil from a higher grade. I've come to replace your teacher, and since I don't know how to teach like her, I'll read you a story.'

'Good, good,' the girls called gleefully.

Sala sat down on the platform. Her back was erect, her stomach tucked in, her neck long, her hair tied back, her skin smooth, her eyes soft, and her voice pleasant. The class fell silent, awaiting the story. Sala placed her sister Hania beside the door. 'If you hear steps, give me a sign.'

Sala, true to the spirit of Pani Zegartowska, chose an ancient patriotic Polish folk tale, about a girl called Wanda, who had been ordered to marry a young German. She, however, loved a young Pole. Wanda refused to marry the German, and since no one listened to her protestations, she chose the depths of the Vistula, where she found her death.

The class was very still. One could feel that the girls identified with the Wanda of the story. Hania returned to her seat and they were all pleased that everything had concluded safely. Had the headmistress heard she might have made a fuss. The Austrians were allied with the Germans. And both hated the Russians. As for the Poles, Pani Zegartowska had once hinted to them, they were awaiting the moment when they could rid themselves of all three.

3 Gunpowder

A year had passed since their mother's death and it was spring again. The spring of 1913. Life in the house in Paulinska Street carried on as usual, with pressures from within and from without.

The world was like a cauldron: crisis followed crisis. It was impossible not to take an interest in what was happening in the world. The grown-ups spoke only of politics and what the children heard was a mixture of rumors. The large states aspired openly to territorial expansion. They ruled the continents outside Europe and sent their armies into weak countries. They forged alliances with each other, suspected each other, and competed with each other.

The Balkan countries too formed an alliance against the domineering Turks who threatened them. These Balkan countries had been a target for all the sides competing for an entrance into the Adriatic Sea. England and France watched the actions of Austria and Germany with concern; they were helping themselves, without armed conflicts, to fat portions of the cake, such as Bosnia and Herzogovina. England and France, who each had their own specific interests, tried occasionally to hold talks with the Germans, but with no success. For the sake of these negotiations, England agreed to form an alliance with France and Russia (the countries of the Agreement), with Austria and Turkey, Germany's allies (the countries of the Center) in the middle. Germany did not accept England's rule over important sea passages – Gibraltar, Suez, Singapore, Bermuda, which connected England with her colonies – and began to develop a military navy with great urgency.

Generals began to draw up war plans, in the knowledge

that war was inevitable. The arms race rushed on in full frenzy.

France, though sparsely populated, increased the period of compulsory military service in her army from two years to three.

In the Austro–Hungarian monarchy too the mobilizations increased.

These things reached the children's ears, but they didn't give them much thought. Their father was the only person in the household who sensed the impending catastrophe. A great change had occurred in him since his wife's death, and one could see that incessant worrying was eating away at him. There was a lot of white now in his beard and at his temples, he stooped more, and his thin body had become even thinner. His shoulders drooped, his back curved and his sad eyes were sunken in their sockets. He had tried several times to speak with his children about the present and the future, but had not found the right moment for such a conversation. The girls had their own world. He understood well how much effort each of them expended in looking after him and little Haim and the whole apartment.

And indeed the apartment was kept spick and span, the meals were served at fixed times, and the girls excelled at their schoolwork. How could he upset their equilibrium, which was delicate enough as it was, by speaking to them like a prophet about the disasters that threatened the world, about the worries that consumed him?

Menashe, the eldest, was the first to leave home. One day, dressed in weekday clothes, an old black kapota and a small hat, he took his Sabbath clothes from the wardrobe, a new silk kapota and a bigger hat, and went out.

After some time he sent a letter home. He had reached the small village of Chszanow and presented himself to the wealthy Reb Leibusz, the same man to whom his father had come on his arrival in Galicia some 20 years before. Reb Leibusz, who was still in his prime and directed his sons and the many-branched affairs of his family, had found a place for Menashe too. In another letter, Menashe wrote that he had been offered a match in the village. Now the letters came one after the other. Menashe wrote that the bride's family was taking care of everything, and that a date had already been set for the wedding.

The bride's father, who was Reb Leibusz's younger brother, came to town, and the two fathers closed themselves in a room for a long conversation. At the end of this conversation, the bride's father rubbed his hands together in satisfaction and invited the whole family to the wedding.

Mania was the only one who knew Menashe's bride.

'She's young and bashful,' she told her sisters, and they wanted to know more: Was she beautiful? Nice? Fat or thin? How was it that Menashe himself didn't know her?! Rozia almost went out of her mind. How can you take two people who don't know each other and tell them to live as one? There'll be lots of weeping afterwards.

'Sometimes weeping, sometimes laughter. Nothing is permanent in such things.'

The day of the wedding arrived. The family divided into two groups. The father and the daughters sat in a comfortable carriage, with a hired driver holding the reins and the whip. Father, in his best clothes, gleaming and polished, tried to straighten his bent posture. The girls, tastefully dressed and elegantly turned out, excited the attention of passers-by.

There was no room for Hesiek, Hania and Haim in the carriage, so they joined their cousins on their mother's side, who had hired a large farmers' wagon and a horse, and held the reins themselves, in turns.

Hania was the only girl in this merry wagon. Apart from her brother Hesiek, there were another two Hesieks, another Menashe, Szewsek (Shavtai), big Lejbek (Arie Leib) and little Lejbek (Yehuda Leib). Szewsek gave Hania a strong pinch on the cheek.

'It's a sign of affection,' he said, smiling.

They all behaved like gentlemen, and offered her and Haim the best place, and competed with each other in caring for them. Hania felt embarrassed but full of self-importance. She liked these boys. There was something different in their behavior and dress.

31

It was a three-hour drive. The boys talked about strange subjects, which Hania had never heard about before. She heard about the untimely death of Doctor Theodor Herzl, of a broken heart. He had not succeeded in his political struggle, but nevertheless had paved the way for modern Zionism. They spoke of pioneers in the Land of Israel. And suddenly the Carmel brothers started talking to each other in a language she didn't understand.

'It isn't nice and it isn't polite to speak in company in a language which not everyone understands,' she dared to remark.

'It's very nice to speak Hebrew!' little Lejbek said ardently. 'Hebrew is our language, not Polish!'

Hania was bewildered. One of the Hesieks came to her assistance: 'It's time that people everywhere learned Esperanto,' he said.

The wagon swayed along the unpaved roads, its wheels sinking in puddles in the muddy parts and rising again when back on the stone road. The passengers bounced from time to time and fell onto each other, laughing, but all of them grew tired. 'To think that we'll have to come back all this way,' said Hania, worried. Her pretty dress was creased and the velvet ribbon Hela had tied had slipped into the wrong place. How would she look at the wedding?

Finally they reached the place. The wedding was being held in the courtyard of Reb Leibusz's house. Here the men stood in one group and the women in another. Hania found her sisters, who had arrived before her and were standing aside. The city girls kept apart from the girls of their own age from the village. Her father and her brother Hesiek blended into the surroundings. The cousins, those who had arrived in the wagon with Hania, formed another group, and they didn't know what to do with themselves. After the ceremony, when the *hassidim*[1] started dancing in circles, with small steps, the city boys too were drawn into the dance and the joy beamed from their eyes. The young couple disappeared inside the house. Towards the end of the evening Haia, Menashe's young wife, came shyly up to her sisters-in-law and tried to make conversation with them. The conversation didn't flow – Haia spoke Yiddish and the girls answered in Polish.

Menashe remained in Chszanow. The mobilizations in the Austro–Hungarian Empire increased. More and more Jews received mobilization orders. If they didn't obey, they were considered cowards and evaders. If they obeyed, the Poles, on receiving independence, would accuse them of treason against the homeland.

Under the surface everything was in a ferment. The Jews began to awake from their long slumber, many centuries long, and were forced to take a stand. They had to ask themselves difficult questions:

Jews, who are you?

If war breaks out, on whose side will you fight? Whose victory will be your victory?

Reb Moshe Weinfeld couldn't sleep at nights. And when he did fall asleep, he had troubled dreams. In his dream he ran from door to window, from window to door, in vain. All exits were closed. He was imprisoned in a trap and there was no way out. Again and again he woke from his uneasy sleep, passed his hand over his eyes, tried to think straight and logically, to get things clear in his mind.

He spoke to himself as if he were the authorities: 'You Jews, there are many of you here in Galicia – when will you finally decide who you are? A nation?

A nation, or not a nation. He remembered very well the difficulties the authorities had made for him on his arrival in Galicia in his youth: he had had to pay a lot of money for his residence permit. His wife's family had paid the sum for him. At that time there had been 'purges' in Galicia, and in order to reduce their number the Empress Maria-Teresia and her son Kaiser Joseph had promulgated cruel and degrading decrees: Jews were obliged to pay a 'head tax', and, worse, Jews were forbidden to marry without a special permit from the authorities, and such a permit was purchased for a lot of money. All in order to decrease the birth-rate, to suppress, to stifle, to erase. Many Jews could not afford to pay such huge sums, and then a new decree came: whoever didn't have money was declared a 'beggar'. Many paupers were declared 'beggars', and an order was issued to deport them from the monarchy. Where to? Across the border from the monarchy Jews suffered much more. There were only certain places where they were allowed to live, in 'the Pale of Settlement'. True, things had changed now. The Austro–Hungarian monarchy was not as strong as it had been. Reb Moshe read in the newspapers that it was growing weaker, that it would collapse like a house of cards if it did not grant rights to the nations of which it was composed. And the Kaiser, who understood the problems, fearful that the Empire would indeed disintegrate, promised rights to the nations.

And then the Jews in Galicia awoke and said:

We too are a nation.

Reb Moshe passed his hand over his eyes again, as though chasing something away in the darkness. But the black mass did not move from before his eyes or from over his heart. How did they dare? We, Jews, how could we make demands? We know better than that. We'll be punished immediately for our impudence. Better to sit quietly and not anger the authorities. Otherwise there'll be pogroms. History will repeat itself.

What kind of a nation are you? Reb Moshe said to himself in the name of the Austrian regime, what kind of a nation are you when you don't have a land?

True, we don't have a land, because we were expelled from it many years ago, but we have many other things in common, Reb Moshe replied, as if he were one of the 'Folkists' who believed in personal autonomy.

What, for example?

Religion.

Religion! But we're talking about nationhood.

All right, Reb Moshe continued talking to the authorities, we have common qualities. We have a common language.

A language, you say! What language?

What language? We have the holy language, the language of prayers.

The language of prayers? But we said that we aren't speaking about religion, but about the everyday, at school, at work. We have one for that too! Our common language is Yiddish! Yiddish! A language! It's a jargon, a dialect, you know that!

What happened in the population census? In the population census citizens were ordered to declare what nation they belonged to and what their mother-tongue was. His daughters, those who were already of census age, said without hesitation: nationality Polish, language Polish, as if it was self-evident. But that was not enough: they were also asked about religion, and only then did they say: the Mosaic religion. But this had to do not only with his daughters. Many Jews from small towns and villages answered differently: we are Jews, they said, and that was their answer to both questions. And when they were asked for their mother-tongue, they said: Yiddish.

'There is no such language in the lexicons,' said the officials of the regime, and the fuss began. Jews assembled to take counsel. In the synagogue they talked a lot of politics. Reb Moshe cleaved to the traditional orthodox camp, to the Jews who didn't want any changes. What characterized them was an absence of political awareness and a tendency to passivity. But they too had to take a stand. The Zionists had begun penetrating into every corner, demanding that the Jews unite and appear before the authorities of the Empire as a single nation. These Zionists were activists, and had a lot of initiative. They were the continuers of the way proposed by Doctor Herzl, who had died of heartbreak, an outstanding man without doubt, but a strange man. He had thought that a Jew was like any other human being. It was interesting that so many were enthused about this idea. He had died before seeing his tremendous efforts bear fruit. Reb Moshe had followed his career in the newspapers, which carried reports on the Zionist Congresses. He kept at home a clipping from a newspaper which had a description of the Zionist convention in the Finnish city of Helsingfors. Where had they found the daring to assemble in a strange city, to conduct themselves there as if they were at home, and to pass resolutions? They're different from me, thought Reb Moshe. Different Jews, but

Jews all the same. There, in that Helsingfors, they had decided that the Jews were a nation. And this nation – the resolution read – will strive to regain its historical homeland, the Land of Israel, and to settle in it. Until then, until the homeland is regained and settled, the nation will go on living in the places where it lives and will prepare for migration and settlement.

Reb Moshe started arguing with himself again:

Nonsense!

Such nonsense, said the wise heads in the synagogue. The Jews have always lived a special life, of religion and of the spirit, and that is what matters.

The great rabbi assembled his followers and raised their spirits. In the synagogues they wrapped themselves in their prayer shawls, raised their eyes to heaven, their lips muttering prayers.

But from the mass of people who not long ago had been united around the God of Israel, individuals and groups had begun breaking away: some circling around the old ways, some caught up by other religions and beliefs, most continuing to seek, alienated, and everything began to disintegrate. People tried to convince each other: A common destiny? Peculiar qualities? True, that is what unites us. Not necessarily on religious grounds. More and more people supported the idea of spiritual autonomy for Jews, on Galician territory. There were 'Autonomists' with a class orientation. The members of the 'Bund' also wanted autonomy of education and language within the international. Others were far from identifying with the working class and called themselves 'Folkists'. To them, only the idea of Jewish autonomy, not religious only, was important. And there were also assimilationists.

Reb Moshe remembered that in 1910 a conference had been held, in Krakow, of all the Jewish parties in the area ruled by the Austrian Empire. At the time, young people had come to his house in Paulinska Street and had tried to persuade and influence him, each towards his own direction. He had sent them all away. He read a lot and knew what was going on, but he followed the rabbi. And the rabbi said not to get involved for the time being. His daughters looked on sadly as he sent the ardent young men away.

The conference's purpose was to unite all the Jewish forces in the Empire to struggle for rights for Jews. Rights had then been granted to other nations and this was an opportunity for demanding official recognition of Jewish nationhood. Deep in his heart he knew he should act. At that conference it was decided to establish a Jewish National Organization in the Austrian Empire, which would comprise all Jews who belonged to political organizations. Because of the passivity in the religious circles, the lead was taken by the Zionists, who since Herzl had been well organized politically. The conference proclaimed that the Zionists alone were the bearers of Jewish nationhood. Then grave conflicts arose. The Folkists were also for nationhood. The assimilationists went with the authorities, against the Zionists. The religious were against the Zionists: let everything be as it has always been. But the census was approaching, and it was necessary, nevertheless, to decide who we were! what was our mother-tongue? They said Yiddish, but Yiddish was not recognized as a national language. What a mess!

The nightmare continued. Moshe knew that a stand had to be taken. For himself too, but mainly for the children's sake.

'All is lost', again he spoke to himself. 'My daughters are already swimming with the stream. Each of them is drawn in a different direction. They're caught up in Polish patriotism. They don't have a more exalted or more important goal than to participate in the rise of an independent Poland. And me? What would I do if I was called to serve in the Kaiser's army?' For with the civic rights which the Jews were granted together with all the other citizens of Galicia, duties had been imposed on them too. 'What would I do then? And what do I actually care' – he continued his conversation with himself – 'who rules in the Balkan countries?'

'Father,' Hesiek had asked once, 'what will we do if we get a draft notice? You're still of mobilization age, and in another year I too enter the lists.'

The father was silent for a long while, his forehead creased with deep wrinkles, his back bent. Hesiek looked at his father's beloved suffering face, and his young heart swelled with love, admiration, and pity for him.

'We won't go,' the father finally said.

The boy said nothing. He understood the gravity of the matter. To go was dangerous and not good, but when one received an order, one had to go.

'What will we do then?'

The father repeated his son's question.

'What will we really do? I wish I knew.'

'I heard that Jews find ways out,' Hesiek said. 'I heard that one of our uncles is stuffing himself with potatoes and basins of noodles to make himself fat. A man weighing 100 kilos will not be mobilized. So he's swallowing more and more ...'

The father's face showed disgust.

'It's true that there are medical committees,' he said. 'Perhaps they'll release me ... Perhaps they'll be considerate ... We'll see ...'

Hesiek, who had never gone to a regular school, only to *heder*, enrolled in a *yeshiva*. Rabbis and *yeshiva* students were exempt from military service, as were priests and novices in the priesthood.

The news was not good. The newspapers reported unceasing disputes among the European states. Diplomats and statesmen ran about from place to place and tried to save Europe from the impending disaster, but without success. In the great cities people gathered in the street and talked about the situation. Everyone knew about the preparation of the armies, and the increases of armed force. Everyone knew that a tiny spark would blow up the barrel of gunpowder on which they were sitting.

One day a red-bearded Jew arrived at their home. His name was Leizer.

'I have to see your father,' he said emphatically, and they all understood that Reb Leizer wanted to speak to their father in private.

When Father come into the large room, all the children scattered in different directions. Reb Leizer watched them leave the room, giving special scrutiny to the eldest daughter, Mania.

Reb Leizer was a known matchmaker in the city, and he had come to propose a match for Mania. At first the father wanted to protest; Mania was like a second mother to her sisters and brother, she ran the household here, what would he do without her? While he hesitated, Reb Leizer began detailing his proposal, speaking very highly of the prospective bridegroom.

'Who is he?' asked the father.

'A great scholar, a follower of the Rabbi of Bobowa.'

The Rabbi of Bobowa was highly esteemed in hassidic circles, and his followers made pilgrimages to the little village, Bobowa, where he dwelled.

'A true scholar,' the matchmaker continued, 'and a noble person, and well established.'

'What is his livelihood?'

'Abundant. Forests, sawmills, various timber enterprises. That's your branch too, isn't it, Reb Moishe? You could open businesses together and help each other. It's a good match I'm offering you, believe me.'

'I'll speak with my daughter. I can't promise her to anyone without her agreement,' said the father, heavy-hearted.

'Speak with your daughter, Reb Moishe, and tell her that a good bridegroom is hard to find in the city, and not only in the city, but in the whole country. Even though he is divorced, and has a son.'

'What did you say?'

'Yes, he's divorced. A *hassid* of his standing is entitled to receive a suitable wife. The first one wasn't suitable, she didn't keep the commandments properly.'

'So why did you come to me, Reb Leizer? Go find yourself a wife for your man somewhere else. Why did you come here? What do you know about my daughter?'

'She is truly a pearl, but even for pure pearls it is hard to find good bridegrooms. And no dowry is necessary. The bridegroom is wealthy. He has everything.'

'That makes no difference. Did I say I would not give my daughter a dowry?'

'But perhaps this is really a good thing for you, Reb Moishe? Keep the dowry for your other daughters. I won't be able to offer a match like this to all of them.'

'Now go,' said the father, depressed. 'I have to think.'

Reb Leizer left. Reb Moshe was inclined to forget the whole thing. What was the hurry? They could wait for other offers.

That day he saw his daughter through new eyes. What sweetness there was in her personality, in her ways. Her grace, and her beauty. All his daughters were beautiful, but she was the most beautiful.

What had Leizer said? Perhaps this was really a good thing for her? She had already reached puberty, true. Was he trying to keep her at home for selfish reasons? Mania sensed that something was being woven around her. Or had the cunning Reb Leizer thrown her a hint, something to think about?

During that day and the next the father and the daughter kept out of each other's way. It was Mania who spoke first.

'I saw Reb Leizer visited you, Father. Did he propose anything?'

'Yes, he has a bridegroom for you, Mattel.'

'For me?' A dark flush spread over her face.

'Yes, my daughter. Do you want to get married?'

'Do you think it's time, Father?'

'Your mother at your age ...'

'I know, Father.' And she added quietly, 'I'm ready too. If you think it's good.'

The father said nothing.

'What is it, Father?'

'Nothing,' he answered, absently. 'We'll sleep another night, tomorrow we'll talk.' He went to his room.

Mania remained in the large room, and didn't know what to do. What was she – a piece of merchandise? A tremor passed through the fibers of her delicate soul and body.

Hesiek was standing beside her.

'I know everything,' he said.

'How? Did Father tell you?'

'What difference does it make? What matters is that I know.'

'Hush, lower your voice, I don't want Father to hear us. Who is he?'

Hesiek went from the light to the heavy. 'A scholar, good family, wealthy ...'

Mania sat before him, but very distant. This was the first time in his life that he had seen her like this, distant, enclosed within herself.

'What should I do,' she asked.

Hesiek had come to tell his sister everything he knew, in order to make things easier for her, to help her. But when she asked him so simply what to do, he had no answer.

'I don't know,' he said finally.

Mania spent a sleepless night. Fear or yearning? Yearning for what? To not get up any more every morning to take care of her brothers and sisters, to live a life of her own. Not to share her bed with Hania any more, to be a woman, a wife. Not a daughter, not a sister. A wife.

The next day her father didn't speak with her. He too had not slept that night. In the morning he looked at her once, then another time, and saw the light and the yearning in her eyes. He went to meet the bridegroom. Naturally enough, things didn't remain secret.

'What's happened?' people kept asking.

Something had happened. For the first time they saw Mania absent-minded. Floating in clouds, day-dreaming. After a short while the engagement was held. Reb Shlomo's mother and sisters were captivated with the young bride-to-be, and also won her heart.

She already knew his family. Him she would meet only on the wedding night, when she was already a married woman. And then there would be no way back. Whether she would be happy or miserable in her marriage – time would tell.

Mania adapted herself to her husband's demands, in dress and head-covering too, and went to live with him in the Podgorza Quarter, on the other side of the Vistula. Only the river separated Kazimierz, which had a wholly Jewish population, from Podgorza, where the Jews constituted a large majority. The other quarters, at the other end of the city, where one would not see a single Jew and life was completely different, could be reached by streetcar, crossing the bridge. But the residents of the two quarters didn't need the streetcar, and didn't use it. They crossed the bridge on foot, both ways, as and when they needed to or felt like it. The distance was not great.

Podgorza, in Polish, means 'under the hill'. The quarter lay at the foot of a green hill alled Rekawki, which means 'sleeves'. This was probably because ridges of the hill looked like a pair of sleeves. A funny name, but famous. The Rekawki hill was green and fragrant in summer and white and soft in winter. Its slopes had known centuries of Jewish children's games.

Until her children were born, Mania visited her father's home daily, and looked after both households., but the scepter of the firstborn in the house had passed to Sala now.

In the village of Chszanow, Haia, Menashe's wife, gave birth to a boy. They called him Meir.

In the spring of 1914 people spoke only of politics. Special editions of newspapers came out one after the other. It was difficult to keep up with developments. The Serbs had dared to enter Bosnia and Herzegovina. In the Jewish streets, people asked questions: What did this mean? Would the Hapsburg rulers in Vienna and Budapest sit still and not respond? Surely not. Austria, Hungary, and a large chink of Poland – Galicia – were not enough for these rulers. They would not withdraw from the Balkan States.

'They've increased the draft in Austria,' somebody said.

'Tomorrow there'll be new draft notices in Russia too,' said someone else.

'And in Germany?'

'Germany has been preparing for war a long time. Her arms industry is working at full steam. They're planning to land a decisive blow on all their enemies.'

'Who are Germany's enemies?'

'All her neighbors! Except Austria.'

'And why this hatred?'

'Is it good for the Jews, or bad for the Jews?'

Shrugs of the shoulders. Wonder and dread in the heart.

Hesiek came into the room, holding a special edition of the evening paper. 'The British Navy is strengthening its guard on the sea-crossroads ...'

His three sisters, Sala, Hela and Hania, leaped up to meet him and grabbed the paper from his hands. 'Gibraltar, Suez, Singapore and Bermuda are being patrolled by ships of His Majesty's Navy ...'. 'His Majesty's Navy ...' – the words sounded so romantic, and Hania repeated them like an echo. 'All these places are very far away from here', said Hela. Sala was absorbed in reading the news and apparently didn't hear her sisters' remarks. Hesiek had vanished. He had probably gone to listen to the talk in the streets, and to examine the most important question of all: was it good for the Jews or bad for the Jews?

The three sisters remained in the room. Twilight had begun to cast its shadows on the walls. It was almost summer, but the walls of the house were saturated with dismal cold. The summer of 1914.

'You mustn't read in the dark. You'll ruin your eyes,' said Hela to her sister Sala, and took the newspaper from her. 'Leave all the politics.'

Sala stretched her tall body.

'All this excitement may be to our good, that is to Poland's good,' she said.

'Our teacher said so too,' Hania put in. 'She dared to teach us Maria Konopnicka's 'Rota'. That poem has become an anthem. Our teacher said that now that they're all quarrelling with each other, we, the Polish nation, should find an opportune moment to revolt. Poland has to be independent and united again.'

'We have to find an opportune moment,' Sala repeated, echoing her younger sister's words.

'Yes, but that doesn't mean you or me. The men, they're already preparing ...'

'Meanwhile our Menashe has been drafted into the Austrian army. It's so awful. We don't know whose side we should be on. The Austrian regime has been fairly good to the Jews, relatively speaking ...'

The news about Menashe had arrived several days before. A Jewish acquaintance had arrived from Chszanow and given them the details: Menashe had found no way out. He had tried to prove that he had to support his family, his two little children who had been born one after the other – his son Meir and his daughter Rela – but nothing had helped. They had said that that was not sufficient grounds for exemption. Every soldier had a family, the army paid the families of its draftees a sufficient wage, and the families were also insured in case of a disaster. If, God forbid, anything were to happen to Menashe, the family was insured. Hesiek, who was 18 at the time and studying in a *yeshiva*, traveled to Chszanow after the news came, to see how his sister-in-law was getting on with two infants on her hands. Menashe's children were part of the family. It did not seem long ago that he had quarreled with Menashe about who was to sleep in the bed. Maybe it was because of the cramped conditions at home that Menashe had left at such an early age. And he had been fortunate, and had managed to establish a family of his own. Now he had been forced to leave it. So Hesiek set off for Chszanow to ask his sister-in-law if she needed anything. But Haia, who, after giving birth twice, remained as bashful as she had ever been, only blushed, and assured him that she lacked nothing. Her sister Mircia lived nearby, she said, and was always ready to help her. Hesiek felt that he was only being a burden to his young and bashful sister-in-law. Little Meir hid among the folds of his mother's dress, and wouldn't deign to even look at the uncle who had come to visit from the great city. The baby Rela cried, and Haia had to feed her. Hesiek gave her regards from his father and his sisters, and returned to the city, sad and downhearted, missing Menashe and concerned for him and his family.

On his return everyone was depressed to hear about the visit.

'Where have they sent him?' his father asked.

'They don't know exactly. To the Italian border, I think.'

'Did your teacher really say that Poland would be free?'

'Yes,' said Hania, enthusiastically. 'Do you want me to teach you the song "Rota"? Everyone's singing it today. There isn't a Pole who doesn't know it by heart.' And without waiting for a response from her sisters, she brought an exercise book in which she had written the words, and started singing:

> We'll not give the land, for it's our homeland,
> We'll not let our language be buried under sod
> We're the Polish nation, we're the folk of Poland,
> Help us, God, please help us, God.
>
> We'll not let the Germans spit upon our faces
> We'll not have our children forced, German
>   to speak and heed
> We'll defend our honor, and all our country's
>   places,
> Us God will lead, God will lead.

Hela sat curled up on the corner of her bed. She felt a stifling in her throat. Here was her 15-year-old sister Hania enthusiastically singing a patriotic Polish song, while her brother Menashe had been drafted into the Austrian army. Her other brother, Hesiek, was growing a beard and side-curls, as befitted a *yeshiva* student. Father walked around the house stooped, sad-eyed, and sallow-faced. There was a feeling that their troubles were just beginning. Hela was now the 'mother of the family', even though, apart from Hania, all her sisters were older than her. Mania was married, and already had a home and a family of her own. Sala was fragile, always dreaming, never practical.

Rozia they hardly saw at home now. She met with Polish girls, perhaps even with Polish boys, and was taking a course in first aid. On the few occasions when she was at home, she didn't answer her father's questions directly. Everyone knew there wasn't a word of truth in her answers. One lie led to another, and there could be no going back. It pained Hela to see her father's distressed face, and she felt the insult to him. Father didn't deserve to be treated like that. But Rozia wasn't to blame; she simply couldn't tell Father the truth, because he wasn't prepared to accept it. It would break his heart even more. What, after all, was Rozia guilty of? She was only going out with people of her own age, who lived only a few streets away. Was that so terrible? Once Hela had tried to talk about this with her eldest sister, Mania.

Hela had set out in the direction of Podgorze, the attractive suburb on the other side of the Vistula, where her sister and brother-in-law lived with their new baby in a rented two-room apartment on the ground floor. She had passed through the crowded streets of Kazimierz, moving out of the way of bearded Jews and furtive youths. As she reached the bridge she was passed by a tram full of soldiers headed for somewhere, perhaps the front. Under the bridge the water of the river flowed silently, and several birds circled slowly above. The plants on the banks had already opened up to the approaching summer, like brides preparing for their night of love, but the willows stood weeping, swaying and sighing gently into the wind. Hela quickened her pace, expelling sad thoughts from her mind. She always tried to visit her sister when her brother-in-law was not at home. She and her sisters felt ashamed in the presence of the religious brother-in-law, who wore a long *kapota* and a broad-brimmed hat over his skullcap. When he was there they would always pull at the sleeves of their dresses, to cover their exposed arms as much as they could. Hela felt as if she was between a hammer and an anvil: not only was she ashamed to be seen by her religious brother-in-law, but in a way she was also ashamed of him. And of her sister too. She loved them, but was ashamed of them. How could this be? Mania, wonderful Mania, so clever, so gentle and industrious, and he, the learned Shlomo, the scholar, how could they be so alienated from the environment they lived in, how could they ignore the world around them and resolve everything by saying: It is the will of God!?

This time Hela screwed up her courage and tried to speak with Mania about what was happening at home between Rozia and their father. Fortunately for her, Shlomo was not at home. Mania was busy, as usual, but was very glad to see her sister.

'Ah, what delicious smells!' said Hela as she came in.

The apartment was tidy, fragrant food was cooking in the kitchen, the baby was playing in its cot, satisfied and clean, and Mania was calm, more relaxed and beautiful than ever. She was 22 now, and her second pregnancy was already evident, adding special softness and sweetness to her already gentle and delicate form. Hela thought of the many tragedies now befalling millions of people in the world, while here, in this house, time seemed to have stopped, and everything proceeded as it had in the past.

'I can't bear to hear all the lies Rozia flings at Father,' Hela said, stroking the hair of her little niece, Rela (Menashe's baby daughter in Chszanow was also called Rela, both of them named after their grandmother who had died so young).

Mania sat at the table folding laundry. Her wig lay beside the mirror in their bedroom, combed and ready to be worn when Mania went out. At home Mania wore a kerchief over her head.

'Don't pay it any attention, my dear. It was quite predictable.'

Hela was amazed and disappointed by the equanimity of her sister's reply.

'Is it all right to lie?'

'It isn't nice to lie, that's true. But if it's not to hurt someone, not to hurt Father ... Do you know what? We have to pray, we have to ask God to forgive her. We'll try to be better than we've been ... We have to try to please God ...'

Hela looked at her in amazement. She hadn't said: to please Father, she'd said to please God. Was her faith really so strong? Had someone else said this to her, Hela would have suspected hypocrisy. But her sister's face radiated faith and sincerity. Hela sighed. She feels good, she thought, but we don't have a common language. If righteous people like Mania approve of lying, who is justified in drawing a boundary between good and evil, in determining what is permitted and what forbidden? Whom could she speak to? To who could she open up the secrets of her heart? Would she be able to talk with her sisters only about children, food, and clothes?

'My father's been called up to the army,' Bronka blurted out.

'What?! Your father?!' Hela had forgotten to ask Mania how their house had been spared in the most recent wave of mobilization. Shlomo was of army age, and much younger than Bronka's father, but it seemed he had a certificate of exemption provided by the Rabbinate.

'Yes,' said Bronka. 'He's already been to the recruiting bureau, and got his uniform and all the rest.'

'Did he get a rifle too?'

'Yes. He'll have to go through training. At first he'll be in a camp not far from the city. After that they might even send him to the front.'

'To the front? That's impossible!' Hela stopped. 'I can't imagine your father in a soldier's uniform.'

'It's a fact. Mother cried awfully. She said she wants to go to the army too if he's going.'

The girls continued talking, when suddenly they heard moans coming from behind the closed door of the room where Hela's father was. The girls fell silent. Hela grabbed Hania's hand.

'Something's happened to Father.'

Suddenly it was deadly silent. Walking on tiptoe, Hela approached the closed door and opened it a fraction. Then she screamed.

On the bed lay their father, white as a sheet, a blood stain spreading under his head. Hela and Hania stood petrified, trembling all over. They didn't notice that Bronka had vanished, had gone off without saying a word.

Hesiek came as quickly as he could.

'One of Bronka's brothers called me from the *yeshiva* and said that something had happened to Father. What's happened to him?' he asked anxiously.

Dread filled the house. Hania led him into their father's room. She poured water over her father's pale face, and he regained consciousness.

'*Tatysi*', said Hesiek, not restraining his tears, '*Tatysi vos iz gescheyen?*' (Daddy, daddy, what's happened?)

On the father's face an expression appeared which could be construed as a faint smile. Hela and Hania smiled through their tears. The three of them bent over the bed.

'A little water,' he requested.

The two girls darted off. A moment later Hela returned with a glass of water. A glass with a saucer. The father had taught his daughters never to serve a glass without a saucer. Hania brought a wet towel to wipe his face. Hesiek supported his father's head and helped him drink. Hela removed the bloodstained sheet from under his head and Hania spread a clean sheet. All of them stared at their father, the same question in their eyes.

'I stabbed myself in the ear,' the father confessed, in a weak voice.

'Daddy, daddy, why did you do that?' Hesiek blurted.

'I was afraid I'd be called up.'

'We have to call a doctor', said Hela. 'The ear has to be treated.'

'No', said the father, weak but firm. 'There's no need. I took care to get drops that stop the pain. And we have to put some cotton wool into the ear. That'll stop the bleeding. Until I appear before the medical committee there's no need to do anything.'

On seeing their alarmed faces, he added: 'It really doesn't hurt all that much ...'

Hania and Hela were still petrified, paralyzed with fear.

'Daughters,' the father said to them in Yiddish, 'I have a request of you, my daughters. Not a word about this to anyone. We'll tell everyone that my ear hurts and bleeds, and that's all. Was any stranger at home when I fainted?'

'Yes, my friend Bronka was here', Hania whispered in Polish. Hela almost said: 'Her father's been called up,' but at the last moment she stopped herself and didn't say anything.

'Little Bronka's like a member of our family,' the father said. His weary eyes rested for a moment on Hesiek's face and then closed again.

In the kitchen, Roh'cze the cook was preparing lunch. Fortunately she hadn't heard anything. Roh'cze was deteriorating of late; she coughed incessantly and almost didn't hear a thing. Her ears must have been blocked with dirt, or maybe she was deaf? For a long time they had thought of dismissing her. But how could one let such a miserable creature go when she was sick? Who would give her food to eat? One couldn't throw a person to the dogs just like that. True, they also needed her. Especially Haim, the youngest. A thousand times they had told her: 'Roh'cze, when you cough, at least put your hand over your mouth. Don't cough on the food you serve us. And don't kiss Haim. He's a big boy now!'

On 28th June 1914, in a world charged with explosives like a pomegranate, there came a stunning piece of news: a young Serbian had shot and killed the Austrian Crown Prince Fritz Ferdinand and his wife. The event had occurred in the town of Sarajevo, in Bosnia, where the royal couple were making a private visit.

'This is the last straw. Now nothing will stop the war,' people said in the Jewish streets. 'Perhaps great statesmen will still manage to prevent the outbreak by diplomatic means,' came the faint replies of the few optimists.

The majority knew that there was no chance. The reports streaming into the press incessantly pointed to the fact that war was inevitable. And indeed, three days after the dramatic event, Austria declared war on Serbia. Several days later, Germany declared war on Russia which before that had formed an alliance with France and England, and the three as allies immediately declared war on Germany. The whole world was in a ferment. The war was already raging, it was impossible to stop it; millions of people were threatened with destruction, and no one knew why or wherefore.

The winter of 1914 was a hard one in Kazimierz. Conditions in Krakow were terrible. Here and there the civilian population was completely cut off from supply routes, and the city lacked food products and fuel. The Polish winter struck mercilessly. Bitter battles were fought on the very outskirts of the city, and hospitals were filled with the wounded. During the first year of the war, the Russians launched a strong attack on Galicia and fought on their own land against the Germans.

The Austrians retreated from the eastern regions of Galicia, as far as Krakow. The town of Pszemysl, not far from Krakow, passed from hand to hand several times.

That year, Jozef Pilsudski, an energetic young Pole and an enthusiastic patriot, established the Polish National Council, in Krakow, under the auspices of the Austrian regime.

Against the background of the awful bloodshed among the three conquering nations, the dream of Polish national independence began to take shape. The Poles, and with them the Jews of Poland, found themselves in an unbearable situation. They served in different armies, and on more than one occasion brother found himself fighting against brother. Austria, Germany and Russia were all interested in encouraging the Poles to fight on their side, and so they competed with each other in the promises they made to the Poles, and promised them independence and freedom after the war.

No one promised the Jews anything.

Bronka's house became a kind of hostel for Jewish soldiers who had been transferred here from other places. They came mainly on Friday evenings, the Sabbath Eve, when they were given leave for one day. Bronka's father also came home every Friday, and always brought with him a lonesome young Jewish soldier, who was willing to sleep on the floor and make do with leftovers, but was not willing to forego family warmth and the Sabbath atmosphere.

Since the beginning of the war, Bronka's mother had been out of her mind. When her husband was drafted she had had a nervous breakdown, and had not stopped crying since.

'You see, Aharon? We were not clever enough, we were not cautious enough. Others sit at home, while you ... What good can you do as a soldier, anyway? And what will I do without you?'

He tried to pacify her. 'It's impossible to be clever enough in these times ...'

'How will you manage?' she complained. 'Alone in the cold? Soon they'll ship you far away, and our Bronka won't be able to get to you with the kosher food from home. How will you manage?'

'I'll manage, don't worry. I'm not the only Jew in the company.'

Aharon's answers angered her, and she changed direction.

'Fine for you, you're going and you don't care what will become of me. How will I manage alone with the house and the shop?' Sheva wailed.

The mother's strange behavior did not pass unnoticed by the children. Bronka lived in dread of the future. How could Mother blame Father for going into the army?! Wasn't it his duty? What were all those hints about others who had been more clever and had not gone? Because of such people they had been told at school that the Jews were not fulfilling their duty as citizens, that they were parasites. Bronka was proud of her father in his Austrian army uniform She would have been even prouder had her father been a member of Jozef Pilsudki's organization for a free Poland. But that organization, Bronka thought, did not accept Jews. Or perhaps they did, but other Jews, not like her father.

Bronka, now 16, decided to release her mother from the burden of housework. Perhaps when her mother saw that they could more or less manage, she would calm down. Bronka and her brothers stood in line for hours for food products, and on more than one occasion came home empty-handed. Twice a week she would walk a long distance to visit her father, carrying in her freezing hands parcels and pans of kosher food for him. The cold was terrible, and her hands ached and swelled up. The ache would extend to her heart, and gave her no rest. Vainly she would rub her hands together and try to warm them with her breath. Her swollen hands lost their flexibility and their resistance; chilblains spread over them, and she found it hard to use them to do the housework.

Sheva was nervous and abstracted, and didn't notice her daughter's swollen hands. The shop became a center of political gossip. People would come in to chat, to interpret and to speculate, not to buy.

'Have you heard, Pani Plessner, a new Pope has been elected in the Vatican. Perhaps he will influence the Christian states not to slaughter each other.'

'What Pope? What Vatican? They have no influence at all!' said one of the people in the shop. 'The *goyim*[2] know how to go to war in God's name, but not how to halt the destruction in His name – that's too much for them!'

'Sha, Sha, don't blaspheme, don't take God's name in vain!'

'Have you heard that Japan has declared war on Germany? Japan! They couldn't sit back quietly, the slant-eyed yellow-skinned Asians! But who knows, maybe it's good for the Jews? What do you think, Pani Plessner, *iss gut für yidden, oder schlect für yidden*? (Is it good for the Jews, or bad for the Jews?)'

'... and Belgrade has been taken by the Austrians, and Paris has almost fallen into our hands!'

'What do you mean our hands? What nonsense are you talking? Who are you and what are you? Are you the Hapsburg monarchy? Or are you just a little Jew from Kazimierz? Enough of this talk. I want all of you out of my shop!'

'I am indeed a Jew, but why did you say "a little Jew"? Hasn't your husband gone to serve in the Kaiser's army? So if the Kaiser has victories, they're our victories too, aren't they?'

Sheva thought how could one know if the Kaiser's victories were our victories too ... In the apartment, Bronka sang Polish patriotic songs all day long, and these were against the Austrians. Or were those people right who were asking when we would finally know what is good for the Jews?

One day Sheva closed the shop, locked and bolted the door, and said that there was no point in opening it any more. No one came to buy merchandise, no one wanted embroidery threads and delicate weaves. Money was losing its value from day to day, and Sheva was not managing with the accounts. People exploited her, asking her for cash loans. In the better cases they returned them when the money was worth far less, in the worse cases they simply didn't return them. She only knew how to run the store in peace time, when her husband stood behind the till.

'I have nothing to do in the shop any more,' Sheva said when she got home. 'I'm going away from here. I'm leaving!' The dustcloth dropped from Bronka's swollen hands. The first thoughts that passed through her mind were: 'in another few days Father is being transferred east, far from here. And Mother doesn't even notice that my hands are swollen.

'Grandma'! she suddenly called. 'Grandma, Mother's leaving us!'

Sheva's step-mother dragged her sick legs from the kitchen, to stand, hands on waist, facing the rebellious daughter. 'Where are you going? What are you talking about?'

Sheva didn't reply. She went to the wardrobe and started taking out various garments and packing them in a small suitcase. Tears sprang in Bronka's blue eyes.

'Mama, Mamusia, don't go! I'll help you ... I'll do everything ... the boys are still small ... how will we manage alone? ...'

Bronka hated this situation. Why did she have to plead? Were the boys not her mother's sons? If Mother wants to go, if we're not important to her, let her go.

Sheva sat down on the bed, beside the open suitcase, and cried. On one of the chairs sat Grandma, her elbows on the table and her head between her hands. Sheva said some fragmented things in between outbursts of sobbing. Her shoulders and her voice trembled.

'In any case I'm of no use to you, in any case the burden falls on you two. I have to go after him. That was my vow. Where he goes – I shall go.'

Bronka understood that she was talking of going with Father, with the regiment of soldiers in which he served.

'But what use can you be to him? They won't let you in.'

'I'll get in. I'll help him and other soldiers too. I'll knit them caps and gloves.'

'You've never even knitted a cap for one of your four children,' Grandma said, angry and pained.

Bronka felt that Grandma's words had hurt Mother. Truth hurts more than a lie – who was it that had spoken about this not long ago?

Sheva, hurt and torn, remained adamant. 'After this Sabbath they are transferring Father's regiment to the east. I'll go with them.'

'Does Father know?'

'No, we mustn't tell him because he won't agree. But I've decided.'

'Have you gone crazy?!' Grandma shouted. 'You're abandoning us, you're abandoning your children, you're abandoning me!'

Grandma burst out crying. Bronka stood between the two women, and didn't know whom to support. Sheva returned to her packing. The older woman muttered under her breath: 'Modern times. Modern women. When I was young such a thing was unheard of!' She dragged her sick legs to the kitchen and continued talking to herself:

'... Fela is about to give birth any day. I'll have to leave this place and help my daughter when the baby is born. She, after all, is my real daughter. This one, my step-daughter, I wouldn't care for at all if it weren't for these children. What will become of them?'

Friday. Bronka's father came home, with a soldier, a pale and thin young man who had never been here before and would surely never be here again. After the Sabbath he would go the front. His name was Srulek. Father was very excited. This was the last Friday. The last Sabbath. After this, who could tell when he would see his family again. He knew nothing about Mother's decision. Mother had pleaded with her children not to tell him, not to spoil his last Sabbath at home. The boys, to Bronka's surprise, had accepted their mother's decision with understanding, even with admiration. Little Moshe had said: 'Our mother's a heroine. She's going to war like Emilia Plater.'[3]

Mother's eyes and cheeks burned with emotion. The boys were washed and dressed for the Sabbath, a clean tablecloth gleamed on the table and the Sabbath candles were alight in their silver candlesticks. The first guest to arrive was Fela, who barely managed to come in through the door in her advanced stage of pregnancy. Her arms and legs were swollen and there were yellowish stains on her face, which was swollen too. Grandma hurried to tell her daughter the dramatic news of Sheva's decision. At the very last moment Bronka managed to pull the older woman aside.

'Grandma, grandma, not now, please! She'll make a

scandal, and there'll be screaming and yelling here! We can't let Father go to war so upset!'

Grandma and Fela went into the main room, where other guests had gathered in the meantime. Bronka could only hope that her request would be respected. The small apartment was full of people. The boys darted between the room and the kitchen, doing small errands for the grown-ups.

Bronka was washing the dishes after the dinner when she suddenly sensed that someone was standing behind her, very close. She froze. Cold lips pressed to the back of her neck, and she felt the scratch of bristles. She turned around sharply, pulling her hands suddenly out of the washing basin, and sprayed drops on the face of the soldier called Srulek.

'Have you gone mad?'

'Forgive me,' he mumbled in confusion. 'You're so lovely.'

There was a knocking at the front door and Bronka darted off to open it. Paula and Stefa, two of Aharon's sisters, had come to say goodbye to him.

'Only for a couple of minutes,' said Paula, and glanced from Bronka's wet hands to the figure of the soldier standing with lowered head beside the basin.

From the main room came the sound of conversation. Everyone was talking at once, in Yiddish, Polish, and German. Stefa gently grasped Paula's hand and whispered in her ear: 'What a noise! What a din!'

They stood in the doorway from the kitchen into the room, not daring to go in. Aharon came to greet them, and Paula repeated: 'We've only come for a couple of minutes, just to wish you a safe journey – go and return in peace.'

He very rarely saw his non-religious sisters, so their appearance now moved him deeply.

'How is Henryk?' he asked in Yiddish. He could think of nothing else to talk about.

'We received a letter,' said Stefa in Polish. 'He is in Antwerp.'

In Aharon's view his younger brother, Henryk, who had left the religious environment at 14 and had gone West, was a traitor.

'And how is he?' he asked, generously now.
There is war there too. He and his wife Mary are thinking of migrating to America.'

'America!' Everyone repeated the word in chorus. Even Srulek, in the kitchen, called out with longing and yearning: 'America!'

Aharon was abstracted and pensive. He was not accustomed to such a crowd of women. Already he wanted to be alone with his wife and children. After all, they only had the one day left to be together. Paula and Stefa turned to go. At the door they met their third sister, Dola. The three sisters exchanged kisses, and Dola said: 'I've come just for a couple of minutes ...'

Bronka stifled a giggle. Smiling, she looked at Srulek. His eyes, hungry and pleading, smiled at her.

'Just imagine,' said Dola as she went through into the apartment. 'My husband Isidore and my son Wilhelm went to Berlin. Wilhelm was accepted into the Conservatorium.'

A glass fell from Bronka's hands and smashed into fragments. Srulek carried on drying the dishes and the three sisters helped gather the fragments of glass.

'Did you hear that? Wilhelm's been accepted into the Conservatorium. I wanted to study music too but I wasn't given the chance – my destiny is to wash dishes,' said Bronka, with a trace of bitterness.

'Perhaps you'll still get the chance,' one of her brothers consoled her.

'When? In the next world to come?'

'No, after the war.'

'After the war!' Srulek repeated, and angrily slammed the cutlery drawer shut.

'... and then the war broke out, and they're stuck in Berlin!' Dola continued. 'Just imagine, I have no news of them, I'm here alone with little Liz and we're so distraught, I'm so terrified, and the distance between Berlin and Krakow now seems infinite. Who knows when we'll be reunited. And you, Aharon, where are they sending you?' She had suddenly remembered to take an interest in her brother.

'East.'

'God! What will become of us? Isidore's brother is serving as an officer in the Russian army. What a situation we're in!'

The apartment slowly emptied. The last of the guests remained in the main room. The three boys were already in bed. Bronka and Srulek had finished the dishes and were standing by the kitchen window. Outside the window the night was dark and cold. A fierce wind blew snowflakes from the treetops. In neighboring windows the Sabbath candles had gone out. Here and there a small weak flame flickered. The night was quiet but charged with explosive.

'After tomorrow I'll be there all the time, on the other side, in the cold and dark,' said Srulek.

'My father too ...'

'They'll be considerate with him, perhaps they'll give him a good place, indoors. But no one will take pity on me. I'll be sent straight to the front line.'

Bronka's heart pounded; perhaps a caress, perhaps a little kiss would make him happy?

At that moment her mother's voice came from the main room: 'Go to sleep now, it's late.' Mother is giving me orders. In another two days she won't be here and she won't care if we have enough to eat or if we die of hunger, and now she's giving me orders.

The boys were snoring loudly. Mother's footsteps were approaching. Srulek hastily grasped Bronka's shoulders and her lips met his. She wound her white arms around his neck.

1915, the second winter of the war. Conditions were growing worse; the population of the city – mostly women, old people and children – moved through the streets like ghosts, frightened and frightening shadows. Most were dressed in rags. Water from stinking puddles penetrated the body through broken shoes. Stomachs churned in perpetual hunger. Somewhere far away were the men who had been taken from here. They sat densely packed in wet black trenches, drawing warmth from each other's bodies, waiting. A gigantic human wall dividing Europe. This wall surrounded Germany and separated it from its neighbors to the south and west. And on the other side, in similar trenches, sat amazingly similar young men, who just spoke a different language. And they were all awaiting the order to kill each other.

Moshe Weinfeld suffered great pain. The lymph glands in his neck swelled up and he had terrible headaches. The family took care of him devotedly. All his children tried to ease his pain and to free him from feeling guilty or that he was a burden upon them.

Once, in a rare moment of weakness, he confessed to Hela: 'Today I saw your mother in a dream.'

'I dream of her often,' said Hela.

'She asked me to hurry and take care of your future before it's too late.'

Hela felt a dread. She knew very well what her father meant.

'This is a bad time to think of permanent plans for the future,' she said. 'People are talking about an evacuation of the population. Only a special permit from the security authorities will enable one to stay in the city.'

'I know all that, my child, but I don't have much time. And apart from that, life must go on. Many people are dying, other people have to be born. I was thinking of your sister Sala, who doesn't seem able to find herself.'

This distressed Hela. Father was right; Sala – who knew her? Who knew what she had experienced in her childhood, or what were her hopes and dreams now? She was such a lovely, charming creature, always hiding in the shadow of others, as if she was apologizing for her very existence. What had caused her lack of self-confidence, her endless skepticism, such a repression of sensations and impulses?

'What do you have in mind to suggest to her, Father?' she asked, heavy-hearted.

He lay outstretched in clean and tidy pajamas, large pillows under his head.

'There is a good man,' he finally began, slowly, 'who has been released from the army because of the state of his health, and his family is interested in asking for the hand of one of my daughters. I thought of Sala.

Hela leaped up as if she had been struck. She had a good mind to say some harsh things to her father, but she restrained herself. The father's position demanded respect, and his poor physical condition demanded consideration. She remained silent, holding the harsh words inside.

With the coming of the twilight, Rozia, who had completed a municipal course in first aid and an accelerated course in nursing, returned from work. The city's hospitals were being filled with people with skin wounds and torn limbs. The treatment given them was superficial – the authorities responsible for hospitalization would dismiss the hard cases in order to make room for even harder cases. Trained and industrious hands such as Rozia's were always in demand. She was exhausted by the hard work, but was not willing to slow down. She was born to work, she said. And others said of her that she was born to help others.

'I've brought something good, something new which will ease your pain,' she said to her father, as she expertly examined the swollen lymph glands in his neck. He let her do as she wished, and this submissiveness was a new feature in his proud deportment, and was very moving to see. He lay there, absorbed in his pain. Hela thought of telling her sister about the conversation she had just had with their father, but she was afraid that Rozia would explode. Rozia knew how to proffer help to the body, but she didn't have the delicacy and sensitivity needed for the soul. Her hands could smooth wounds and mend torn parts of the body, but her tongue would lash and wound.

Hela and Hania sat in the living room, in the dark. Their father had fallen asleep in his room under the influence of the sedative.

Rozia had gone back to the hospital.

Sala was staying with Mania and Shlomo, to whom a sweet baby had been born in the meantime – Rivka'le, a sister to little Rela.

Sala had taken Haim with her, hoping that it might be good for the bored boy to meet Naftali, a boy of his own age, Shlomo's son from his previous marriage.

Hesiek came into the room. Almost every day he took time off from his studies at the *yeshiva* of the Rabbi of Gur, and came home to see what was happening.

'Why are you sitting in the dark?' he asked as he came in.

'Because we feel dark inside!' Hela burst out. 'Because you yourself said we have to save on electricity and paraffin, and the food supply in the house is running out, and there's no news from Menashe; who knows, maybe he's rotting in one of those damned trenches, and it breaks our hearts to see Father suffering and ... what else to you want to hear? That Father's decided to marry Sala off? There's some news to rejoice at, isn't it?' she ended, ironically.

'What did you say?!' Hania leaped up from her seat. 'To whom?'

'To whom? To someone who's been released from the army because of the state of his health, and his family's interested in asking for the hand of one of us. Nice, isn't it? Maybe you're interested? Or maybe we should offer it to Rozia?'

Hesiek came nearer to his sisters and sat down at the table. 'Don't make fun of this, it's a serious matter. Father worries about us. And he feels that his time is short.'

All the harsh words Hela had intended to release now stuck in her throat. The three of them sat there, deep in sorrow.

'Who is the man?' Hela finally asked, assuming that Hesiek certainly knew. Father had no secrets from him.

'His name's Schiffman. Natan Schiffman, from a good family. A decent man, I think.' It was evident that he did not know much more than this.

'But how is it possible? How can one give a girl like Sala to a man she has never met? Would you be willing to be married to a woman you'd never met?'

Hesiek gave his sisters a sidelong glance and said light-heartedly, as if by the way,

'That won't happen to me because I already know my future wife.'

His sisters looked at him open-mouthed, and he smiled. Then he got up and turned towards the kitchen.

'I'll bring a glass of tea,' he said.

'Ah, you're probably thinking of that silly little Bronka,' Hela tried to guess.

He didn't respond, and left the room quickly.

'That was a poor slip of the tongue on your part,' Hania remarked. 'And you're quite wrong. Bronka, like me, is almost 18. She's a full-grown woman. And not at all silly. Even if she is innocent in may ways, that has nothing to do with stupidity. She's doing the job of head of her family now, and she's changed a lot lately. We've all changed ...'

'I'm sorry,' said Hela. 'I didn't know, that she and Hesiek ...'

'I didn't know either. She's become very reserved lately. I only know that she doesn't have a permit to stay in the city. Everyone in Susser House, where she lives, has to leave. She hasn't managed to get the necessary permit. Now she has to start wandering on the roads with her old grandmother and those three brats, her brothers. I don't envy her.'

Hesiek came back with the glass of tea, which wasn't tea, just water spiced with something strange. They talked about their father's condition.

That night Hela couldn't sleep. She was riled at herself for having made that sharp remark about Bronka, whom she liked and admired. She seemed to have hurt Hania even more than Hesiek.

The next day, early in the morning, Hania slipped out of the house and set off for the Guesser House, to see Bronka. Suddenly she had felt a longing for her friend who recently, because of the many things she had to do and the many responsibilities on her shoulders, had rarely come to visit them. With rapid steps she crossed Krakowska Street. As she approached the corner of Rabbi Maizels Street she noticed an unusual commotion. The residents of the large building were vacating it, with their children and belongings. People carrying bundles were coming out of the house one after the other. Children helped to carry various items, and the little ones swarmed around the grown-ups' legs. Horse-drawn carts waited outside the building, and Austrian officials supervised the evacuation. Hania felt grateful to God, or to the Higher

Providence, or to whoever, for having brought her here today. A tremor went through her body at the very thought that she might have come too late and have missed seeing her friend before her hasty departure. She quickened her pace and climbed the stairs, taking them two at a time. At a turn of the staircase they met and fell into each other's arms. Bronka put down the things she was carrying and they sat down on the steps. Suddenly Bronka embraced her again and burst out crying. Hania too felt her eyes misting up. These were brief moments of weakness. Bronka quickly wiped her tears and smiled at Hania, her eyes full of meaning.

'There were a thousand and one things I wanted to tell you, and now – I can't find the words, and there's no time left.'

Hania thought that Bronka might find the time to tell her what was going on between her and Hesiek.

'Did you want to tell me something especially important?'

'Lots of important things,' Bronka sounded evasive.

'To do with boys?'

Bronka blushed, and Hania pressed: 'I already know.'

'How do you know?' she asked in a whisper, and the blush turned crimson.

I'm guessing.' Hania was stepping on thin ice.

'... It isn't at all serious... And anyway... there's nothing tying me to him.'

'But Hesiek said he was going to marry you!'

'Hesiek?!'

'Who did you think I was talking about? Who were you talking about? You're a riddle to me. What were you hinting at?'

'God, I'm so confused!' Bronka felt the taste of Srulek's kiss on her lips. Perhaps she could have told her friend about him, but the time wasn't right for that kind of conversation.

'I'm so confused,' she repeated. Then she pulled herself together, and added: 'There hasn't been anything between Hesiek and me. You can rest easy on that score.'

Hania shrugged, as if to say that it was none of her business and she didn't care anyway, but Bronka didn't let her interrupt.

'We have no time for idle talk. We have to say good-bye now. They're already waiting for me. I'll write to you, I'll write you all the things I wanted to tell you. I hope the mail will work properly. These days one can't know. Take care of yourself, and I hope we'll see each other again soon. Tell your father I hope he gets better and give my regards to your brothers and sisters. Be well, my dear, till we meet again.'

She ran after her depleted family, who were making their way through the crowd: the old grandmother and the three boys, her brothers.

Hania remained where she was, with doubts and longing in her heart.

Some two months later Sala was married to Natan Schiffman.

In the negotiations conducted before the wedding between the families of the bride and groom, Schiffman's parents had promised to take care not only of all the needs, but also of all the additional wishes of the lovely bride. They displayed generosity towards and understanding of her interest in the arts, and promised that after the war, when the troubles were over, she would be able, if she wanted, to travel to Vienna, Paris and London, to feast her eyes on the art treasures and to absorb the advanced western culture that interested her so much. She would be able to live the life of a lady, the resources would be adequate for that. They also made no fuss about the dowry that the bride might bring to their family; Natan was their only son and in any case everything they owned would pass to him.

Sala received the news of her forthcoming engagement with her characteristic submissiveness. Her sisters had expected an outburst on her part, or resistance, but there was no sign of either. Hela quietly observed her sister, wondering what was going on inside her.

As the days passed, and Hela got to know the Schiffman family, her anxieties subsided. Suddenly Sala's future started looking quite good to her. Deep inside, she began to think that her first judgment had been hasty. After all, it was not easy to find good husbands, or families who were willing to generously take care of all one's needs, including trips abroad. Hela had always been attracted by the thought of traveling. Since her earliest childhood she had dreamed of Paris, London, Rome ... In her imagination she saw herself touring these famous places, meeting interesting, wordly people. Secretly, she even started hoping that a similar opportunity might arise for her, not something worse.

Rozia was cautious about the future. Speaking forcefully, as she usually did, without mincing her words, she said: 'His parents' promises aren't worth much. It's not his parents she's marrying, but him. We'll see what happens after their first night together!'

Of course even the brave Rozia didn't dare to say these things in the presence of Father or Hesiek. Her audience was limited to her two sisters, Hela and Hania. The eyes of both girls grew wide with amazement. Hania lowered her gaze to the floor.

'These are very intimate matters. They're things one doesn't talk about,' said Hela, uncertainly.

'Really? So we've been taught, that's true, one doesn't talk about them and afterwards one pays the price. Things one doesn't talk about!' she scoffed.

'And I think,' Hania said hesitantly, 'that in the choice of a partner one needs a lot of luck. Even without a matchmaker one can make mistakes. Except if one falls in love.'

She blushed.

'But how can you fall in love, if you're not allowed to even touch before the wedding?' Rozia scoffed. 'Oh, how innocent you both are! In every generation, in all times since Adam and Eve, mankind has known sin. Good is always involved with evil, pleasure with suffering, and doing with mistakes.'

'Or perhaps, perhaps what is thought of as sin isn't really sin at all?' Hania asked, pensively.

Rozia's words had been prophetic. Something was wrong between Sala and Schiffman. A week after the wedding, during the 'Seven Blessings', the two of them walked about among their guests like shameful shadows, afraid to look into each other's eyes. The family had gathered in the

Schiffman house. The new husband's parents were affable and despite the difficult times had made every effort to receive their guests graciously. But that was not the most important thing.

Natan Schiffman was about 30 years old, thin and pale of face. The hair on his head was something between blond and ginger, and his beard was yellowish and thinning. His pale eyes evaded a direct gaze, and his face was sealed. On one side of his back a hump stood out.

Hela attributed the tension between her sister and her brother-in-law to their natural shyness, and hoped it would pass. But days passed, and Sala, who had always held her head high, now let her head droop, like a flower whose stem has lost its sap. And the light in her eyes went out.

The shock came two weeks after the wedding, when she came home, carrying her bundle of clothes. Her face was pale, her eyes were red from crying. Her sisters didn't ask her any questions.

Father was told that she had taken a short holiday from her new home. He asked no questions either.

Schiffman came to visit his wife in her father's house. Embarrassed and shy, he rang the doorbell. Hania let him into the room where his wife Sala was sitting, beautiful and stone-like, like a statue of Venus.

He stopped beside her, crushing his hat in his hands.

'Please, sit down,' she forced herself to say.

'Will you drink a glass of tea, Natan?' asked Hela, trying to make her voice sound merry.

After a long pause he replied. 'No, thank you. Really no.'

'Then I'll go and make the tea.'

Hela got up and Hania followed her. They went out quietly, leaving behind them two people whose continued life together was threatened by a serious problem which they did not know how to cope with.

Sala stayed a long time in her father's house, and her fear of returning to her husband was palpable. What was she afraid of? No one knew.

'These are things one doesn't talk about,' Rozia jeered.

What also amazed everyone was the fact that Schiffman's parents had stopped interfering and had vanished from sight. One day Schiffman came, and Hela, who opened the door, immediately understood by his behavior that he had decided to be forceful and practical. Even before he met his wife he asked to speak to her father.

At first Hela thought to spare her sick father unnecessary excitement, but Schiffman insisted. Hela understood that the matter was serious, and that it was impossible to refuse Schiffman. And perhaps Father would have something to suggest, perhaps they would decide to consult a rabbi?

Schiffman went into the father's room. Sala waited tensely, her eyes aflame and her cheeks burning. Hania and Hela sat beside her, like two faithful bodyguards. From the next room came the sound of speech, unclear, fragments of words in Yiddish. And then - silence. Finally Schiffman came out and stood in front of his wife.

'You're coming home with me. Right now!'

Her two sisters stood up and placed themselves between the couple. Hela spoke.

'She won't come against her will. Don't command her.'

Sala got up too. She stroked Hania, who was crying profusely, on the head, and said gently to Hela: 'You two don't have to do my fighting for me, I have to manage with my problems by myself.'

Schiffman, his eyes turned down, said quietly:

'I want what's good for you,' and burst out crying.

The four of them stood there, unable to raise their eyes. From the next room they heard the sound of their father's stifled sobbing.

'I'll go with you,' Sala said quietly.

One day, to relieve the tension a little, Hania, Hela and Haim decided to visit their sister Mania. The new baby, who was already three months old, was a marvel in their eyes. The first-born daughter Rela, was a year-and-a-half old, and also sweet, chattering in two languages – in Polish with her mother and in Yiddish with her father. When they arrived at their sister's house they found Sala there. They knew that Sala often visited here lately, to find relaxation in the chores of which here there was always an abundance.

They all stood around the cot and the baby raised her gleaming brown eyes to them, and shifted her gaze from one person to the next. A radiant smile spread over her little face, and her tiny hands and feet waved vigorously in the air.

'How cute, what a sweetie! I could stand and watch her for hours!' said Hania.

Hela went up to the elder girl, who also wanted attention from the guests, and Sala, who was like a member of the household there, took the baby out of the crib and spoke to her.

'Now I'll wash you nicely with soap and water, and then I'll put baby oil on your skin, and I'll dress you in nice clothes and I'll comb your hair into a cock's comb, and you'll be the most beautiful baby in the world!'

Mania smiled at her good-naturedly.

'You talk to her as if she understands.'

'Perhaps she does understand, who knows? See how she laughs and reaches her hands out to me. She loves me.'

Mania went into the kitchen to prepare dinner for everyone. Hania and Haim sang songs to Rela and Hela told her stories, and they all imitated the voices of forest animals and walked around on all fours to make her laugh. The little girl laughed fit to split, and demanded 'Another story! Another song!'

Suddenly an awful scream resounded through the house. Everyone froze. The scream had come from the bedroom, where Sala was supposed to be washing the baby. Little Rela was the first to run to where the scream had come from. All the others stood stock still, afraid to make a move. Within seconds they heard the hysterical crying of Rela. Mania came running from the kitchen, holding a large wooden spoon, with remains of dough sticking to it. Four pairs of eyes stared in awful silence.

It turned out that the large pot of boiling water which Sala had prepared for the baby's bath had slipped out of her hands, boiling water had spilled over the delicate body. The baby had no time to make a sound – her small body had turned instantly into a wretched bundle of torn and crinkled tissue. Someone ran out into the street to call for assistance. All the Red Cross ambulances were now in the service of the military hospitals.

Hania ran as quickly as she could to the first-aid station. Panting, choking with emotion, she told them in broken sentences what had happened. They promised to come quickly, but told her that she would have to wait patiently until one of the doctors was free. In the meantime they asked her for the address where the awful accident had happened. When she said 'Krakusa Street, Podgorze', the station-worker looked at her with cold eyes and hissed:

'What are you getting so excited about, little Jewess? Do you think we don't have more important problems than one of your vermin getting scalded and dying?'

In the meantime a Jewish children's doctor – who had in treated the children of the family – arrived at the house Krakusa Street. By the time he arrived, the baby was no longer alive.

Sala kept shouting: 'I murdered her!'

The doctor tried to pacify her, and gave her an injection. Mania sat unmoving, and mumbled: 'Good God, have mercy on us ... The Lord giveth and the Lord taketh away ... O God, who are we compared with You ...'

Haim and Hela took little Rela to the kitchen and went on telling her stories. The child listened quietly, tears dripping from her intelligent eyes.

Hania had vanished, as if the earth had swallowed her up.

Krakow, April, 1916
Dear Bronka,

Yesterday, quite by accident, I met a woman who brought me news of you. I was awfully excited and asked her to tell me as much as she could about you, but she didn't know much, only that she'd seen you in Bratislava. She's quite sure it was you and not someone else. She even described what you looked like: 'An exceptional figure among the Jewish refugees in Bratislava: blond, round-faced, blue eyed and pug nosed', and I felt everything inside me tightening up with excitement, I so wanted to see you. The woman told me she'd seen you together with your three brothers. She described them to me and said that one of them, apparently the biggest, was wearing the old cap of some discharged soldier, and the smallest was sporting an amusing straw hat, while the third, the middle one, even there, in Slovakia, had on the traditional skull-cap and was growing his side-curls. The description fitted what I remember of your brothers, and a stone rolled off my heart on hearing that you are all alive and well. I didn't know what to tmake of your absence and your silence. Everyone who leaves this city seems vanish like a stone in the ocean. The evacuations are continuing all the time, for the battle area isn't far from here, and people are hanging on with their fingernails, looking for all kinds of ways to avoid becoming refugees.

At home we are sad. We still don't know where Menashe is. My skin goes prickly when I think of him. It's almost two years since we've had a sign of life from him, and he hasn't seen his children. They no longer remember him.

Not long ago my sisters made a little party for me for my eighteenth birthday. I missed you there terribly, I thought of you all the time and I remembered that in November you too will reach this lovely age. Perhaps by November the war will be over? I remember our last meeting on the stairs at the Susser House. Almost a year has passed since then. You promised you'd write me all the things we didn't have time to talk about. You haven't written, and in the meantime new things have happened, compared with which everything that happened before then just pales. Or am I wrong? For above all, it's the personal things that I'd like to talk to you about. War or no war, we're just flesh and blood. Do you remember that then, on the steps, you started telling me something? You hinted at some meeting you'd had? And you got confused. When will we be able to see each other again and to talk face to face? Not long ago I had a terrible shock. It's connected to the tragic death of my sister Mania's baby daughter, and an insult I got from a stupid worker in the first aid station of the Red Cross. 'Little Jewess,' he said to me. I can't write about it, I'm ashamed because I don't know what hurt me more, the death of the baby or that insult. I feel like a sinful straying creature. I would like to believe in a free Poland, as Zegartowska taught us. I feel the need to belong to something noble, to heroes and achievers, but now suddenly I'm not sure that my choice has been right. I'm afraid of encounters with people like that station worker. I'm writing you without knowing your address. I simply had to get some of this distress of my chest, I won't go on until I get your address or until I receive a letter from you …

Yours, Hania

Not many days later, the long-awaited letter from Bronka arrived. Hania kissed the envelope before opening it. 'From Bratislava, from Bronka', she said to Hesiek, and watched his response. 'Want the stamps?'

'Stamps, no. What does she write?'

'I haven't read it yet,' she said, and went to find a quiet place for herself where she could be alone with the letter.

Bratislava, April 1916
Dear Hania,

I don't understand why you don't reply to my letters. I've already written two or three and I've had no reply. Of course it's not impossible that you didn't receive them, and that they have vanished somewhere along the way, in all this chaos that rules in our turbulent world.

Now I simply don't know where to begin. In my earlier

letter I described to you the place where we're staying. It's a kind of refugee camp where you have to fight tooth and nail for every inch of space and for every crumb of food. I don't need to tell you that there are people who know how to do that much better than me. But we too have learned to manage. In the end the five of us received a place that isn't too bad, in a vacant storehouse, and we've done what we could with it. We've even decorated the place with all sorts of things we found. Our grandmother, Grandma Herrstein, is our savior really. From various peelings and crumbs she makes us 'variegated' meals, and the main thing is that we don't starve. As refugees we do get financial assistance from the government, but without Grandma I couldn't manage. She has all kinds of strategies to keep the money, which loses its value from day to day, exchanging it for corn flour, potatoes, and the like. My brothers are working, and add to our livelihood. They've changed a lot. I watch them and see how different they are from each other. It makes me doubt the theory that education, environment and conditions are what determine human character. I think that every human being comes into the world with spiritual capacities unique to himself. Take my brother Wowek, the eldest of the three. He's a real thinker. People here call him 'Philosopher'. Someone gave him a discharged soldier's cap and he refuses to part with it. He's only fifteen, but people treat him with respect, a little, perhaps, because of the cap, but mostly because of his capacity to explain and develop thoughts and because of his knowledge of politics. Politics, that's an inexhaustible subject here. People talk and interpret from morning to night. Is it the same with you?

My second brother, Shaye, has become more religious than before. He's really fanatical. He watches over us lest we deviate from the way of the precepts, and reminds his brothers of the times for prayer. Yesterday I cried because someone stole some good soap that I was keeping for myself, and now I have to wash myself like everybody else, with coarse laundry soap. Perhaps it's childish to cry over a silly thing like that, at any rate I cried and said 'What a life, what a world!' Shaye explained to me that we're still not living our real lives, that we're only in the passage-way, in the corridor to the world-to-come, and that whatever happens now, in this world, we should accept with equanimity. Wowek scoffed at him. Wowek believes that everything depends on people. The existing regime has indeed failed, he believes, but the communist revolution is what will redeem mankind. Because in the communist regime there will be equality and no one will need to steal anything. They started quarreling and the distance between them was abysmal. I promised both of them that I would make do with the coarse laundry soap, but neither of them was satisfied and they continued philosophizing.

I was amazed to hear Wowek's views. He will have trouble with our parents. They have surely never imagined that in their petit-bourgeois household a red revolutionary was sprouting.

We of course miss Father and Mother, and worry about them. Especially Moniusz, my little brother, he's absolutely sick with longing. It's Mother he misses most. I never knew he was so attached to her. Before the war I used to feel a bit of resentment towards Mother for being always so busy, and not with us. Now those complaints seem silly. She is what she is, and she's our mother, and we all love her very much. If only we could see her already, and Father too. Moniusz doesn't stop talking about them. In Mother he sees a symbol of self-sacrifice and initiative. He amuses us with his songs and his jokes. He's a spoiled child, and when there isn't anyone to spoil him he spoils himself. Everyone here loves him.

My brothers work distributing newspapers. Every day they go to the press, help in arranging the pages in place, and then distribute the newspapers to subscribers. This work of theirs gives us a threefold benefit: first - they're occupied, second, they earn money, and third, they're always the first to know the news.

I worry a lot about you and your family. According to the news, the area of Krakow and Galicia is all disputed territory which keeps passing from hand to hand. Now the Austrians are again in Lwow and Stanislawow, and the Germans hold Warsaw and have also entered Kovno and Vilna. It frightens me that the war is spreading so!

Wowek says that the British army has advanced on Mesopotamia, in the direction of Bagdad. And the Turks have gained control of the Suez Canal. All these places are far away from us, yet they're still near. For the Land of Israel is in that region. The Land of Israel, and Jerusalem, which we have heard about since our earliest childhood. I feel that the fate of the places close to the Land of Israel is important to me – it seems that the Land of Israel is very important to me.

Yours, Bronka

Krakow, August 1916
Dear Bronka,

I'm so glad that at last we can correspond. It's quite clear to me that not all the letters reach their destination, but at any rate there is now contact between us.

Here it's a crazy world. They're still evacuating civilians from the city. Every day people are evicted, supposedly for their own security, but at the same time they bring other people here, from different areas. It's an endless moving of peoples. Masses of homeless people live in temporary edifices, refugees like yourselves. You know what that kind of life is better than I do. We're still hanging on somehow, and still have our apartment, I hope so much that we'll be allowed to stay here. My father's condition has improved slightly, but it's unlikely that he'll ever be himself again. If he could only hear something about Menashe, that would surely do him some good, but unfortunately we have no news at all, apart from the general reports about the millions of soldiers who, in the

74

best case, are now spending their third year in the defense trenches – if they haven't been killed at the front.

People talk a lot here about Pilsudski's regiments. There is no doubt that Pilsudski is a great man. He is preparing the ground for Poland's independence.

Sala is going through divorce proceedings. Schiffman is a decent man but it seems that in relations between two people that isn't enough. I think she can't bear to have sexual relations with him. We two have never spoken directly about love and sex. Sometimes it may be easier in writing than in speech, to pass barriers created by habits and education. Schiffman forced Sala to return home with him. She went, but their relations didn't improve. On the contrary, there was a further deterioration. Rozia says that we're very backward in our way of life, that a woman has no rights in our society, we are like the husbands' maid servants and they can do whatever they like with us, while modern women in the world of today are striving for emancipation.

And on the same subject: Hela has fallen in love! I discovered the fact only a few days ago. It's still too early to tell you about it. She herself hasn't told anybody anything, but I'm close to this sister of mine and I can feel that something great is happening in her life. Perhaps in the next letter I'll write you more.

By the way, I met your Aunt Fela. She's an exceptional woman and manages to 'fix' everything. The authorities ordered the evacuation of the house where she lives, but she managed to get a permit to remain. Her child is developing marvelously, and he looks very intelligent. She looks after him like a model mother. Who else haven't I written about? Perhaps it will interest you to know that Hesiek has stopped studying at the *yeshiva*. At present he isn't down for conscription, and he's building on the chance that he'll manage to evade it. He sits with Father a lot. I suppose Father is telling him the secrets of the business.

Yours, Hania

Bratislava, (no date)
Dear Hania,

It's so good to get letters from you. Life has become better since I've started waiting for the mail, and not in vain. You have no idea how much I miss you all, and the city, and home.

Yesterday we received a brief note from our parents. They're both well. Mother is managing to stay near Father, and is taking care of him. We're all proud of her. We laughed, and cried, in turns, and we wanted to know more about them, but the note was very short, it must have been written in a hurry. But that too is good.

I was glad to read about my Aunt Fela and little Itzik. We all knew, from the day he was born, that he was a 'little genius'. He really is a gifted child. I remember her with great warmth; actually it was she who raised me and my brothers. She is rough with her tongue, but she has a heart of gold. Grandma Herrstein, her mother, told me in utmost secrecy – God forbid I should tell my brothers – that Fela too hasn't succeeded in her marriage. She thought she would find a man who would be able to understand her, to work together with her, build a life together. But actually there is no love or attraction between her and her husband. It's marvelous how out of a marriage like that such a child was born. But their case is different to the one Rozia described. In their home, Fela is the dominant one. She is the industrious and talented one, and she's the one who earns their livelihood. And he – he devotes all his time to the holy books. I think that with him it's an escape from reality, an escape from life, which he can't cope with.

Whom has Hela fallen in love with? I'm dying of curiosity. I'm relying on you that when you can you'll write me about it. You know I have a lot of affection for your whole family, and feel that that's mutual.

As for antisemitism, we feel it here too. We keep to ourselves and don't mix with the local population.

Yours, Bronka

During the third year of the war, Menashe was sent back from the Italian front, and the family was notified that he was in one of the hospitals in Krakow. Hesiek had already stopped studying at the *yeshiva* and spent all his time in the business. For hours he would sit bent over papers, while his father lay in bed and gave him instructions. The relationship between father and son was a wonderful one during this period. At the father's request, a desk had been put in the large dining room, which now also served as an office.

'We have to let Hai'cze know, so she can come and look after her husband,' said Rozia, who had managed to find out which hospital Menashe was in.

He had a slight wound, but his general condition was very bad, frighteningly so. 'You'll be alarmed when you see him,' said Rozia, the only one of the family who had seen him since his return from the front. 'He looks like a shadow of his former self.'

Hesiek took time off from business and traveled to Chszanow to tell his sister-in-law that her husband was alive and in Krakow. He came back quickly.

'Hai'cze and the children are not in Chszanow,' he told them on return. 'They've left, in the direction of the Carpathians. That's all I could find out. There's panic and terror in the villages there, and everyone who was able to, fled.'

'Fled? With the children? How is she managing, the poor thing?'

'She'll manage,' said Hesiek. 'Children in wartime have small demands.'

'Yes, but afterwards they'll remain frightened and introverted all their lives.'

They looked at each other, worried and in silence. Their father got up quietly, and slowly walked to the flowerpots that stood beside the window. He inspected the leaves, turned the soil, wiped and watered them.

His children watched his actions affectionately.

'If only people might receive the treatment of a loving hand the way your plants do, Father,' said Rozia.

'Plants, like people, need looking after,' said the father pensively. 'Which of you will go and visit Menashe tomorrow?'

'I'll go to the hospital tomorrow with Rozia,' said Hela, and Rozia nodded in agreement.

The next day they set out for the hospital. Hela took a set of implements with her, with hot food for Menashe, who Rozia said was really starved.

'Many soldiers die not of their wounds, but of blood-poisoning, or simply of exhaustion or of lack of treatment.'

Hela felt a tremor run through her body.

'You speak of it so calmly, and it's so awful!'

'If you'd seen what I've been seeing every day these last years, you would be the same.'

'Will he die?' Hela asked, and regretted it at once, but it was too late to take back her words.

'Are you asking me? What am I, God? If he had a good doctor beside him, perhaps it might be possible to save him.'

Entering the hospital was a shock for Hela. For the first time in her life she saw horror close up. Young men with torn bodies, missing limbs, some blind, some half burned, screamed from every side and asked for help.

Following Rozia's instructions, Hela went through the entire hospital to look for a doctor and to try persuade him to come to Menashe's bed. Menashe himself lay there quietly, he was so exhausted. Hela didn't succeed in her mission, and the two of them stood beside Menashe's bed not knowing what to do. Hela felt a slight nausea.

'You're completely pale. You look as if you're about to faint. You'd better go, or they'll have to treat you too. Go on now, go!' Rozia almost threw her out, scolding her forgivingly.

Hela felt a dizziness in her head.

'I'll come again tomorrow,' she promised, and smiled weakly at Menashe. He smiled sadly back at her.

When she was outside again, she breathed in deeply. The fresh air filled her lungs and the sense of nausea passed.

She walked through the city streets, in the twilight of evening. She was not in a hurry to return home. When she passed through the tree-lined avenue called the Planty, she sat down on one of the benches and closed her eyes, trying with all her might to banish the dreadful sights of the hospital from her memory.

Before her inner eye there passed, one after another, the figures of people close to her who were in danger: her sick beloved father, Menashe lying helpless in his hospital bed, and Aleks, what would become of Aleks? How much longer would he stay in the city? When would she be able to speak with him alone?

Aleks was a young Jew who had deserted from the Austrian army. He was not the only deserter.

* * *

The third year of the war saw a worsening of the situation of the Austro–Hungarian Empire, because of differences of opinion between Vienna and Budapest, but even more because of division among the annexed nations. While the German nation and the Russian nation stood behind their warring armies – and after the heavy casualties identified even more with the fighting men – the nations that had gone to war on the side of the Hapsburg monarchy had started aspiring for independence. The longer the war lasted, the more acts of betrayal and cases of desertion struck at the Austrian army.

Aleks wandered around the city without a permit, without a food-card, without any papers at all. He was a good-looking young man with a lot of personal charm. Tall, with an athletic build and smiling eyes, he was every sensitive and delicate woman's dream man.

Hela fell in love with him at their first meeting. Aleks was always surrounded by people; other deserters grouped together around him. This was a group with no fixed address. Its members kept themselves hidden, and evaded even people who were on their side. Hela volunteered to act as contact between them and Jewish families in the city's institutions who wanted to help them. Hela knew quite well that the members of Aleks' group did not deny themselves the company of women. The more she came to know them, the more she learned about the other side of life. She discovered that there were always girls who were willing to spend time in the company of soldiers.

Prostitution, too, flourished in the suburbs. Doctors who specialized in skin ailments and venereal disease were overburdened with work. A great number of the poor easily became victims of syphilis and other terrible diseases. Wealthier people became impoverished by the expensive treatment of their organs, which were affected by the widespread diseases, and especially by the sums they paid to keep their treatment secret. For Hela, this was her first sight of a world she hadn't known existed. Until this time she had only known young men who were part of her close or distant family. Aleks was different to them all.

She didn't know how she could invite him to her home or initiate a meeting between him and her father. Aleks, for his part, didn't take her seriously. 'What do you want?' She said to herself privately. 'Do you want him to propose to you? This is neither the time nor the place.' Deep inside she knew quite well that with a fellow like Aleks she could develop a friendship even without a proposal of marriage. 'But perhaps he has other girls,' Hela tormented herself. 'Perhaps he's looking for another kind of girl, not one with "a good upbringing" like me?'

She opened her eyes. It was quiet in the avenue, and the evening chill penetrated through her thin blouse and made her shiver. The figure of Aleks did not depart from her inner eye.

She returned homewards full of guilty feelings. Everyone was waiting for her, wanting to hear how Menashe was, and she had been sitting on a bench in a public park, dreaming of her beloved.

Father and Hesiek were still sitting bent over the desk.

'What's the news?' they asked in unison.

She described the situation, trying to tone down the dreadful truth.

'We'll have to bring him here,' their father decided. He turned to Hesiek.

'Next week take care that the goods are delivered according to the orders we've received. This is an important deal and if you handle it responsibly and manage to keep to schedule, there'll be other orders after it. You'll have to be quick – to get past the sea blockade, to overcome the disruption of transport routes, and to supply our building timber to all who want it.

Remember, son, there will be a great boom in building soon. One can sense the new state about to be born, and at such times there is always a tremendous demand for building materials. And ask the girls to take care of getting Menashe transferred home.'

The next day Father's condition became more grave. Rozia didn't go out to work and stayed constantly beside his bed. Expertly and professionally she changed his sheets and washed him as he lay there. He suffered in silence and asked for nothing except analgesic drugs.

He was several weeks dying, but nevertheless when merciful death finally came it was a shock to the whole family. They bore their grief in silence, each of them feeling a strong sense of responsibility for the others. Each of them kept the image of their beloved father deep in their hearts.

From here on everyone's main concern was for Menashe, who during his stay in the military hospital had contracted severe pneumonia. The doctors in the hospital did not come to his bed, and it was impossible to obtain a private doctor. Hesiek and Rozia brought him home, and spent nights and days trying to save his life, but to no avail. Their devoted care was not able to master the disease – which in those days was not yet curable – and Menashe grew weaker and weaker. The critical hour arrived. The whole family were gathered in the large room: Mania and Shlomo, Sala, Schiffman, and all the others. Hela and Haim both had severe cases of influenza, and lay burning with fever in the girls' room. Menashe lay in his late father's room, struggling for his life. Mania was once more in the last months of pregnancy.

Suddenly jets of blood sprayed from Menashe's mouth. Rozia and Hesiek supported him, in a hopeless effort to ease his suffering.

Just then there came the sound of a body hitting the floor. Mania had fainted, and lay there helplessly, while inside her the baby moved. Her husband Shlomo rushed to her, and Hania fled from the room emitting broken sobs, which she could not control.

That night Menashe breathed his last.

He was buried beside the fresh grave of his father.

4 An Impossible Love

They remained alone. Two brothers and five sisters, one of them married to a hassid, a scholar years older than herself, and another wretched in her marriage and planning to get divorced. When the war ended, Menashe's wife and two children were supposed to return.

The apartment in Paulinska Street, with all its contents, remained under the control of the five who were still unmarried. In order of age, these were Rozia, Hesiek, Hela, Hania and Haim.

The business, in its entirety, passed to Hesiek, but he was obliged by his father's will to provide for the three who were younger than he: Hela, Hania, and Haim. Sala and Rozia each received a sum of money as their portion of the inheritance.

Mania received a pair of antique silver candlesticks and other objects of value.

Meir, Menashe's first-born, would – on reaching bar-mitzvah age – receive the *Humash* and the *Shass* (the annotated *Pentateuch*, and the set of the Six 'Orders' of the *Mishnah*), which Moshe Weinfeld had brought with him from his father's house on the other side of the Carpathians.

'He got all the property,' Rozia said to her sisters.

'Who?'

'Who? Hesiek, of course.'

They remained silent. After a while Hela spoke.

'The apartment belongs to all of us.'

'Can one turn one apartment into five? How much longer will we go on living together?'

'I wish we could move. Too many terrible things have happened in this apartment. Three people have died here already.'

'Four,' Rozia corrected. 'Don't forget our Roh'cze.'

'Leaving Haim her tuberculosis as a parting gift,' one of them added cynically.

The sisters were troubled, and suspicious. Hesiek worked from early morning until late at night, and the less they understood of his doings, the more their suspicions of him grew.

Time passed. One day Haim came in from the street with a sensational piece of news:

'America has declared war on Germany and her allies!'

'At last! The Germans were provoking American ships, not letting them pass. It's amazing that a great country like America has put up with that for so long!'

'That's because the Americans are originally from Europe. There are people there from Germany and Austria, from France and England and Holland. In America they all live under one flag, but they have families in the countries they came from, and those countries are in conflict with each other. Maybe that's why it has been so difficult for the Americans to mobilize an army.'

Haim spoke excitedly, standing in the middle of the room. His sisters looked at him in amazement. Where did he get all this knowledge about what went on beyond the ocean?

He was trembling with excitement.

'Great things will happen now. America's the land of freedom, the land of democracy!'

Hela slipped out of the house. She felt a need to hear some of what was being said in the streets. The Jewish part of Kazimierz had begun to look different. The war was still raging, but in the background there was a sense of disintegration. Among the ultra-orthodox Jews who filled the streets of Kazimierz now walked soldiers, deserters, wounded and bandaged men who had been released from hospitals, and homeless people who had come here from villages and smaller towns. All spoke of a great movement of peoples on the roads. People in rags fleeing from starvation and war, gathering in the big cities, seeking a roof over their heads and some bread to eat. In the courtyards of the houses, on the sidewalks, people gathered, listened, argued, interpreted and sighed. A great exhaustion and weariness could be felt, also a restrained joy, and a dread.

Hela reached the place where Aleks lived.

This was a dark room, without a single window. It was packed with excited young people, enthusiastically arguing. They were a secular crowd, though many of them wore skull-caps or hats, and some wore parts of army uniform – cap, jacket, or trousers.

Aleks was quiet and serious. He wore khaki army trousers, and his chest was bare, covered with curly hair. His stomach was smooth and white, and his shoulders broad. He was absorbed in some carpentry,   making some kind of small box or crate, and didn't notice her come in. She sat down in a corner and listened to the talk.

'Now that America's in the war the Germans will be defeated quickly. Turkey, her ally, will leave Palestine and the Jews will be allowed to settle there. That's what was decided in London.'

'And "our" Austria will have to break up.'

'It's already broken up. All the peoples that make up the monarchy are all demanding independence, and they'll get it too. It's already been discussed in the parliaments.'

'What, will Galicia become independent?'

'Galicia? We will gain independence. The Jews as a people will get independence.'

'How? We don't have a country.'

'We don't need a country. We'll be a free people even though we're scattered.'

'Don't talk nonsense!'

'It's not nonsense. It's been discussed in parliaments too.'

There was a bewildered silence. The young men didn't know how to respond to this staggering news. They didn't have enough information about what was going on. A short red-haired fellow climbed onto a chair and spoke excitedly: 'I tell you that a great hour is coming, and soon. So much blood has been spilled for nothing. Now Wilson will teach the Europeans something about democracy. He will demand freedom for all peoples. International co-operation. No more wars.'

'Idiot!' someone scoffed. 'Where did you read those beautiful words? This war isn't over yet. Millions of people are far from their homes. And the masses of degraded prisoners will also have something to say when they get back.'

'He's not an idiot at all,' someone else defended the redhead, who was still standing on the chair. 'What you said doesn't contradict what was said before. A great hour is coming, an opportunity that mustn't be missed. Poland will gain independence. That has already been promised her. And as for us, the Jews, I've heard that in Warsaw there's been a great awakening among the Jews. They're writing declarations and calling meetings. They're consolidating stands to be taken. The Zionists are the ones taking most of the initiative. Even before the war they had started looking after the interests of the Jewish people, and held international conferences and congresses. They had a conference in Helsingfors in Finland where they passed some important resolutions. Now, when a free Polish state comes into being, we too, the Jews, will make our demands to the free Polish government. Our comrades in Warsaw are planning for that fateful hour. We too are a people!'

'Yes, and the Poles have been waiting for almost 200 years for the moment when they regain their independence – you think they'll have nothing to do but listen to our demands,' someone scoffed.

'They've already said that there isn't room for two peoples on the banks of the Vistula!'

The argument reached a dead end. They knew parts of facts and each of them interpreted these differently. The Bundists argued with the Zionists while the assimilationists looked on in contempt. And what would the religious Jews say?

Hela made her way through to where Aleks was.

'What's going on here?' she asked.

'As you can see, they're yelling and arguing.'

Is that all he has to say to me, she thought. And aloud she said:

'What are you thinking of doing?'

He stopped working, put down his tools, and looked at her.

'You know what? It's too noisy here. Let's get out of here. We'll find a quiet spot and sit down and talk. OK?'

They passed through the disputants, who continued yelling and arguing.

In the Planty avenue spring flowers were blooming in all their glory, as if they knew that this was the last spring of the war. They sat down on a vacant bench. Aleks spoke.

'I'm leaving Krakow soon.'

'Why?'

'There's nothing here for someone like me to look forward to. Soon Galicia will be liberated, and then all Poland. The Polish army will be organized. But before that, when the Polish regiments come home from abroad, their first aim will be pogroms against the Jews. They'll accuse the Jews of treason, of supporting the enemy, and who knows what else. It's an old story. You'll see that I was right. And then a Polish government will arise. But the Poland of Pilsudski that will come into existence is not the summit of our dreams. I look to Russia – there great things are happening. The weaklings who ruled there until now and ruined the nation have fallen, and great men have taken over at last. Great leaders. The Russian people want peace – they want freedom. Lenin promises freedom, and he will know how to make it happen. He has put the regime in the hands of the workers and the soldiers who have suffered so much and he's already planning the nationalization of the lands and their distribution to the people. My place is there. I'm as convinced as he is that the revolution in Russia is the first step towards a great revolution throughout the entire world.'

Hela heard him in astonishment. First Wilson, now Lenin, and in any case these were not the subjects she wanted to talk about with Aleks. She felt that the belief he held was no less strong than a religious belief. She already knew, from her conversations with her religious sister, that people who believed could not be made to think in any other way.

'When are you thinking of leaving here, and for how long?' she asked quietly.

He took her hand and brought it to his face.

'Don't be sad', he said gently, 'I'm not leaving tomorrow, I'll try to let you know when it's to be.'

She wanted to fall into his arms, to bury her head in his chest. But he sat there distanced and pensive. His great plans occupied him more than anything else, and separated him from her.

She sat there taut, restraining herself, waiting.

He got up. 'See you soon,' he said, and left.

5 Happy is He Who Believes

'Hania! Haniusia!'

'Bronka? Is that you? God, how I've missed you! When did you get back?'

The two friends fell into each other's arms and tears came to their eyes.

'How I've missed you!' Hania repeated, almost choking with excitement.

'What about me? I've been counting the days ...'

They fell silent, both at a loss for words. There was so much to say, but suddenly it seemed that a curtain had fallen on all the memories, all the events, all the thoughts. Everything was compressed somewhere inside, closed and locked, and they could find no words to express their feelings.

'What have you got to tell me?' Hania asked.

'A lot! So much!'

'Then speak, speak ...'

'I missed you, I missed you ...' Bronka repeated.

'Let me see you. Show me how you look.' Hania overcame her excitement and scrutinized her friend. 'Not bad. You haven't got fat, you haven't got thin, you haven't changed a bit!'

'What did you expect? That I'd be old already?'

They laughed, the laughter of 20-year-old girls, and walked through the streets arm-in-arm, bumping into the people coming toward them, swaying, taking two steps forward and one step back, like drunks.

'Oh, how good it is to be home again! Come, let's get outside Kazimierz for a bit. I have to see the city I haven't seen for so long.'

They walked past *di alte shule*, an ancient building dating back to the fourteenth century, its gothic style making it stand out from all the other buildings in the area. Beside the synagogue there was a stir – more Jews than usual seemed to be going in and out.

'What's happening here?' asked Bronka.

Hania shrugged. 'I don't think there's anything special going on. Probably it's simply that lots of people have come back from abroad, like you have, and they're coming here to pray.' She wasn't certain of her reply, however, and added: 'When I've come here I've seen many Jews gathering and standing around other synagogues too. But you wanted to get away from the Jewish streets, didn't you? So let's go.'

It was the autumn of 1918.

Bronka and Hania straightened their clothes, fixed their hair, and blended into the Polish streets.

In the Planty avenues which bordered on Ditlowska Street, stood oak and chestnut trees, grand and erect. Their gleaming fruit had long since fallen, and now they stood decorated in their colored autumn leaves. Here and there a leaf broke off and dropped gently, to join the carpet of fallen leaves that rustled under the feet of the passers-by. From some distance away church bells rang. There was excitement in the air.

'How I love this city!' said Bronka, clasping Hania's arm more tightly.

'How beautiful the autumn leaves are!' They brought their heads closer..

The gentle breeze,that was mixing the green oak leaves with the red chestnut leaves, now mixed Bronka's fair hair with Hania's dark hair. Their dresses flew up all the wind got strongert.

'Where will we go?'

'Come, let's go with the flow. I feel as if this whole street is streaming like a river – everyone's going in the same direction.'

They merged with the stream of people who were indeed hurrying with special purpose. The stream pushed them towards the Jagiellona University. Two Austrian officers came walking casually against the stream. Suddenly some Polish children, about 10 or 12 years old, came up to them, stood on tip-toe, and pulled medals off their uniforms. The officers smiled and patted the children's heads, an idyllic picture! Similar scenes were now occurring all over the place. From a side street some boys ran out with a special edition of the evening newspapers:

'The Austrians are moving out of Galicia! Polish legions are taking over their positions ...'

By the Government offices, large groups of Austrian officers and soldiers could be seen dismantling their command-posts, vacating offices, hurrying to leave.

'They sat here so many years and now they can't wait to leave,' came voices from the crowd.

By the main entrance to the University, a large group was assembled of students and other people, and in a spontaneous gush this whole group began to sing, loudly and in unison:

> Poland is not lost yet
> As long as life is ours
> What was taken from us by force
> By force we'll make it ours
>
> March, march, Dombrowski ...

Hania and Bronka stood to attention like everyone else, paying homage to the song that was to become Poland's national anthem.

'Come on, let's get back to our district,' Bronka said suddenly.

'I'm sure that by now the people there also know that the Austrians are leaving the city.'

'Not yet,' Hania pleaded. 'How about going to the big market square, to Sukiennica. I'm sure they're celebrating there, beside the Kosciuszko tablet.'

Bronka was wary. 'I don't feel like getting into a crowd. I remember things I heard from customers in my parents' store. They used to say that every change involves danger for the Jews, that Jewish people don't like changes.'

'You're talking nonsense,' Hania scolded her. 'The war's about to end, maybe it's already over. Shouldn't we be happy?' Then she suddenly remembered the crude words of the first-aid station attendant: 'Why should we get excited by one of your Jewish vermin dying?' And this Jagiellona University – how many troubles had Jewish students suffered inside its walls? How many Poles had borrowed money from Jews, with interest, and had then accused, insulted, and debased them because of this contemptible occupation of theirs?

'Yes,' she said finally however, 'I'm happy. A new day is dawning for Poland and for us.' They withdrew from the excited crowd and found a secluded bench in one of the quiet sections of the Planty.

'We've been talking and talking and we still haven't said a thing to each other,' Bronka remarked.

'My father died,' Hania said sadly.

'I heard. I cried. I'm sure you know I admired him very much.'

Hania nodded. 'And Menashe's dead too.'

'I'm sorry,' Bronka mumbled. 'That I didn't know.'

'Our family isn't the same any more. There's quarreling all the time.'

'Who quarrels with whom?'

'My sisters have ganged up against Hesiek.'

'Why?' Bronka asked in a whisper.

Hania shrugged slightly. 'I don't know. I don't understand what's going on at home. Envy, suspicion, the inheritance, money ... I don't know.'

'Pity,' said Bronka pensively. 'And what about Hela? Is she engaged?'

'Engaged? No. She's still in love, though. And she suffers. When it isn't mutual, the suffering can be very great, it seems.'

'Who is he?'

'I don't know. She's never brought him home.'

They sat there quietly, paying no attention to the tumult in the streets not far away. Hania rubbed a dry leaf in her hands and went on:

'Sala's involved in divorce proceedings, I already wrote you that. Our Roh'cia died, and Haim has tuberculosis. We wanted to put him into a sanatorium before he infects all of us, but the institutions are all chock-full, and until his turn comes … Hesiek's checking out the possibility of putting him in a private sanatorium, in Zakopane.[1] It'll cost a fortune. Each day there costs the equivalent of what a small family can live on modestly for a month. And the way there is blocked. Maybe now that the war's ending it'll be easier.'

'Where will Hesiek get so much money?'

Another shrug.

'That's his business. Now you tell me. It's your turn.'

'We were lucky. True, we suffered, and we wasted the best years of our life, but we've come back, and all of us are more or less all right.' Instinctively, Bronka lowered her eyes and her gaze rested on her fingers, which even now in the relative warmth of autumn, were swollen and red. The cold had caused them permanent damage. 'My parents came home, both of them well. I think that Mother really did do a great thing in going to be with Father. Many men who were alone simply got lost. No one knows if they're alive or dead. For the time being, I'm happy to be home together with everybody. But I know well enough that very soon I'll feel cramped there. If I want to do something and my parents won't let me, I won't be able to be obedient the way I was in the past.'

'I'm in a good situation,' Hania said bitterly, 'I can do whatever I feel like and nobody will care. With all the quarrelling going on at home now, especially between Hesiek and Rozia, I don't believe anyone has either the desire or the strength to keep an eye on me and on what I do.'

Bronka stroked her hand and smiled at her.

'Don't worry,' she said. 'What do they quarrel about?' she asked again.

'Everything. Come on, let's go.'

When they reached the Jewish quarter they immediately noticed the changed atmosphere. The large groups of Jews, which had earlier seemed like people come to pray in the synagogues, were actually groups organizing for self-defense. A rumor had spread through the streets of Kazimierz, that with the return of the Polish legions, pogroms against the Jews would break out. The Austrian regime was no longer functioning, and the Polish regime had not yet organized itself. At times like these, of changes in power, there is anarchy, and a good opportunity is provided to strike at the Jews; for the excited masses needed to be given a goal, there was no better scapegoat than the Jews.

The paradox was that among the Polish soldiers returning from many places of exile there were also many Jews, not a few of them officers. These had repoted that on the way, when they passed the Jewish quarters of Polish towns, the soldiers would attack the Jews, plundering their property, calling them traitors and informers who were unfaithful to Poland. The Jewish soldiers were torn by dual loyalty – between their obligations to the legion in which they served and their identification with their Jewish brothers in the villages and towns on the way. Most of them had left their camps and hurried on ahead of the regiments to warn the Jews in the towns of the approaching danger.

A Jewish officer who reached Krakow after deserting from the regiment of General Haller, who was returning as the head of regiments of Polish soldiers from exile in France had confirmed these things. Haller was known as a sworn hater of Jews, although the Jews who served under him were always treated well.

'You Jews are different,' he used to say. But they knew his jokes, and they also saw with their own eyes what his soldiers did.

'Jews! Don't be passive! If we don't defend ourselves, no one else will!' said the Jewish officer who had fled from General Haller's regiment. 'Jews! Defend yourselves! They will loot your property, rape your women, shear your beards. I've seen it with my own eyes.'

And the Jews were inclined to listen to him.

The main activists were the Jewish soldiers who had returned from the front, who knew how to handle weapons, and who had seen what had happened in the smaller towns. These were joined by religious Jews and *hassidim* with long beards and sidecurls, dressed in *kapotas* – all as one man they lent their shoulders to the defense of their families and their property.

'Come to our place,' Hania said to Bronka. 'I have to see what's happening at home.'

'I have to go home too first. As soon as I can I'll come and visit.'

They parted. Bronka turned towards Suesser House, and Hania towards Paulinska Street.

Jewish youngsters went from apartment to apartment, distributing leaflets of instructions prepared by the civil guard of Kazimierz. The leaflet told all families to provide themselves with iron rations of food and to hoard as large a supply of water as possible. It was possible that the quarter would be surrounded and isolated.

There were also instructions to firmly close the windows and doors of the houses and the shops with iron bars, and to prepare additional means of defense. Hania came in through the gate. It was already late, and the staircase was in total darkness. She groped her way up until she reached the door of their apartment. The bell wasn't working. She knocked and knocked and no one answered. She felt suddenly alarmed. Where was everybody? Without realizing what she was doing, she started kicking the door and banging it with her fists. When she'd already lost hope, she heard soft steps inside, and the hoarse voice of Haim asked:

'Who's there?'

'It's me, Hania. Open, Haim! Thank God you're home.'

He spent a long time on the lock and the bolt, and finally the door opened.

Haim stood before her, a youth of 18, handsome and tall, with flushed cheeks, looking a very symbol of health. On a momentary impulse she forgot his tuberculosis and fell into his arms, but he gently moved her aside, far from him.

'What's happening here? Where is everybody?' she asked.

'What everybody?' His hoarse voice immediately revealed his secret. 'Rozia hasn't been home for two days, she hasn't even come back to sleep. Hesiek was called by the block commander to serve as his deputy in the defense operation. You know what's going on, don't you?'

'I know, I know,' she said impatiently. 'And Hela?'

'She's gone too.'

Haim had an attack of coughing, dry, straining his lungs.

Hania felt hopeless. She would gladly have returned to the street, to join some active group, to do something. Or she would have gone to Bronka, or to Mania. But she couldn't leave Haim alone.

'I'll make you a glass of tea,' she said, and when he didn't object, she quickly asked:

'Have you eaten at all today? Or has everyone forgotten you?'

'I don't have any appetite, anyway.'

She went into the kitchen, and when she came back with a tray of food and drink, she found him sitting on the bed, rolling up laundered bandages.

'Several hours ago someone threw this in here and asked me to roll them up, in case there are wounded.

'Eat now,' Hania ordered.

He obeyed. Then they both sat and rolled bandages.

Later that night Hela returned. Her face was pale, and her eyes sunken. Hania and Haim looked up at her, but she wasn't inclined to tell them anything. Some time later she said:

'The attack will come tomorrow, Haller and his men are advancing on Kazimierz.'

'How many are they?'

'Very many. And there's always a rabble that's willing to join in, when it's a matter of looting a Jewish quarter.'

'Who did you see out there?' Hania asked cautiously, guessing what was bothering her sister.

'I'm worried about someone I didn't see,' Hela replied, and said no more.

'Go to sleep, Haim. We'll all go to sleep. We'll need all our strength for tomorrow.'

The next day General Haller's troops reached the gates of the Jewish quarter of Kazimierz, and met strong, massive, and well-organized resistance. At first they were scornful and thought to repulse the 'cowardly Jewlings', but when these drew knives against them, Haller's soldiers turned on their tracks. No blood was spilled.

Hesiek came home exhausted.

'We can open the windows. The danger has passed,' he said.

Other people came into the room with him – relatives and neighbors, all of them talking about the recent events.

'Poland is reborn. Today we had our first encounter with our new landlords.'

'Don't jump to conclusions. What happened today is still the continuation of the war. It'll take time till law and justice take over.'

'Law and justice? Here?'

'Yes. Here. We'll receive legitimate rights and the law will protect us.'

'Happy is he who believes. I think, that if we want to build a new life, then not here. Why do we need landlords? We have to go to Palestine.'

'To Pales-vuss?' someone joked.

No one was excited about the idea of going to Palestine.

'Desert, blazing heat, malaria. Whoever wants to, let him go. I believe we'll be granted autonomy here, and we'll be able to conduct our affairs and lead our Jewish life. We, not they, will be the landlords!'

Hania didn't know if this had been said jokingly or in earnest.

'What are we – Poles or Jews?' she asked.

'Both,' someone replied.

She sighed deeply.

'I'd like to be one thing, not two.'

They were so concerned with themselves, with their personal and family problems, with the defense of Kazimierz, that they didn't pay attention to what was going on in the Jewish world around them. After all, Krakow was not the only place in the world. Krakow was indeed the biggest city in Western Galicia under the Austro–Hungarian regime, which had collapsed like a house of cards at the end of the war. But the most important city in Galicia, situated in the east of the province, was Lwow, and this city became an important center in Jewish political life. During the war Lwow had passed from the Austrians to the Russians who were fighting them, and back again. During these times extraordinary suffering had been caused to the local civilian population, and the Jewish population suffered sevenfold, for they always, whoever ruled and whoever was defeated, were accused of treachery on behalf of the enemy.

But the center of Jewish life now was in Warsaw, and from there exciting news arrived.

When the city passed from Russian occupation to German, the Jews in Warsaw were accused of having brought in the Prussian enemy by means of telephone calls in which they spoke to the Germans in their jargon and revealed to them all the secret places. Among other ridiculous accusations, it was also said that the phylacteries which Jews wore on their foreheads, were actually secret and sophisticated instruments for the communication of information.

Towards the end of the war the population of Warsaw increased astoundingly, especially the Jewish population. Oppressed and persecuted Jews streamed into it from the 'Pale of Settlement', seeking shelter from starvation and pogroms.

During this period industry began to grow in the large cities, especially in Warsaw and Lodz, and Jews who had no source of livelihood tried to find jobs, either to establish themselves in the place or to learn a trade and languages and to prepare themselves for migration, especially to America. A large proportion of the houses of commerce and industry were owned by wealthy Jews who had lived in the place a long time. This was only of slight help to the Jewish refugee who had just arrived and constituted the poorest class – a phenomenon previously unknown in Warsaw – the new Jewish proletariat. The wealthy Warsovians had little time for them, especially since these Jews didn't speak Polish and didn't know Polish manners or Polish culture.

'They call them "Litvaks", the Jews who have come to Warsaw from the "Pale of Settlement". They're more funda-mentally Jews than we are even though they're not all religious. They were never "'Poles", because Polish culture is not their culture. They're simply Jews, and the leaders of the movements work hard to influence them,' said the man who had arrived from Warsaw with a suitcase full of leaflets sent by the Zionists of Warsaw to the Jews of Galicia.

Galicia and Poland were about to unite into a single Polish state.

The Jews too had to unite, to organize, to demand representation in the new Polish government. That was what the leaflet said.

There were those who thought that the best thing was to sit back quietly, that Jewish-national activity would arouse the ire of the Gentiles at this time, now that the Poles had important national tasks of their own.

At Bronka's, life started returning to normal. The parents opened their store downstairs again, and the brothers were already able to help in several chores connected with the family income.

'The most important thing we have to do now,' said the father, 'is to find a husband for Bronka.'

She blushed to the roots of her hair and said:

'You might present me to the brother of my friend Hania. Her eldest brother.'

Her father looked at her in amazement.

'You've already chosen?'

'Yes, Father,' she said, and remembered that before her exile to Bratislava Hania had told her, when they were sitting on the stairs of the house: 'He said that he'll marry you.'

'Yes, Father. I've chosen.'

6 A Black Sheep and a Pair of Doves

Rozia had vanished. At first they thought that her disappearance was only temporary, and that she would reappear when the days of alert in the Jewish quarter ended and life returned to normal. But the days passed and she didn't return. They waited for her anxiously, apprehensively. What could have happened to her? They started reconstructing every detail of her life before her disappearance, every conversation, every word spoken by her or by others in her presence. But her disappearance remained a mystery.

'It's because you, Hesiek, kept making remarks to her all the time and she couldn't stand it. You forgot that she's older than you.'

Hesiek's general mood was bad now. Rozia was older than him, and Sala was older than him, yet when they needed something, especially in material matters, they came to him. He was the address for all their demands, desires, and needs.

'Could I have kept silent when I saw her going to work, counting money, and writing in her notebook on the Sabbath in this house?'

'Yes, you could have. You shouldn't have said anything, because you knew she wouldn't listen to you anyway. She's an adult, and it's her right to do as she thinks fit.'

'Not in this house.'

'There you are! You threw her out of the house. Are you satisfied now? What will we do now?'

'Shouldn't we notify the police?' asked Hania, hesitantly.

'What police? The Polish police?'

Silence.

'We have to ask all her acquaintances. Maybe somebody knows …'

'We've already asked. Nobody knows, and when we ask, it feels like a kind of scandal – people start supposing things. Of course it's nonsense, just talk. Or they give stupid advice.'

'We have to go to the hospital where she worked.'

Outside snow was falling, covering the street with a gleaming film of white. Icicles dripped from the drainpipe under the roof, and the window-panes were ornamented with drawings made by the frost. Hela and Hania decided to go to the hospital.

The hospital where Rozia had worked was in Copernicus Street, a street of hospitals and clinics. There was probably not one ordinary residential building in the whole street, just various clinics, large or small, general or specialist practices, and hospitals. In the courtyards of the buildings were living quarters for doctors and other health workers. One also saw many nuns working industriously in this area, as nurses or assistants in all branches of medicine.

The nuns in Copernicus Street did not wear black or dark blue as did their sisters in the convents. They wore a pale blue dress with a white apron over it, and a long train descended from their white head covering, which was decorated above the forehead with a pin in the shape of a red cross.

In the winter months both the doctors and the nurses, when they went out into the street, usually put a dark cloak made of thick felt over their clothes.

After asking numerous questions they finally found the place where Rozia had worked. Hela had already been here once and she recognized the building. They were greatly surprised when the secretary said she didn't know of anyone by the name of Rozia.

There's no one here by that name and never has been.'

'But I know for sure that she worked here. I came here with her once … I saw her working here, in nursing clothes …'

The secretary sent them to the deputy director, who called in the head sister for assistance. Finally one of the sisters said:

'I know, the ladies must mean Janina.'

'Janina?!'

The sister drew a small photograph out of her pocket,

placed it on the table, and pointed to a figure standing among a group of hospital workers .

'Is that her?'

Hania and Hela looked at the photograph.

'Yes,' said Hela, almost whispering. 'That's Rozia.'

'She didn't tell us that her name is Rozia. Here she was Janina.'

Hania felt a growing discomfort. The nurse whose photograph it was reached her hand out to the two girls.

'I'm Sister Ursula, deputy head sister.'

Hela and Hania introduced themselves. Sister Ursula said affably:

'I can see grave concern in your faces, ladies. I'll be glad to help, if only I can. But why should we stand here, in the passage? Come to my room, ladies, and we'll talk. I can give you 20 minutes.'

They followed her to her room. Sister Ursula told them what she knew.

Rozia had been a good worker, much liked by her fellow-workers. She hadn't used to tell the others about her private affairs, or about her family. Lately she had become friends with a medical student in his fourth year who worked in the hospital as a sanitary attendant. Everyone knew about this friendship.

'And where is he?' asked Hania. 'Perhaps he knows where she is?'

Sister Ursula smiled and looked at her visitors, sympathizing with their distress.

'The trouble is that he isn't here either. Now that I reconstruct the events, I realize that he left the hospital on the very same day. I'm almost certain that they're together somewhere.'

The 20 minutes the sister could devote to them came to an end. She looked at her watch, and that was a signal that their time was over. She did not give them the name or address of the medical student, but promised to help:

'If I find out something that might interest you, I'll let you know.'

She noted down their address in Paulinska Street.

'Janina gave us a different address,' she said.

They went out into the cold street. Here, in the street, Hania released her pent-up feelings, and exploded:

'I'm burning with shame, I wanted the earth to swallow me up, I feel I'm going crazy!'

Hela tried to calm her.

'Easy, easy,' she said. And after a long silence, she asked:

'Why were you so ashamed – because she went with a man without getting married?'

'No.'

They continued walking through the snowy street. The soft snow had become firm under the feet of the passers-by and the street was covered with a layer that was hard and slippery.

'Be careful not to slip,' said Hela, trying to ease the tension. Hania sighed.

'Even the fact that she went with a non-Jew, even that isn't what made me so ashamed.'

Hela didn't ask any questions. She understood her sister's feelings, though she had different views.

Hania clenched her fists and hissed through her teeth:

''t's the falseness, the pretence. Who are we? Are we allowed to be what we are, or aren't we? Is this our place? Is this our home?'

They came out of Copernicus Street into Stefan Batory Street. On one of the corners there was a pleasant-looking cake shop.

'Come, let's go in,' Hela suggested. 'Let's think quietly about what we've heard, and work out what and how to tell Hesiek.'

They went in, took off their coats and shook off the snow that stuck to the soles of their shoes. They sat down at a little table and ordered cake and tea for two.

The place was indeed pleasant. A merry fire glowed in a hearth in the corner, its tongues occasionally leaping up and spreading light and warmth throughout the room.

Hania calmed down a little. She looked at her sister and saw the expression of suffering on her face. A wave of love rose in her heart and she clasped the lovely delicate hand that was resting on the table.

'And you, what's happening with you?'

At first Hela tried to ignore the question. She was not accustomed to opening up her heart's secrets to anybody.

'I'm not your "little sister" any more, as you always call me, said Hania. I'm already 20,' Hania said. 'And you're 21. At our age the difference isn't significant. You can tell me.' The waitress came and placed before them the glasses of tea, sugar, lemon, and cakes.

'There isn't much to tell,' said Hela. 'Rozia's vanished, and Aleks has vanished too. He's gone to Russia, he said his heart is drawn there, to their revolution. In Russia, as you know, peace hasn't come yet. The wars are still going on, and there are different upsets. I have no news of him. He went, and left me, just like that.' Her voice broke, and several minutes passed before she recovered.

'I think of him day and night without knowing if he even thinks of me at all.'

Tears stifled her.

'You don't have to wait for him,' Hania said quietly.

'I know I don't have to, but I want to.'

Hania sipped the tea and tasted the cake.

'Excellent cake,' she said.

Hela moved her plate aside.

'You can eat mine too. I'm choking.'

The waitress came by. 'Is everything in order, ladies?' she asked.

'Everything is fine. The cakes are excellent.'

The waitress moved off.

'What will we say at home?' They had to get back to immediate matters.

'I think we have to tell the truth. Especially because of the Gentile.'

'Look, I'm sure she has taken that into account and has chosen her own priorities. She'll get along. Fortunately for her she has a trade, and in any case she's more practical than the rest of us,' Hania said optimistically. 'I wish I too had a trade and could do what I want without depending on anyone. I too think of my future; I'm worried, I don't want to end up like Sala.'

The waitress took the dishes from the table. Hela paid. They got up and put on their coats.

'We have to look after ourselves,' said Hela, with a sigh. 'We have to make use of the long winter evenings and study something useful.'

'Or maybe travel?' Hania tried. 'Maybe join some movement, a socialist one, or a Zionist one?'

'I always wanted to travel. Paris, London ... But travelling costs a lot of money. Apart from which, I can't go far from here – maybe he'll come back. I want to study something useful. To work. To earn money.'

They went out into the street. A winter wind blew with threatening wails, and whirled the dense snowflakes. The sky was the color of lead.

They hastened their steps and put up the collars of their coats. 'I'm thinking of joining the Bund movement,' said Hela.

Hesiek and Bronka sat on either side of the large table that stood in the center of the living-room in the apartment on Paulinska Street, not speaking. He looked at her, straight into her large eyes, their color like that of the bright spring sky. She bore his prolonged gaze with brave pride. A smile, light and gentle, hovered on her lips. A golden curl slipped from her braid, twisting mischievously over her high forehead. Her hands rested on her knees, under the tablecloth.

He sat concentrated, looking. His strong and well-built hands, so like his father's, supported his bearded chin.

They sat like this for a long while. Finally she burst out laughing and he smiled. His smile revealed an attractive dimple in his right cheek, under the thin plumage of hair.

Again they became serious.

'Would you stand up?' he asked, in a tone of request.

She got up shyly, and stood by the table, cheeks flushed, her round breasts rising and falling with each beat of her heart.

104

He got up too but didn't approach her. He kept looking at her from across the table, full of wonder and earnestness.

'Would you turn around?' he asked again, in the same tone.

She picked up the hem of her dress and turned gracefully like a ballerina, and burst out laughing. He smiled, and again they sat down as before, on either side of the table, not speaking.

'What next?' she asked finally.

Hesiek sighed.

'Patience. We must be patient.'

'What have you and Father agreed on?'

'I asked your father for time. I explained to him that first I have to take care of the family affairs, the money matters. I can't bring you into the mess that the family is in now. A little patience, that's all we need.'

'You know I won't be a burden on you. I'd try to be a help to you.'

'I know,' he said, and he spoke it with sincerity.

Hela and Hania came into the room, and the wonderful magic was immediately dispelled. They hinted that they had important things that had to be discussed with due gravity in the family circle, but gave no details. Bronka felt uncomfortable. Hesiek suggested that she stay for dinner, but his sisters ignored the suggestion and Bronka said quickly: 'Thank you, perhaps another time. I promised I'd be home early.'

No one protested. Even Hania, her bosom friend, seemed far from her just then.

Bewildered, Bronka left them, and went to her parents' home.

One day Hesiek took his fiancée to his late mother's family home. On the way, he told her that the spacious house was always bustling with activity and was a center for the entire family. Many older people dined here every day, and with them about a dozen children of all ages. Every day, too, there would be a guest for dinner from among the poor of the community. You might see one of them eating without a knife, blowing his nose at the table, not speaking, embarrassed.

Around the table many conversations flowed. From time to time there would be outbursts of laughter, or even of dispute, and the guest would sit there, with his eyes on his plate.

Hesiek told Bronka that his young cousins were exuberant revolutionaries, who tried to throw off the customs of their forefathers, their ways and their dress, and not infrequently there would be tension between fathers and sons.

In the Carmel house they didn't know a thing about Rozia's disappearance. The elders had a bad opinion of her behavior. The uncles didn't like the fact that a young Jewish woman from a good family was working as a nurse in a hospital. Woe to the daughter who had to work for her living. And work in night shifts was shameful, immoral. Hesiek decided to hide what he knew about Rozia from his uncles.

'Disgrace of this kind should not be taken outside the house,' he said to Bronka, as they walked towards the Carmel house.

As they entered the apartment they were immediately enveloped in the special atmosphere that this family radiated. Father, mother, children, grandchildren – a good family in which the succession of generations had not yet been impaired.

Hesiek introduced his lovely fiancée to everybody. She was bewildered and worried:

'I'll never remember all the names and I won't know who belongs to whom. There are so many of them.'

'With time you will,' he consoled her. '"Krakow wasn't built in a day".[1] You'll get to know them all.'

The aunts and uncles were very friendly to Hesiek's young and somewhat bashful fiancée. She passed the test of their scrutiny, and received much praise. The younger ones, however, were more reserved. They conducted active conversations on many subjects. The elders here spoke Yiddish mixed with German and Polish, while the youngsters spoke Polish and Hebrew.

Bronka didn't dare to open her mouth. She listened with gleaming eyes. When those present began asking how her brothers were doing, Hesiek found an excuse to get up and leave, and together with Bronka went out of the house, which was humming with life like a beehive.

In the street he said to her earnestly:

'We too will have a big house. We'll raise a big family, and have at least a dozen children!'

'A dozen?!' She burst out laughing. 'A dozen children!' she repeated, and laughed again, dancing around him like a little girl, like a bird just released from a cage. Then she grew serious. They stopped and looked at each other. With his gaze on her, a flush came to her cheeks. Her hands moved forward, and then returned to her sides. His strong hands came towards her, but suddenly she darted off. He stood there, watching her go, her laughter echoing in his ears like the chiming of bells.

At long last a letter arrived from Rozia, and then another, both from Stanislawow.

The letters were addressed to Hela and Hania, and Rozia forbade them to show them to anyone else.

... I fell in love with a young gentile. His name is Anton. I was so much in love that I found it difficult to concentrate on my work. It took great effort not to mix up the medicines, not to bring a patient a chamber-pot instead of the glass of tea he had asked for, and so on. When I walked through the corridors of the hospital I was always hoping to meet Anton. Every young man I saw from a distance seemed to be him. I kept looking at my face in the mirror, more than ever before, trying to make my hair suit what might be Anton's taste.

When I examined my body, I found to my sorrow that it was too heavy and I wondered what to do to make my figure more delicate. I was saddened by the sight of my muscled legs and my large hands. With pain and envy I thought of you and of my other sisters, for all of you are more beautiful than I, and each of you has a more feminine and delicate body. My consolation was that I too have an interesting face. I've been told that more than once, and though my hands are big they know how to work and don't need any favors.

Several days after I met him for the first time, he surprised me as I was sitting by a desk in the nurses' room writing summaries in the work book. He walked quietly up to me and stood behind me, and I felt certain that it was him. I wasn't surprised to see him – since our first meeting I always imagined seeing him beside me. Now our eyes met. Anton reached out his hands and gently clasped my head. We stayed like that for several minutes, looking at each other. Then he brought his face to mine and pressed his lips to my lips. My body filled with a sensation I'd never known before. A sweet warmth washed through me, and all I wanted was that this should never cease.

Anton broke away first. I was still in the same place, and I felt that the slightest touch would be enough to throw me into his lap. He said he would wait for me by the hospital gate at the hour I finished work, and I agreed. In the evening we met and walked in the shade of the trees in the Planty. Our bodies were quivering with desire. He invited me to his room. I didn't want to go. I wanted to tell him about myself, about my family, about you. I started telling him twice, but I didn't say what I really wanted to say, I just felt that my body was melting and that I was losing control of my thoughts. We went to his room. On the threshold he promised that he would be good to me. In bed too, after the event, I tried to tell him about my origins, and my family, but he closed my lips with his kisses. After that felt a great dread. I thought I'd never be able to come back to my family and to look you in the eye. I started crying. He didn't understand what was wrong with me and I found it difficult to explain. I asked him to promise that he would marry me, and he laughed, which hurt me. He said that I was behaving as if I'd grown up in a Jewish ghetto. And when I said that I really had grown up in a Jewish ghetto, he seemed really shocked. He was silent for a long time. Then he lit a cigarette, and puffed on it slowly. He said

that he had nothing against Jews, and that he didn't
mind, but that his parents mustn't find out that I'm
Jewish. The weeks that followed were weeks of bitter
conflict between impulsive desire and rational, logical
thought. At first I didn't want to live with Anton unless
he promised that he'd marry me, then I realised I didn't
want to marry him at all. I knew it was impossible, but I
was willing to sacrifice everything for the moments of
happiness his closeness brought me. From day to day our
love became more tempestuous, and left no room for
rational considerations or for spiritual intimacy. In our
snatched brief meetings – the result of the decision not to
live together – we would swallow quickly, without
digesting properly, arrive at brief moments of satiety
only for our hunger to return immediately, to awaken us
and trouble our rest. We hardly had a single real conversation. And my questions, if I did manage to ask them
once or twice, remained unanswered.

I'm writing you in the hope that you'll understand. I
forbid you to show my letter to anyone else.

Hela finished reading and breathed in deeply. Hania sat
down opposite her and took the last page of the letter. When
she had finished, the silence in the room continued. Hela
quoted, in a voice other than her own:

'It is good for a person if once in his life he has had a great
love, if once in his life he has been agitated by a blazing and
miserable emotion. For that gives, at least, a kind of justifica-
tion to the feelings of despair which press upon us.'

'Who said that?'

Hela fled from the room without answering.

In her second letter Rozia wrote:

Time does its work though not to our advantage. I
started emphasizing my Jewishness, out of feelings of
guilt towards our departed parents, blessed be their
memory, and towards the entire family. This angered
Anton. He demanded that I hide my origins. He said that

there wasn't much to be proud of in being Jewish. Once he exploded and said that my Jews had crucified Jesus. They had pierced his living body with nails and tortured him. I was astounded. I told him that even if we supposed that was true, it had happened 2,000 years ago. How many generations had been born and died since then, how many people had suffered and been tormented! And Anton said that the Jews should go to Palestine. I was shocked. He asked me to forgive him, but the rift was already deep and there was no way of sealing it. It deepened even more and gave place to a contact that was chilly and lacking in passion, which afterwards seemed never to disappear.

I put together my personal possessions and left Anton. He didn't stop me and didn't look for me. I reached Stanislawow and I still don't know what I'll do with myself. I assume that there is no possibility of my returning home. I wouldn't be able to make a place for myself there again. Soon I'll write you about what my next steps will be, and I'll send an address. Meanwhile don't look for me, but don't forget me. Pass on my enduring love to all the members of the family. I trust you, and believe that you will know what to tell the others about me. There's no need to hurt people we love. Be well, all of you.

Lovingly, Rozia.

They finished their reading of the letter. The room seemed to be filled with Rozia's presence.

Outside the window a weak sun fought with the leaden clouds, occasionally peeping through them and sending a faint ray towards the earth.

Hesiek came into the room. Hela quickly folded the pages of the letter and thrust them into the pocket of her gray sweater.

From the expressions on their faces he understood everything.

'Is she well?' he asked.

'I imagine so,' Hania stuttered. Rozia had not written a word about the state of her health.

He understood that his sisters had no intention of telling him more details. Sighing, he said:

'Business is starting to move.'

He expected them to show some interest in his affairs, to ask who he was doing business with, who was helping him, what profits he was making.

But Hela said:

'I've found a job. Looks like I'll start doing clerical work for the Freilich–Carmel firm.'

This was good news, though Hela herself didn't know much yet about the work that she had been promised by these relatives. It was unlikely that it would hold much interest for her, and the wages too would probably be very small.

They sat absorbed in their thoughts. Hesiek said:

'I'm not satisfied with the institution Haim is in now. We must transfer him to a good sanatorium in Zakopane.'

There were wrinkles on Hesiek's young face. His sisters didn't reply. He continued:

'Sala has expressed the wish to travel to Switzerland. Perhaps the trip will rehabilitate her.'

Suddenly he remembered something. From a pocket of his jacket he drew out a watch on a gold chain, his father's gift, and said hastily:

'I must run. I have an important appointment and I'm already late.'

Spring again.

The third spring after the war. A spring of national rebirth in Poland and Czechoslovakia. A spring in which new concepts were being spoken of in the world: equal rights for every human being by virtue of his or her humanity; full national rights to minorities – which the young state of Poland had an abundance of.

Events succeeded each other rapidly. Hesiek's agile mind did not rest for a moment.

At nights, during the few hours he allotted himself for sleep, he would wake in alarm, remember something, leap up from bed, make a note, erase what he'd written, and write again. His notes were not ordered, his drawers were in a mess. The important things were in his head, and his head was always busy.

Returning to bed on these chilly, clear spring nights, he would think of Bronka. His conscience troubled him about his repeated postponements of their marriage: he was harming her, and himself too. She felt cramped at her parents' house, he knew that. Indirectly and without accusations she told him about the friction between her parents and herself, about how annoyingly cramped the place was since her three brothers had grown up, and about her wish to move out of there as soon as possible. And he? Wasn't he flesh and blood too? Sometimes his desire for her would drive him out of his mind, but he controlled himself. His day's routine was so full that it exhausted his desires. During this time he had received a large order for timber and building supplies from someone close to General Sikorski. The order was very tempting, but he was quickly disappointed when he heard that there were differences between Sikorski and Pilsudski, the leader of Poland. This troubled him. Had he not amused himself with the thought that in the near future he would receive a large order from someone close to Pilsudski? Supplying the order of Sikorski's friends might sabotage that. But he had to be quick! The government was planning to establish co-operatives, and these, it was said, would mercilessly supplant the Jewish merchants.

Obligations lay upon him from all directions. His sisters constantly needed money. The sanatorium cost a fortune. Taxes to the government, taxes to the community, the purchase of merchandise, investments in the business. The Polish currency wasn't stable, inflation was rampant. People ran about in circles and the struggle for survival was hard.

Industriousness alone wasn't enough. You either have or don't have a special business sense, which is a gift of God. Hesiek knew that God had endowed him with this special sense and he was grateful to Him for it.

His full day began with prayer. At this time he prayed in the little synagogue close to Paulinska Street, which was in the same courtyard as another synagogue which the Jews called the 'Stiebel'. In this Stiebel his brother-in-law, Reb Shlomo, prayed among the *hassidim* of Bobow, who all wore *streimels* and white socks. They were very orthodox, and would spend whole days in the Stiebel, praying earnestly and fervently, their whole bodies swaying forwards and backwards and to the sides, moved by unearthly inner forces, their eyes raised to the sky in pleading, and closing themselves off from outside influences. After prayer the *hassidim* would remain, studying *gemarah* and repeating verses of the Psalms. Among these Jews there were several who had come from distant places, who had left a wife and children somewhere, in order to free themselves from the burden of a family, to seclude themselves far from interruption and to delve deeper into the Torah. They discussed questions of the fear of heaven, spoke about the world-to-come, the coming of the Messiah, and the return to the Holy Land, to Jerusalem. These *hassidim* were totally divorced from the outside world, and had no interest at all in the social upheaval that was taking place before their very eyes in all of Europe and in Poland in particular, nor were they interested in the aspirations of the Jews for equality. They wanted to live apart, and the national aspirations were absolutely alien to them.

Several of these *hassidim* were wealthy merchants and other Jews worked for them and ran their businesses. Most of them were small shopkeepers, owners of small stores mostly run by their wives. Only when political organization began in the Jewish community too, and Jews were given an opportunity of being represented in government institutions, were these ultra-orthodox Jews forced to consider who they would support. They had a revulsion for the socialists and they opposed the Zionists. Who then would gain from the votes of these electors?

In Hesiek's synagogue the atmosphere was different. Here too most of the congregants were small merchants, some of them artisans, very few somewhat wealthy, and the rest – poor vendors. After prayers the Jews would divide into groups. Some of them remained to go on studying *gemarah* and *mishnah*, and others would heatedly discuss the affairs of the local community, always knowing who had said what, who had gained and who had lost. Others discussed politics.

In the *'mizrach'*, the eastern side close to the holy ark, sat the

Jews of well-known families, educated men with firm financial status. Beside them sat very old Jews with silver beards. These loved reminiscing about bygone days, when they were close to kings and princes in Poland before it was divided.

Nor was there any lack of idlers in this synagogue, Jews who took no part in any activity, ignorant and low people. And there were also victims of fate, and people who had not managed to overcome the difficulties of earning a living under the burden of taxes and expenditures.

Outside the synagogue gathered beggars and charity collectors.

At first Hesiek had used to stay in the synagogue after prayers too. He would continue leafing through the old yellowing pages of his *siddur*, which he had received from his father, and repeat chapters of Psalms, or join the study groups. There were certain things in the holy texts which he did not understand, and he would go over them again and again until their meaning became clear to him. And when he understood, he would smile to himself. There were chapters that aroused his imagination and gave him inspiration. Once when he was in synagogue he wrote a poem to his beloved, taken mostly from the *Song of Songs*. Afterwards, at home, during one of his sleepless nights, he got up and copied out its words: 'Thy love is good', and 'Thy lips are like a thread of scarlet', and 'thy temples are like a piece of a pomegranate within thy locks', 'I long to see thee ... Come!' He wrote the poem in the notebook in which he wrote his columns of figures of income and expenditures, debts and loans and interest. Without thinking twice he tore out the page, put it in a closed envelope, and after prayers in the synagogue handed it to one of Bronka's brothers.

It was the middle brother, Szajek, and he refused to do the errand.

'What's inside?' he asked suspiciously.

'It's none of your business,' Hesiek said to him. 'You just deliver it. It's very important.'

'In synagogue one doesn't write letters,' his brother-in-law-to-be scolded him.

Hesiek fumed.

'No such prohibition is written anywhere,' he said. 'Today's a weekday, not the Sabbath.' And looking at the stubborn lad he asked:

'Where were you when intelligence was distributed to humans? They skipped over you, did they?'

Hesiek was in a hurry to get to his business affairs, and because he hadn't succeeded in getting the assistance of Szajek, he had to go by Bronka's house himself and give her the envelope. Within two minutes he was next to Suesser House. He saw her from afar, sitting on a window-sill, cleaning the windows in her parents' apartment, and singing. In the windows all around stood women and girls, listening to her singing.

She saw him from a distance and ran to open the door. When she stood facing him she took off her kerchief and released her golden hair.

'Hello,' she said, and crumpled up the dust cloth together with the kerchief.

'I have to run,' he said instead of a greeting. 'This is for you!' He handed her the envelope and went.

As time went on Hesiek shortened his stays inside the synagogue, and immediately after prayers would go off to his business.

In the mornings, before going to pray, he would spend several minutes washing himself meticulously, brushing his clothes and shoes, and trimming his beard, which with the passage of time grew shorter and shorter, and began to resmble the foppish beards of the Polish intelligentsia.

The traditional black hat had been exchanged for a new modern hat, and his suit too was tailored according to the latest fashion. One morning Hela said to him:

'Have you too adopted the slogan: "Be a Jew in your home and a Pole in the street?"'

He replied:

'"A dawn hour lost is high in cost", we won't waste it in long conversations and explanations. You're in a hurry to get to work too.'

'Yes,' said Hela, 'I've started working. You know, Sala was

here yesterday. She didn't speak about her divorce. She was very low, thin and pale, but I had the impression that she's starting to get used to it and to become resigned.'

'I hope so,' said Hesiek. 'If she stays with Schiffmann it'll save me a lot of money.'

'You and your money. Money money and again money. You're not interested in anything apart from money!' Hela complained.

'I have to go now,' he said, and went.

Bronka's younger brother, Muniusz, agreed to be their letter-bearer. He brought her letters to the synagogue, where he would hand them to Hesiek and receive letters for her from him.

Their main problem was where to meet. At her place there were her parents and brothers. At Mania's there were two little children. At his place there were his sisters. On a bench in the Planty – not respectable. In a coffee shop in the Polish quarter – not customary. And there was no coffee shop in the Jewish quarter.

'At my Aunt Fela's,' Bronka suggested in one of her letters. 'She's a progressive woman. And her husband, the fanatical Uncle Herzig, doesn't have a say there. And their Itzik is still little, and Grandma Herrstein won't bother us.'

Hesiek refused. He suggested they meet at his Aunt Idess'.

'There, in all that din, nobody will pay us any mind. We'll find ourselves a little corner in that big apartment and we'll talk.'

'All right,' Bronka wrote, 'I don't really feel free there, but let it be as you want.'

Bronka and Hesiek sat in one of the rooms in Aunt Carmel's apartment. It was the twilight hour. In the mainroom the aunt was speaking with people who kept coming and going as though it was a railroad station. In the adjacent room two people sat playing chess, someone was studying Hebrew, and someone else was secretly studying Latin.

'I had a scene with my father,' said Bronka, when she felt sure that no one could hear them.

116

He waited for her to continue, but she was in no hurry to give details. Then he said:

'What do you think about us getting married next month?'

She leaped up from her seat.

'Already?!'

'Why, is it too soon?' he asked.

'No ... But it is very sudden. You surprised me.'

'I think,' he said gravely, 'I think it's time. Rozia won't come back home, that's certain. For the moment we don't know where she is, but even when we find out, she won't come back. Haim's in the sanatorium, in a good place. Sadly they won't be releasing him soon, tuberculosis is a long-term disease. I wish they'd find a cure for it. Sala seems to have decided to stay with her husband, or so it seems at present. She's starting to get used to it. As for Hela and Hania – well, we can't wait until they make a place for themselves in the world.'

'With Hania I get on fine,' Bronka whispered. 'Recently we've become even closer friends. We spend every day together at the *hachsharah*.[2]

Hesiek looked at her with curiosity. 'Where?'

'At the *hachsharah*, the agricultural training center run by the Zionist movement. That's what I quarreled with my father about.' Bronka was quiet for a moment, and then asked:

'Do you think Hela will accept me nicely?'

'What kind of a question is that? You'll be the first lady in my house!'

'Where will we live?'

'Ten people once lived in the apartment on Paulinska Street,' he said, with determination.

'Oh, Hesiek!'

He took her hand, brought it to his heart, and then kissed it.

Hela worked in the iron and metal wholesale house owned by her mother's relatives. The company was called by its proprietors names, Freilich and Carmel, and had been established in Krakow by these families in 1817. The company's offices were in Kazimierz, and operated in a modern manner, with telephones and telegraphs, bank accounts, and a regular clerical staff. Hela was taken on as a kind of servant of two masters: as an assistant to the woman who was head accountant and to the man in charge of public relations. As such, she sat between the two of them.

'Bring me that please!'

'Copy this please!'

'Add up this column of figures!'

'Take this down!'

'Put that up!'

'File this!' – all, of course, spoken good-naturedly and with the addition of words such as please and thank you. But the work held no particular interest for her. The 'bosses' were her uncles and cousins, and they treated her with warmth, but even this very closeness and familial treatment made her feel frustrated – did they need her, or were they pitying her?

She decided that she would keep this job only until something more interesting turned up, and started learning French, so as to prepare for the possibility of a journey abroad in order to learn a real trade.

At work Hela met many people. The great movement of peoples after the war had not yet concluded, and many families were still separated from their loved ones and had no news of them.

The head accountant, Elsa, was waiting for news of her brothers.

'Of my two brothers,' she once said to Hela, 'one went to Warsaw, an assimilationist, and the other went to the Russian side.'

Hela swallowed, and said nothing.

'The one who went to Russia left his fiancée here. The girl gave up hope and married somebody else. Now he's a loser both here and there.'

'Perhaps he'll marry too?'

'Who? A Russian girl? Or one of the Litvaks? His fiancée was right. There's a limit to how long a woman should wait for a man.'

Hela said nothing.

A man who came to the office said he had been on the

Russian side and had met someone there who knew someone else who had met Aleks.

'Where? When?!' Hela wanted to know.

The answers were vague and contradicted each other. Someone else said that he had met someone who was a close friend of Aleks who had not been separated from him for many years, but he had died.

'Who?' Hela yelled. 'Who died?'

'Nu, the one who was with Aleks.'

'And what happened to Aleks?'

'How can I know, if this friend of mine who was with Aleks all the time is dead?'

'How many years have you been waiting?' Elsa asked her.

'Many.'

Now Elsa said nothing. She was a very forward woman, and as time passed Hela noticed the strange and special relationship that existed between her and the public relations man, Misha. At the end of the day's work, both of them would stay in the office, working. Once Uncle Fishel, who was the big boss, had said to them:

'Why are you still sitting here? You won't get paid for overtime.'

They ignored his remark and continued working quietly and industriously. There was never any lack of work. They spoke little, and their silence did not invite speech or questions.

'Can I help you with something?' Hela dared to ask at the end of the working day. She knew in advance what the answer would be; they made no attempt at all to hide their desire to remain alone.

Hela left and turned towards her home. As she walked she changed direction. Her private French lesson would start in another two hours. What to do until then? At home, in Paulinska Street, preparations were already being made for Bronka's arrival after her marriage to Hesiek.

She would have gladly stayed in the office, to continue working or to write a letter to Aleks; another letter, one of very many she had not sent.

But she couldn't return to the office. As she walked a

church procession passed her. Boys and girls marched in white, and at the head of the procession walked a priest carrying a large cross. Only then did she notice that she was outside Kazimierz. A handsome young man came walking from the opposite direction and she had the feeling that he was looking at her with a special look, one that penetrated her, seeing everything. She trembled and suddenly remembered Rozia. This was how it began. This was how it could begin. She didn't want troubles of that kind – she mustn't wander about alone. She hurried back to Ditlowska Street, where her French teacher lived. She rang the doorbell and went in. Inside there were already several young women who studied with her in the same group. A few minutes before the class was due to begin, Bronka arrived. Her eyes were red with weeping.

'What's happened?'

Without saying a word Bronka handed her a typewritten anonymous letter .

'Beware,' the letter said. 'You are endangering your happiness. Save yourself while there's time. You are about to marry a hard man, tyrant, a pursuer of profits and of women (!!) Your life with him will be a dog's life.'

The two women stood facing each other, petrified. 'Do you have any idea who could have written me such a letter?' Bronka finally asked.

'Why are you asking me??!!' Hela's eyes blazed with fury. 'Are you out of your mind?'

'I'm sorry,' Bronka mumbled miserably. 'This letter has upset me so … Only three weeks before the wedding.'

Bronka fled from the classroom.

Hela sat down gloomily and waited for the teacher. What to do? Where to flee to? How to get away from here? To get away and forget everything! To forget Aleks, Bronka, Hesiek, and all the others.

After the lesson one of the women came up to her and said: 'I've got hold of the prospectus for the course for X-ray technicians. Do you remember that we talked about it? My relatives in Switzerland sent it to me.'

'Oh yes, of course I remember.'

'Here, it says: a new branch ... they're looking for people ... knowledge of German a requirement, French desired ... It could become a profession much in demand, good and interesting work. And it takes only six months to learn...'

Hela took the prospectus in her hand, and the woman continued:

'My father has already promised to finance my journey. And my relatives in Switzerland will help me. I've decided to go. And you?'

'Good for you,' said Hela bitterly, and added: 'I'll give it some thought, and give you an answer soon.'

On her way home she visited her big sister Mania. Sala and Hania were there. Hela noticed a great change in Sala. She really was wilting by the day. Today in particular, her face was pale and her eyes lowered.

'Now it's he who wants a divorce,' she said in a feeble voice. 'We have no children.'

'Hell!' Hela hissed.

Then the four sisters sat down and discussed the future. Mania's two daughters were already in bed, fed and washed. 'Hesiek and Bronka are getting married and they're going to live in the apartment in Paulinska Street.'

'Bronka cried today at the *hachsharah*!' Hania interrupted.

Hela didn't say a word.

'She's nervous before the wedding,' Mania said gently. 'I remember myself. They'll get married. Hela will go to Switzerland to learn a trade. Sala will go with her to rest. And Hania will come and live with us here,' she said, looking affectionately at her youngest sister.

Hania smiled lovingly at her, but Hela clearly saw how her face fell.

If it was her, Hela, she would never agree to go and live with Mania and her family. What an idea!

The sisters continued talking in whispers, so as not to disturb the children's sleep.

Suddenly the door opened and Reb Shlomo came in, unusually excited. With him were his eldest son, Naftali, and his younger brother Mendel.

'The Poles have won!' he said in Yiddish, and the two youngsters added:

'It's unbelievable!'

'What? What's happened?' the women asked in Polish; they had no idea what they were talking about.

'They've defeated the Russians!'

Ah, yes. Hela remembered that there'd been another war. Elsa had told her in the office:

'It's the same thing all over again, brother against brother. My brother in Warsaw with the Poles, and my other brother with the Russians.'

The excited Naftali told the story very concisely:

'The Russians charged with all their might to repel the Polish army, which is still in its diapers – that's how they contemptuously spoke of it. The Russians thought they would advance wherever it was possible. And miraculously, the Poles held back the Russian offensive and then pushed the Russians back to their border. The Poles are talking about a miracle. A miracle on the banks of the Vistula.'

The news was astounding, but Hela felt that it couldn't make her and her sisters forget their personal worries.

In the streets everyone was excited and spoke about the 'miracle'.

7 Tuberculosis

Two sets of preparations were set in motion: for the wedding, and for the journey to Switzerland. Hesiek and Hela spent many hours together going over the syllabus of the course she had decided to take. They decided to 'cheat' Sala and to tell her that the cost of the journey was much less than it really was so that she wouldn't feel guilty about taking so much money from the family's funds. They also agreed that Hela would find a way to consult a good doctor, and would spare neither time nor money in helping their sister.

'She needs treatment, like a plant that hasn't been watered. Have you seen how her eyes have dulled? She used to be so beautiful, so tall and radiant. And now!'

They booked railroad tickets and a hotel room to live in until they could find cheaper accommodation.

They obtained foreign currency, and put a sum aside for clothes for both of them for the journey.

Hela was excited. She remembered Bronka's eyes, red with weeping, and her distress over the slanderous letter she had received.

Did Hesiek know about the letter? She didn't dare ask. In another month he and Bronka would be living in the apartment in Paulinska Street. He was sending them to Switzerland. That surely suited him. 'Oh, you're so suspicious,' she said to herself: 'what's this jealousy that's got into you, eating away every good part of you? No one owes you a thing. After all, what would we do without him, all of us?'

He sat before her, absorbed in tiresome calculations, his face weary and tense. 'You're so busy,' she said to him, trying to cheer him up. 'You forget to eat, you forget to sleep, I hope you won't forget to show up at the wedding.'

The wedding was to take place in two weeks time at Suesser House. Bronka's family had taken responsibility for all the arrangements.

'If I forget, I hope there'll be someone around to remind me.' A dimple appeared in his cheek when he smiled at her.

'It's good to see you smiling,' she said.

The sisters were to travel to Switzerland immediately after the wedding. All of them were waiting for Haim to arrive, but a letter came from Zakopane, to say that his doctors could not allow him to take part in the family celebration.

'I must see him before I leave,' said Hela.

'Go to Zakopane,' Hesiek suggested. 'Six hours on the train and you're there.'

She agreed. She tried to convince Sala to join her, but Sala was too depressed. How could she travel? How could she visit sick people in a sanatorium? Tuberculosis bacteria are always on the lookout for good soil to grow in, and she might fall victim to the disease. Apart from which, her mood wouldn't cheer Haim at all.

'I'd go with you,' Bronka said, uncertainly. 'I like Haim, and I know he'd be glad to see me, but my mother's called in a seamstress and I have a lot of work to do now, in both homes.'

Hela said nothing, and Bronka continued:

'I want you to tell Haim that if he gets permission to leave the sanatorium for a while in the future, our home – I mean this home – is always open to him. I'd be glad, very glad, if he came!'

Her light blue eyes were moist. Hela looked at her affectionately.

'All right,' she said. 'I'll tell him what you said, word for word. It's no secret that he likes you very much.'

Hania considered the possibility of joining Hela on the trip to Zakopane. But with her too things didn't work out. Her group at the *hachsharah* was in the midst of important activity, and a young man from Lodz, who was studying law in Krakow, had begun courting her.

'I can't go with you in the near future,' Hania said regretfully.

Hela couldn't change her schedule, and so she boarded the

train alone, equipped with sweets, little gifts, money, and long letters.

The resort town of Zakopane lay in the Tatra Mountains, which are part of the Carpathian range that extends through south-eastern Poland and northern Czechoslovakia. The town was surrounded by high mountains, the most distinctive of which was the 'Giewont'. The slopes were partially covered with dense, ancient forests of pines, cypresses and firs, and partly with gleaming bare rocks of granite. They surrounded Zakopane like a crown studded with colored stones. Constant running streams engraved forms in the rock as they descended, and their fresh water joined with the many brooks of this region, moving like silver ribbons as they made their way to the rivers.

The sound of the water mingled with the chirping of birds – mainly cuckoos and hoopoes – and a cool breeze caressed the wildlife and the landscape. The fresh fragrance of plants and trees was borne by the winds in all directions. Herders walked on the slopes; the bells tied to the necks of their goats and kids rang as they walked, and the herders play flutes. On the grassy stretches, where daisies, poppies, and star-thistles grow, were country houses built of wood, with sloping red roofs.

The men of the mountains were called 'Goraly'; the name comes from the word 'Gora', which means mountain. The 'Goral' wore shoes made of thin, printed goatskin, black trousers narrow at the ankles, an embroidered white shirt, a black felt pullover and a broad black hat ornamented with a band made of small shells that sported an impressive feather. 'Goraly' spoke a special language, different from that of the city-dwellers, and their dress is different too.

These 'Goraly' brought their goods to market in horse-drawn carts, or drove horse-drawn carriages for visitors and tourists, and these horses too were decrated with a fine feather or a flower. In winter, when the temperature dropped to 30 degrees below zero, all this wondrous landscape was covered in a thick layer of snow. The dense whiteness blots out all the other colors of nature, leaving only the blue of the sky and the glow of the sun.

The wheels of the carts and carriages were then replaced by pairs of skids, to slide on the snow when pulled by horses. The town filled with skiers. People in colorful sportswear skied expertly from the tops of the high mountains, gliding down for many kilometers, and when they reached their destination they retraced their steps and climbed up to ski down again. On the smaller slopes, children slid gleefully on bobsleds while other children built funny snowmen. One of these, called a 'Balwan,' had a stomach made of a huge snowball, a head made of a smaller snowball, eyes of coal, and a red juicy carrot for a mouth.

Hela, enchanted by the wonderful landscape and intoxicated by the fresh air, had no difficulty finding Dr Doleski's sanatorium, which was located in one of the beauty spots of this region.

She was excited at seeing her brother, and delighted to discover that the fresh air had done him good and had improved his appearance. He had put on weight, his pallor had gone, and he looked extremely healthy. But he told her that the X-rays continued to show the deep vacant spaces that had formed in his lungs, and that the doctors did not hold out much hope.

There were about 30 patients in the sanatorium. A few of these were confined to their beds because of the gravity of their illness, but the majority were able to walk about in the fresh air. Three times a day their temperature was taken and noted down on their cards. Once a week they were weighed, and their weight curve was noted too. Occasionally, when necessary, they were called to examinations in the laboratory or in the X-ray rooms. Every day, Dr Doleski, his assistants, and the head sister, did the rounds of the patients' wards, stopping by every bed, asking each patient how he or she felt, studying their cards and writing down instructions. After the visit by the doctors the patients were permitted to dress and to move to the light camp beds that were spread around the cultivated garden of the sanatorium. Everyone was allowed to select the bed that appealed most – some of them were next to each other, and others were apart, for those who liked solitude.

'At first I liked being by myself,' Haim told her. 'I used to lie there, with a newspaper or a book, reading, thinking, drowsing. A nurse would come up and wrap my feet in a warm blanket, and bring me a glass of hot milk at ten o'clock.'

Gradually Haim had come to know the other patients. Most of them came from the Polish intelligentsia and middle class, for the poor could not afford to pay the high cost of residence in this private institution.

About half of the patients were women, who would come out to take the air with their sewing or knitting. There was no sign in their appearance of the disease that was eating away inside them.

Haim had noticed a fragile girl with a sallow face, who would lie for hours on end not doing any reading or handicraft. There was always an aluminum spittoon beside her, which she would spit into during long and exhausting fits of coughing.

'Her name was Rachel,' Haim told his sister. 'I happened to glance at her. I was sure she was Jewish. She would get to her camp bed supported by a nurse, or in a wheelchair, that's how weak she was. As time passed, when she had her coughing fits, I too began feeling a burning pain in my chest. Once I picked a bunch of wild flowers and gave it to her, and she invited me to sit down in an easy chair beside her bed. From then on we would spend our "air time" together.'

Haim paused.

'Does this interest you at all?'

'Oh, yes, Haim, go on.'

'She spoke freely, and would mix serious subjects with trivial things, skipping from one subject to another. Rachel taught me that the red patches on my cheeks represent as it were the spaces in my lungs. "You can depend on me", she said, when I didn't want to believe it. There was no trace of doubt in her voice and I believed her. Once she said to me: "see that couple walking over there? They too are convalescing here, like us. She's the wife of a famous doctor in the city of Katowitz, and he could easily be her son. A young and inexperienced fellow. If only her husband could see them."'

Hela smiled, pleased that her brother was sharing his experiences with her.

Haim continued:

'I told Rachel that I wasn't interested in them, that I don't like gossip. "Neither do I", she said. "It's just boredom." Rachel was very sick. Her hands were thin and fragile.' His voice became very sad. Yellow autumn leaves fell on the heads of the brother and sister as they talked.

'She told me that she'd been here a very long time, and felt that it was a pity that her parents were wasting so much money on her. I wanted to cheer her up, so I told her about all of you. I told her I had five sisters. "Five sisters!" she exclaimed. She had wished for at least one sister, but had not had that fortune. She was an only child. We talked about social injustice, about different regimes and political movements. Rachel was a socialist, even though her parents are very wealthy. And I didn't know how to present myself to her. I don't know what I am. I don't have a defined political stand or outlook. What about you?' he suddenly asked his sister.

She was surprised by his unexpected question. 'Me? I've been thinking of joining the "Bund", which is a Jewish social-ist movement, a movement of the Jewish proletariat seeking Jewish national autonomy here in Poland.'

'I know what the "Bund" is, I'm not all that ignorant,' Haim interupted.

'But,' Hela went on, 'I'm not acting out the movement's path in my own life. I'm going off to Switzerland to learn a profession. The members of the movement can't afford luxuries of that kind.'

'I told Rachel about you all,' Haim repeated. 'I told her about Rozia who ran away from home, after getting involved with a non-Jew. Rachel said that she saw nothing tragic in that.'

'Oh, Haim,' Hela interrupted him. 'I forgot to tell you some important news that arrived only yesterday. Rozia has written to us from Palestine!'

'From Palestine?!'

'Yes. She's in one of the *kibbutzim*, working as a simple laborer, building roads.'

'Oh, I'm so happy that she's got there,' Haim said musingly. 'At least one of us has.'

'Hesiek's not so happy. Men and women live together there, instead of getting married – they move into a tent together.'

After a long silence Haim went on:

'Rachel taught me a lot. She said that we, the Jews, are a strange nation, full of contradictions. Every day we yearningly remember Jerusalem, but we don't go there. We support the Zionist pioneers who are returning to the soil there, but we don't join them. We understand the proletariat that is awakening and demanding its rights, but we choose to live as bourgeoisie. We speak the Polish language and we love Polish culture, but we aren't Poles. And so I too started asking myself: Who are we, actually? Once, when I was sitting in the grove close to Rachel's easy chair, the wife of the doctor in Katowitz and the young man walked by us. Both of us, Rachel and I, heard their gay laughter, and we saw how the young man put his arm around the doctor's wife's shoulders. They moved out of sight and hearing. And I took Rachel's fragile hand and held it in both of mine. She smiled at me, sadly.

'The next day she didn't appear at "air time". She was lying in bed with a high fever and struggling with her cough. Suddenly, with her absent, the beauty of the landscape seemed to turn ugly, and the air didn't seem fresh any more. I felt lost outside. I wanted to be near her, beside her bed. I read to her, extracts of *belles-lettres*, and poems.

'As her condition worsened it grew more difficult to talk, and she lay there silent and helpless.

'Several days passed, and Rachel didn't get up. Once I went into her ward with a letter I'd received from you and Hania. Inside the envelope you had put a dried flower and a color postcard with a drawing of Wawel Castle. Rachel reached out her thin, fragile hand, and asked to see the postcard. "Krakow", she said in her faint voice. "The beautiful city I so wanted to see, and which I'll never see now." She asked me to read her your letter. I sat down and read it to her and didn't notice that she'd fallen asleep as I read. I folded the letter and left the room on tiptoe. And so she hovered between life and death, until it ended.'

His voice broke. The story was ended.

Hela didn't know how to console her brother as he mourned the first girl, and perhaps the last, he had grown attached to in his lifetime.

They went for a walk and she told him about everyone. Haim wanted to know more details about Rozia, but there were no more details than she had already given. She spoke about the preparations for the wedding and for the journey, gave him all the gifts and letters, repeated to him what Bronka had said.

He asked her to send his blessings to everyone, especially to bride and groom.

When they were about to part she felt a pinching in her heart.

It was sad in the sanatorium. Death lurked everywhere.

'Soon summer will be over,' Haim said, 'and autumn will come. It'll be my second autumn here. In autumn an unseen brush will change the hues of nature, and the green will be covered with gold. A leaf that falls will never grow again.'

They parted and she returned to the city.

8 On the Threshold of Womanhood

Hania was perhaps the most beautiful of the sisters. She had exceptional charm, and every part of her body was in perfect proportion. She had beautiful skin and a long neck, an entrancing face, and long, soft, black hair in which a tint of auburn played like sunbeams.

And it was not only in her physical appearance that she was charming; each of her movements was graceful. Her light walk, her sweet enchanting smile – which revealed perfect teeth – her pleasant voice, and above all her bright merry eyes, which nevertheless had trace of solemnity and even sadness.

She was very intelligent, not proud, but well aware of her qualities.

Small wonder then, that she was often bothered. Such a flower inevitably draws butterflies and bees who want to play, to suck the honey and leave a sting.

She lived in a number of worlds. The apartment on Paulinska Street was one world, Mania's house was another. The Zionist *hachsharah* was a different world again. And as for the 'bees', Olek Orbach, Witold Zborowski, and Shmulik Kahana were very different from each other. Olek was a young man from an economically well-established Jewish family in Lodz – a good and highly educated family, completely assimilated. He was studying law at the Jagiellonska University, and had asked her to marry him.

Shmulik Kahana, a young man at the *hachsharah*, made her feel that she interested him.

And Witold Zborowski interested her. It had all happened at once.

The *hachsharah* was located in a Quiet Nooklet. A nooklet,

not a nook. The Poles like to pamper their nouns. How did Witold speak? 'Sunlet shines, rainlet falls, heartlet aches.'

The Quiet Nooklet was about an hour's walk from the city center. The way there was along a broad tree-lined avenue called the 'Blonia'. In the middle of the Blonia were about six traffic lanes that served streetcars, buses, and horse-drawn carriages, and beside these were broad sidewalks, with benches for pedestrians.

On one side of the Blonia was a permanent amusement park, a swimming pool, and a large park with the unusual name 'Park Jordana'. But the name of this beautiful park, which had many benches hidden in its pretty nooks, was not connected to the river in the Holy Land; it was named after a person.

On the other side of the Blonia stretched a vast expanse of green, on which there were carousels, swings and a Ferris wheel. What flights, what joys for children! And at the edge of the lawn and all along it, from the Quiet Nooklet to the Vistula, flowed a small brook called the Rudawa, which means 'redhead'. The residents of Krakow, in love with the Vistula, scoffed at the Rudawa and insulted it, calling it 'a channel, not a brook'.

The Quiet Nooklet could be reached by tram, bus, carriage, or on foot, along the sidewalk or along the lawn. Or by boat, on the Rudawa.

In this Quiet Nooklet the young Jews erected a work camp, a kind of small agricultural farm which was also a branch of the large farm at Czestochowa.

The building was surrounded by tents. A blue and white flag flew over its roof and a striking inscription in Hebrew appeared on the door: '*Kavod La Avodah* – Honor to work!'

The young people worked the land which belonged to the farm, planted flowers and green vegetables. Bronka taught them to sing while they worked, and they sang in Hebrew and in Polish. Bronka taught them all her favorite song of spring:

> A rose-wreath round my ringlets –
> O harp-strings in my fingers,
> Play me a song that's merry,

Play me a song of love –
All the flowers are blooming –
Violets and tulips –
Aromatic fragrance
Wafts now through the fields.

Dancing, I'll go smiling, beaming,
In this enchanting measure
And in the ring of love.
My ears hear joyous singing
Because the Spring, the Princess,
So beautiful and radiant
Wanders through the fields.

When Hania and Bronka first arrived at the Quiet Nooklet and presented themselves to the person in charge of the farm, Shmulik had appeared from somewhere, taken one look at Hania's face, and since then had not left her alone.

He found all kinds of excuses, changing his jobs, working overtime at the farm, just to be near her as often and for as long as possible.

She, of course, was immediately aware of his attempts. She felt like saying to him:

'Listen, fellow, leave me alone, find yourself another girl, you won't get me.' But she didn't say anything. She just became tense, every time he appeared.

He walked around in slovenly clothes, barefoot, with long hair. But it was not only his appearance that disturbed her. There was something difficult to define about him. Something superficial in his character, something that wasn't serious, as if he'd come to the *hachsharah* just to have fun. There were many like him here: pioneers in words only.

During their breaks from work the comrades would sit around and discuss contemporary topics.

Among these they spoke of the proposal made by the special emissary of Baron Hirsch, that Jews should migrate to Argentina. 'The Pika Company will finance it.'

'We can establish a Jewish state in Argentina too!'

A great tumult arose, people shouting to high heaven, and the proposal dropped.

'Then let's talk about Madagascar! We must arrive at a clear stand!'

'The Polish government is planning to send envoys to find out if Poland can send her Jews to Madagascar.'

'What's this about sending? No one sends us anywhere. We go when we decide to go, and where we decide to!'

'Don't try to be clever! You haven't grasped the real problem. Where will you go?'

'To Palestine, of course!'

'So go ahead! What are you waiting for?'

So they disputed. For Hania this way of living and thinking was completely new.

The man in charge of the farm, Ephraim Ben-David, got up and spoke in favor of Palestine. Palestine, he explained, was the one and only place on earth for which there already was political backing – the Balfour Declaration. 'Doctor Herzl, Doctor Weizmann, Nahum Sokolov and other Zionists have prepared the ground for us,' he said, 'We only have to make it come true – to get up and go there.'

This was the truth! Their speaker was a real man! And Shmulik kept circling around Hania, guiding her in her work, showing her how to hold a hoe, finding work-clothes for her. He said to her:

'Don't you care about your lovely delicate hands? What do you need all this for?'

What did he mean, 'what for?' Yes, she did care about her hands, and maybe 'all this' was really not for her, but he shouldn't ask her such a question. If he's here, one of the old timers and activists, then let him be a pioneer, let him go before the van, let him encourage, let him arouse enthusiasm. And if he doesn't like that, let him find some other kind of framework to be active in.

I wonder if he'll go to Palestine, or if he'll just talk about it. Who goes to Palestine? Only those who are absolutely fed up. Those considering the journey are all kinds of misfits:

134

unemployed, people in strife with their families, confused people. And those who actually go are a handful of idealists.

To avoid exposing herself too much to the fervent attentions of Shmulik, Hania tried to stay close to Bronka. She knew very well that their appearing together upset him.

'Maybe you're wrong about him?' her future sister-in-law said to her once. 'Maybe you just don't know him well enough?'

Hania didn't reply. How could you really 'know' someone? Did Bronka know Hesiek? Did Hesiek know Bronka? One hardly knows oneself.

Once, when Bronka had already stopped coming to the *hachsharah* and was busy with the seamstress sewing her wedding gown, Hania walked some distance from the farm and found a quiet 'nooklet' of her own, in a field, among corn and alfalfa. Here and there some daisies sprouted. She took one of them in her hand. Its little petals tickled her hand as if pleading: Pluck us and we'll tell you your future. She started plucking them the way she remembered from her childhood: Three positive petals: he loves me, he likes me, he respects me, and three negative ones: he doesn't want me, he doesn't know me, he scorns me. She sat there discarding the little petals until the white flower was no longer a flower. Its white head was almost bald, a few petals still holding on, but Hania's hand removed them too:

'… doesn't want me, doesn't know me, scorns me.' The last petal dropped.

Angrily she threw down what remained of the flower. Who scorns me? Who dares? Surely not Olek, Yesterday he'd brought her a bunch of roses.

'A rare color,' he said. 'I looked for tea-colored roses, especially for you.' Olek's a gentleman. He had already told her about his family, and his studies.

'It's hard, studying,' he said. 'I don't want them to even know that I'm a Jew. I behave like them, I attend classes on Saturdays, but they know. They placed me in the special seats, a ghetto inside the university. I might stop studying next year.' Olek spoke in a monotone, and his movements were somewhat clumsy. His brown eyes showed both his lack of self-confidence and his good-naturedness.

No, Olek doesn't scorn me. Nor does Witek.

If only Witek were a Jew! If only he were a Jew! Actually, what difference was there between him and Olek? Olek didn't observe the Jewish precepts, didn't know a thing about Judaism, didn't even keep the Sabbath. So what was the difference?

Yet there was a difference. Her family would accept Olek, but not Witek. She had met Witek by chance. Two strangers who had noticed each other. Witek – tall, blond, well-built – was walking briskly and confidently in an open raincoat, the wind blowing its flaps to the sides, when he saw her from a distance. He smiled at her with his blue eyes and said:

'I kiss your handlet, lovely miss!' Then noticed her new dress, and said:

'What a lovely dresslet the miss is wearing!'

And another time when they met, he was carrying a shopping basket with bread, butter, and eggs in it. He said:

'Here's breadlet and butterlet. When I saw you, these almost turned into an omeletlet.' He pointed to the eggs.

Another time he said: 'Perhaps I might be permitted to invite the lovely miss to a theatrette? We could see a good playlet?':

Oh, Witek. If you were a Jew, I'd go to a theatrette with you, we'd see a playlet, we'd make us an omeletlet, and all kinds of other pampered things which you seem to like. Maybe a kisslet? Maybe a huglet? But I must forget you, and quickly, Witek. You'll take the mountain path, and I the valley. You'll become a priest, and I – a rabbi's wife. No. I won't be a rabbi's wife, but it looks like I'll be the wife of a law student who won't complete his studies because he's persecuted in the University because he's a Jew. By the Rudawa, frogs croaked.

She had no desire to go back to the farm. Bronka wasn't there. Shmulik would start pestering her, boasting as usual. Yesterday she'd been asked if she wanted to go to the market to sell flowers raised on the farm. She'd said no. She'd been shy. Witold might have passed, and seen her selling flowers in the market together with the peasant women.

She ought to have been proud. Of working the land, of

growing flowers. Rozia was in Palestine - she had returned to the motherland, she was building the country, and could be proud of her deeds. If Hania were there, she wouldn't be shy either.

Olek would not want to go to Palestine. He'd already told her that.

At the University he felt out of place and would certainly leave. That's what he'd said. He would manage; one can live without an academic education. And a person doesn't have to define himself, Olek had said. He was simply a human being, and by virtue of that he could live wherever he felt like living. I'm a cosmopolitan, Olek had said to her.

Crrr crrr crrr. Those frogs again. She felt chilly. The sun was setting. Suddenly she heard footsteps.

She got up in alarm from among the corn and alfalfa, and a thorn stuck in her leg. She let out a thin, restrained scream.

'At last, there you are!'

Shmulik was standing over her, and she was touched by the concern in his face.

'Everyone's looking for you.' He sat down beside her on the grass.

'It's wet here,' he yelled. 'Get up at once, you'll catch cold!'

'You fusspot!' she laughed. 'We're pioneers, we're not supposed to be so pampered!'

He took off his sweater and spread it on the ground. 'At least sit on this.'

His cotton shirt had various stains on it. He caught her glance and said:

'That's not dirt. They're marks of work.'

'Good for you Shmulik. Today you're OK.' And after a pause, she added:

'Shmulik, I don't feel like going back to the farm, I don't know why.'

'So what do you want?'

A silence. It was so hard to answer this very simple question. she was aware of being inside the high grass, the corn and the alfalfa, which swayed gently in the breeze. It was very quiet all around.

'… No, Shmulik … No … I don't want to …'

The water of the Rudawa slowly washed over the wild grasses, and the frogs continued their symphony. A big red sun dropped below the horizon.

The next day Hania went to see Ephraim Ben-David. It was eight o'clock in the morning. He had already worked two hours in the field. He was sitting in the place which might be called an office, and was busily writing articles for newspapers, in Polish and in Hebrew.

Ephraim Ben-David was a poet. He wrote his poems at night, for there wasn't time enough during the day. He was fluent in Polish, knew Yiddish, and was now attacking Hebrew. He had mobilized all his forces of soul, body, and spirit for the struggle to conquer the language. He worked at it, he used all the knowledge of it he had gained from studying the holy books, he translated and delved into every character, and knew the language inside out.

Ephraim Ben-David was the best of the workers on the farm. He was versed in every branch and his hand showed in everything. The least popular jobs were always done by him.

Hania stood before him feeling like a traitor.

'Please sit down,' he said.

'I've come to say good-bye,' Hania said. 'I'm leaving the farm.'

His face was hard, uncompromising.

'What are your plans?' he asked.

She blushed, and the words burst out. 'I haven't made any yet,' she said.

'And you've already decided to leave? Pity. But one must do what one wants. I wish you all the best.'

What was there to say? Every minute of his time was precious. Hania got up and said in Hebrew:

'*Shalom! Lehitraot b'Eretz Israel!*' (Peace [good-bye], see you in the Land of Israel.)

She could see that his thoughts were no longer with her. Nevertheless he smiled and replied:

'Let's hope we do see each other in the Land. Who knows … all the best and *shalom*.'

She left his 'office' and started walking away from the farm. Good-bye, Quiet Nooklet, I've spent some beautiful hours here. Perhaps I'll come back one day, on a walk with my children. A daisy peeped out from among the wild grasses by the sides of the path and she bent down to pick it, but at the last moment she changed her mind. Let it grow in the field instead of telling her future.

She looked behind her. The blue-and-white flag waved in the wind, and she stood to attention, and then set off on her way.

At home she found no place for herself. Everyone was busy. Hesiek, Bronka, Hela Haim and Sala, the wedding, the journey, illness and depression.

And Rozia was in Palestine, working hard on the road or in the field, or perhaps sick with malaria?

And Mania? She wouldn't understand; the most she could tell her would be to trust in God, or to go and see a rabbi and ask him for advice.

Hania's nights became nightmares. There were decisions to be made, and quickly.

In the meantime she didn't even have a corner to herself, to live in, to be alone. And not a penny to her name.

A day before the wedding Bronka came to her, looking restless.

They walked over to the window and looked out into the street. Bearded Jews stood in groups talking, with their hands as well as with their mouths. A group of children with sidecurls, chattering loudly in Yiddish, came out of one of the houses, where the heder hour had apparently come to an end and the rabbi had dismissed his little charges. On the corner someone was selling hot chestnuts and seeds:

'*Frische, heisse, koifts*', ('Fresh, hot, buy!'), called the fat woman vendor from under her black hat.

It was a hot stifling evening.

'I've left the farm,' Hania said in a hoarse voice. 'I don't want to see him any more.'

'Who?' asked Bronka, but immediately touched her friend's hand gently and added:

'You don't have to. What did Ben-David say?'

'He said that with soldiers like the ones he has he'll never be able to make progress. We'll never succeed.'

The street below darkened. The bearded men, the children, the chestnut vendor, all vanished. From Miodowa Street Hela came towards them, with a thin, tired-looking man beside her. They were having a lively conversation, which ceased the moment Hela caught the glances of the two girls by the window.

Bronka retreated a little into the room, and Hania raised her eyes to the sky. A star fell. It flashed, glided, and vanished so quickly that she didn't have time to make a wish.

PART II

In the Heart
(1927)

9 Quests and Loneliness: Hela's Story

The winter of 1927 was a cruel winter. Waves of snow swept through the streets, fierce winds whirled them and turned them into solid pillars reaching high into the sky. These pillars then twisted amid the howling whistling wind, rising and disintegrating into cascades that brought down trees and houses, and wiped entire villages off the face of the earth.

January was the hardest month.

The roads were covered with snow, means of transportation were paralyzed, and many places were completely isolated. Villages were doomed to destruction; many people froze to death or died of starvation or disease. Others survived, but only just, preferring to sleep until the spring in some protected corner, body to body, animals with humans.

In Paulinska Street Hela had lived alone for several years now, she and the ghosts of the past.

It had gone on since the death of the child.

At nights she would leap out of bed, her shoulders trembling, her head dizzy. She could hear something was knocking in the kitchen.

She ran there and heard voices gurgling, and whistles. There was no one in the kitchen. She ran back, barefoot, and crash! – a chair fell in her path, or something else. From the kitchen impudent voices laughed. The apartment was full of ghosts. Hela would return to her bed and slip under the blankets. The bed was cold and empty, the sheets and blanket-covers stiff and cold. Through the cracks in the windows the cold winter and the dark night would steal in.

She didn't hold out. She couldn't go on living alone any more.

At first they had lived together: the two of them, and she. They had come here after the wedding, radiant with joy. They filled the apartment with a kind of atmosphere it had not known before. They started making changes, moving the furniture, adapting the apartment to their needs. They would close themselves in the bedroom, the room that had once been Father's and Mother's, the room in which Mother, Father, and Menashe had died. The room which was wrapped in a kind of sanctity, that even they, the children of this household, had never allowed themselves to enter. Now merry laughter resounded from it.

Bronka's laughter, coming from the closed room, used to drive her out of her mind. Everything turned over inside her. She couldn't bear it.

'You're here in my home, not in yours,' she occasionally reminded her sister-in-law. And at once she regretted it. She was surprised and pained to see how easily she had upset her, clouded her joy, chased the smile from her face. She hadn't intended to hurt her so, she'd only wanted to protect her own rights. It was hard to accept the fact that this woman had rights here too.

The trip to Switzerland had been most timely. She had gone, and they had remained alone in the apartment. But the whole thing was for one year only. Where did she have to come back to from Switzerland?

There, in Switzerland, towards the end of the course, a professor had taken an interest in her. He was from Berlin, and was working in Switzerland as a lecturer in the medical school where she was studying. His name was Edward Kurtz, and he had many fine qualities. But Hela had reservations. She didn't know Aleks's fate. And deep in her heart she thought of him all the time.

Only when she returned to Krakow, after year in Switzerland, did she find out what had happened to Aleks. He had returned, but not alone. He had brought a pretty little woman, who spoke Russian in a thin musical voice. Aleks and the woman had married, and a short while after the wedding a little daughter was born, who they called Maja.

Hela had tried to avoid meeting Aleks, but such a thing was impossible in a city where all the Jews knew each other. Aleks was with her everywhere all the time. She did not succeed in getting him out of her life. He kept returning.

The Swiss doctors had been unable to help Sala, who sank deeper and deeper into her depression.

When the sisters had returned, there was nowhere for them to go.

To Paulinska? No. Hela well remembered the tension between herself and her sister-in-law, and didn't want to go through that again. They spent their first night back in Krakow in a hotel room.

'Very nice,' Hela said to her sister. 'We've come home, and we haven't got a home. A fine situation, isn't it?'

Sala was so downcast and apathetic that Hela was immediately sorry that she had touched on such a sore spot. In an attempt to get her out of her depression, Hela said:

'Have you noticed how our lovely Krakow has become smaller? After Zurich, Lucerne, and Berne, it's not as impressive as it used to be. Now I understand Aunt Matilda. If you come here from the west, nothing here is going to make any impression on you.' Sala remained quiet for a long while, and suddenly said:

'That's not true. Krakow's the most beautiful city in the world!'

They stayed in the hotel room for several days, and then representatives of the family arrived and brought them home almost by force.

'Everything's prepared for your arrival, your beds have been made,' said Bronka, smiling. Hela scrutinized her from head to toe, and Bronka blushed.

'You've put on weight,' said Hela. 'I have a healthy appetite,' Bronka smiled, embarrassed, and looked around for her husband. Evidently she could feel comfortable in the company of her sisters-in-law only when he was beside her.

One day, while they were still in the hotel, Schiffmann came to visit his ex-wife. He had aged greatly since they'd seen him last. His body had shrunk and his deformity stood out more than before. In his pale face his eyes were very red, as if he suffered from lack of sleep. Beside him stood a short woman, wearing a winter coat with a fur collar, and a hat with a muslin veil that came down over her face.

Sala went to meet them and reached her hand out to greet them, and Hela retreated to a corner, full of admiration for her sister, who showed great self-control, acting so politely to the man who was the cause of her bitter suffering.

A quiet weeping suddenly set Schiffman's chest quivering. His wife brought out a handkerchief, wiped her eyes under her veil, and passed the handkerchief to her husband.

Silence descended upon the room. The four of them sat there, their heads lowered, gazing at the floor.

Hela was not a part of this and felt superfluous. Schiffman's little wife had lost her self-control and her whole body was trembling as she sobbed. Schiffman sat with lowered head, his hat pulled low over his eyes, his hands caressing the delicate white hands of his ex-wife Sala, who didn't ask to be released, but sat there petrified, like a still Greek statue.

A short while afterwards Sala died. Her death came quietly, unexpectedly and mysteriously, and shocked those who remained alive.

After Sala's death, Hela returned to the apartment in Paulinska Street. Bronka was pregnant.

'I beg your pardon,' Hela said without looking her in the eye. 'I said you'd put on weight, I shouldn't have, I didn't know.'

'How could you have known?' Bronka laughed. 'Your brother wants a dozen children, he told me, so we have to get on with it.'

Hela didn't reply. She noticed all the changes they had made in the apartment. Everything looked different. Again it was hard for her to bear it.

Hesiek was busy outside the house most of the time. He would come home for quick meals, kiss his wife, ask about his sister's health, gulp down his food, and go off again. Bronka was not confident as she moved around the rooms; she was confused, losing her balance, perhaps because of the pregnancy. Yellow patches appeared on her face, and her feet became swollen.

A spirit of malice came over Hela.

'It's still my home, not yours,' she blurted. Bronka turned pale, and the yellow patches on her face became more distinct. She looked around for a chair to sit on. Her hands trembled. Hela was sorry for what she'd said, but it was already too late. 'But there's room here for all of us,' she said, more gently. They sat facing each other. Bronka tried to smile.

'I've started to feel the baby,' she said shyly, ignoring what Hela had said before. 'He's really kicking inside. I have a feeling he's going to be a fine fellow of a man.' Her eyes beamed.

Hela felt a deep regret.

'You have to look after yourself,' she said. 'I'll help you. Today I'll make dinner.'

Bronka didn't respond, and asked:

'Have you found work yet?'

Hela's face grew gloomy.

'Oh, it's terrible. There are hardly any vacancies, and there are so many applicants for every job. You get so many rejections, it's awfully exhausting, and degrading.'

'Even in your profession?'

'Who looks at your profession? I don't even get to the places where they consider the professional aspects. Some people say that before going off to study I should have changed my name and perhaps also my religion.'

'No!'

'There are private places, of course. There are Jewish employers. I heard that a private X-ray center is being opened in Smolenski Street owned by a Jewish doctor. But they pay ridiculously low wages. That's why I haven't applied. But, not to worry! I won't become a burden upon you.'

'But Hela, that wasn't why I asked.'

That was how it was always, a kind of venom babbling inside Hela.

This venom was destroying Bronka, and Hela knew it. If

only she felt some relief afterwards, but the opposite was the case.

This Bronka, what does she know about the struggle for survival going on in the streets? About the scarcity of jobs, which were always kept for other people. Who was it that had spoken of equal rights for the Poles and for all the minorities? All that existed only on paper.

Throughout these years Hesiek was busy making money. Hela knew that he had made it his sacred goal to get rich, come what may.

'With money you can buy anything. Status, and respect,' he used to say.

'Rubbish!' Hela replied, resentfully. She was still running about looking for work, only rarely talking of her disappointments.

'You can really expect a lot of respect here, I'm sure,' she mocked him. 'Your Polish neighbors for example – do they give you respect?'

'Socially I have nothing to do with them,' he answered. 'They don't interest me in the least.'

She interrupted him with a vigorous gesture of dismissal: 'How can you say a thing like that? What do you mean you're not interested in them in the least? Don't you live among them?'

'So what? They have their belief and culture, and we have ours. We have to preserve our uniqueness.'

'I don't know,' she said, more moderately now. 'If we preserve our uniqueness, they mock us, and if we try to be like them, they suspect us. What solution do you see?'

'What does it matter? Let them mock, let them suspect. What matters is what we feel. And I don't feel myself inferior to anyone. On the contrary.'

'Those are ostrich tactics. You don't understand the world you live in.'

The views of the brother and his sisters were so different. It was impossible to talk to him about Jewish matters. To him, Judaism was beyond all argument, and after that, second and third on his scale of priorities, came his family and his business. And that was that. That was his world.

Bronka understood nothing about his business. She ran the household, and at the most could write down housekeeping expenses in a little notebook she had bought for the purpose. He allotted her a sum of money for these expenditures, always saying as he handed it over:

'Spend as much as you need. Don't feel limited.'

But she tried to save. That was her nature. Hela said to her:

'He isn't going to get rich on what you save. Those wretched pennies won't buy the beautiful big house you both dream of.'

'I don't dream of a big house at all. I'd be quite content with a small apartment that was all mine!'

Hela was astounded. Was this her innocent and submissive sister-in-law?

In contrast to her brother's bourgeois aspirations, Hela felt an affinity with the socialist movements that had begun making their presence felt, even though that year the regime was firmly in the hands of the 'all-powerful' ruler Jozef Pilsudski, and the Communist Party had been outlawed and had gone underground.

Masses of young people were seeking a way to a better future.

The state was young, moulding itself after long years of subjugation. Everything was in motion, in the process of becoming. Many young Jews had knocked down the walls which had closed off their lives in the townlets and the quarters reserved only for them. Education had reached many, but its influence was not uniform. Some saw it as a light for the perplexed; others saw it as a danger to Jewish wholeness, which was centered primarily around the Jewish religion.

Since her return from Switzerland, Hela had sought a framework in which to fit. At first she joined the 'P.P.S.', the Polish Socialist Party, and after that the 'Bund', the Jewish labor movement.

Most of her friends had at first been active in the P.P.S, but anyone who wanted to preserve his Jewish identity, even a little, felt foreign and discriminated against here. Very few were willing to completely deny their origins. Thus, against this background, tensions arose, and crises of faith began. The Bund, as a branch of the general socialist movement, encompassed a Jewish workers' movement in Poland, Russia, and Lithuania, and supported the Socialist International. It didn't recognize a connection between the Jewish diasporas, and did not view the Jews as a nation. This movement suited many who chose the path of class struggle as a solution to the problems of mankind, and tried in this framework to solve their own personal problems.

In the Bund clubhouse in Bochenska Street, cultural evenings, discussions, and lectures were held. Here Hela heard about the convoluted fate of the Jews, their history from the distant period of the Bible, until the destruction of the Second Temple.

Here was a new page in this history – the Exile, Spain, a glorious new period of fine co-existence of Muslims and Jews – then its tragic end with the coming of the Christians – the Marranoes – the assimilationists – the Rambam (Moses Maimonides), Spinoza, and Moses Mendelssohn – Shabtai Zvi and other false messiahs – the persecution of Jews all over the world – Herzl. Shivat-Zion – Achad Ha'am and Jabotinsky – Y.L. Gordon, Sholem Aleichem and Sholem Asch, Mapu, Mendele Mocher Seforim, Bialik and others.

But in the main the Bund concentrated on the development of class consciousness. They taught the theories of Marx and Engels. They studied the ideologies of Lenin and Trotsky, and obliged everyone to read Gorky and Mayakovsky. They got in a tangle over the question of 'Who is a Jew?' and found difficulty in defining the language of the Jews. There was no end to the arguments. 'Assimilation? No, we don't want that,' said one of those present. 'On the contrary, education gives us tools with which to examine ourselves. Who are we? Where are we heading? We must examine the values of our people, not only from the religious perspective. We have to distinguish between Jewish religion and Jewish nationhood. We have to develop our literature, our language.'

'What language? What nationhood? What are you talking

about?' Tumult in the hall. Some yelled: 'Yiddish!' Others yelled: 'Hebrew!' Some yelled out that they belonged to the Jewish nation wherever it existed, and others yelled: 'A geographic homeland!'

'If so,' asked Hela, 'if a geographic homeland, then why Yiddish? Why not Polish?'

She didn't speak Yiddish, and barely understood it.

'Why Yiddish and not Polish? Because there are very few Polonists like you. Because the masses of Jews whom we hope to reach, and help, and organize, don't know Polish, they speak only Yiddish.'

'And Hebrew?'

'Hebrew is the holy tongue. Yiddish is a secular language.'

Everything was confused. Not all the Jews spoke Yiddish. She sank into thought, while many got up angrily and left the hall.

'You want to identify with all those miserable retarded people in the towns and villages? That's no solution for us.'

Hela recalled the family at her brother Menashe's wedding in Chszanow. She remembered her sister-in-law, who then had looked at her relatives from the city as if they were a group of arrogant self-important strangers. There was no doubt that Cracovians felt themselves superior to the town-dwellers. Hela felt a pinching in her heart. They had heard nothing from Menashe's family. What had happened to them?

It was hard for Hela to consolidate a view and a stand of her own. She only knew that these things were important and complicated. And that one could not be apathetic about them. The literature of the Jewish Enlightenment flourished in two languages – Yiddish and Hebrew, but Hela read only Polish: Antony Slonimski, a Jewish author who wrote in Polish, and of course Julian Tuwim. For her, the favored language was Polish. Her sister Rozia, who had already been in Palestine for eight years still couldn't write Hebrew without mistakes. Rozia, who spoke perfect Polish, and wrote in an excellent style – she had even written poems in Polish – found difficulty in putting a simple sentence together in Hebrew.

One's language too is one's homeland.

She did a lot of hard soul-searching before deciding to formally join the Bund. No one in her family supported the idea or helped her make the decision.

The center of political and cultural life had now passed from Galicia, to Lwow, to Krakow, to Congressional Poland – and then to Warsaw. There, Jewish printing houses, schools, clubs, and theaters had been set up. Jewish writers and poets all concentrated in the capital too.

Many of Hela's new friends traveled all over Poland, trying to win converts to the Bund, and they drew their inspiration from Warsaw.

Although Hela was already an official member of the Bund, she continued with her soul-searching. Her fellow-members were people with class consciousness, and were becoming fanatical in their ideas. They saw their movement as the only solution for the Jewish masses, and condemned the awakening Zionism with the claim that it was causing harm to the Jews of Poland.

'You, the Zionists, go ahead and go to Zion. You can't stay here in the Polish state and be loyal to another state, even if it's a state that is only just coming into being.'

The members of the Bund accused the Zionists of causing anti-semitism. The assimilationists accused the ultra orthodox of causing anti-semitism. The ultra orthodox in turn accused the Zionists of causing anti-semitism.

One member of the club used to say: 'What difference does it make who's to blame? There are facts that exist. Anti-semitism exists. A situation has arisen which does not augur well. Let's all get out of here!'

Everyone treated him as if he was mad. 'Where will we go? Why should we go? Weren't we born here?'

Rozia wrote from Palestine, long letters in Polish, and between the lines details appeared of her hard life in the desert country. The difficulties were off-putting. But there was elating news too. In 1925, the Hebrew University had been opened in Jerusalem. Rozia wrote a lot about this event. Hela sent presents to her with the Carmel brothers, who went there to be present at the inauguration ceremonies. Shabtai and Menashe Carmel had gone to prepare the ground for their migration to Palestine. Deep in her heart Hela envied them. Uncle Fischel too, the opponent of Zionism, had traveled to Zion that year too, to prostrate himself upon the graves of the saintly *tzadikim*. His long and enthusiastic letters, in fluent Hebrew, which he sent home from this trip, became famous among the Jews of Krakow. Hela asked for a translation. A melancholy descended upon her. What was there in this land, so distant and yet so near, so repulsive and so attractive, so yearned for and so threatening, and so full of contradictions? Why could one not stop thinking about it?

The University of Warsaw sent an official representative to Jerusalem. This was Professor Mazdrzakowski, a doctor of medicine, and with him traveled Professor Schor, the Chief Rabbi of Warsaw.

The Zionist movement was the most organized of the movements in Poland, and aroused wonder and excitement. The Polish intelligentsia were curious about it, and the antisemites supported it. The Jewish pioneers preparing themselves for *aliyah*, the 'going up' to the Land, were quite different to the Jews the anti-semites hated. Thousands of Jews signed up for *aliyah* every month, and it was impossible to remain apathetic in the face of these facts. Hela was angry that no one in her family advised her what to do. What was this apathy? Could you let day follow day without stopping for a moment to think where all this was leading?

She decided to stay in the Bund. Here she met people whose company somewhat eased her loneliness.

Elsa, the accountant she had worked with just after the war, was one of the people who had drawn her to the Bund. Elsa had found her alone and depressed, looking for a job and not finding one. She had said to her:

'Come to us. Among us you'll find interesting people who won't abandon you when you need them. They'll help you find work, give you guidance about your rights, and defend you when you need it.'

Elsa was a courageous woman. While Hela had been in Switzerland, she had become pregnant by Misha, the public-relations man, and had given birth without being married. Unashamedly and openly they were raising the child while each of them lived apart, keeping their previous surnames and their own freedom.

'Emancipation!' Elsa would say, raising her head high. Misha would smile forgivingly and understandingly. Elsa and her sister Bianca, with the baby, Philip, rented a room in Polish Krakow, far from their angry parents, who were deeply ashamed of Elsa. Elsa and Bianca would stroll in the Planty, with the well-fed and well-groomed Philip in a splendid pram. The baby's father, Misha, would join them on these strolls, play a little with his son, and then accompany them to the entrance of their house, where he took his leave and went his way.

Elsa, Bianca, and Misha were active members in the Bund. During this period a small Jewish theater opened in Krakow and new faces appeared in the Jewish scene in Krakow. They were talented and energetic young people, enthusiastic and devoted to the project. They had to perform. They had to succeed. At first they appeared on a rickety and primitive stage, and the acting was poor, more suitable to elementary school standard. But the audience was forgiving, and many people came to see the plays, which were performed in Yiddish and were based on the stories of Sholem Aleichem, Mendele Mocher Seforim and other Yiddishists. Gradually the theater's standards improved. The Jewish public was proud of the troupe, and Polish dramatic circles began to evince interest in it. Relationships of mutual encouragement and support arose. The Jewish theater won the place it deserved. It and its actors introduced a new atmosphere, artistic and bohemian, into the Bund clubhouse.

One day, when Hela was at the clubhouse, she found Bianca there. Bianca was also one of the actors. She was sitting at a make-up table, wearing a long dress which reached to the floor, the costume for her part .

'Everything's falling apart,' she said. 'It's all hopeless! Our theater won't survive without municipal support. All our efforts are in vain!'

She was on the verge of tears. Jozek came up to her to console her: 'Don't you worry, my fair lady. We have come through harder times, we'll manage somehow. We'll make do with less.' Turning to Hela, he said: 'I don't think you've met my good friend Neufeld. Neufeld the painter.'

Neufeld and Hela shook hands and the painter immediately returned to his work, sitting in concentration in front of an easel. Hela stood there bewildered, not knowing what to do with herself, and Jozek turned to his friend.

'Listen,' he said, 'you can't live on painting alone. True, you're a man who makes no demands. A piece of bread, a brush, and a pair of pants will do, as long as you can get yourself out of the gray mediocrity which the artists of the academy are engulfed in today.'

'No, you're wrong,' said Neufeld, without interrupting his work. 'Actually there are some very interesting experiments being made in our academy these days. They're trying to revive various trends in art. Especially successful are the attempts to revive Impressionism. In our academy there's a feeling of progress, a sense that we're *avant-garde*.' He was quiet for a while, and then he added: 'Colors have to create something new and to complement nature, and not necessarily to copy it.'

'He's right,' Bianca interposed. 'What, for example, do you feel when you look at works by Gauguin? Something wild and primitive, full of instinctual drives. Isn't it so much more wonderful and stirring than all the conservative banalities?'

'That, of course, is a question of taste,' said Jozek. 'But what is certain is the more troubled the artist soul, and the further he is from serenity, the more fascinating the power to be found in his works.'

He and Hela stood looking at Neufeld – at his thin, sagging face, and at his restless hands.

'Do you think you've discovered America?' the painter replied, and got up, looked at his painting, and asked:

'What do you think of it?'

They moved closer to the painting.

'Do you like it?' Neufeld asked Hela. She, who had visited

several great museums during her year in Europe, looked at the painting with a critical eye.

'Not bad,' she said cautiously. 'One has to get used to the style, of course.'

'Isn't it interesting that the great artists are always men?' said Jozek, knowing that the remark would arouse indignant replies.

Elsa and Bianca got to their feet and attacked him sharply. They flung a disordered *mélange* of names of famous women at him – Madame Curie-Sklodowska, someone called Olga Boznanska, and winners of international prizes – and anyway, they said, why would you say such a thing, you of all people?

It was Jozek who had helped Elsa find a room in the city when she was in the last months of her pregnancy with little Philip.

The poor fellow already regretted having spoken.

'Yes, you're right,' he said. 'Actually we men are the inferior sex. No man is capable of doing what every woman can do.' Bianca and Elsa calmed down.

Hela was amused. She liked the atmosphere in the clubhouse. She looked at the clock.

'I have to go,' she said.

'Where are you hurrying to?' asked Jozek. 'No one's waiting for you at home … I'm sorry,' he immediately apologized: 'I'm sorry. We're all of us lone wolves here: Neufeld, I, you.'

Hela smiled at him.

'You're a good friend, Jozek,' she said. She said her good-byes and left. She hadn't noticed that in the meantime Neufeld had packed his gear and had gone out about a minute before she did. They met in the corridor and came out into the street together.

'I know where you live,' he said. 'I live around there too.'

'I've never seen you!'

'I've seen you,' he smiled. 'And I hope we'll meet again. Good-bye.' He walked off, and she noticed his neglected dress and appearance. Was it accidental or was this his usual style? And the way he spoke, and the way he related to her or to

Jozek, for example – was it all natural, or staged?

At this time, Hesiek and Bronka were living with her, on Paulinska. Their baby was ten days old. They had called him Moshe, after Hesiek's father.

The infant and the mother seemed to fill the whole apartment. Wherever you looked there was laundry clean and dirty, and new smells pervaded the air.

Hela was delighted by the birth of her little nephew. At the same time, everything annoyed her. Everybody's attention now centered on the baby. She couldn't even have a chance to invite acquaintances home for a glass of tea.

Again there was a quarrel between her and Bronka.

Bronka was weak and hysterical after the birth; her breast-milk was not flowing properly, she suffered terrible pains and the baby was always hungry.

Suddenly Haim wrote from the sanatorium that he was being given a short period of leave before his journey to Vienna for a complicated lung operation, which the doctors had decided to try.

Bronka insisted that Haim should come home, even though everyone knew that she and the baby must not expose themselves to the presence of someone ill with tuberculosis.

'He must come here,' she said stubbornly. 'This is his home as much as it's ours. It's not his fault that we healthy people don't get along with each other.'

'If you weren't here with the child,' said Hela, 'I would take Haim in and there'd be enough room here.'

The next day Bronka and Hesiek decided to pack their belongings and to prepare the child for moving.

'Where are you going?' Hela asked, in despair. It was already too late.

'We'll have to sell the apartment,' said Hesiek. 'We'll divide the money into four parts. Hania and Olek need money too. A quarter of the sum will go for Haim's operation. We have no other source for these expenses. A quarter to Hania, a quarter to us, and a quarter to you. You'll have to find another place to live. You can stay on here another month. We're leaving

157

here tomorrow.'

Hela was dumbstruck, 'Why so suddenly?'

'It's not sudden.'

Bronka tried to protest. 'The baby's still small ... he won't be able to fight the germs ...'

'We're moving,' said Hesiek, in a tone that left no room for contradiction.

The worst period of all was the brief one during which Hela lived by herself on Paulinska, with ghosts wailing in the night and feelings of loneliness and guilt oppressing her.

From a drawer she took out the album of photographs taken in Switzerland and on the trip she had made to Egypt at the end of her course. In many of the pictures Professor Edward Kurtz appeared beside her: by the Sphinx and by the pyramids; on camels. Rozia had sent similar pictures from Palestine. Sand, sand, and deserts. Everything looked distant and unreal.

Hania and Olek needed money. They were living in a rented room, which they would soon have to leave.

They asked Hela to lend them her share of the proceeds from the sale of the apartment on Paulinska Street.

'And what about me? Where will I live?'

'You can live with us,' Hania said. 'If we don't pay at once we'll miss the chance to buy the good apartment we've been lucky to find. There's a lot of people who want it.'

Neufeld painted Hela's portrait. Her face, he said, made a good model. Its lines were like those of Venus. Yes, Venus. That was what he said. She sat in front of him, and he looked now at her and now at his canvas and the picture came into being.

So it was several times. These were pleasant hours. They didn't talk much, a word here, a word there. They learned to understand each other by hints.

As she sat there before him while he was absorbed in his work, she was able to observe and examine the features of his face, his delicate and supple hands, his whole bearing. He seemed to her to be suffering from under-nourishment, and even more from a lack of attention. She wondered if there was a woman in his life. True, Jozek had declared often enough that 'we're both lone wolves ...' But even lone wolves usually met some she-wolf. Would he ever tell her about himself?

Neufeld finished his painting. The portrait was amazingly beautiful. 'What a success!' Bianca cried. She and Jozek were considered a couple at this time. 'What a success! You've really managed to get something of the depths of her soul onto the canvas!'

'Oh, don't exaggerate! I wish I knew what goes on in those depths,' said the painter.

Hela smiled. He wanted to know what was in her heart.

'Things there are less complicated than you think,' she said. At that moment she was willing to open herself up. A rare moment; the gentlest touch was enough. Neufeld came up to her and with a ceremonious expression handed her the painting.

'This is for you. A gift from me. A souvenir forever.'

'A present? But you've put so many hours of work into it!'

'For you,' he said.

When Neufeld left she continued sitting where she was and looking at the picture as if hypnotized. A warmth flooded through her when she thought of him, of his words, and of the amount of work he had put into the painting. For some reason her thoughts returned to Professor Kurtz and to Aleks. Jozek came into the room. She gave a start.

'Why the alarm? I've got good news. Have you found a job yet?'

'No. It's hard to find one. I can't obtain a government position.'

'I've found a fantastic job for you. A Jewish doctor, who's an X-ray specialist, is looking for an assistant. He's opening a private institute. I can put you in touch with him. I've already told you about him.'

'Oh, Jozek!' Hela said. 'You're so good to me!' Again the same feeling she'd had before. Just the gentlest touch. Jozek put a finger on her mouth. Then he came up to her and kissed her.

At that moment Neufeld came into the room and Jozek

broke away and looked for a cigarette. Hela was totally confused.

Neufeld looked at the portrait he had given her before, took some of his equipment, blurted out a 'Good-bye' and hurried out.

'Wait!' Jozek ran after him.

As quickly as she could Hela hurried back to her empty apartment. She threw herself onto the bed and burst out crying.

The next day she told Hania that she was accepting her invitation and would go and live with them.

They were living in two rooms only, but the feeling of warmth created an illusion that there was a lot more space than at Paulinska.

Hania made room for her in a wardrobe and said: 'Feel at home here.'

The apartment on Paulinska Street was sold, and Hela's portion was given to Hania and Olek as a loan. They began repaying their debt by giving her free lodging. Hela said to Olek:

'You take care of the accounting. I hate all that.'

He opened a notebook and wrote down:

'Hela – rent, on account of the loan.'

He figured out the interest they would owe her if they didn't return the loan quickly. He explained to her various things connected with this and she listened with only one ear, giving him her complete trust.

In the meantime she continued looking for work. The job in the private institute which Jozek had mentioned was an actual possibility, but the Jewish doctor was offering a ridiculously low salary. He wanted a split work day for no more than pennies.

'That's exploitation,' Olek said angrily. 'Don't take that job. That bastard knows that it's difficult to find jobs and he's exploiting the fact. It's always a matter of supply and demand.'

Olek and Hania's apartment was close to Copernicus Street, and to St Lazarus Street, that street of hospitals and clinics where Rozia had worked many years earlier when

Hela and Hania had gone looking for her after her disappearance.

'Why don't you try your luck in one of those hospitals?' Olek encouraged her.

Hela applied at various places in Copernicus Street. Krakow was a scientific center at this time, and even had a medical school. In the clinics and hospitals local doctors and surgeons were employed, and – when necessary – specialists would be called in from Lwow and from Vienna. These institutions were religious – Catholic – in character, and nuns worked in them as nurses. Both workers and patients were Catholics.

Jews were hardly ever given medical attention here. There was a kind of ancient arrangement, according to which Jews had to pay double for services, so they had no alternative but to go to private doctors.

At that time, true, the Jewish hospital on Skawinska Street – which had been built with the aid of contributions from wealthy Jews, mainly from America – had just been renovated. Jewish doctors had taken it in hand and set up new departments, but the standard of its equipment was far below that of the university departments in St Lazarus and Copernicus Streets.

Hela didn't tell anyone about her experiences while looking for work.

Sister Ursula, whom she had good memories of, was no longer working in the hospital on Copernicus Street, and she had no one to turn to. Nothing came of all her attempts. She felt depressed, and realized that without someone's help she would make no progress.

With Hela's arrival an upholstered sofa had been put into the dining room of Olek's and Hania's small apartment. Here Hela slept at night. Hania did all in her power to make things easy for Hela and to make her feel at home.

Hela was an easy lodger. She was out of the house most of the day. She took the job at Doctor Lustiger's private institute on Smolenski Street, and they hardly ever saw her.

Her new employer, Doctor Lustiger, was a serious doctor, with a passion for his profession. He ran the X-ray institute where she worked, and also worked in the Jewish hospital in Skawinska Street. During his absences from the institute Hela ran all the institute's affairs by herself, with the help of auxiliary manpower and a maid-servant, to her employer's satisfaction. During her midday breaks she would handle all her private affairs in the city, and in the evenings, after work, she would mostly go to the Bund club house. She would come home only to sleep.

Nevertheless, after a child was born to Hania and Olek, Hela started feeling more and more uncomfortable about staying at her sister's. She was very fond of the baby, Irka, and the little girl became attached to her with all her being. Yet, surprisingly enough, dispite the trust and understanding that existed among the tenants of the small apartment, strange tensions were created among them.

Olek did his best to be pleasant to his sister-in-law. He manouevered things well in the little apartment in which he lived with two women and a child, but nevertheless the situation deteriorated. Hania started getting suspicious and to remove any shade of suspicion Hela took care never to remain alone with Olek, not even for one moment, and restrained and stifled the warm feelings she was developing towards little Irka.

She finally decided to put an end to this situation. She resolved to speak candidly with Neufeld. Once she had been able to read his thoughts.

'What's the matter with you, my lady? Why are you so deep in thought? Have you been musing about some great work of literature, or about reality itself?'

'Nothing,' she said, and blushed. 'Literature and reality, did you say? Don't they reflect each other?'

'Not precisely and not always. Modern art is the product of thought, composition, selection, and so on. So it is in painting, anyway. I imagine it's the same in literature.'

'In life too. A life too has to be a product of thought, don't you agree?'

'Perhaps, perhaps,' Neufeld replied, somewhat abstractedly. He had finally become aware, it appeared, of Hela's prolonged and questioning gaze at him.

'I thought,' she said hesitantly, 'that it might be good if we talked.'

'Come, let's get out of here,' he said. 'I'll walk you home.'

They walked in the street, not speaking. Neufeld led her towards Paulinska Street.

'I don't live here any more,' said Hela. 'I left here quite some time ago.'

'I didn't know,' he said in surprise. 'Have you let your apartment?'

'I didn't let it, it wasn't mine.'

'What, wasn't the apartment yours?'

She heard a strange tone in his voice. The importance he attached to the matter of the apartment annoyed her, and suddenly something snapped in her heart.

'No, that apartment wasn't mine and I don't have another one. I'm living at my sister's, I don't have rich parents, I don't have parents at all, and I don't have a dowry.'

Neufeld continued to walk beside her, and didn't utter a word.

She was silent too. This artist, modest in his desires, who needed no more than a piece of bread for his artistic soul. Villain!

'You don't have to accompany me to my sister's apartment,' she said dryly. 'You needn't trouble.'

'Hela, understand.' He stopped, and spread his arms to the sides. 'I live alone like a dog. I have practically nothing to live on, there's no income from the paintings yet. Please, understand me.'

'Yes, I understand.'

She stood facing him, her back erect, and gazed straight into his eyes. The chill of the night crept into her bones and her body trembled.

'Of course I understand. It was nice meeting you.'

With quick steps she walked off and was swallowed up in the darkness of the street.

10 Who Are We? Hania's Story

During the winter of 1927 the angel of death hovered above the apartment on Paulinska Street, reaching his long arm out towards the tenants. They held their breath in dread, waiting to see who would be taken next in the bitter weather.

The war had ended long ago, but there was no end to disasters, especially in the winter, when the world lay in darkness. In the long black nights, and in the days that resembled the nights – dismal and foggy, oppressively cold – you felt that the war hadn't solved a thing, and that the end of the world was at hand.

Disasters continued to visit the tenants of the apartment on Paulinska Street, as though a special fate had spread its net over them and they were caught in it one by one.

The first to go was Sala. She departed this world quietly, withdrawn upon herself, as if apologizing for her very existence as a living creature. She had been 11 years old when her mother died, 16 when the war broke out and the dreadful tragedy that befell her father had occurred before her very eyes and she had been a witness to his suffering. Before her eyes, too, her brother Menashe had died, and her sister Rozia had rebelled. And she – Sala – had been given to a stranger in a hasty marriage that had made both her and him miserable. She hadn't asked for even a little happiness for herself. There had been no one to ask it of.

Several years after this, Hesiek and Bronka's first child died. This baby, at whose birth there had been so much rejoicing, and whose short life had filled the gloomy apartment with new freshness and hope, had been the fruit of their love, restrained as it was under the gaze of jealous eyes. So much effort and suffering and pain had been involved in the baby's birth – and all in vain.

When the baby died, Hesiek broke down, like a firm, flourishing and flowering branch suddenly breaks without warning.

And his fragile wife – whose open womb bled and whose breasts were like two heavy stones that hurt terribly, full of milk no longer needed – strengthened his spirit.

Before three years had passed, while they had barely managed to get over the loss, two more babies were born to Hesiek and Bronka, one after the other, and then there was another disaster – their Haim, whom everyone loved so, who was so handsome and on the surface looked so vibrant and alive, who had struggled so desperately against his disease since his early adolescence, and had allowed the doctors to perform various surgical experiments on his body, didn't survive the last treatment and died on the operating table. This last operation, according to the famous Viennese professor they had found, was supposed to cure him once and for all from the awful disease.

The professor had encouraged them when they had come to consult him.

'If the operation succeeds,' he had said, 'your brother will come back to you completely healthy. We will try to remove the affected parts of his lungs. It is indeed a new experiment, but I see no reason why it shouldn't succeed.'

Why hadn't he had the strength to come through it? Why had he been the one chosen to be a guinea-pig? He had so hoped for the chance of being completely healthy, he had been so glad. With a smile on his face he had surrendered his body to this complicated experiment, and on taking leave from his family, had said: 'Don't worry, this operation will solve many problems.' These last words of his screamed in their memories after his death with a hidden despair and a sense of mockery.

The disasters that had come one after the other had not fortified them: on the contrary, they broke their capacity to see things in the right proportions, and drove happiness from them.

Again it was Hesiek who took it all harder than everyone else. Life had lost its meaning, and in his mind death had taken up a central place. He waited for death to come and take him and reunite him with the rest of his dear ones.

'In what way am I better than my brothers? I'm not meant to have a long life,' he would say over and over again.

He neglected the business affairs which he had put so much effort into. He worried too much over his little children whom he saw as potential orphans. He pitied them, and in his imagination foresaw all kinds of disasters awaiting the poor things. And his wife? What would happen to her when he would no longer be able to protect her?

Hela suffered some severe disappointments. Hesiek and Bronka moved and went to live in a spacious apartment in a beautiful quarter of the Polish city, not far from the Juliusz Slowacki Boulevard. During the lonely nights, her body became rigid with fear of the ghosts who walked in the empty apartment. Holding her breath, she would hear strange whistlings, chirpings and gruntings, and among them the ringings of Bronka's innocent laughter and the heart-rending crying of the baby. To the loneliness and regret were added her degrading disappointments in her quest for work, and her bitter disappointments from her relationships with men. All this so affected her that one day Hania found her on the verge of total collapse. Hania looked after her with gentleness and with understanding, and took her to her home.

Olek and Hania couldn't afford the kind of luxury enjoyed by Hesiek and Bronka. It was thanks only to the money from the sale of the apartment on Paulinska, and to Hela's share (which they had received as a loan) that they were able to pay key-money for their small apartment, and to furnish it modestly. They still had to face the burning question of a source of livelihood. This was the crucial issue in Poland during the first stages of its existence as an independent state.

Olek remembered the period well. What chaos there had been all around him. There hadn't been a family which had not suffered severely. Sick and famished people, shadows of men, had kissed in the streets and cried with joy:

'The war's over! The war's over!'

A spontaneous joy swept through all the suffering people living in ramshackle and unheated houses, the people on the roads returning from the front or from imprisonment, the victors and the vanquished alike. The borders of countries had not yet been determined, but it was known that several large states would disintegrate, and that new or renascent states would come into being. Exalted slogans rose in the air, implying that all men were brothers, and that now a new world would arise in which there would be no more war.

In those days Olek walked around the streets of Krakow ready to kiss and embrace anyone he met.

'Hey, friend,' someone pushed him in the street. 'Poland is being born again, have you heard?'

'Yes, yes,' said Olek. 'A free and independent Poland.'

At that time he was living in a rented room in Krakow, next to an assimilated family, who were friends of his parents. It was their son Tadeusz who tried to get him involved in political activity.

This Tadeusz had been raised as a Gentile. His parents were petits-bourgeois, very prim and proper, who acted as though they were 'pure' Polish aristocracy. They had not troubled to tell him of his Jewish origins. But he had caused them much misery. Against their will he had joined the P.P.S. (the Polish Socialist Party) and become an enthusiastic fighter for the working class.

'It's a pity that you're wasting your intellectual potential and your personal charm,' Olek said to him. Olek was jealous of his friend's graceful personality and witty tongue.

'It's you, my friend, who are completely wasting yourself and not doing a thing,' he rebutted.

One day, to the delight of his family, and of Olek too, Tadeusz came back from a P.P.S. meeting and said:

'To hell with them! I've had enough. Let them fight their own battles.'

Tadeusz's parents sighed with relief. Olek could see by their faces how relieved they were. They preferred not to ask him what had happened at the party meeting, or who in the party had shown lack of confidence in him, or had slighted

him. None of that mattered. It was better that the disappointment had come early. He would get over it. Olek too was
pleased. From now on Tadeusz would be free for discussions
about good books and pretty girls.

And now, at the end of the war, Tadeusz surprised everyone by coming home one day carrying piles of mysterious
papers. Various people came to visit him, long discussions
took place in his room, which became the headquarters of an
important movement. To his parents' consternation, Tadeusz
had joined a Jewish movement that was fighting for national
rights for the Jews.

'Now is the time to act. Now. While everything's still flexi-
ble, and the borders aren't fixed yet, the constitutions are not
yet written, now is the time for us to demand rights. The
League of Nations, which is to discuss national demands, will
discuss ours too.'

His parents were staggered.

'What kind of adventure are you sticking your head into
again?! Haven't I explained to you that we mustn't draw
attention to ourselves? We are small, unimportant people. The
Polish leaders and politicians will know how to arrange their
state without us. Poland will be represented in the League of
Nations and will legislate its new constitution.'

Tadeusz made an impatient gesture.

'They're looking after themselves – and we must look after
ourselves!' he said, almost raising his voice.

'Tadeusz!'

Olek slipped out of the room, not wanting to be a witness
to the family scene. Several minutes later Tadeusz joined him.
'They don't understand a thing. Listen,' he said sharply to
Olek, 'there's news about pogroms, about expropriation and
looting. Co-operation with the Poles? I've already tried that.
They won't give full trust to anyone with Jewish blood in his
veins. They'll always suspect you of treachery.'

Again he tried to draw Olek into political activity. This time
he suggested that he join the Zionist movement.

'Forget it,' said Olek. 'I'm not a political person, I just want
to be an ordinary citizen.'

'But what kind of a citizen, my good friend? You'll always be a Jewish citizen. Inside Poland's new borders there will be lots of minorities. They're talking about 40 per cent, as against 60 per cent Poles.'

Tadeusz tried to explain to Olek the Zionists' aim of consolidating a delegation to represent the Jewish nation at the League of Nations in Versailles, and to demand recognition of the Jews as a national minority. They were in close contact, Tadeusz said, with the Zionists in Warsaw. And not only in Warsaw. Jews all over the world were organizing and sending delegations to Paris.

'That means that there'll be two delegations from Poland?'

'Yes, right, because two nations live here.'

Olek gazed for a long while into his enthusiastic friend's eyes. 'I don't know ... something about it doesn't seem right to me ... and anyway I have no time for politics. I want to study at the university. And apart from that I have a girlfriend.'

Tadeusz was unmoved by this important announcement. His mind and energy were absorbed in the Peace Conference in Paris, and in the preparations for it, while Olek, what did he have to do with a Peace Conference? His heart thought only of his Hania. What a lucky man he was!

He didn't complete his studies at the law faculty at the university, despite – or perhaps because of – the fact that in this faculty there were more Jewish students than in other departments.

Everything there was too difficult, in fact unbearable. All the arrangemeats in the university were administered under the 'minorities charter' which had been forced upon Poland at that Peace Conference in Paris which Tadeusz had talked about. The Poles had signed the charter under pressure exerted upon them by other delegations, and saw this as external interference in Poland's internal affairs.

'I don't know,' Olek used to say. 'I'm not an idiot, gentlemen, [every second word of Olek's was 'gentlemen'] but there are things I couldn't get over. All the time there was trouble at the university: about who was a Jew and who isn't. There were special benches for Jews. They counted us like so many head of cattle. I didn't particularly identify with the Jews, I didn't even want them to know I was a Jew, but they always knew. Elections to the Students' Union were always on a percentage basis. The Jews claimed that they were victims of injustice, because even though most of the Jewish population after the war live in the cities, yet the percentages were figured in terms of the total population of Poland. Since when does a Polish peasant send his sons to the university?'

Hania listened to him.

'There's another side to that coin,' she said.

'Anyway,' he went on, 'I didn't even want them to know. Sometimes you want to be like everyone else.'

'With a face like yours you can't hide your origins,' she said, looking at his semitic features and his dark complexion, his black hair, brown eyes, and Jewish expression. Without intending to, she recalled Witold, the tall, blond young man who had courted her with distinctive Polish elegance while she was still single.

'I can't change my face,' he replied sadly, as if guilty of something.

Olek stopped studying at the university, and tried to find a government position of some kind.

'Don't be surprised if they refuse you everywhere you go. After all, you haven't completed your studies,' Hania said to him, not sure herself whether she was strengthening or weakening his spirit. 'We suffer from a kind of persecution complex. No one's persecuting us.'

'You can't judge these things objectively,' he replied, gently and without confidence. 'You sit at home, you're not struggling out here.'

'I do know,' she said firmly. 'I have eyes and senses too, I'm a living being, just like you.'

'All I wanted to say was that there's a particular and difficult reality ... but you mustn't get angry, my dear. You must think only of yourself and the baby. By the time it's born I'll find work. I promise.'

A shadow passed over Hania's lovely face, and she repressed a sigh.

Hela's money helped them very much, and gave them time to get organized. They decided that when the child was born they would put its crib in their bedroom.

Sometimes the three of them would go to the cinema or to the theater. They preferred the good Polish theater to the Jewish theater which Hela tried unsuccessfully to promote in her family.

All three of them enjoyed the evenings they spent together in the pleasant apartment, in the small family circle.

Olek was a real gentleman and displayed sympathy and much affection towards his sister-in-law.

'It's in my nature. I've been like that since birth, gentlemen,' he would reply whenever his sister-in-law made comparisons between him and Neufeld, complimenting him.

He took care to make them both feel good, so much so that Hania sometimes felt that he was going too far.

I'm the happiest of women, one voice inside Hania would say, attentive to Olek's pleasant manners and the wonder of the new life forming inside her womb. I'm happy, I'm happy. The pregnancy filled her with joy and a feeling that since she had become pregnant she was more beautiful than before, and that everything around her was organized and arranged.

But there was also another inner voice, which alternately troubled and warned her.

Since their move to Topolowa Street there had been a hint of hidden tension which had accompanied her every step, every hour of the day or night. Other people too felt her tension, but they attributed it to her physical condition, her pregnancy.

She alone knew that the tension was connected mainly to the change of apartment. Her desire to blend into the new environment was so strong, that it confused her. When they climbed the stairs, speaking to each other, she would demand that they lower their voices: 'Let's not make a noise.' And in the apartment too she would walk around on tiptoe and speak in whispers: 'Let's not disturb the neighbors.'

On Paulinska it had been possible to occasionally shout through the open window, or to whistle on the staircase, but here red lights flashed and dazzled her eyes, and prolonged or broken sirens, like those heard during the war, resounded in her ears, regularly reminding her of something unclear and unknown even to herself.

Olek and Hania did not understand Hela's socialistic–Bundistic leanings.

'What have you got to do with them?' asked Hania. 'If you want to choose a Jewish labor movement, then why not a Zionist labor movement? Look at what is happening there in the Land! Pioneering, settlement, communal life in the *kibbutzim*. Is there any better socialism than that? But the Bund? If we're to go on living in Poland, then why stress our Jewishness?'

'Hania's definitely right, gentlemen, we're making problems for ourselves.'

'Olek, you yourself told us what happened at the university!'

'Yes, but I think it's just a question of time. If we're smart, gentlemen, and learn to adapt...'

'Who'll adapt?' Hela raised her voice. 'Do you want people like our Shlomo and Mania to adapt? They're religious Jews.'

'Who's talking about the religious?'

'Quiet!' Hania pleaded. 'Please don't shout. The neighbors will hear us. Please speak quietly.'

'All right,' said Hela, lowering her voice. 'You don't like the Bund? Do you know any better solutions? And I like the Bund. Do you know why? Because I've found good friends there. I don't have any other friends, and that's a lot. I like spending time in their club-house.'

'That's something else, gentlemen,' said Olek. 'I don't like any movements or organizations. They're all demagogues, gentlemen. I believe in man as man, and in his right to live wherever it suits him, gentlemen. I don't know a word of Yiddish or Hebrew – what has all that to do with me?'

And again two voices spoke inside Hania. One voice sang to her in Hebrew, lines from the songs they had sung in the Quiet Nooklet:

172

'There in the Land the delight of our fathers, all our hopes will come true.' And the second voice said: 'Madness, it's absolute folly to go to that hard desert land, when here it's comfortable and good. Maybe Olek's right. We must adapt, not make ourselves prominent, we must please the Poles. Ben-David, the leader of the Zionist *hachsharah* had said the opposite: with soldiers like you we won't get far. The children of Shmulik the gardener were born in a kibbutz, and my child will be born here.'

Outside, the rain came down in torrents. A snake of light flashed in the black sky. Hania let out a stifled scream and blocked her ears, to protect them from the thunder that would come after the lightning. Hela and Olek leaped up in alarm.

'What's happened to you? What's the matter?!'

He embraced her shoulders, in concern.

'All these arguments, I hate them. They harm you, and your health's the most important thing of all to me!'

She looked at him. He seemed to be moving away from her, becoming smaller. He doesn't see or hear a thing.

Hela went into the kitchen and came back with a bowl of apples. 'Take an apple,' she said to her sister, and handed her the nicest one. 'You need a lot of vitamins now.'

During this period Hela worked in the private institute of Dr Lustiger, the Jewish doctor recommended by Jozek. He made her work a split day, and also on Saturdays, so that her only free day was Sunday. In compliance with the Polish constitution, Dr Lustiger's institute was closed on Sundays. Olek too had a day off from work on Sundays. With the help of his family he had opened a small import–export office and dealt mainly with the transfer of various goods between Krakow and Lodz or Warsaw. He aspired to develop the business to a larger scale, perhaps even internationally.

Saturdays were ordinary work days for him, and Sundays were rest days. At first this disturbed Hania, but she got used to it with time. On Sundays, Hela would spend a lot of time in the bathroom, pampering her body with creams and fragrant scents, and when the church bells rang and the citizens of Krakow streamed in their multitudes to morning services, the

three of them would sit themselves down to a family breakfast, and enjoy little Irka's cleverness.

Afterwards it was Olek's custom to go to the city, to the
Phoenix café, where he would meet his acquaintances, who
like him hovered between two worlds.

'If you want to go with him,' Hela said hesitantly, 'go, and
I'll stay with Irka. You can rely on me – in Switzerland they
taught me how to look after babies.'

Hania didn't respond. She hadn't heard, or she pretended
that she hadn't. Hela stood there confused.

'I'll gladly stay with her,' she said.

They never let her hold the baby. She felt so strongly for
the little creature, so soft and warm, its little heart beating so
fast, its little lungs breathing so regularly, and its plump tiny
hands reaching out towards her. She so longed to touch her,
at least for a moment, to wash her, or dry her, but Hania
always stood between her and the baby, saying:

'I'll do it myself.'

Hela would swallow and hold back her tears, feeling
unwanted. Now a flutter of hope rose in her.

'Go on, go with your husband. It's a long time since the two
of you went out together.'

'Ah, it doesn't attract me at all. They sit in the cafe, smoke
cigarettes, and talk only about business and politics. It'd be
better if the two of us went for a walk with Irka in the Planty.'

'It really is a nice day for a walk. And when we get tired,
we might pay Hesiek and Bronka a short visit.'

'A wonderful idea.' Hania was in a good mood, 'I haven't
visited them for ages.'

The spring weather was just right for them. Irka, dark and
charming, happy and dressed up, was put in her pram, and
the two sisters proudly carried her down the stairs and into
the street.

Hania wore a light-colored coat which suited the season,
and had a sportive green hat on her head. Beside her walked
Hela in a pale blue spring suit, with a matching floral blouse
in pastel hues.

The sun shone, the air was fragrant and caressing, and Irka

smiled from her pram at the passers-by. On the corner stood a balloon-vendor and Hela bought a red balloon and tied it to the little one's pram. They made their way along the Planty. The chestnut and acacia trees were blossoming and the scent of lilac rose in the air. Squirrels jumped from branch to branch, and children fed nuts to them. White swans floated on the lake, and the drops of water spraying from the fountain changed colors in the sunlight. Among the lawns and flowers children played. Sunday, a day off from school and work.

'Here's Pani Zborowska,' Hania said suddenly, and returned a smile of greeting to a handsome lady with fair hair sitting on one of the benches .

'I meet her almost every day when I go walking with Irka,' she explained to Hela.

They continued standing there a little while longer, exchanged a few polite words, and continued on their way.

Hesiek and Bronka's apartment was completely different from Hania's. To enter the apartment was to be enveloped at once in atmosphere of abundance and good taste. On the wall in the vestibule hung a stuffed deer's head with magnificent horns. Opposite it were faces of Jews in framed pictures, among them the famous picture of Shmuel Hirschenberg, the 'Eternal wandering Jew'. The apartment was divided into two wings. The front included three large light-filled rooms, adjacent to each other. In the back there was another room, completely separate, and beside it, a long and illuminated corridor led to the kitchen. The bathroom and toilet were along the corridor, and the kitchen, which could also be reached through an additional door on the rear staircase, had two more small rooms attached to it.

Hela and Hania carried Irka's pram up the broad front staircase. Breathing heavily, they stood outside the door of their brother's apartment.

Bronka opened the door herself. It was Sunday, a day off for the help.

Two little children stood beside her, clinging to her skirt. She was pregnant again. She caught the critical glances of her sisters-in-law, and said with a smile:

'I've already given up on having a lovely figure. I have a lot of work on my hands, and this pregnancy took me somewhat by surprise. To tell you the truth I don't have the strength any more.'

They went into the large living-room, where the furniture was black, upholstered with red leather in antique style. Delicate objects made of alabaster and bronze stood on top of the buffet, and through its glass panes came the gleam of silver and crystal. A lamp with 12 pearly bulbs was hung above the large table, and there were fine pictures on the walls. In a corner, by the entrance to the porch, house-plants grew in flowerpots, and around the porch, in colored window-boxes, geraniums flowered. Good taste and a sense of spaciousness. The lady of the house, shy and embarrassed, invited her guests into the room.

'I'll bring you coffee and biscuits. I baked only yesterday.'

'Don't bother about coffee or biscuits, come and talk a bit,' said Hania. 'I've missed you.' And as she gazed around the room at all its luxuries she added:

'Do you remember how we used to walk every day to the "Quiet Nooklet"? And how we worked in agriculture there, and how you taught songs?'

'Things have changed,' said Bronka, pensively.

'You've got nothing to complain about,' Hela remarked, trying to speak affably.

'I'm not complaining,' Bronka said quietly and looked at her swollen hands.

This time Hela didn't say anything offensive. She tried to be nice and friendly to her sister-in-law. She was sorry to see her distressed, standing there, heavy and stolid, facing them.

'We have to go,' said Hania.

Bronka took a step forward and apologized once more:

'I didn't even serve you coffee.'

Hania and Olek did not observe the Sabbath. On Saturdays life in their home went on as usual. Olek would open his office as on every other day, 'for the usual clients', as he used to say.

They watched the different stages of assimilation of Jews

among the Poles. Some days the problem of assimilation seemed very simple to them, and on other days they understood that the problem was insoluble.

They themselves had moved away from Judaism in a circuitous path: they had emerged from one world without being absorbed in the other. At first they had observed Sabbaths and the High Holy Days. After that, only the Day of Atonement, Yom Kippur. With the passage of time, even this day was not properly observed in their home. Hania tried to convince herself that it was possible to be Jewish without being religious – why, even Rozia in Palestine didn't observe the religion – but deep in her heart she knew it was not the same thing. Hania knew families in Krakow in whose homes both Hanukah and Christmas were celebrated. While they, Olek and Hania, celebrated neither. They lived in a vacuum, in a loneliness they had imposed on themselves.

One of Olek's assimilated friends, who aspired to political influence in the state, and especially in the Jewish community, explained that for him the community served as a springboard to state institutions, to which his only chance of participation was as a representative of the minority; then, thanks to his broad education and his knowledge of the Polish language, he would be able to advance in the political hierarchy. This man told them that there had been occasions, in the outlying places of the new Polish state, when the Ukrainians had given their votes to assimilated Jews who had promised to represent the interests of all the minorities in the Polish administration and institutions.

Another of Olek's acquaintances had cut all his connections with Judaism and was apparently on the way to religious conversion. Olek and Hania knew that this was escapism, and they also knew that there was nowere to escape to. The destination of this escape was an alien world that refused to accept those escaping into it; the way back was blocked to a large extent; and the attempt to straddle both sides of the fence was unlikely to succeed.

Hania felt contempt for herself for not having the courage to demonstrate her Jewishness. Most of the Jews of Krakow, including those living in the Polish quarter, would go every Sabbath to the little synagogues they called a *shule*, which were scattered throughout the entire city. There they would wrap themselves in prayer-shawls and pray in a language they hardly understood. When asked about the meanings of these prayers which they recited so fervently, they would reply: 'All our prayers are praises of God and pleas that He hear our voice and not forget us.'

When Irka was a bit bigger the help will surely take her to church, where Irka will kneel like everyone and cross herself. A tremor went through Hania's body at the thought of what her father would have said had he known how his grandchild was being brought up. And perhaps the best thing Hania could do would be to start visiting the Reform 'Temple'?

The Reform synagogue was located in a beautiful modern building and served a large section of Krakow's Jews. Most of them went there not for the prayers, but to hear the sermons of Doctor Oziarz Thon, the famous Zionist leader, who also served as Reform rabbi in Krakow.

Olek didn't visit these places. He probably didn't know how to hold a *siddur* in his hands. There were no religious requisites in their home, no skull-cap and no *siddur*, let alone a prayer-shawl and phylacteries.

'Didn't you have a *bar-mitzvah* when you were a boy?' Hania once asked him.

'What's a *bar-metzvah*?' he asked, mispronouncing the Hebrew words.

'A Gentile stays a Gentile,' Hania smiled, partly in disappointment.

She knew that since coming to live in Topolowa Street she had separated herself from the family of her religious sister, Mania. It was impossible to imagine that her brother-in-law Reb Shlomo, with his sidecurls and beard, would come and visit her here, in Topolowa. At the same time Hania was not at all willing to give up her closeness to her sister and her family.

So sometimes, on Saturdays or Sundays, she and Olek would visit them in Podgorze. To reach Podgorze they had to cross the Jewish quarter of Kazimierz.

On Saturdays the Jewish street was crowded with Jews in hassidic garb and *streimels*, the children speaking Yiddish and wearing skullcaps under which their long sidecurls dangled. Noise and din. Many Jews wrapped in prayer-shawls argued vehemently with each other while they interpreted the words of the sages.

'A most exotic world,' Olek said to Hania, bewildered and confused as he walked beside her in his European suit, on their way to Podgorze.

'You're delicate in your choice of words. I see that you're really disgusted.'

'At any rate a strangeness, gentlemen, a great strangeness.'

'We're strangers in two worlds,' she said sadly. 'You know, Zborowska has invited me to visit her in the country. They have a large estate in Mazowsze. She urged me to come with Irka, for a week or more. There's lots of room there – I'd be glad to go. She told me that the place is charming. The house stands on a small hill in the midst of plain country full of lakes and forests. You know how I love nature, I'd go, but how would I feel there? The way of life there would be completely foreign to me. They have different customs, their own folk songs and dances, and they go horseback riding and hunting. We think that we've assimilated, but in fact we haven't. We've remained strangers. I would like to be a friend of Zborowska's, but I sense the distance between us.'

Olek was silent. Two little children with ritual fringes protruding from their jackets stopped in front of them and said something in Yiddish. Olek didn't understand a word and blushed.

'They're asking what time it is,' Hania explained. He told them the time in Polish and tried to smile. The children gave him a strange look and ran off.

'Goy! Goy!' he heard them laughing.

When she first met Olek, she had feared the response of her family. 'A man without a bit of yiddishkeit in him!'

But to her great surprise they had accepted him warmly, and had told Hania explicitly that they were all very relieved, and that they preferred Olek over one of those irresponsible and unrealistic madmen from the Zionist movement.

Hania was happy. She too felt relieved. Mania, to her, was like a loving mother, caring and beloved. She was full of understanding and consideration. She, who herself had missed out on her youth, could understand others, and the stormy emotions which belonged to adolescence. And Shlomo? How relieved Hania had been when she got to know this man, this scholar who was clever and understanding in his own way, good hearted and with a good sense of humor, who despite his uncompromising devotion to the religion of Israel, understood secular matters much more than she could have imagined. In their home there was an atmosphere of wholeness and acceptance, of faith and authority.

They didn't concern themselves with the problems of the hour, and accepted things as self-evident.

Shlomo ran extensive timber enterprises. He had large sawmills on the outskirts of Krakow and in Rabka. His brothers and brothers-in-law helped him in the business. He had attained the status of a unique and respected head of family, surely because of his wisdom and also because of his good and close relations with the rabbi.

It was amazing to see Shlomo and Olek conversing quietly. They talked of politics. Shlomo read a newspaper in Yiddish, Olek in Polish, but both newspapers reported the same events. The economic boycott that had been declared on Jewish merchants troubled everyone. Shlomo explained to Olek how the boycott was harming his business, how it did not allow him to make an honest profit, for Shlomo had big sawmills. Olek nodded his head submissively and shrugged his shoulders.

'What can one do, gentlemen, what can one do?'

Hania shifted her gaze from her brother-in-law's face to her husband's, and felt bitter: they talk only of the outcomes of the boycott, and they don't think of its causes. It was good, at least, that Shlomo was capable of conducting a secular conversation. He showed more understanding of secular matters than she had believed him capable of. A warmth enveloped her in her sister's little apartment. Everyone spoke quietly here, in low tones, calmly and peacefully. Something of this is lacking in our apartment on Topolowa. We too speak quietly, but serenity is far from us.

Rays of light broke on the window-pane of her sister's home. Where did they come from, how did they get here, these rays of light? There was no sky to be seen, because the houses were so close to each other. The courtyards between the houses looked like tiny cracks from here. Through them the light penetrated and flooded the apartment. Mania sent her a warm smile.

'What are you thinking about?' Hania asked her.

'Oh, nothing, I was thinking about the children.'

Shlomo and Mania had four children – two girls and two boys. The boys were *yeshiva* students. The elder was clever and witty, like a demon, the little one was loveable and a dreamer. The elder always spoke for the younger, even though the younger did have something to say, but the elder got in before him. 'We' – he always spoke in the first person plural. The boys were in the middle, between the girls. The youngest girl was six and the eldest was seventeen.

'We're already looking for a bridegroom for her,' Mania said to her sister.

'Already?' Hania was astounded. Had Mania forgotten how she herself had felt when she was 17? When their father, blessed be his memory, had married her through Reb Leizer the matchmaker? Had she forgotten how she had gone like an innocent lamb, from her father's rule to her husband's, without knowing what was awaiting her, without even tasting the taste of youth, of freedom? Why was she condemning her daughter Rela to the same fate?

'Yes, already,' said Mania, calm and quiet. 'What can a girl like Rela do? Wander around? Look for butterflies in the field? Or, God forbid, something worse? When a girl reaches the right age there's no point in keeping her a virgin. A woman, from the day she is born, has one function to fulfil in life: to be a good wife to her husband and to bear children. All the rest is worthless.'

Hania controlled her anger. Inside, she was fuming. It was a good thing Olek hadn't heard. To be a good wife to her husband. A good thing he hadn't heard. Mania had added:

'It is God's command.' Ha! A good thing Olek isn't a believer, then.

She looked at Rela. A delicate lass, still small, she should still be playing with a ball, studying something, getting to know the world ...

'It looks like it'll be Shlomo's younger brother,' said Mania, as if by the way.

'What? But he's her uncle!' Mania spread out her hands.

'But he's suitable. From the point of view of family. From the point of view of a livelihood. She agrees"

'She agrees? What does she know?'

'We've told her.'

What did she know about life? Hania got up, depressed. So what use to me is all their wisdom, all their serenity? What's going to happen to all these people? How far will this decay go?

Mania was saying something to her now about little dresses in good condition which had been her younger daughter Renia's. 'They're in perfectly good condition, just like new', which would be good for Irka.

'Here's a parcel that Shlomo has prepared for you. It's all clean and pressed, and it only gets in the way in our wardrobe.'

Hania sorted the little dresses and looked at her sister's beautiful calm face. How could she know what was in her heart? Shlomo and Olek were playing chess. Renia, Mania's younger daughter, was playing with little Irka, with dolls. A family idyll. Hania caught fragments of the men's conversation: they were cursing the government, the high taxes, and the Zionists.

'They're the ones who will bring disaster down upon us.'

'After their activities the Poles really may throw us out of the country.'

'Come, Olek,' Hania said to her husband. 'We have to be getting back.'

'Checkmate!' Olek said to Shlomo. The game was over. 'Checkmate!' Olek repeated, rubbing his hands together.

'Look, it's already dark outside. It got dark all at once.'

The sisters exchanged kisses and hugs and parted. Shlomo gathered up the chess pieces.

'Until next time. Next time I'll beat you,' he said.

'Or it'll be a draw,' Olek laughed.

They went out into the street, Olek pushing Irka's pram. Hania put her arm through her husband's strong arm.

'I must tell you something,' he said, without looking at her.

'What do you want to tell me?'

'What?'

'You said that you wanted to tell me something, didn't you?'

He bent down towards little Irka and made her laugh.

'Look,' he said. 'Her mouth's already full of teeth.'

'Is that what you wanted to tell me?' They continued walking in the direction of their home. An evening breeze blew on their faces.

'You've never noticed before this that her mouth is full of teeth?'

'I did notice,' he said, confused.

Hania shrugged her shoulders.

'I haven't told you about my family yet,' said Olek, several days later .

'You've told me a bit.'

They were sitting in their apartment on Topolowa. On the table lay socks to be darned. She pushed a mushroom-shaped wooden darning block into a gray sock of Olek's and started darning. He didn't speak.

'Quiet,' said Hania, though no-one had spoken. 'I think Irka's sneezing.'

They both listened. No. She was sleeping.

'My mother's family derives from the Jews who were expelled from England. They were expelled from there in the fourteenth century. And my grandfather on my father's side came here after being expelled from Russia.' She said nothing and he continued. 'That's how it is, gentlemen, that's how it is.'

Then he fell silent again, and got up and poured himself a glass of water.

'My uncle, my mother's sister, the one who owns textile plants in Lodz – which are second only to those in Manchester in England – changed his religion.'

Olek played with the glass of water he was holding, trying to slant it in various directions without spilling any of it. He didn't take his eyes off the glass.

Hania felt the blood rising to her face. She recalled Rozia.

'Is that what you wanted to tell me when we were walking back from Podgorze a few days ago?'

'Did I want to tell you? I don't remember any more. Perhaps. At any rate, that's it.'

'So he's a Catholic now?'

'No … I don't know. He's not a Catholic … Look, I left home a long time ago. I haven't seen him since then. And my sister Sonia, she left home right after me and went to America.'

Hania folded the socks. They were all mended now. Socks were easy to mend. Where now was Shmulik the gardener who loved taking care of the soil and the flower beds? Had that been she, who had walked with Bronka everyday towards the 'Quiet Nooklet', had worked there in agriculture, had sung Hebrew songs, and had felt a new excitement every day on seeing the blue and white flag? And what had become of the leader, Ben-David, the stubborn idealist? His troops had disappointed him already then.

'All right, gentlemen,' said Olek, and rubbed his hands together. 'We'll continue, gentlemen, slowly but surely.'

'What are you talking about? And what are you so happy about? What's sure? Nothing's sure. Except death.'

He thought she was joking.

'No, I'm not joking,' she said, and smiled wistfully. 'Here, in the heart, it's not funny at all.'

Occasionally the two sisters would have frank conversations. Hania knew almost everything about Hela's friends. She knew about Elsa and the illegitimate child she had had with Misha. She also knew about Aleks, and about his return from Russia with another woman, and she also knew, from Hela's own stories, about the sad episode with Neufeld.

'What a bastard!' Hania fumed when they spoke about him. 'A member of the Bund! What kind of a socialist is he when money is the most important thing to him? It's all phoney, I tell you. I hate all those fake idealists who use beautiful and exalted phrases, and pretend to be the world's most righteous people, saviors of humanity, while they're nothing but materialists, and choose only what's good for themselves. I prefer people who have the courage not to pretend.'

Hela sat on the sofa, one leg over the other. Her long finely shaped legs in their silk stockings gleamed in the light, and looked very feminine and at the same time very brave. A new dress made of a soft material emphasized her figure and suited her eyes, which were dark blue, like deep pools. Suddenly Hania noticed a new curve in her sister's back, like the beginning of a humped back, which until yesterday had been straight and proud. Was Hela tired? Or was this the beginning of ... No. She was still very young.

Hela spoke pensively:

'To tell the truth, I never loved him.'

'Who's talking about love?'

Hela stole a glance at her and went on:

'He's in love with his painting, his art, and himself. I doubt if I could have been happy with him.'

They were quiet for a long while. It was not Neufeld who had caused the deep wound in Hela's heart. Not Neufeld.

'You must meet new people,' said Hania.

Hela stretched her neck, straightened her curving back, and looked at Hania with sadness in her eyes. Hania reached a hand out to her sister and drew it back. 'You spoil Irka too much,' she said, puffing salt on her sister's wounds. 'It's not right that you're nicer to her than I am!'

Suddenly Hela felt angry about everything. Well-meaning people sometimes drove you mad. Like Olek, for example, he felt much too considerate to her. And suddenly the apartment was too small and cramped.

'In the summer Rozia's coming to visit. Where will we put a bed for her? We can't send her to a hotel!'

185

Hela's face turned pale, then red.

'Maybe I'll take a trip somewhere.'

'Where can you go for a trip?'

Hela said nothing. Hania placed before her a yellow envelope bearing a stamp of the British Mandate.

'Read it,' she said, in an appeasing tone.

During the two years since 1925, Rozia had been writing to her sisters. She boycotted Hesiek completely. Hania's eyes fell again on certain parts of her letter:

> ... I'm torn between two worlds. My longings for you, my dears, don't leave me for a moment. They exhaust me. I long for home. Did I say home? Yet home is here. Yes, this is home, and I can't give up the little I have here. Actually I don't have a thing. I haven't learned the language of the place yet. It's a difficult language. I do speak it, but I can't read without the vowel signs. One word can be read one way but also another way, it can have three or four different meanings. And to write it? I'm completely illiterate. True, one can manage with Polish and German. I've also learned English here, quite easily. But Hebrew – no. There is no lack of zealots for the Hebrew language here. Some of those look at me as if I'm stupid, others treat me as a traitor. Despite all that, from day to day I feel myself more and more a part of what is coming into being here.
>
> ... He's much younger than me. A *yekke*. Have you heard the expression? A Jew born in Germany. He's tidy, polite, meticulous, wears glasses. Ten years difference between us. How did it happen? It just happened. His parents have separated and he's supporting both of them. He's in love with his family and I love my family. His sister, after two years of university in Germany, raised chickens here. One day she vanished, leaving her husband and children, and went off on a ship with an English seaman. But what has that to do with me? From where you are you probably see me as a light-headed adventurer. Do you remember the talks we had when we

were children? About social conventions and all that nonsense? I've always scoffed at those things ...

... After I left the Schiller kvutzah, not far from Jerusalem, I settled in Tel Aviv. We live in a dark apartment on the ground floor. Not far from the beach. Beyond the sea is Europe, my old world, which both attracts and repels me.

The sea is calm here, smooth as a mirror, reflecting the blue of the sky, and the waves break only on the shore, striking it forcefully and raising white froth. Along the beach the sand is golden and warm, and in it you can find thousands of shells, little ones and big ones, white, orange, and brown – marvels of nature. Who made these beautiful shells, the little homes of creatures that existed once and exist no longer? The masses of shells bear witness to something that existed and has vanished. And what will remain after us? Have you thought of that? Here in the Land we're at least preparing a home for those who will come after us.

... I'm worried by the wrinkles in my face. The sun here destroys and exhausts. An hour on the beach, and your body is tanned all over, your skin is salty, sticky, and dry. If it weren't for the wrinkles, I would feel a lot better. They're my greatest enemies. I work hard and don't have help in the home. Our cousins, Arie Liebek and Yehuda Liebek, have established a large kibbutz in the Jordan Valley. The place is close to the Jordan River and the Sea of Galilee. It looks out on the Golan Heights and the summit of Mount Hermon. They're raising livestock and children. They eat olives and salted fish, and the mosquitoes bite them. The mosquitoes come from the Huleh swamps, and bear malaria parasites. Many good people die of malaria ...

The children born here are called *sabras*, they're spiky and coarse on the surface, but sweet inside like the core of the ripe cactus fruit. Education here is based on an eye for an eye and a tooth for a tooth. It's completely different from the education we received at home and from the education you're giving your children. At first I was astounded. Later I understood. The world is full of dangers and evil intentions. In Europe the Jews would escape from pogroms, beaten and degraded. From here there's nowhere to escape to. This is the end of the line. Here the rule has to be 'He who rises to kill you, make haste to kill him first'. Here there is no alternative, because we don't want to go back to being what we've been.

I'm planning to come to Krakow in the summer. On my own, I expect. I long for the coolness of the Polish city, for the touch of the river waters that flow from the mountain peaks, for buildings that are well built, where it's warm in winter and cool in summer. From far away everything looks beautiful to me, a wonderful radiance. I know that when I come to you I'll feel a strangeness and I'll long for this place. My dears, please send me pictures, to let me see what you look like now. I'm working hard and saving every penny I can for the trip. Be well …

Hania folded the letter. Her eyes were moist. The Golan Heights. The Jordan. Galilee. Jerusalem. A tremor passed through her. There was an incomprehensible hidden magic compressed in each of those words. Longings and yearnings. Galilee, the Jordan, Jerusalem.

Shmulik, in which kibbutz are you and what are you doing now? How many children do you have? Irka pulled at her dress.

'Mama!'

From her round, serious face, the gray-brown eyes of Olek and herself looked out at her, with the addition of a gleam and hue that were the child's own. Irka was dressed like a baroness and had the manners of a princess. And her fate? Her future? The *sabras* there in the Land ran about barefoot in the *wadis*; they were being taught to grow a spiky exterior. Irka's face looked pale to her.

'There's not a bit of sunlight here,' Hania said aloud, and

undid a ribbon which was tied in a butterfly knot on her daughter's head. Irka looked at her in astonishment. 'Mama!' she said again.

Hania picked her up and pressed her close to her heart. The little one made faces, as if she could feel her mother's distress.

'My dear daughter,' said Hania. She relaxed her embrace, put the child down on the floor, breathed deeply and went into the kitchen to prepare a meal.

Hania spared no effort and devoted much thought and work to her daughter's physical and spiritual development. Irka had dark hair and brown eyes, with fair skin; plump, full of joy and merriment, understanding and alertness. Her whole being bespoke gentleness. She had, as it were, two mothers. When Hela came home from work, the little one immediately ran to her and greeted her happily:

'Aunt Hela! Aunt Hela!'

Then the aunt would raise her high in the air. Irka would wind her little arms around her neck, and Hela would lavish kisses on her soft and fragrant neck and face.

'You pamper her a lot more than we do,' Hania would remark, with a trace of annoyance.

'That's because I don't see her much,' Hela justified herself.

One evening they planned to go out early, and Hela stayed behind as baby-sitter. The evening meal was all ready for Irka on the little table. Olek, dressed in a dark gray suit, glanced with satisfaction from his daughter playing with an armless doll to his wife standing in front of the mirror.

'Does this hat suit me?' She had become very clothes-conscious recently.

'You're beautiful in any hat and without a hat too!' Olek said fervently.

'Thank you very much,' Hania said without a smile. She took off the burgundy hat and tried another one, pale green, shaped like a man's hat.

'That's better,' she said with satisfaction. 'We can go. But what about you, Olek?' she suddenly asked. 'What about your hair? It's gleaming, as if you've put brilliantine all over it.'

'I haven't put anything on it,' he said, and went up to the mirror to look at his smooth black hair. 'That's what my hair looks like, I can't change it.'

'But you shouldn't have put hair cream on it.'

'I didn't.'

'But...'

'Don't quarrel,' Hela interposed, and brought Olek a gray hat with a feather in it.

'He can wear a hat too and everything will be all right.'

From the threshold Hania said severely:

'Don't force Irka to finish her meal!' Let her eat as much as she wants. She's fat enough already.'

'I'm afraid that if Irka's allowed to eat as much as she wants I'll have to give her a second helping.'

'Don't you dare!' Hania warned.

When the door closed behind them Hela and Irka's fun began. Both got down on all fours.

'You're a bear!'

'And you're a forest!'

'How does a bear go?'

'How does a bear go? Not "moo-moo-moo", not "bow-wow-wow", not meeow-meeow-meeow".'

'How does a bear go? So don't be a bear, be a bird. A bird goes "cheep-cheep-cheep".'

'Don't want bird. You be a horse.'

'All right. Come on, get on. Gee-up gee-up little horse. I've no strength left. Come, I'll tell you a story. Once upon a time...'

Irka already knew all the stories by heart and made sure that Hela didn't skip a single sentence or a single word. Then she begged: 'Another story!' And then another and another. The time flew. According to Hania's instructions, Irka should already have been in bed. But the illustrated book by Hans Christian Andersen contained so many stories. And what of the Brothers Grimm? And the *Arabian Nights*?

'Afterwards you'll dream of demons and witches,' Hela said in alarm, 'and your mother will be angry at me. Go to bed now.'

'Another story!'

190

'One more and that's it.'

The little girl hugged her and gave her a kiss.

'You're sweet.'

They didn't even notice when Hania and Olek came home from their visit to their friends. At once Irka slipped off into bed and covered herself up to her head. Hela was embarrassed.

'What is this? The child's not a sleep yet at this hour?' Hania asked severely, still standing with her hat on and her handbag and gloves.

'It's nothing, gentlemen, it's nothing,' Olek said gaily.

After that no one spoke. Hela took a few steps towards door, as if she wanted to go out. Where to?

Hania started undressing quietly.

'We were playing.'

'Ladies,' Olek said merrily, 'may I invite you to a glass of tea?'

'Oh, yes,' said Hela at once. 'I'll gladly have tea.'

'I won't, thank you,' Hania said curtly.

He went into the kitchen to make the tea, humming a tune from Carmen. Hania went into the bedroom.

He came back with two glasses of tea. Hela sat stooped, melancholy written on her face. He placed the tea before her and stood silently looking at her hunched shoulders, not daring to move. Without raising her head, she said:

'Thank you.'

He continued standing there and saw that under his gaze a light blush rose in her face.

Then he put the second glass on the table, sat down, and gently touched her arm. They looked into each other's eyes for a long time, saying nothing.

Hela had read Rozia's letter from Palestine. 'Social conventions', and all the rest. Olek had read it too.

What did it matter that her husband's sister had run off with an English seaman? My sister Sonia, didn't she do the same? Not with an English seaman, but with an American stage-director. So what? Hela should have run off too. With a seaman, a director, someone. I myself would ...

191

He moved the chair he was sitting on slightly. 'Did you say something?'

'Hania must have fallen asleep.' He looked towards the bedroom.

'She may not have. Tell me something, Olek. Tell me about your business.'

'My business?!'

'Yes. Your business.'

Obviously they couldn't just be silent all the time. What could he tell her about? Before, she had told Irka stories. Now he would tell her something. How do people become close to each other? Is there a way to become close other than by physical contact? Or did people always remain alone with themself?

'Well, they already know me, gentlemen. My word is respected, and the business is expanding...'

The door of the bedroom opened and Hania stood in the doorway. Her hair fell in waves onto her shoulders. An unbuttoned dressing-gown covered her night-dress. Olek stopped in mid-sentence.

'I was telling Hela a bit about my business ....'

She buttoned her gown, brought a chair for herself, and sat down. She had never taken an interest in his business.

'I think I'll have a glass of tea.'

He got up and went to bring her a glass of tea.

Again Hania leafed through the letter she had received from her sister.

'What do you think,' Hania asked when he came back with her tea, 'what could be the reason for her marrying a man so much younger than herself? Love? Lust? Either way, it'll pass quickly. Every stage of getting old will be a nightmare for her. That is, life will be a nightmare for her, because one gets older every day. Poor Rozia!'

They were silent. Hela sighed. She got up and started preparing her clothes for the next day.

'When Rozia gets here,' Olek said, 'we'll know everything.'

'That's not true. We'll never know. Come to sleep, Olek.'

'It drives me crazy, how cramped it is in our apartment,' said Hania, when they were in their beds.

'She has to leave here.'

Olek was quiet for a long time.

'We can't throw her out,' he finally said.

'You always take her side.'

'I don't know what to say to you.'

'The two of you go off to work every morning and nothing bothers you, and I stay home with all the mess, and it's so cramped it makes me sick!'

'Perhaps we should look around for a bigger apartment? We just can't throw her out, we've committed ourselves to her.'

'We haven't committed ourselves to anything. We should just give her back her money and that's it. Actually, why shouldn't she go and live at Hesiek's? There's a lot more room there than there is here.'

'Soon they'll have a third child. She won't find it very comfortable.'

'Do I find it comfortable? There's lots of room there. Bronka will be needing help and Hela loves children.'

'You arrange other people's affairs very easily. It has to be her decision. I won't tell her to go.'

Hania fell silent. He lay with his hands under his head.

'Now you probably look down on me,' Hania said in the tone of a remorseful, spoilt child. 'I'm an awful woman, wicked, jealous and egoistic.'

'You're the most wonderful woman in the world,' he soothed her gently, and waited. He too was thirsty for a sweet word from her, some kind of gesture of affection.

A blue night spread outside the windows; in the cold sky a full moon was surrounded by glinting stars.

Irka's regular breathing stopped for a moment and the little one emitted a mischievous chuckle in her dreams.

In the other room, Hela turned from side to side and let out a silent sigh.

11 Man's Home is his Castle: Bronka and Hesiek's Story

The rays of a cold winter sun broke through the window-pane. He lay in his wide bed, in the modern bedroom of their fine and spacious apartment, holding a newspaper and not reading it.

Saturday. A quiet hour of the afternoon. A rare moment of rest. He looked outside, at the strip of blue sky. The sun had already slipped westwards and was about to set. He closed his eyes and sank into musings.

Echoes of noise reached him from the children's room in the center of the apartment. Bronka was there with the children. She had ordered him to rest.

'You don't know when to stop. A man is not a machine. You can't work 24 hours a day. It's a good thing that God created the Sabbath.'

The tattered nerves, the inner disquiet, the constant tension, the persistent willingness to struggle. For what? Till when? Lately he had dared to think that a respite had come. That perhaps this was it. They had paid the full price, they had given their share to the angel of death and to all the devils and ghosts. Perhaps at last it was the turn of the good, ordinary, normal life? When he walked in the street he sensed the glances of people raised to him in silent wonder and open envy, as if asking 'How did you do it?'

Not one of those who envied him knew what it was like to be him. He remembered well the bitter day when he had left his father's home on Paulinska Street. With a weak woman and a sick infant. They had almost had to live in the street. With the money he had available then it was impossible to obtain an apartment. He had approached his father-in-law but the latter had given him nothing.

'I have nothing left,' Reb Aharon said. 'During the war our

store was closed. For three years I wasn't here. When I came back, they almost confiscated it. I had to struggle to get it back. No Gentile buys from me. And our people – they're paupers. I still haven't developed a business. And I have no reserves. You're not the only one who needs money, Hershel, all of us need money, my three sons too.'

Hesiek stopped his speech. His three brothers-in-law – he knew them. No help would come from them. His father-in-law stood before him, stroking his beard in embarrassment, and looking at him with his big pale blue poet's eyes. 'I'll speak with Mother,' Reb Aharon said. 'She holds the money in this household.'

'No,' said Hesiek. He couldn't fit the word 'mother' to his mother-in-law. 'No. I'll manage somehow.'

Bronka's three brothers who were no longer adolescents had remained without trades and without education, and were looking for wealthy brides.

'You don't have to speak to anyone,' he repeated. 'I'll manage somehow. And in the future, we'll do business together yet!'

He and Bronka and the sick little one moved into a temporary apartment, and only afterwards did the house come their way, the house they lived in now. The whole house was to be sold, and it was a rare opportunity, an offer that would not come their way again. What was needed was a speedy decision and immediate action, because the next day there might be a devaluation and it might be too late. Times in Poland were unstable, the economy was unstable. This was the last chance.

'Listen, sir,' the previous owner of the house, who urgently needed money, said to him, 'either you get me the money, or I put an advertisement in the newspaper.'

He got the money and bought the house. Loans from banks, high interest, private loans, even higher interest, nerves, tension, nightmares at night. The apartment in Paulinska was sold, and the money divided among the heirs. He pawned several objects made of silver, remained without a penny, saw in his blackest dreams how his wife and son asked for shelter at his mother-in-law's, and would wake up in alarm, bathed in a cold sweat. He overcame his pride and again went to see his father-in-law to ask for a short-term loan. For a day or two. Reb Aharon went out into the street with him. His wife did not need to hear what they were talking about. The two men spoke for a long time. *'Efshar, tumer, meiglich?'* (Is it possible, tell me, maybe?) They paced forwards and backwards, and again stopped and argued with their mouths and hands. Hesiek drew a little notebook from his pocket, wrote down sums and figures; Reb Aharon checked what he had written and again they walked forwards and backwards, and then Reb Aharon disappeared for a short while, and when he came back he had the money with him. 'It's all your responsibility. I'm not telling you to buy. You could lose all the money. We've already seen such things happen,' said his father-in-law, adding worries to his already troubled heart.

Hesiek ran as fast as he could to conclude the deal with the proprietor, who already had his emigration papers ready. Only after the event was there time to really see what he had bought. The house was far from Kazimierz, far from his parents-in-law, a bit far from the center of the city, but close to the area of the academies and the park, in a quiet and well-cultivated quarter.

It was in a quiet street, opposite a Jesuit monastery. The monks cultivated their garden, which stretched in all its glory outside his windows, though it was hidden from the street by a high wall that surrounded the monastery.

In the front part of the house were eight spacious apartments which faced the street, with venetian windows and round balconies hanging over the two rose-bushes that grew in front of the entrance. The front of the house was covered with wild creeping vines, their dense leaves creating a green carpet through which the clear window-sized patches gleamed with the shine of the panes. The kitchens of these attractive front apartments faced an inner square courtyard, where they met the windows of about sixteen smaller apartments occupied by middle-class families.

All the apartments were occupied, except for one in the front, the best of them all. He examined the entire house, saw the front yard and the back yard, spoke with the janitors – a man and a woman who lived in a small inner ground floor apartment – who smiled in embarrassment and submission at their new landlord.

After this he climbed the broad stairs of the front level and entered the empty apartment.

The light and radiance dazzled his eyes. The four large rooms smiled at him with their white walls. He passed through them all, peeped into the large modern bathroom, the toilets, walked along the corridors, opened the glass door of the round balcony and peered down.

The rose-bush was blooming.

He went into another room and opened a broad venetian window. Green leaves of wild vines grew around the window. Opposite stretched the monastery garden. Industrious monks in brown cloaks, with brown skullcaps on their heads were working there. Quiet and cleanliness reigned all around.

'We shall live here!' he decided.

Here he would bring Bronka and the baby. Here their other children would be born. He put his head and most of his energy into the business. He checked exchange rates, followed the changes, alert to every movement. At the appropriate moment he sold the entire house and kept this apartment only. The apartment of his dreams.

'Where is he dragging you and the baby?' Bronka's mother asked her. She had returned to her wool store and had become a respected merchant, a businesswoman. 'Where is he dragging you? To the end of the world? How will you live there among the Gentiles?' 'How will we live there?' Bronka was weak after giving birth. 'Differently from how we live here, that's for sure. Here it's so cramped. Here it's like living in a ghetto.'

Hesiek said that the Gentiles would not interfere with them. Inside their apartment they could behave according to all the Jewish customs and precepts. It was nobody's business if they cooked kosher food or not, if they lit Sabbath candles or not. But the children would be able to breathe good clean air. They would like nature. They would get accustomed to beauty. They would learn music.

'My children, Mother,' Bronka said, 'will ride horses, climb mountains, swim in rivers.'

The mother was close to fainting, and looked for a chair.

'Oy, it's not good for me to hear all these things. How will you live day by day there, I ask. Where will you buy? Who will you talk with?'

Bronka looked at her mother out of her weary blue eyes. Before her mind's eye there passed, as in a movie, pictures from Suesser House, the cramped and disordered apartment in which she had no real space for herself. The smelly lavatory on the porch, shared with other tenants. The noise, the bustle and the crowd in the Jewish street and in the courtyard. She answered slowly:

'I'll buy in shops owned by human beings. I'll speak with human beings.'

They started furnishing their apartment in Lobzowska (the name of the quiet street) room by room, item by item. They delighted in their home like two children delighting in a beautiful toy.

The remainder of the money Hesiek invested in business. He bought a white horse and called it Hirsch, his own name. He bought a cheap vacant lot on the outskirts of the city and started filling it with merchandise. At the beginning he did everything by himself. He led the horse himself, and loaded and unloaded the goods himself. He organized an office and kept the accounts himself. His willpower was tremendous, and his deeds filled him with satisfaction.

And then the baby, little Moishele, died. The world became suddenly black, and grief twisted his face. Bronka wandered around the silent beautiful rooms with lowered red eyes, the flowers wilted on the rose-bush, the monastery garden was covered with a gray cloud, and through the broad venetian windows a chill crept into the apartment.

Hesiek walked around depressed and sad. But when Bronka became pregnant again he recovered and with renewed strength looked after her and his business affairs.

Large sums from his income went to the doctors who were treating his younger brother Haim, who was then still struggling for his life.

Haim's death was a terrible blow for Hesiek. He sank into a real depression. Nothing made him happy any more. Not his property, not his business affairs, not even the beautiful apartment he had so delighted in. Everything seemed vain and futile to him. Life had neither joy or purpose. Sunken in despair and gloom, he sat down and wrote out a detailed last will. He bequeathed everything to his beloved wife, and hoped she would not need the favors of her parents. Poor Bronka. His heart ached when he thought of her and of the child that was to be born to him, but he had no strength to go on fighting. Let the True Judge come already, let him come and take him.

And then Bronka, with feminine gentleness and the intuition of a loving wife, managed to revive his will to continue.

And now there were already two little ones moving around the apartment, filling it with noise. Life pressed forward, the children made endless demands, it was necessary to look after them and to be around them day and night, and to work outside to supply the growing needs of the household. The bigger girl already had a governess, the little boy had a wet-nurse, and in the kitchen a housemaid stood over a basin of laundry and dishes.

The daughter was beautiful. She had soft silken hair, skin as smooth as velvet, and her eyes were cornflower blue. Whenever he held this wondrous creature in his arms, he felt his heart go out to her, and he could have gone through fire and water for her, just so she would not lack anything. He would stand for hours beside her crib, looking at her enchanting form, at the motions of her tiny hands and feet, at her smiles, and in his heart the icebergs melted, to be replaced by a wonderful warmth.

They called her Rela, after his mother, Rela née Carmel, the melancholy young woman who had been matched with his father when she was still a little girl, who had borne him eight children and had passed quietly from the world.

Very quickly the name Rela became 'Reli', and when they felt like pampering her especially, which happened very frequently, they would call her 'Relinka'. They expended a great deal of concern upon her. They would be alarmed by the slightest cry she might emit, and gave in to all her demands.

When the boy was born, Reli was two-and-a-half years old, a beautiful girl who was quite spoiled.

The boy was fairer, and plump. He was also calmer, perhaps because they were more experienced by now and looked after him less anxiously. They called him Szaja.

'Why? Why Szaja?' Bronka tried to protest, very weak after the difficult birth. She had given birth at home, in the presence of an experienced private midwife. At the last moment the midwife had been afraid of complications and had suggested that a doctor be called. The two of them, the doctor and the midwife, worked hard to help the tormented mother, while in the other room Hesiek rocked little Relinka in his arms.

'Why Szaja of all names?' Bronka asked in a weary voice. 'We're not in Kazimierz, the boy will suffer when he grows up.'

Hesiek stroked her perspiring face and kissed her white hand. After a long pause he said:

'We must prove to everyone and especially to ourselves that we are not headed towards assimilation. What I received from my father I will pass on to my son. It doesn't matter where I may live. My Jewishness is my identity, and it's also the boy's identity. His name will always remind him of his origin.'

'You're cruel, Hesiek,' Bronka said to him. He started back in surprise. How had such hard words been spoken by her weak and tender voice?

'You're tired now. You must rest. Did you want us to call him Stanislaw? Or Tadeusz?'

She closed her eyes. She knew that there was no point in arguing. He had decided on Szaja, it would be Szaja. Nothing would help. She had spoken seriously and he had scoffed. She closed her eyes. The baby cried. Bronka's breasts were empty because of the high fever after the birth, and the wet-nurse had not yet managed to pull out her huge abundant breast. A moment later the boy started sucking greedily. Reli pulled her little hand out of the governess's grip, and stood beside the sucking infant.

'At least at home, among ourselves, let's call him something else,' said Bronka, in an appeasing tone.

'Let's call him Izio.'

But she thought – what's the difference? Out of the frying-pan and into the fire. But little Reli had picked up on the word. She pointed to the baby and chirped:

'Izio?'

They both laughed, happy and charmed by Reli's cleverness. And so things remained.

On his return from work Hesiek would immediately devote himself to helping his wife. While she fed little Izio, he would take care of Reli, who now demanded maximum attention. Or he would make the children's beds and arrange their clothes. He learned to sew buttons, to put elastic into trousers and to lengthen hems. He would lengthen the hems of little dresses, of pajama pants, and of sleeves. Stage by stage until the last millimeter. Lengthening of hems became a hobby of his.

A regular housemaid took care of the house cleaning and the kitchen work. Another girl was in charge of the laundry and the ironing and other difficult chores. In Hesiek's business it also became impossible to manage alone. He hired a worker, whose name was Antony. Antony looked after Hirsch the Horse, but Hesiek continued as before to visit his friend every morning and bring him a large cube of sugar, which he would put right between his teeth while stroking his mane. Hirsch and Hirsch stood facing each other, looking directly into each other's eyes with a friendly gaze. Antony would object that the stallion was treated better than a working man who staggered under his load and no one cared. And here was the master, pampering the horse, making sure that the wagon to which Hirsch was harnessed was not overloaded.

Antony worked with Hirsch in the yard, and in the office sat Wowek, the eldest of Bronka's brothers, keeping the accounts. Hesiek employed him in a full time capacity – he needed someone to keep the accounts and answer the phone while he himself was out on the road. Wowek had gladly accepted his brother-in-law's offer. His two brothers had gone into their parents' wool business. The wool and embroidery threads shop had expanded, a large storehouse had been added, and the business was now called A. Plessner and Sons. Wowek, who had leftist tendencies, refused to become a partner of his father's, because such a status was opposed to his world outlook, which called for the suppression of capitalism and the development of the proletariat. He would explain Marxist theories to people he spoke with, telling them about the Communist Manifesto and *Das Kapital*, the red flag and the revolution, the exploited and the exploiters, the working class and the state as a tool in the hands of he revolution, and about the dictatorship of the proletariat, which was the only way to the creation of a better world, internationally. His brothers admired his erudition in these secular topics, but found it difficult to follow him, to enter a world so strange and so distant from their own Jewish world. Hesiek would scoff:

'A passing illness. He's full of slogans and theories, but theories are one thing and action another.'

Rumors had reached him that although Wowek was employed by him in a full time capacity, he also demanded his share of the income of the family company which had begun to prosper. His brothers objected to this, and tension rose in the family, dissolving only when Wowek decided to get married.

Everyone forgave everyone else and all came to the wedding. Wowek returned to his place of origin, the wool shop. He came to terms with his fate, which had destined him to be a property-owner and an employer (two hired employees were already working there) and not a proletarian worker. He was a pale-skinned, physically soft young man, with a delicate face, who wore spectacles. A thinker, short-statured and narrow-shouldered. He met his wife Adela for the first time under the wedding canopy. She was soft and feminine like himself. She was very quiet, and you had no way of knowing if she was bashful or if she simply had nothing to say.

'One thing is for sure,' said Bronka when they got back from the wedding, 'she'll know how to cook a meat soup with noodles, she'll know how to bear children, she'll never say "no" to her husband, she'll never make demands for herself, and she'll never revolt. She won't know that a woman is also a human being, who may think and express views of her own.'

Hesiek looked at his wife, a prolonged glance. Was she speaking about Adela, or about herself? Her eyes slipped away from his gaze. Or had he imagined it?

'And you?'

'What? Am I like Adela?' She sounded offended.

'I didn't say that.'

'It's true, I'm like that, I know how to cook, to bear children, and not to say "no".'

He sealed her mouth with a kiss.

Wowek left Hesiek's office, and in his place came a young woman, a secretary who could also type. Antony wasn't sorry.

Despite the declared policy of the Polish government, which had proclaimed a boycott of Jewish firms, there had been considerable movement in both businesses – in Hesiek's building timber business, and in his father-in law's wool business.

Hesiek followed the developments and was aware of the boycott process. The rise of the Polish state at the end of the First World War was accompanied by difficult tensions between the Polish majority and the large Jewish minority dwelling in its midst. In previous centuries, when the Jews had arrived in Poland in the course of their wanderings, they had enjoyed the auspices of the Kings of Poland, whom they had served as land agents, suppliers of rare merchandise, and moneylenders. In those times the Jews had made no special demands as a collective, and they had conducted their religious activities among themselves, within the synagogues and communities.

Many things had changed since then.

The Jewish minority had suffered persecutions, hardships, and changes of all kinds. Persecuted and unwanted, the Jews had gathered in various parts of Poland, which was a less stable country economically than were her richer neighbors, with a large proportion of her population living in feudal backwardness. Poland struggled heroically for her freedom and independence, attacked as she often was from the north, the east, and the west. She lost her independence, and Russia, Prussia, and Austria divided her up among themselves. The conquest had been long, lasting for seven or eight generations. In the conquered land of Poland people died and were born, Poles and Jews alike, the two nations side by side increasing, in enslavement and frustration. The Poles aspired to political independence and cultivated their feelings for the glorious history of their nation, for its language, its literature, and its poetry.

And the Jews? These were no longer the same Jews who had served the Kings of Poland and had made no demands. The Kings of Poland had long vanished and with them those Jews had vanished too. The developments and the changes had affected everyone. Among the Jewish minority there had been a consolidation of secular – and even national – elements. The Jews too cultivated their feelings for their glorious historical past, for their language, their literature, and their poetry.

The First World War had ended. Wilson had spoken about freedom for all nations. About a great democracy. Several states had attained independence. Among those who had attained independence there had been no Jewish state, such as the one Herzl had dreamed of. Against this, the Polish state had been among those states that had received independence.

The Jews in Poland constituted a large ethnic group, and they had demands. They demanded national autonomy.

The Poles, emotionally aroused about the great historical moment in which their nation had received independence after so many years of subjugation, concentrated all their resources on the building of their homeland. They demanded that all citizens unite around this main goal. Extremist groups in the new Poland, among them the Endeks – members of the anti-semitic National Democratic Party – incited hatred against the 'treacherous' Jews. The Jews defended themselves by seeking international support for their demands. At the Paris Conference, when the peace treaty was signed at Versailles, the Poles were forced to include the 'minorities charter' into their constitution. They saw this international pressure as interference in their internal affairs, and this put a further strain on the relations between the majority and the minority. To protect themselves from the Jews 'who are selling us out, proliferating, and taking control', the boycott on Jewish businesses was declared. The government opposed violence against the Jews, but encouraged the economic boycott against them. Skladkowski said: 'Pogroms – no; economic boycott – go ahead.'

The government of the new Poland established co-operatives, which were closed to Jews. It created a monopoly on essential materials, and thus closed the way to Jewish commerce in these materials. But it was impossible to close all the ways. And the borders to international trade remained open, despite all the hardships.

Hesiek conducted business deals with Germany, Austria, Italy, Hungary, and Yugoslavia. On his journeys to these countries he also made contacts for his father-in-laws' business. In this way he also became a partner of him and his sons in a certain sector. In his own timber business he already had a small team working for him. Now, as a partner in A. Plessner and Sons, he put great momentum into planning an expansion of the business. With his young brother-in-law Monius, who for business purposes was called Marek, he planned a business trip to the western countries, but first of all to Warsaw. Warsaw was an important center, impossible to bypass.

One day Bronka phoned his office in alarm:

'Come quickly, there are men here who have come to confiscate our property, the furniture in the living room, and the pictures.'

Within five minutes he was at home.

He threw open the doors and stood in the living-room. Bronka stood there, as pale as chalk. Her third pregnancy was clearly in evidence, Beside her were Reli and Izio, quiet and frightened. The strangers walked about in the room as if it was their own, moving a table and chairs.

'Stop!' he called, standing there in the entrance to the living-room, and the strangers gave a start and retreated.

'Put everything back in its place, please!' he ordered.

The strangers showed him a slip of paper from the Treasury, to which was appended a summary of his debts.

'This is not a correct account,' he said.

The two men shrugged their shoulders.

'We don't write the accounts. We carry out the orders.'

Bronka felt a slight dizziness. He apologized, and led her and the children out into another room.

'Don't worry,' he said to her, 'I'll arrange everything. Everything will be all right.'

Bronka took the children in her arms and started singing to them: 'Once upon a time/ There was a great king/ And a princess too…'

Several minutes later he came back.

'OK. They accepted a bribe. Everything's all right now.'

'Didn't you pay income tax?'

'Of course I did.'

'So what happened?' She understood nothing about his business. What had happened today was not to her liking. 'I don't want anything like this to ever happen again. Do you know what one of them said? "Take a look at what we have here! I'm from here, I was born here, have I got an apartment like this? Or furniture like this?" I felt the blood rising to my head. I was trembling all over, and I heard myself reply: "We're from here too. We were born here too." Let's leave here, Hesiek,' she suddenly said. 'Let's go to Palestine. If we sell the apartment they'll give us a visa.'

He dropped onto a chair that was near him, as if his legs had suddenly collapsed beneath him. He lowered his head to his chest, his young face suddenly covered with deep creases

– or perhaps the previous appearance of his face, smooth, smiling and vigorous, had been only a mask?

'With the children? When they're so little?' he asked softly. Her heart filled with pity for him, for herself, and for the children.

'I only thought...'

'And you're pregnant. You'll be giving birth soon.'

'True. This isn't the right time. I'm just making things difficult for you.'

'You, making things difficult for me?! If there's anyone in the world who helps me, it's you. I have no one but you.'

'It's time to wash the children,' Bronka said, and got up, heavily. He got up too.

'You stay here. I'll wash them. I'll go and fill the bathtub with water.'

For Bronka, this pregnancy was the hardest of all. So much so that towards its end she was unable to function.

'Can your mother come and help us a little?'

Every morning he got up at five o'clock, washed his body in cold water even in winter, as his father had done when he was his age, put on phylacteries, prayed the morning service, woke the children with a deluge of kisses, fish oil, and a sweet, brought Bronka milk coffee and a buttered roll in bed, told the housemaid to take good care of the lady of the house, and ran off to his business.

'My mother? Have you forgotten that she didn't even look after us when we were children? And now you expect her to look after our children?'

He nodded. Better not to say anything.

'But she's a woman of valor,' said Bronka. 'She's saving the shop.'

'Or the shop's saving her.'

'You were never in love with her!'

'In love with her?! Have you seen a normal man who was in love with his mother-in-law?'

'Oh. Hesiek, you know very well what I mean. You can't stand her.'

Tears dripped down her face, washed over the yellow

stains on her face, and dropped onto her heaving belly. He sighed, but before he responded, she said:

'She's my mother. And I won't have you saying a bad word about her. Even if she doesn't come to help us now.'

Grandma Herrstein, Mrs Plessner's step-mother, was still alive. She lived with her daughter Fela Herzig, and responded gladly when Bronka asked her to come and stay with them until after the birth.

Grandma Herrstein was a tall thin woman, with a severe face and pursed lips. Her dresses came down to her ankles. Beneath them one could see high boots, tied with laces, and with flat heels. On her head she used to wear a Turkish turban, which generally did not rest in the proper place but somewhat to the side. Her face was very wrinkled and on the right side of her chin was a brown mole from which grew a clump of hard black hairs.

Bronka greeted her with a demonstration of love and delight. Her mood improved at once and the apartment again resounded with the sound of her merry laughter.

'Dear Grandma! How good it is to see you!'

Grandma Herrstein had arrived exhausted and out of breath after the long trip from Kazimierz, which she had made by street-car.

'I changed "tramways" twice! It's so dangerous! You've certainly found yourselves a place to live in! Beuberick!'

In the meantime she scrutinized the apartment.

'It's like at Napoleon's.'

Bronka laughed till the tears came. Reli and Izio looked at the old grandmother, curious and full of anticipation.

'Where's Beuberick, Grandma? How was it at Napoleon's?'

'Good. No need for talk. Time to roll up sleeves and get to work! There's no time to waste on idle chatter!'

'Tell us more, Grandma?'

She didn't want to tell all her stories at once, for fear she might run out of the words she had available and would have to finish her life in silence.

'How old are you, Grandma?' everyone wanted to know.

'How can I remember?' she would reply to the inquisitive.

'I was born so long ago that I've forgotten myself.'

The children pressed themselves to her at once, and sank into the folds of her long dress. She would seat them on her knees, one child on each knee, sway slightly, and tell tales.

When she had got married she had been six years old, two years older than Reli, so she told them. And her heart's chosen had been seven. They had played five stones and had walked hand in hand from his parents' apartment to her parents' apartment and had been afraid to walk in the dark.

Reli and Izio listened open-mouthed to her amazing stories.

'They're too little to understand,' Bronka said, but the children wanted to hear more and more.

'We were lucky,' the grandmother continued, with the same severe expression on her face. 'We were lucky that we started playing father and mother early and that everything worked out well. But many children were very miserable. There was a girl whom her parents married to a boy who was drafted into the Russian army when he was ten. He served for 25 years and she was forced to wait for him.'

'It's so good that Grandma's with us now,' Bronka whispered that night. The children were already asleep in their beds, and the old grandmother had been given the fourth room, where she too was in bed. They had taken care to give her comfort and even luxury such as she was not accustomed to.

'It's good that she's with us,' Bronka repeated, not sure if Hesiek had heard her. He lay beside her, very tired after an exhausting day's work. Regular snores came from his mouth, and his eyes were half closed. Almost asleep, he said:

'I hear.'

She turned from side to side, not easily finding a comfortable place for her distended stomach. A night lamp beside her bed cast a faint light onto the room. In the large mirror opposite were reflected their two beds with their white coverings and two shapes under the covers. The mirror returned each of their motions and the faint light of the lamp increased the size of the shadows that floated on the walls of the room.

Bronka gave the drowsy Hesiek the latest report on the Herzig, Plessner, and Mantel families. The grandmother lived with her daughter Fela Herzig. This was the same Fela who had combed Bronka's plaits and had ironed the white collars that she had had to wear to the Austrian school.

Now Fela was married to David Herzig, a Jew with long beard, sidecurls and *capota*, and she had little joy in her marriage. But she got a lot of joy from her son Itzik. Itzik was born during the war, while the grandmother and Bronka and her brothers had been in exile in Bratislava. Itzik was a gifted boy, and was going to a Polish school. Despite the fact that he was a Jew (so Grandma said), he had jumped two grades at once. When Grandma talked about Itzik, her face was radiant and her severe expression vanished. Itzik had a good grasp of mathematics, physics, and chemistry. His mother Fela did not allow his father to influence him: she didn't want him to become like his father. She was proud of Itzik and understood that he had to study.

Fela worked hard to support her husband, who recited passages from the Mishnah and verses from the Psalms from morning to evening, and her son who studied mathematics and chemistry from morning to evening. She embroidered wonderful tablecloths and curtains for wealthy people's windows. Her embroideries were works of art. The shop run by A. Plessner and Sons gave her embroidery threads on credit and at cost price, and thus the two step-sisters, Bronka's mother and Fela, no longer scoffed at each other and lived together in peace.

Aharon Plessner's two spinster sisters – Panna Paula and Panna Stefa – would never marry. They hated all the Jewish husbands. The trouble was that there was nothing in the middle. Marriage with non-Jews was also out of the question. So they lived alone, two beautiful, cultivated and elegant ladies. One year Paula would work in the bank while Stefa ran their household, and the next year Stefa would work in the bank and Paula would run the household.

Reb Aharon's third sister, Pani Dola Mantel was married and had three children: Wilhelm, Liz, and Fredek. All of them were lost souls to Judaism. The eldest, Bronka's cousin

Wilhelm, had been sent to study music in Berlin and there he had been caught up by the war. But despite the war he had finished his studies at the academy successfully, with excellent results. He had specialized in music theory and had done his doctorate in this discipline. Now he was a professor at the conservatorium in Krakow, and gave concerts all over Poland, with his name appearing on large placards. And the daughter Liz was spoiled, because she was too beautiful and had things too easy. Fredek was a student.

Bronka spoke, and Hesiek, half asleep, half heard what she said. Her voice grew more and more distant, more and more dim. Then still. Absolute silence. She turned off the night lamp. The shadows descended from the walls of the room and seemed to gather in their beds together with Grandma's tales. She turned her face to him and smiled. Imagination blended with reality, he felt light as a feather and floating in air; he seemed to have fallen from space into the bed. Her hand touched his shoulder:

'You were snoring so loudly,' said Bronka.

In the morning the apartment filled with the smell of freshly ground coffee. Industrious Grandma had got up early and reached the kitchen before Marynia, the housemaid.

'Jesus Maria!' cried Marynia and quickly went back to put on a working dress and an apron. 'The old lady gets up so early!'

Grandma looked her up and down and the girl blushed in embarrassment.

'When I was your age I didn't go to sleep at all. I didn't permit myself such a waste of time.'

Hesiek, who was already in the kitchen having prayed and shaved, was now enjoying the dialogue between the two. His shoes stood polished and gleaming beside the kitchen door. A Jewish milkman from an adjacent village brought milk and cheese, and the Pan Wirt's grocery store delivered fresh rolls and butter. Marynia brought a bucket of coals up from the cellar of the building. Blocks of wood for fuel were kept on the kitchen porch, and Hesiek helped her prepare fine kindling and old newspapers, to make it easy for the fire to be lit with a lighted match. The two of them, he with the wood and she with the coals, hastened to light all the stoves.

From the children's room came sounds of merry laughter, and the stern and serious voice of Grandma.

'Now at last I'll be able to make the trip to Warsaw,' thought Hesiek. Bronka and the children are in good hands. He phoned his brother-in-law Marek and they decided to take a train to Warsaw the next day.

Unusually for him, he arrived at the station early, and noticed uncommon activity there. Something had happened or was about to happen. Polish policemen in blue uniforms walked in pairs in all directions. They wore white gloves and had on their full gear, ready for action.

He and Marek had agreed to meet about an hour before the train left. They had to conclude and arrange several things before the journey and had decided to travel second class on an express train because they hadn't had time to reserve seats for themselves. In the first and second class there were always vacant places, because most of the population could not afford to travel better than third class, since the difference in price was so great.

Marek came towards him. This pampered child, his in-laws' youngest, who had once made trouble for Bronka and had demanded constant attention, had grown into a real man. He had fair hair, a high forehead, blue eyes, and a candid gaze. His lower lip was slightly thick and protruding. He was clean-shaven and wore a light-colored suit and a raincoat, and on his head was a peaked cap, worn on the side with dandy-ish casualness. He was carrying a large suitcase. Hesiek, taller and more supple, though he was at least ten years older, wore a dark suit, a white shirt with cuff-links and an elegant tie, a coat and a sportive hat.

'How's Bronka?' Marek asked.

'Heavy. I hope she'll wait until my return for the birth.'

They started talking about business. There was little time. The policemen hurried about the station in a suspicious manner. Marek too noticed the uncommon activity. They turned towards the ticket-office.

'Listen,' the young man said to him as they walked, perhaps wanting to take his mind off the policemen. 'Szajek has been offered a bride! And she's exceptionally beautiful!'

Hesiek displayed impatience. They had come here for business and work, not to talk about beautiful girls. What did the youngster understand about these things? Probably another one like Adela.

'A flower, not a woman.' Marek spoke enthusiastically. 'Her name's Rachel and she's a real flower, I tell you. What a body, what legs!'

'Enough of that,' said Hesiek, annoyed, for some reason. This Szajek, of all people – the '*bocher*' with no spice in him, who swayed in prayer and rolled his eyes, who had refused to deliver his love-letters to Bronka, who didn't have much sense in his skull, the '*shlemazel*,' the '*shlumiel*,' the failure – he of all people!

'Is it serious?'

'Very serious. They've already discussed "conditions." '

'So let it be with *mazel tov*,' he said, and looked at the clock.

In the meantime they had neared the ticket-office. People were standing in line. The longest line was at the counter marked Warsaw. Hesiek and Marek joined the line. An additional group of policemen arrived at the station. Among the Polish crowd hurrying on its way could be seen orthodox Jews hastening in the direction of one of the trains. The policemen turned after them, in the same direction.

'What's happening here?!'

In front of them in the line for tickets stood a man and a woman most elegantly dressed, asking for first class tickets to Warsaw. To their surprise there were no tickets.

'First class!' the elegant man repeated, and drew from his pocket a visiting card with a symbol of the aristocracy embossed upon it.

The ticket-seller nodded. He had no first class tickets for sale.

'Sold out.'

'All the tickets?'

'The Jews bought the entire carriage.'

'The Jews bought ...' .

'No point in asking?' said the ticket-seller. 'I'm not here to give explanations. There are no tickets. If your honor has questions he may take them to the police.'

Hesiek was no longer standing in line. He was running after the group of Jews who were hurrying in the direction of the train to Warsaw.

'Jews, what's happening here?' he asked in Yiddish.

'The Rabbi from Gur is travelling, the Rabbi is travelling.'

Hesiek, excited, returned to the line, where he had left Marek to keep their place. The Rabbi from Gur was travelling from Krakow to Warsaw! His *hassidim* had bought up the entire first class carriage for the Rabbi and his entourage!

Hesiek's excitement was great. They barely managed to get tickets in the third class. Everything had become mixed up.

The Polish aristocratic couple made do with the second class. The policemen kept order and the Polish public gazed in astonishment and wonder at the *hassidic* entourage accompanying their adored Rabbi. Some of them turned away in disgust and contempt, while others, on the contrary, approached and stared at the unaccustomed sight.

When the train moved off, Hesiek pulled his young brother-in-law in the direction of the first class carriage. They pushed their way through among the peasants who packed the third class, squeezing past a woman wearing a large colored kerchief, her face round and smooth and her body smellings of dairy and stable, the milk of cows and goats, the smell of fodder and straw. The peasants noticed the two strangers making a way for themselves, and sent suspicious glances at them, while they cursed softly. The women crossed themselves.

'*Zydy* (Jews)', Marek heard, or perhaps he imagined it, but he started, and the whole adventure no longer appealed to him.

'Don't pay any attention,' Hesiek said to him, and continued forward. 'It's all worth it.'

In the first class carriage, the Rabbi's Hasidic bodyguards were suspicious. Hesiek and Marek had to prove that they too were followers of the Rabbi from Gur. Whoever wished to approach had to plead for permission to be in the Rabbi's presence.

The carriage was black with *capotas*, some gleaming, some saturated with grease. All the hasidim looked alike. All struggled to get as close as possible to the Rabbi, and some fell upon the remains of his dinner. Even Hesiek obtained a few crumbs from the Rabbi's dinner, and offered some of them to his companion. Marek flashed him an astonished glance.

'You? I wouldn't have believed it. Why is it so important to you?'

Hesiek didn't reply. What could he say? There were things which could not be explained.

The train did not stop at towns. At cities it stopped for several minutes: Kielce, Radom. At each stop the stations were packed with Hasidim who strained to touch the carriage, and gathered around the Rabbi's window.

In Warsaw, Hesiek changed back to a different person, wholly European. He led Marek, who was visiting the capital for the first time, along the 'Jerusalem Boulevard', by the president's place (the 'Belweder'), to the Lazienki Park and the market in the Old City. Then they went into a cafe to refresh themselves with a large cream cake and a good cup of coffee. Here they met some fellow businessmen, and from them they heard news about developments in the Sejm (the Parliament) and the Senate, in the state as a whole, and in Jewish circles in particular. Immediately after the coffee, the politics, and the gossip, they got to work.

*   *   *

Very quietly she came into the room where he lay. The winter sun had already disappeared from the window and had set somewhere behind the monastery garden. The high stove made of ceramic tiles sent heat into the room. Bronka placed her hands on the stove, then turned around and placed her back against it.

'Are you sleeping?'

'No. Just lying here thinking.'

'What were you thinking about.'

'Just things, about what we've been through. About your family. I was recalling my trip to Warsaw with your brother, and my concern for you and your health. I won't travel again until you give birth.'

She lay down beside him, her large belly rising high above the level of the blanket. He placed his hand on her and they both became attentive.

'Feel it?'

Gentle knockings made his hand tremble. They came from inside her stomach. Something that belonged to him, that had come from him, was moving there inside her body. Tying them in a connection that could not be undone.

'Do you want a boy or a girl?'

'And you?' he asked.

'It doesn't matter to me. I just wish it was already born.'

'It doesn't matter to me either. I just wish it health.'

Years before, when he'd wanted 12 children, he hadn't known what a child was. Or what a woman was. It was strange that he had wanted so many children. The commandment 'be fruitful and multiply' had been spoken in another time and another place. Where? How had God imagined it would be? And who was God? Suddenly a fear descended upon him because of these heretical thoughts. And that it was just now, right before the birth, that he had started to have fears. He hoped God would not punish them again. He was all-powerful. God gives, and God takes away.

'What's the matter with you?' asked Bronka. 'You're trembling all over. I'm the one that has to give birth, and you're afraid. Shame on you. I haven't seen your sisters since that Sunday when you weren't home. But I've heard that something's happening there. Hania's terribly nervous and Hela's looking for a room for herself. She says she has to get out of there. Something's happened. You're all so sensitive and extreme, the lot of you!'

'True. We're like that.'

'So?'

'So nothing. What are you saying?'

216

'I'm saying that we should ask Hela to come and live with us. With the money she's earning she won't be able to pay rent for a decent room. Especially since I've heard that that character Aleks, or whatever his name is, is meeting her again, and he's married.'

Hesiek turned over and lay on his back, quiet, stiff, as if he'd swallowed a stick. How could they bring Hela here? She'd bother Bronka, just as she had at Paulinska.

'Here it is different,' said Bronka. 'The apartment's big. There's an extra room with a separate entrance.'

She's already forgotten. She's too good and forgiving. It would be hard for her. And he wouldn't be able to help.

'Who's with the children?' he changed the subject. 'Why are they so quiet?'

'Grandma's there, telling them stories. Hela loves children too.'

'Hela loves children, that's true. She should have had a child of her own. Her relationship with Irka is one of the reasons for the tension between her and Hania. People exploit her. Her boss exploits her at work. He makes her work very hard and pays her starvation wages. Aleks exploits her too. To his little Russian wife he gives everything: children, a good home, and a good name. And from Hela he takes everything. People exploit Hela, her loyalty, her honesty, and her loneliness. But if she comes here she'll exploit Bronka, Bronka's goodness and innocence. Wowek said that the society we live in is based on exploiters and the exploited. The regimes are decadent and only communism can bring redemption. I don't like that idea. Communism is foreign to my spirit and terrifies me.'

A great weariness descended on Hesiek and he fell asleep.

Saturday evening. The children were making a noise in their room. They were sick of being quiet. Bronka came into the room. Soon Hesiek would go to the little synagogue on Dluga Street. After that, on his return, he would make *havdalah*,[1] she would hold a colored plaited candle and he would rub his fingernails near its small flame and let her smell scents from the antique silver box. Only then, with the end of

217

the Sabbath, would they turn on the electric lights in the apartment, for Marynia, their *Shabbes-goy*, was not at home. Bronka would put the children to bed, and would be able to indulge herself in listening to the music she loved, which she would hear on the special instrument he had bought her – a radio-phonograph with earphones especially for her. He would go out to arrange some affairs, meet some people, and then he would come back home to her. If he found flowers on sale in the street he would surely bring her a flower, and if he didn't find flowers, he would bring her a good cake or some chocolate. Even though she'd told him that she didn't want to put on weight. What a spendthrift he was! She would tell him:

'A thousand times I've told you I don't want to put on weight, and I even baked for the Sabbath!' 'Your cakes are the best in the world,' he would say, 'but the one I've brought you is something special.'

They would sit and talk about the children, about their future, and make plans. They would also talk about Bronka's mother, the mother-in-law, and say that she was selfish and didn't see how sweet her grandchildren were, and that it never even occured to her to bring them a block of chocolate.

They had decided to invite Hela to come and live with them. They'd decided to do this right away, as soon as possible. They would tell Hela that they needed her, so that she couldn't refuse. She was very sensitive, and had suffered enough. Now they would say to her, before the birth, that it was important to have another close person in the home, to keep an eye on things. Grandma Herrstein had to go back to her daughter Fela, to help her with the housework, for Fela was working for her family's livelihood. And Grandma was too old, anyway. They needed Hela. There was an extra room here with a separate entrance: modern showers and toilets. It would be good for all of them. And that man too, it would be good if he knew that she had a home, and support.

Bronka's time to give birth had come, according to all the signs and calculations, but nothing happened.

In the apartment all the preparations had been completed. They had arranged for the experienced midwife who had delivered Reli and Izio to come. Pans and basins stood ready. A small stove had been brought in especially and placed in one of the corners of the bedroom. Water could be boiled on it. Also implements, sheets, towels and diapers, everything had to be boiled. The microbes would die in the boiling water before they could cause harm. In a period when aspirin was the only medicine to prevent infections and inflammations, every birth was a grave and dangerous test, and the slightest complication could lead to a struggle between life and death. Many cases had ended in disaster. No small number of infants were still-born, or died during birth from poisonings or various infections. That was the least of the evils. The worst was when the baby was condemned from its first day to a life of orphanhood. Women in childbirth caught high fevers or lost a lot of blood, hemorrhages were frequent, and could not always be stopped.

There were of course also easy cases, when babies 'leapt' from their mothers' wombs before it was time, healthy and whole.

Bronka had stopped feeling the baby and the midwife was worried.

'We can't feel the child, and the lady is anemic. If there's a hemorrhage I won't be able to stop it.'

Hesiek was alarmed. Perhaps God was punishing him for the heretical thoughts he had been thinking lately. All the doubts he had had. He promised himself that he would never again dispute God's judgment. He prayed fervently. In the synagogue he organized a minyan of Jews for a special prayer. Bronka asked for her mother to be beside her.

'I want my mother. Ask Mamale to come.' She spoke like a little child.

He ran to Kazimierz, and burst into his in-laws' shop like a tempest.

'Quickly, quickly!' he urged his mother-in-law.

Alarmed, she gathered her things, and straightened her wig. At that moment there were no customers in the shop. Reb Aharon sat by the till, writing a poem in the holy tongue. It was in high and ornate language, the blessing of the father to his middle son on his marriage, which was to take place in several months. Reb Aharon's eyes gazed straight ahead and saw what others did not see. The nib of the pen which he dipped in ink drew the Hebrew characters that none of those present knew how to read properly. He wrote and erased, playing with words and lines. He had not even noticed the entrance of the young man who had burst into his shop and grabbed his wife.

'What's happening here?' he asked, as if returning from a different world.

'Poems he writes now! Our daughter's life is in danger, Lord of the Universe!'

Reb Aharon smiled. Apparently at this very moment the thought he had been seeking, or the rhyme he needed, had come to him. He made a pacifying gesture with his hand, as if saying – wait a minute, dear people, wait a little while with your bad news, I have to finish the poem. Five stanzas, each of six lines, had already been written. Reb Aharon's lips muttered the opening lines:

> A father's blessing to the beloved son
> On your leaving my rule for a roof of your own
> A precious gazelle has fallen to your lot
> A gift of God ...
>
> (Krakow 1933)

'I've finished. It's ready to be printed. Now tell me what has happened.'

They told him briefly and left the shop. The streetcar stop was close by, right opposite the shop, but as if to spite them the streetcar didn't come.

'So far away you wanted to live,' the mother-in-law grumbled.

A black horse-drawn carriage rolled by. He tried to stop it but it passed quickly, leaving a train of cold air behind it. It began to grow dark. Opposite them a lighted streetcar stopped, people got off and on, and the streetcar moved off in the direction opposite to the one they wanted. Among the people who had got off, there flashed the figure of a woman in white, who skipped down the steps like a gazelle. White shoes, white hat and coat. The whiteness stood out among the black-garbed people in the dim twilight.

Meanwhile, Hesiek had stopped another passing carriage. It had five comfortable seats, and on them were soft blankets to put over one's legs. Over the seats was a huge umbrella-like canopy. The driver hauled at the reins and the two horses slowed down, brought their forelegs close to their hind legs and trotted on the spot, their shoes knocking on the stones of the road.

The mother-in-law hesitated. In such cases, he explained to her, one can't rely on public transport. If there were an airplane for hire he would have hired it, just to get home as soon as possible.

'I'm paying,' he said.

He put his hand into his pocket to draw out his wallet. The mother-in-law said something about waste and wastefulness and about how they had chosen to live at the world's end.

Suddenly the air filled with fragrance. A street lamp had been lit and it sent its light all around. The figure in white, which had appeared before on the other side of the street now stood between his mother-in-law and himself. A white fur collar surrounded her head. Pink cheeks, glinting eyes, an enchanting smile. The two women, the elder and the younger, discussed something in whispers. The carriage turned around and the driver got down to help the elder lady to mount. The younger one stood beside him. In her eyes there was embarrassment, and also a mischievous spark.

'What are you waiting for? You rushed me out of the shop. I didn't even say goodbye properly, and now you're just standing there.'

A blush came to the younger woman's face, and she lowered her eyes.

The driver lifted his whip. 'Wista,' he called, pulled the reins, and the horses moved off.

He got into the carriage and sat down beside his mother-in-law. The figure in white was swallowed up by the crowd.

'That's Rachel, Szajek's betrothed,' said the mother-in-law. 'It was in her honor that Father composed the poem.'

A father's blessing to the beloved son
On your leaving my rule for a roof of your own
A precious gazelle has fallen to your lot
A gift of God ...

Marek had mentioned her too, when they'd gone to Warsaw.
He hadn't been exaggerating. A gift of God indeed to Szajek.

When they reached home the midwife came out to them.
She looked disturbed.

'The water's broken,' she said.

The water had broken. A warm liquid poured from his
body as if he were the mother. He hurried to the bathroom,
changed his clothes, and returned to the room.

The water had broken but the delivery was not progress-
ing. The doctor was on his way. 'I called for him,' said the
midwife. Bronka lay there quietly, her mother stroking her
face. He didn't know what to do with himself. The children
were in the kitchen with Marynia and the old grandmother.
'There too I'm not needed.'

The doctor said that it would be best to move Bronka to a
hospital. It was possible that a Caesarian operation would be
necessary.

Bronka's mother burst out crying.

'Mother, it isn't the end of the world, I'm not the first woman
to go through such an operation, and I won't be the last.'

Bronka tried to appease her as if she was the one having the
operation. 'Just don't lose control,' Hesiek said to himself. 'God's
punishing me. That's certain. I have no doubt about it.' But he
postponed the accounting. Now he had to think well and
quietly. Slowly, to do the correct thing. Hela had good connections with doctors and with hospitals. She worked with them.

'I'll run and get Hela. She'll know which hospital to
approach.'

Again he hired a carriage, and urged the driver to drive
quickly to Topolowa. It was already late and he got them out
of their beds. Irka burst out crying. Hania, Hela, and Olek
stood around him in their pajamas, concerned.

'What's happened?'

'I told you,' he said to Hela. 'I begged you, I pleaded with you to come and stay with us.'

'What are you talking about?' Hela interrupted him. 'You didn't say a thing to me.'

'I didn't? I'm totally confused. We talked about it between ourselves, Bronka and I. Well, if I didn't say it, I'm saying it now. Come at once! Bronka has to be taken to a hospital. It looks as though she'll need an operation.'

Hela dressed quickly and they hurried out.

'Let us know what's happening!' Hania and Olek shouted after them.

Again the two horses galloped through Krakow's quiet streets. The lamplighter had lit the last of the lamps. A faint flame glowed inside it, closed inside the glass of the lamp, struggling to continue its existence.

They arrived. While he was paying the driver he thought he heard Bronka screaming from the second floor.

'I can't take this.'

'Calm down,' said Hela. 'She's allowed to scream now and you're not allowed to get hysterical.'

They took Bronka to a private hospital, one of the best in the city. The three of them, her mother, her husband, and her sister-in-law, waited all night beside the delivery room.

Early in the morning the doctor came out to them. 'We'll have to operate,' he said.

A black curtain fell over Hesiek's eyes. He had wanted 12 children, fool that he was.

The doctor waited for a reply.

'But she'll live?'

The doctor spoke quietly.

'If we don't operate, her life is in danger.'

They signed their approval of the operation.

'The baby's less important,' Hesiek mumbled,. 'The main thing is to save my wife. Please!'

The doctor looked at him with equanimity.

'We'll try to save them both,' he said.

PART III

Memory and Imagination
(1934–39)

12 First Memory

A table set for dinner stands in the middle of the large room. Three children and their mother sit around it. The room is full of sweet warmth and of children's chatter, the mother's laughter and the chirping of a bird. The mother has a smooth round face, sleek fair hair, laughing blue eyes. The children know that she's incapable of anger. Father isn't at home and they're permitted to do anything.

In the middle of dinner Izio grabs a book out of Reli's hands. 'No reading at dinner!'

'You're not going to tell me what I can do!'

They start quarreling. Mother tries to quieten them.

'Stop it,' she asks.

They quarrel, shout, and fight. The little girl begins to whine. She doesn't want to eat. She's had enough. The mother asks her to eat more.

'Just three more spoonfuls. Just three.'

The walls of the room are painted pink. The ceiling is white. There are two white cupboards, and between them a bed covered with a spread that looks like a lawn with flowers. Above the bed is a large picture. In the picture there is a beautiful princess wearing a white crown made of narcissus flowers. She is walking on the banks of a blue river and a golden sun sends its beams down upon her. The picture is embroidered with tiny beads, each bead the size of a pinhead. 'I embroidered it,' Mother said, 'yesterday, or the day before, or maybe even a week ago.' On one of the cupboards stands a cage, with a canary in it. Its feathers are yellow, and its chirping blends with the other voices in the room. In a corner there is a tall, warm, ceramic stove, and beside the stove a white rocking-horse with a thick mane, a saddle and reins. Beside it is a pram, with a cushion and a blanket inside it, and inside the pram, a doll. Opposite them are another bed and a white desk. Outside the window large fluffy snowflakes fall. Gradually the whole world outside is covered in white.

'Will you stop that!' Mother says angrily, but they don't stop. They're not afraid of Mother's anger. They run around the table, chasing each other.

'Give me back my book!'

'I wont'! I wont'!'

'I'll call a policeman,' says Mother. For a moment there is quiet. The race stops. And then Mother bursts out laughing and they all follow suit. Mother is incapable of calling a policeman. She's afraid of policemen herself. Little Ania cries loudly:

'I can't eat any more!'

'Everyone's laughing and you're crying? Silly girl. Two more spoonfuls, and that's all.'

The bigger children are fighting again. Marynia comes into the room and gathers up the dishes. There is shouting and crying all around.

'How little the lady knows how to handle them! They should be beaten! Otherwise they'll be all over the lady.'

Izio pokes his tongue out at Marynia. Mother scolds him and says 'bad boy'.

His eyes become sad. A shadow passes over Mother's eyes and she says:

'Izio's a good boy.'

Reli is reading her book again. Ania yawns among her tears.

Suddenly they hear the sound of a key turning, and then rapid steps. 'Father's back!!' they all shout.

Reli throws down the book, Izio jumps off the chair and knocks it over. Mother runs her hands over her body and her hair and straightens her dress. Ania wipes her tears with the sleeve of her blouse.

Again they are sitting by the table, the five of them. All the children are on top of Father. The bigger ones on his knees and the little one hanging on to his neck.

'You'll choke him,' says Mother. They ignore her. Marynia brings food for the master. He cannot release himself from their embrace. And then he says:

'Presents.'

They immediately let go and stand waiting in anticipation. Ania gets a new doll which opens and closes its eyes and says 'Ma-ma'. Reli and Izio are busy opening their presents. The packaging is lovely, the paper is from abroad. Now Mother sits close to Father and they laugh, embrace, and whisper. Marynia comes in again, bringing tea. Father gives her a new blouse. Marynia leaves the room.

Father puts the children to bed. He scolds them for not having recited the *Shema* prayer in his absence. Today everyone says *Shema Yisroel* and laughs. The words of the prayer sound strange.

Father is not pleased with their ears and their fingernails and starts cleaning them.

'Not everything at once,' Mother says. 'Let them go to sleep now. Let's have a bit of quiet.'

Before they turn the lights off, Aunt Hela arrives. She is dressed so beautifully, a broad-brimmed hat on her head, high-heeled shoes, long fingernails lacquered red. Father gives her a silver or golden hairpin as a present. She takes off the hat, shakes her hair loose, and puts on the pin. Father, Mother and Aunt Hela go from bed to bed distributing good-night kisses. Silence falls on the room, and the darkness is soft and gentle. The grown-ups leave the room and close the door behind them.

Reli is eight, and is keeping a diary. When Mother was taken to hospital and Father went with her and she and Izio stayed with Grandma Herrstein and Marynia, Reli had developed a severe earache. She had cried and cried all day and all night, but her parents hadn't come. They had returned with a new baby and everyone had run about around the baby. To Reli they'd said: Don't come near, don't touch, don't do this and don't do that. Izio sat in a corner and made strange motions with his mouth and hands. He had not made such strange motions before. He probably wanted to get attention, but no one came up to him. Everyone was busy with the baby.

When Reli was five, they kept reminding her that she was a big girl now. She walked beside the baby's pram, bored, and Izio walked on the other side of the pram. Everyone looked at the baby, gushing and smiling profusely, and only at the end did they deign to look at Izio and Reli too. Reli didn't like these boring walks.

Again her ears ached, and she had a high fever. Only then, when she was ill, did they all gather around her. They were truly alarmed. Perhaps they were finally sorry for all the grief they had caused her. The doctor came, Doctor Bujak (a funny name, the word meant rocking-chair), whom everyone praised. But Reli didn't let him approach her. She kicked with her hands and feet. Mother said: 'What sort of behaviour is this?! I'm really ashamed. You know you're a big girl now.'

Even when she was ill they wouldn't let her forget that she was big. It's not my fault they had me first. When the doctor left, Grandma Herrstein came. The doctors don't know a thing, she said. Someone has put the 'evil eye' on Reli and we have to get the evil eye out of her. She tied red ribbons around Reli in all kinds of places, then she opened the little door of the burning stove. Beside the stove she scattered various implements, said some incomprehensible words and made some strange gestures. Reli looked on in wonder and forgot about her earache. Grandma continued with her acts of witchcraft and mystery, and Mother stood beside her smiling. Suddenly the door opened and Father stood on the threshold. His face was very angry. Reli doesn't remember exactly what happened. Father shouted. Mother got between him and Grandma, as if protecting her. Grandma was offended, gathered up her belongings hastily, closed the doors of the stove, and went off. Father fumed and said that he would not agree to have superstitious rites performed in his house. Mother said that Grandma had only wanted to help the children.

'It's especially because of the children that I don't agree.' They quarreled. Reli's ears started aching again.

That year, when Reli was five and Izio was four, they took the baby and went to a resort village. There they lived in a white house with a sloping red roof, and Marynia would bring them water from the well. Father was not with them in the village, he came only for Sabbaths. Once, when Mother and Marynia were busy making jam and drying mushrooms, Reli and Izio went out into the yard and started playing father and mother. Reli sneaked up to Mother's room on tiptoe, and without making any noise took the baby out of its crib and took it with her to the barn, where they had built their 'house'.' The baby didn't object – on the contrary, she smiled at her little 'parents' and co-operated in their game. After some time she fell asleep without tears or fuss and the 'parents' went off to gather plants for 'dinner'. When they returned they met their mother and Marynia who were screaming and distraught.

'Ania's been kidnapped! The baby's been kidnapped!'

'The gypsies kidnapped her. The gypsies wander about around here, kidnapping children and selling them to the circus!' shrieked Marynia.

And Mother said that they had to inform the gendarmerie. Reli wanted to tell the truth, but the words stuck in her throat for fear. Izio opened his mouth but Reli pulled his arm so hard that he yelled with pain.

'Be quiet!' she said to him, herself not knowing why.

After that the policemen came and searched. They found Ania well, in one piece, and sleeping, covered with a blanket in the barn. Mother was very angry at Reli and once more reminded her that she was a big girl now.

When they returned home, after staying three months in the village, they found the whole apartment newly repainted. Father had seen to that. The children's room, which had been pink, had now been painted pale blue. She liked the pale blue better.

When she was six, Mother organized a birthday party for her. Mother baked a lot of cakes and biscuits and dressed Reli in a new dress. Grandma Herrstein's present to Reli was a small coffee set for dolls. There were six little cups and six tiny saucers, a perfect little kettle with a spout and a lid, and lovely little containers for milk and sugar, all fine and delicate miniatures. But Mother decided that it was a pity to give such a beautiful set to Reli and her dolls, and took it for herself. She placed it where 'we can all enjoy it', one of the buffet shelves in the dining-room. Reli was upset. In the afternoon she went to the buffet, and took six little silver spoons from the cutlery drawer. Reli had wanted to play with these spoons for some time, but Mother had said that these spoons were not for playing with, but for mocha. Reli decided that Mocha wouldn't mind, and took six spoons, one spoon for each of the little cups, and threw them out of the window of the children's room right into the street. Three of the six spoons were found and were brought back home, and three were lost. Mother said that Reli was unbearable. And what about Mother taking her coffee set?

Towards evening the guests arrived. Among those who came was Aunt Mania from Podgorze, with her daughter Renia, who was Reli's age, and Moniek. Moniek was already ten. He wore a skullcap, but his ritual fringes were hardly visible under his shirt, and his side-curls were hidden behind his ears. Aunt Mania didn't even taste any of the wonderful cakes. Mother swore that everything was properly Kosher, but the aunt was afraid. Moniek teased Reli. A year ago, when they too had been at that village, Moniek had threatened Izio that he would drown him in a village toilet, the creep. He talked nonsense, boasted that his uncle was also his brother-in-law, because his father's brother had marred his sister whose name was Rela, named after the same grandmother who had died long ago after whom Reli too was named. Reli didn't understand what he was talking about. But all of it together was too much for her, and so when Moniek now rushed to their rocking-horse and wanted to ride it, Reli pushed him hard and said:

'The rocking-horse isn't yours!'

He poked out his tongue at her and jeered: 'Reli Relochee/ Frightened of roaches!'

She fell upon him with clenched fists and fingernails, ready to scratch and to pinch. The mothers came running, and each of them scolded her own child. And even though Moniek was bigger than her, his mother again reminded her that she was a big girl now.

Aunt Mania asked Mother to sing a song. Everyone knew that Mother sang beautifully. Mother blushed and tried to refuse, though it was obvious that she wanted to sing. But what should I sing? Mother asked.

'I remember the lovely days of childhood,' Aunt Mania requested.

Everyone stood around the large piano. Mother sat down at the piano and started singing:

> I remember childhood times so lovely;
> A song of the past revives in my mind –
> Of fabulous fables and marvelous marvels,
> Told by old Grandma so loving and kind:
> Of the black dragon and the sleeping princess,
> Of a regiment of soldiers who fought very bravely.
>
> I heard, I listened, crying in anguish,
> O Grandma, I pleaded,
> Keep telling, tell onwards,
> Until I'm asleep, and continue in dreams,
> And from these songs so entrancing
> Draw out a legend enchanting.
>
> Years passed and a lovely young maiden
> Came to see me, visiting me.
> She offered her mouth to me to kiss her,
> And then she whispered, emotionally,
> Saying she'd never forget me, no never,
> In moments of joy and in times of woe,
> For she thinks of me always, secretly yearning,
> And I softly whispered to her
> Keep telling, tell onwards,
> Keep telling, tell of me,
> I truly love fables so dearly
> I truly love fables so dearly.

Reli thought that she would write about all these events in her diary, with an additional comment that life was difficult. Or perhaps she would write only that life was difficult sometimes ...

13 Children's Games

In Aunt Hela's room there was a special atmosphere, completely different from that in all the other rooms. It was a dark room, its only window covered by a heavy curtain through which fragments of light filtered in from between the walls of the rear of the building. This room had once been Father's work-room, and there remained in it from that time a huge desk, a deep leather armchair, and a book-case of carved wood and glass. These were items that Father had given up for Aunt Hela. She had added more feminine accessories: colored cushions, round vases, rich materials, etc. The sofa, which served also as her bed, was covered with a thick, striped, hairy blanket. Underneath it, on the floor, was a pair of golden slippers. On the great desk, various notebooks and illustrated journals were scattered. Beside the sofa there was a pile of medical journals and of novels in three languages: Polish, German, and French. Along the outer wall stood a large cabinet, part glass and part carved wood, and it hid yet another closet, which was concealed inside the wall. In this hidden closet Passover utensils were stored: pans colored purple, blue, and red, kettles, cups and plates. Aunt Hela had asked the children not to tell anyone what was in the closet. Apparently she didn't like the idea that pans and plates were stored in her lovely room.

This closet was the most secret place in the entire apartment. No one could tell that it was there, nor guess about the pans and plates patiently waiting there from one Passover to the next. The mysterious atmosphere in the room and the knowledge that behind the large cabinet there was a secret closet stimulated the children's imagination.

Aunt Hela used to go to work early in the morning,

without eating. If she were to allow herself a crisp bread-roll every day from those delivered every morning by Pan Wirt's grocery, she would need – so she said – to go to the seamstress and have all her skirts let out. She said that at work she was given a cup of tea, and this had to satisfy her until noon. She would arrive for lunch hungry as a wolf, but she would sit quietly and wait until Father had completed the blessing of washing the hands, and until Mother had given a signal or pressed the little bell to order the first course.

During the day Ania loved to steal into this room and to leaf through the books and journals scattered in it. Once she was surprised to find a cigarette butt in the crystal ashtray. Did auntie smoke?

Mother too sometimes went without breakfast. She would stay in bed, reading a book. Father said that in any case she worked too hard. But sometimes she would get up in the morning, to the fresh rolls and the aromatic coffee. Those mornings the parents would sometimes speak together about some 'he'.

'He's been here again.' Or: 'When did he come?'

'When did he leave?'

'Whom are they talking about? Who's this "he"?' Reli and Izio didn't know. Reli was already going to school, and she didn't have time for such nonsense. Izio and Ania decided that he was surely someone who lived in the secret closet hidden behind the large cabinet. More than once they had tried to move the heavy cabinet to find out who was hiding there. But the cabinet was too heavy.

Mother's eyes were red with weeping, because Grandfather was sick. 'They'll drive him to his grave,' Mother said through her tears.

'Who are "they"?'

Mother didn't answer.

He. They. Grown-ups speak in riddles and are always hiding things. They think their children are stupid.

The next day Ania went with Mother to Grandma's shop. Not far from the shop two new buildings had been erected. In one of them a new trade school for Jewish girls had been opened. It was called *Shalhevet-Amal*.[1] Here the girls were taught sewing, pattern-cutting, embroidery, spinning, and other practical trades. The other building, to which Ania had been coming twice a week since it had been erected and since she had turned five, was the Jewish center for gymnastics, the modern and streamlined center of the ZTG, the Jewish gymnastics association. Mother would accompany her to the ZTG, and on the way they would usually visit Grandma.

Grandma sat in the shop, her eyes red, because Grandfather was sick. Grandma said that the uncles were shortening his life, the way they quarreled among themselves over positions in the other big shop, the one which had 'A. Plessner and Sons' written over it. Grandfather said that only one of his sons was talented enough to be a merchant and to inherit his business. This was Uncle Marek, his youngest son. He had contacts in Manchester, Warsaw, and Lodz, and he ran the business because his other brothers, Grandfather said, had no head for business and only knew how to lose money. Wowek was a philosopher, and ought to be a professor, and as for Szajek ...

During his illness, Grandfather wrote poetry and meditations. In the margins of his volumes of the Talmud were written various interpretations that he had thought up.

Ania went to gymnastics with three of her little friends: Marysia Keller, Celina Krischer, and Dzidzia Hollender. Mother stayed in the shop with Grandma.

About an hour later Ania returned, elated, but she quickly cooled down when she saw the faces of Mother and Grandma. They were crying because the Chief Rabbi of Krakow, the admired and authoritative Rabbi Kornitzer, had died suddenly of a heart attack.

A week later Grandfather died. He had already started feeling better, and then suddenly ...

Mother was very miserable. They tried to console her, but to no avail.

'Father is Father, no one can replace him.' Her handkerchief was all crumpled and wet. Mother disappeared from home and sat *shiv'a* with Grandmother, in the apartment in

Suesser House, where she had grown up. During those seven days Father too was hardly ever at home. Marynia looked after the children. Aunt Hela sat at the table with them at breakfast too and ate rolls even though her skirt was bursting, she said.

There were many people in Grandma's apartment. Grandma, her three sons and Mother sat with their shoes off, on low chairs. Aunt Mantel, the deceased's brother, had sent a telegram of condolence. No one had bothered to read the telegram. To live in the same city and to send a telegram! What kind of a sister is she? Other telegrams arrived from other cities and from abroad.

Aunt Herzig was solemn now, for a change. She was known for her raucousness and her clowning, but this time she was quiet and sad. In the past she had used to scoff at Mother and call her strange nicknames, such as 'Bronka Stupidonka', or in better cases, 'Pani Bronislava, wife of the Graf Potocki'. Father couldn't stand her jokes and nicknames, until Mother accused him of having no sense of humor.

Today Aunt Herzig came up to Mother and said in a choked voice: 'Your father, blessed be his memory, used to give me thread on credit. That enabled me to support my family, and to cover all of Itzik's expenses. I embroidered, I sold, I collected money, and only then did I pay him. That way I could earn a living. Now I must depend on your brothers, each with his thick head, woe is me!' And she started crying.

Mother cried all the time too. Now everyone was speaking in praise of Grandfather.

He had been a wise man. A scholar. Generous. Devout and educated at the same time. He had been a good man. A good husband. A good father. A good citizen. A good soldier. Mother cried and Grandma cried.

'What use to him are all these praises now? When he was alive no one appreciated him properly.'

People came in, people went out. The two spinster sisters, the beautiful Aunt Paula and Aunt Stefa, sat in another corner, by the window, and reminisced about the childhood they had shared. How had it happened that Grandfather had become what he had become? All his brothers and sisters had become completely assimilated. His brother Henry had left Eastern Europe when still a lad, and had traveled west. He had reached Belgium, and later had gone on to America. He had married the niece of Dr Adolf Standt, a great Zionist, the right-hand man of Dr Theodor Herzl. But Henry and his wife Mary had not 'gone up' to Zion, but had sailed from Belgium to America.

Another of Grandfather's sisters, Dola, had been living in Belgium for many years now. Everyone said that Mother was the spitting image of Dola. Dola was an 'anchored wife'. That was the term used to speak of women whose husbands had left them. Dola's husband had left her in her third month of pregnancy. After his disappearance, Stefa and Paula said, their sister Dola had gone to Belgium, and told everyone there that she was a widow. Uncle Henry was still in Belgium when she arrived there with the child, and he had helped them get established and had supported them. Dola was a beautiful, pampered woman and liked to dress up in fine clothes and to sit in cafés. It had been difficult for Uncle Henry. It made him angry that the agreement of no less than 100 rabbis was needed to extricate Dola from the miserable alliance she had made with the man who had disappeared without a trace. Uncle Henry bore the burden and was annoyed that Dola didn't seem to care. Men didn't interest her because she had her son, Odon. Odon grew up quickly, fell in love with his mother, and she fell in love with him. All this was too much for Uncle Henry, and he went off to America with his Mary. When Henry's support ceased, young Odon started to work for a living. He stopped going to school and went to work so that his pampered mother could go on with her life of idling and sitting in cafes.

Grandfather had had another sister, a singer, who had sung in bars and cabarets. At the age of 30 she had committed suicide. Grandfather had never mentioned her name since.

'What's Oedipus?' Ania asked her brother Izio. They went into Aunt Hela's room and he looked the word up in the encyclopedia.

'Not "what's," but "who's".' Izio lectured Ania about

Oedipus and about the famous complex.

'We've got something like that in our family', Ania said importantly, and told her brother what she had heard about Aunt Dola and her son Odon.

Izio leafed through the encyclopedia. He was an inquisitive boy with a thirst for knowledge. Sometimes he would sit for hours reading the encyclopedia, item after item. Everything interested him. He had often heard Marynia's exclamations of 'Jesus Maria!'. Izio read up on the subject and explained to Marynia that Jesus, the Christian God, had been a Jew.

'Our Jesus a Jew?' Marynia crossed herself three times. 'Have you gone crazy? Did you fall on your head?'

He understood that it was impossible to talk with Marynia on these subjects, so he turned to Ania and gave her a lecture about the good man whose name had been Jesus. Many Jews and Greeks had followed him, because they saw him as the Messiah. But the true Messiah would come from the House of David, from the dynasty of kings. Only a few Jews had understood that and had not followed Jesus and we were the descendants of that handful, who awaited the true Messiah, and when the Messiah came that would be the end of days.

Izio and Ania rolled around on the floor of Aunt Hela's room, with the encyclopedia open beside them. Sometimes he would squeeze Ania so hard that she screamed with pain. Sometimes he would choke her and then she couldn't scream. When the end of days came, screaming wouldn't help her. She had to get used to the idea that they might lose each other. There would be total chaos, the sun would cease to shine, there would be absolute darkness. All the buildings in the world would collapse like toys, no trace of anything would remain.

'Like after the deluge?'

He thought for a moment. 'Different,' he said.

As they were rolling on the floor Izio noticed a small glittering object under Aunt Hela's bed.

He crawled on all fours towards the object and picked it up. It was a cufflink made of a fine metal, silver or white gold, an object that belonged to a man's wardrobe. Ania grabbed the cufflink from him. 'Maybe it's Father's?'

'No. It isn't Father's.'

Both of them turned to look towards the large cabinet, as if they wanted to gaze right through it into the hidden closet.

'He,' said Ania. 'It's his.'

Izio said nothing.

'Will we give this back to Aunt Hela?'

'Hocus pocus spiritus,' said Izio, and twisted his hands rapidly. 'Hop! Where's the cufflink? It's gone!'

'What have you done? Where is it?'

He smiled at her mysteriously. He placed his two hands together, the little finger of his right hand next to the thumb of the left, his right thumb to the tip of his nose, and the rest of his fingers were swaying, as if playing a flute.

'Gone.'

Mother was very worried because she didn't know what would happen to Grandma now. Who would she live with? Uncle Wowek and Aunt Adela lived in a small and shoddy apartment in Podgorze, with their son Henry, and Aunt Adela was pregnant again.

Uncle Szajek and Aunt Rachel lived in a somewhat better apartment in Starowislna (Old Vistula) Street. They too had a son, Romek, as handsome as his mother, and Aunt Rachel too was pregnant again. Conditions in both homes were very cramped, and neither had any room to spare for Grandma.

Mother, it seemed, wanted Father to suggest that Grandma should come and live with them, but Father gave not the slightest hint of wanting to do that. Mother was nervous; she shouted at the children all the time. She was sad about the situation and couldn't think about anything else.

Mother had not received anything in inheritance from Grandfather, and Father said that that was very fortunate, because otherwise she too would have got involved in the devil's dance that was going on about the inheritance. Grandma remained in her own apartment, together with Uncle Marek.

'Let's only hope that what happened to Dola and Odon in Antwerp won't happen to them.'

Now everybody spoke in praise of Grandfather, and Mother could not hold back her tears when his name was mentioned. She was very worried about Grandma, and every day, even after the days of the *shiva*[2] she would visit her in the shop.

On top of all these troubles Marynia announced that she was leaving, because she had to return to her village and her family. Her father too had died, two days after the death of the lady's father. Her family had asked her to return quickly because they were short-handed on the farm.

Marynia's little room next to the kitchen now stood vacant, waiting for its new occupant.

Aunt Hela was in a nervous state too and said that things had vanished from her room.

Mother contacted the employment bureau for household help, and they started sending candidates for Marynia's replacement. Mother believed all their stories about how quick and industrious they were and was willing to settle the whole thing there and then, but Aunt Hela said that one had to be cautious and demand letters of reference from their previous employers. They might steal things from the house. Even in Marynia's time things had disappeared.

'Marynia?' said Bronka. 'I'm positive that Marynia didn't touch anything that wasn't hers.'

'Don't be so sure,' said Aunt Hela. 'I tell you things have disappeared from my room. Expensive things.'

'What's missing?'

'It doesn't matter.'

'It does matter. We must know.'

Aunt Hela was blushing furiously. Izio pinched Ania so hard that she could barely keep herself from screaming. Mother said that if something important really was missing they would have to get in touch with the police.

'No!' the children shouted in chorus. 'Marynia wasn't a thief!' Aunt Hela, fuming, left the room.

The train moves off. Mother stands on the platform, wiping her tears. She is crying.

Mother, mother, why are you crying? What are you thinking about? What are you afraid of? That something will happen to your children? That this train will take them to hell? Trains go quickly. Some trains go off the rails, and smash into smithereens. Yes, a fatal accident might happen. A terrible disaster might occur. But accidents can happen to pedestrians too. Who can read the future? Who can know what fate awaits these sweet children? After all, one can't stop life.

If only one could stop life. These trains ...

'These trains frighten me,' Mother used to say.

The children by themselves, being taken from her. That's hard. It's hard for Mother. They're off to camp ... to summer camp.

'They're not alone,' Father would say. For two weeks he had toiled to convince Mother to agree to send the children to the summer camp in Kowaniec. 'They'll be with counselors and instructors. Trained and responsible people. We can't keep them in an incubator. They can travel by themselves this time.'

He talked to her about it until she agreed. And after she calmed down a bit and even liked the idea of having some time to herself for a while. A bit of peace and quiet. She deserved it, she said half jestingly. We never had a honeymoon, she said to Father, you started working straight away. Father always wanted to take Mother with him to the beautiful and interesting countries to which he traveled, and he never took her. It had never worked out. The home, the children, there was always something, and she had not even been to Warsaw. Mother's greatest dream was to travel to Palestine, at least for a visit. We could buy a citrus orchard there – this was one idea she tried to slip into Father's head, which was always full of other ideas. Sometimes they would start making calculations of time and money. The trip to Palestine would 'burn up' a whole week. There and backwould mean 14 days wasted. Father had no desire to sit on the deck of a ship and get a suntan.

It was then that it was decided that Mother needed a rest. The children would go off to camp at Kowaniec. Father would remain in the city, and in addition to his usual business would again take care of the renovation of the apartment, which had again fallen into disrepair. Aunt Hela would go to Paris with her friend Bianca, to see the international exhibition to be held there for the opening of the Eiffel Tower, and Mother would go to Zakopane, to a good hotel with half board.

The directors of the camp sent all the participants a list of instructions. So and so many pairs of socks, shirts, soap, a brush. Everything was organized. The counselors were two girls who were friends of the family. Nevertheless, Mother cried. It was hard to part from the children.

The participants in the camp were about 30 boys and girls, including two 'babies'. It was the 'big' children, those between ten and fourteen, who had given the tag 'babies' to Irka Orbach, the daughter of Aunt Hania and Uncle Olek, and to Ania. From all sides they heard barbed comments directed at them.

It had been stupid to send them here. Kids like them should stay at home and play with dolls.

The camp was organized with the assistance of Pani Mania Carmel, who was the director of a model Jewish kindergarten in Krakow. She had rented a many-roomed house in Kowaniec, and two kindergarten teachers had taken on the running of the camp. The house stood on a green hill on the edge of a wood, not far from a river and some water reservoirs. Around it was a vegetable garden and almond groves which blended in with the large areas of green and gold furrowed land.

Apart from Reli, Izio, Ania and Irka, there was also Renia, the daughter of Aunt Mania and Uncle Shlomo from Podgorze, who was Reli's age. There were also the children from the more distant family on Father's side – the girls Ada, Henia, and Ila Carmel, and the boys Abrasha and Zvika Carmel, and many others, all of them children of one large family.

The atmosphere of Eretz-Israel reigned in the camp. Morning exercises were conducted in Hebrew, and Hebrew words filtered into the Polish that everyone spoke. The counselors cultivated this atmosphere, and taught Hebrew songs, directed performances, and organized hikes and group games.

Only Irka and Ania felt unhappy there. Reli completely ignored the little ones so as not to damage her status in the group. Even Izio, who at home used to play with Ania and read her passages from the encyclopedia, turned his back on her here, carrying out tasks that the group had entrusted him with.

Upstairs, on the upper floor of the house, lived the 'big' ones. The 'babies' lived downstairs. Upstairs they would gather for social evenings, group singing, dancing, fun, parties at night, while downstairs there was quietness and boredom.

Upstairs, the talented Ila Carmel, energetic and nimble, would read to her audience witty skits she had written, and her sister Henia would put on solo performances, arousing everyone's wonder and admiration.

Upstairs also, Zvika and Abrasha would invent discoveries, discovering new planets, doing chemistry experiments in glass test-tubes, while downstairs the counselors would simply go from Irka's bed to Ania's to see if they'd fallen asleep.

So it happened that Irka, the one with the more initiative of the two girls, planned an escape.

Irka was a very special girl. Plump, with smooth black hair like her father Olek's, and her mother's soft velvety gray eyes. Hania's. She was so clever that the 'big' ones might have accepted her into their company to participate in all their activities. But Irka was loyal, and had a sense of justice and rightness. How could she leave a friend in trouble? Not Irka. So one day they both got up early in the morning, equipped themselves with carrots, cucumbers and apples, and went into the forest, their destination being the city, home. Ania walked listlessly behind Irka, who walked ahead, enthusiastic about the idea. For a long time they walked like this in the forest, and saw no sign of the city. Not even of a solitary house. Only tall rustling trees and frightening groaning shadows. When they were starting to feel tired, out from the trees before their weary eyes there emerged some vague long and transparent forms. The wind moved the branches of the trees and as it moved it changed the shapes of these vague forms, adding long arms that stretched forward. The leaves rustled under the children's feet, and when they stepped on them they emitted sounds like the voices of children imprisoned in the depths of the earth in Aladdin's caves.

'Oh!' yelled Ania. 'I saw a wolf! Red Riding Hood's wolf!'

'Sh ... sh ...' Irka tried to soothe her. 'There are no wolves here.'

If only those vague forms would vanish! 'Milka, our household help, told me that there are ghosts and devils, and that there's a heaven and a hell. In hell they burn people alive, they really burn them in fire, and there's smoke ...'

'That can't be,' mumbled Ania, exhausted and frightened.

'Yes, Yes,' said Irka. 'You'll see, you'll find out one day.'

'I want to go home!' Ania burst out crying. 'I want to go home to my mother. I don't want the camp. I want Mother.'

Towards evening the two girls were brought back to the camp by a patrol of local police. They were both put to bed at once. They had a high fever. The counselor telephoned Krakow and told the parents what had happened.

Again the apartment had been freshly renovated. The walls of the children's room were painted mauve this time. The furniture remained light in hue, and the door frames still had the smell of fresh oil paint. In the living room the pictures had been rearranged, with the addition of paintings by the great Polish painters Neufeld and Gierymski. The black furniture in the living room shone with a new gleam, and the philadendrum had grown a new leaf.

At the beginning of the school year Ania would enter the first grade. Izio would transfer from the little school for boys to which he had been going so far, to St Wojciech School, an institution famous for its high standard and its strict discipline. Reli would start taking private lessons in music with Professor Wilhelm Mantel, who had agreed to come and visit her at home once a week, and once a week she would visit him at the conservatorium. She would also take French lessons with Mademoiselle Gautier, who lived nearby. And Izio, in addition to his studies at St. Wojciech School, would also go to *heder*³ in the afternoons. Everyone had returned home with many experiences to relate. Aunt Hela was still in Paris, and kept sending them postcards with pictures of the Eiffel Tower and the Arc de Triomphe.

Mother was tanned, and in a good mood. She told them all, including the children, of her successes in Zakopane. She was mischievous and gay, and Father was pleased. 'You see,' he said, 'how good it is to travel alone occasionally.' And Mother said:

'You haven't even asked who courted me there.'

'I'm quite unconcerned. Barking dogs don't bite.'

'General Haller, in person.'

This name, suddenly thrown into the conversation, upset Father. He was no longer calm.

'What did you say? The man who led the pogroms against the Jews at the end of the war ...'

'The very same.'

'He ...'

'He used to move my chair for me at the dining-table at the pension in Zakopane. And he would smile meaningfully at me. He even asked if he could accompany me on my walk to "the Valley of the Sleeping Warrior". Of course I got out of it. He didn't notice that I was a Jew.'

What a strange mother. On the one hand she so wanted to go to Palestine, and on the other hand she was so delighted to tell how her Jewishness had gone unnoticed. Father became grave and sad, and deep creases appeared on his face. Mother too became serious, and said that every crease on Father's face was like the eternal road of afflictions of the Jewish people, and that his forehead was too small to contain them all. 'You see?' Mother said. 'You should have come with me and not exposed me to dangers. When will you finally keep your promise and take me abroad?'

The next day, after another postcard had arrived from Paris, and everyone was seated around the dining-table, with only Aunt Hela's place vacant, Mother said:

'His wife was at Zakopane.'

'Whose wife?' said Izio, abstractedly and innocently.

Mother didn't answer, but one could see that her gaze was turned towards Aunt Hela's vacant place. Izio pretended that he wasn't listening. He would have gladly pretended to be reading a book, but it was forbidden to read at the table. Reading at table had already been the cause of severe quarrels between Mother and Reli. Only Father was allowed to leaf through a newspaper at the table. There were different rules for parents and for children.

Izio made out that he heard nothing, and Mother said, turning to Father:

'He's in Paris on business.'

'Terrible,' Father sighed. 'How will it all end?'

Aunt Hela returned with many lovely things and presents. She had had a wonderful time in Paris, she said. She had been with her friend Bianca. 'We went to the Louvre and to Versailles and of course to Notre Dame, and to Sacré Coeur, and we walked in the Champs Elysées, and I bought myself a new coat and new shoes even though it's very expensive there.' She showed the children photographs and postcards from Paris, and there were photographs that she didn't show and quickly put in her purse. The children exchanged glances and pretended they hadn't seen.

Mother and Father didn't take part in Aunt Hela's excitement. They looked as if they wanted to say something, but they didn't say anything.

The school year had begun, and Ania didn't go to the first grade. She lay in bed in the mauve children's room, under the picture of the beautiful princess embroidered with beads the size of a pinhead. Ania had a kidney infection. It was a prolonged and tiresome illness.

Mother used to sit beside her, singing some of her songs, showing her pictures from the album, and telling her exciting stories. She wrote down for Ania all the letters of the Polish alphabet, for in Poland too children in the first grade are taught to read. And Irka, who visited Ania every day, would correct Mother. 'The teacher taught us this way, and the teacher knows better.'

Mother would swallow and say nothing, probably thinking that when she herself had gone to school she too had believed that her teacher knew everything better than her parents. For Ania's sixth birthday, Mother baked her her favorite chocolate cake. Aunt Hania and Irka brought her a present – the marvelous edition of *The Wondrous Journey on the Back of the Wild Duck* by Selma Lagerlof, and Aunt Hela gave her Janusz Korczak's *King Mati the First*.

Doctor Dora Rubinstein, of the Carmel-Rapaport family, visited twice a week, to examine Ania and give instructions for further treatment. Mother said that when she had been engaged to Father, he had once brought her to Doctor Dora's parents home. Dora had been a student at the time and had studied Latin in secret. She had completed her medical studies in the city of Brno in Czechoslovakia, and had married a doctor who was not religious and quite assimilated. Dora's face was lovely and her eyes were melancholy. She spoke quietly but authoritatively, and was always in a hurry. Once Mother had managed to make her laugh:

'I looked for you in the telephone directory. I looked under Rubinstein and Rapaport. Do you know how many Rubinsteins there are in the telephone directory? And Rapaports?!'

Then Mother sang her the song that was famous in Krakow:

'Is that Procurator Rapaport?/ Or Collector Rapaport? 'Is this Halina Rapaport?/ Or Celina Rapaport …?'

At first they both laughed, but then Dora suddenly became serious and said:

'Weintraub'? Weinfeld? Weingarten? What will happen to all these people?'

'They are the vineyards of Europe,' Mother said, pensively.

'Europe is not good soil for our vineyards.' Doctor Dora took out the instrument that measured blood pressure. Ania gave her her little arm.

'Will I be able to go to school tomorrow?' she asked. 'No, my dear. Stay in bed and go on eating food low in salt.' She turned to Mother.

'You know,' she said, 'another baby girl has been born to

my brother in the kibbutz. That's four children born to him in Palestine. "*Sabras*." And my other brother has decided to 'go up' to Eretz Israel too.'

'What, really?' Mother seemed surprised. 'What courage, to leave all the good things.'

'My brother says that he's leaving the bad things. You know, a person with undeveloped potential like him is dependent on his wife's parents. Life here, for him, is suffering. And who determines what is good for a person? Even if he doesn't fulfil all his expectations, the important thing is the strength latent in aspiration. He speaks to his son Yossi only in Hebrew.'

'What, he doesn't speak to Yossi in Polish?'

'No.'

'So how can Yossi understand?'

Mother and Dora burst out laughing and Ania pulled the blanket up over her head.

'And you?' Mother asked, serious again.

Dora looked out of the window, with her gentle eyes that were soft and yet hard at the same time. She looked out for a long while, as if there, beyond the panes, she was seeing sights that belonged to other worlds. To the world of the past or the world of the future? On the panes drops of dew had frozen. An uneven layer of frost, thick in places and thin in others, had settled on the glass, and its thick and picturesque whiteness shut out the sights of the exterior world, separating the mauve room from the world outside.

'I?' said Dora with a gentle sigh, 'I will stay here.'

Mother sighed too. Dora wrote out prescriptions, gave instructions, gathered up her instruments, said good-bye, and left.

Reli and Izio came back from school, and noise filled the apartment.

At a quarter-to-two, Hela came home from work for her three-hour lunch break.

At ten-to-two, Father came home for a one-hour break. Lunch was served at two o'clock sharp.

Then all of them – except for Ania – sat down around the

large table, which was laid out perfectly, in the lovely dining room, and the new Marynia (this one was called Marynia too) served the meal. Through the open door, delicious smells reached Ania, who lay in bed with her tasteless and boring dietetic food.

Now they knew for certain that the man from behind the cabinet really existed. Sometimes, when Mother and Father were not at home, they heard him speaking in loud quick whispers, a flowing whispering that was like streaming water: *sh-sh-sh-sh-sh-sh, sh-sh-sh-sh-sh-sh*, and *sh-sh-sh-sh-sh-sh*, very quickly, as if he was afraid that he wouldn't have time to tell Aunt Hela everything he wanted to say. Then there would be a silence, and then the children heard her whispers, quite different from his, quiet and fragmented.

The whisperings died down and again there was complete silence. The man who whispered quickly was not heard or seen, he simply vanished.

'He's probably gone back into his closet.'

'How can he breathe in there?' the children wondered.

'Maybe he's not in there at all?' Reli dared to question the concensus. 'Maybe he comes in from the outside, from the street, and not from the closet?'

'Then why is the hidden closet in Aunt Hela's room?' It was hard to know why it was there of all places. Reli shrugged. She had to get ready for Mademoiselle Gautier's visit. She would be arriving soon and would say in her sweet voice: *'Bonjour,* Reli,' and *'Qu'est-ce que c'est,* Reli?'

Mademoiselle Gautier was the French teacher who lived nearby, in the same building, on the same floor in fact, in the apartment facing theirs. She lived there with her mother, a very impressive French lady, whom the maidservants had to address as 'Esteemed Lady'. Mother used to suppress her smile when she heard Marynia talking about the esteemed lady and about Mademoiselle Gautier. The two women looked as if they belonged to a different world, as if they had stepped out of the paintings of Renoir – all they lacked were the crinolines.

'There are people for whom titles are very important,' said

Mother. 'Here, one floor below us lives Dr Stanowski. His wife never studied medicine but everyone addresses her as "Mrs. Doctor", and for her that's important, you can see it on her face.'

In the morning, before going to school, the children romped around in their mauve room, jumping from the beds and cupboards and making a noise.

'Quiet, for God's sake, be quiet,' Mother pleaded. 'Behind that wall is Madame and Mademoiselle Gautier's apartment, and below us lives Doctor Stanowski's family. Be quiet, or what will they think of us?'

Ania recalled her visits at Irka's. Aunt Hania did not allow talking even in an ordinary voices, only in whispers, for fear of disturbing the neighbors.

What were they so afraid of, these mothers?

One morning Aunt Hela came into the dining-room, dressed to go to work, in her green coat, the one she'd bought in Paris, and a very lovely green *pelouche* hat, and she looked as if she'd been crying. The children were sitting around the table, and Father was buttering rolls for everyone and pouring coffee with milk. For school he would make them sandwiches from dark bread, and between the slices he would put slices of white cheese. He said that there was no need to arouse the envy of the other children in the class, some of whom had perhaps never eaten a bread roll or tasted sausage.

'Hesiek,' said Aunt Hela, with tears in her eyes.

'Yes?' Father asked.

'Nothing,' she said, and quickly left the house.

Father sighed and went on preparing the sandwiches. Mother was still in bed, reading a book. From there she gave instructions to the children about what to wear. Ania refused to put on warm underpants and wanted to wear only short socks despite the snow and the cold. She hated winter clothes, they were itchy, and Mother always got angry.

Father finished making the sandwiches and wrapped them in white napkins.

'What's in the hidden cupboard in Aunt Hela's room?' Izio asked.

'Passover dishes, of course.'

'But apart from that?'

'Apart from that? Nothing.'

'You don't know, Father. There's a man in there,' said Ania. The knife dropped from Father's hand.

The children held their breath.

'A man there?! Don't talk nonsense! And anyway you'd better get going or you'll be late for school!'

Marynia stood in the corridor with sweaters, coats, hats and gloves. They all helped each other to get dressed.

'Come on, let's move,' Izio said angrily to his sisters, who were a long time getting ready. Reli was always looking for something – she was absent-minded and forgetful and lost mainly gloves, by the dozen.

'You need to have them tied on you with a lace, like a child in the first grade,' Marynia scoffed, and pushed the children out of the apartment. 'I wish she'd shut up, this Marynia,' thought Reli. 'Isn't it bad enough that Mother gets angry every time something's missing? It's ridiculous, the importance they attach to a pencil or a ruler.'

'March, march!' Marynia urged them on. 'Reli, don't lose your head.'

Vicious woman.

The three of them skipped down the stairs, taking them two by two. In the street the trio split up and each went their own way. Reli hurried towards the streetcar, Izio vanished into Szlak Street. Ania rearranged the schoolbag on her back and started marching.

The street was gleaming and smooth and a fierce cold pinched her cheeks and toes and fingers. She thrust her hands into a large muff which hung on a lace that ran under the collar of her coat. And if people said 'Like a baby', let them say it. Better to be like a baby than to suffer from the cold. At the corner of Lobzowska and Szlak Streets, two nuns were opening their haberdashery shop. They wore long, dark blue dresses that reached to the ground, and on their heads were blue shawls with white hems. Ania passed by them and suddenly noticed that one of the nuns was young and beautiful. Her discovery surprised her. Until now she had thought that all nuns were old and grim-faced. The young nun smiled at her and Ania returned a bashful smile. Then the two nuns turned towards the shop, raised a heavy iron shutter and opened the door. They sold exercise books and note-books, pencils, stickers and so on. Before Christmas the shop would be filled with stickers in the forms of little angels, fir trees, glinting stars, painted eggs and pink piglets. The nuns said that all the money they earned was given to the convent.

'Try to buy your exercise books in Mr Zyskind's shop,' Father had said once. 'Only if you need something urgently buy from the nuns.' On the corner of Szlak and Krowoderska was Mr Wirt's grocery. This was the shop which sent them daily deliveries of rolls and butter for breakfast.

On another corner of the same intersection, in a dark gloomy house, lived Izio's rabbi. He lived here among Gentiles. Ania had never been in his apartment, only boys were allowed to go in there. Izio said that the rabbi lived with his wife and their eight children in a one-roomed apartment with a kitchen. In this place, every afternoon, he conducted the *heder* for the few Jewish boys who lived in this Gentile environment whose parents were keen that they should study Torah. Ania walked quickly past the building. She had no desire to meet this bearded rabbi now, on her way to the school named after Teofil Lenartowicz. If now she were to turn left into Krowoderska, she would pass by a pharmacy, a women's millinery store, a cake shop and a bakery, and arrive at Father's office, where one could see through the window the large lot where he stored his timber supplies. But Ania didn't turn left. She turned right towards her school, which was right next to the 'Scholastica', another school for girls, and not far from the Municipal Theater building named after Juliusz Slowacki.

In this part of Krowoderska Street lived a friend of Ania's – Halinka Sternlicht. Every morning Halinka would look out her window, and when she saw Ania in the distance she would come downstairs and the two of them would go on to school together. Halinka's mother was a widow. Apart from

Halinka she had another daughter, and an old father, a very quiet man. She earned a living by sewing dresses and suits. Father said that it was a *mitzveh* to give her work, but Mother hesitated, and finally gave her expensive cloths to a more experienced seamstress.

Halinka and Ania walked together and crossed the little market that linked Krowoderska Street with Dluga Street. Dluga Street, as its name implied (*dluga* in Polish means long), started outside the city and ended at its center. Two streetcar lines ran along it. Dluga Street was divided, as it were, into three parts. Its beginning and end were very Polish. It connected with Grodecka Street, which led into the central market square, in the middle of which rose the famous St Mary's Church. From the high tower of St Mary's, every day at noon precisely, a special melody, broken off before its conclusion, was played, in memory of the loyal bugler who wanted to warn the city of danger but was shot to death by an enemy bullet before he had finished playing. In the market square stood tall statues of the great hero Tadeusz Kosciuszko[4] and the national poet Adam Mickiewicz. This was a place always bustling with life, the very heart of the city. The middle part of Dluga Street was very different in character. This was a very Jewish section, crammed between the two Polish sections.

In the middle part of Dluga Street, Uncle Szajek had a shop, which sold wool and embroidery threads. Once, when Ania was returning from school and passing by her uncle's shop, Father came out of the shop wreathed in smiles and in a very good mood, and invited Ania and her girlfriends into the shop. Aunt Rachel stood behind the counter, wearing a lovely woolen dress that she had knitted herself with wool from the shop. She was radiant and beautiful.

'What are you doing here, Father?' Ania asked, surprised.

'Waiting for Mother,' Father said. 'She's gone to exchange a book in the library opposite, and when she's in the library she forgets herself.'

Father bought them all cubes of filled chocolate which were called 'Domajnski Cubes'.

'What marvelous chocolate!' Aunt Rachel said and Father

offered her another cube, but she refused.

'I mustn't,' she said to Father, and both of them laughed mischievously.

Opposite her uncle's shop was the Renaissance Library, where Mother used to exchange books. Reli had a subscription of her own, and the two little librarians, the Blaustein sisters, said that soon there would be no books left in the library that Reli hadn't read. Father and Ania crossed the busy street towards the Renaissance Library. How good it was to hold Father's hand. It was so strong and secure. Ania matched her steps to Father's. She could have walked with him to the world's end, she thought. But not without him. Father said:

'It's a good thing that Aunt Rachel's in the shop. Otherwise they might lose all their money, because your uncle doesn't have a clue about running a business or looking after customers.'

Ania wondered why Father was telling her all this, for she was still a little girl and what did she have to do with such things. But it was nice to feel that Father trusted her and treated her as if she were a grown-up.

Next to the library was Mr Zyskind's little shop. Mr Zyskind was the father of Ronia, Ania's other friend. Every day she would join Halinka and Ania on their way to school. The Zyskind family, five in all, lived in a small apartment on the ground floor, adjacent to their shop. The apartment could be entered from the yard or through the shop. Mr Zyskind, who wore traditional Jewish clothes, spent his life in the shop, except on Sabbaths, holy days, and prayer times. His wife divided her time between the shop and the house. Their three daughters went to Polish schools.

The three girls, Ronia, Halinka, and Ania, walked towards their school. Halinka's mother had told her to go into Mrs Biderman's cloth shop at the end of Dluga Street to exchange a piece of light brown lining for a dark brown piece. But the shop was still closed. Mr Biderman would appear in the shop only on rare occasions. Most of his time he spent in the synagogue and in Jewish community affairs, and Mrs Biderman, a short round woman, was in charge of both the shop and the household.

'I'll have to come back here in the afternoon,' Halinka said disappointed, 'because Mother can't finish her work without this piece of lining.'

'Let's go now,' Ania said, pulling her sleeve. The three girls crossed the busy street and entered the snow-clad Planty. Here the trees slept their long winter sleep, covered by a down of soft snow. The pond where the swans swam was frozen over; the swans and squirrels had taken to their winter homes until the coming of spring.

On the other side of the Planty they could already see the theater building, and from there they did not have a long way to go. As they approached the Scholastica and Lenartowicz schools, they merged with other schoolgirls streaming from all sides and going in the same direction. All wore the same uniform: a dark blue coat with a velvet collar known as a 'monteniak', and a dark blue beret with a school badge and a class number above the forehead. The girls of the 'big Scholastica' looked down on the girls of the 'little Lenartowicz'. There were many more of them so that also made them feel more important.

When the first bell sounded, the girls took off their coats, straightened their dark blue dresses with the white collars, and went into class. Ronia, Halinka, and Ania, and two more Jewish girls – Cesia and Ada – sat in the third bench, next to each other, and all the others sat in other benches.

The teacher came into the class and the girls stood up for the morning prayer. Ronia had taught Ania how to fold her hands during prayer in a way that the two thumbs would not form a cross.

'For us it is forbidden to place our hands in the form of a cross', Ronia had said.

Everyone in class crossed themselves at the beginning and end of the prayer, and only Ania and her four girlfriends did not pray or cross themselves but just stood there doing nothing, as if they had no God.

All the teachers in the Lenartowicz school wore long dark clothes, and Mother said that they were all spinsters.

Ania's teacher avoided ever saying the words Jews or Jewess or Jews or Jewish. Instead of Jews she would say 'Israelites'. She apparently thought that this was more refined and less insulting. She would say, for example: 'On Saturdays we will not make many advances in our studies because the Israelite girls don't come to our school on Saturdays. Nevertheless I would ask the Israelite girls to visit one of our pupils who lives near her every Sunday, and to copy the Saturday lessons. I don't want there to be two levels in my class.'

Every Sunday Ania would go to Krysia Zborowska's to copy the lessons. Krysia's family would have just come home from church, and Ania didn't like to disturb them on their holiday. Krysia was generally busy and didn't trouble to explain the lessons to Ania, but she always let her copy from her exercise books. Once a week the class would be visited by a priest, the only man who ever entered this building, and he would give religious instruction. The five girls were exempt from this lesson, and they would go out into the schoolyard or into the Planty to play.

In place of this lesson they had to go to another school once a week to hear a lesson on Jewish religion. A pale and bored teacher would teach a very mixed class, made up of girls from different schools. He told them about Adam and Eve, Cain and Abel, about Abraham, Isaac and Jacob, Sarah, Rachel and Leah and about Noah's ark – all in Polish and in a very monotonous voice. The lesson was held during the girls' free time, during the hours intended for play or for reading interesting books. No wonder, then, that their absences from these lessons in religion were many, and their interest in them minimal.

Ania's teacher, Panna Zembaczynska, used to choose Ania to appear in class performances, and would have her recite poems, and on parents' evenings she would say to Mother that Ania had to improve only in mathematics. Polish she knew well, the teacher would stress.

On one festive occasion the teacher had Ania recite the popular poem by Teofil Lenartowicz, the poet the school was named after. In the performance hall sat the schoolgirls and their parents. The school headmistress, Panna Amalia Panska, sat at the piano and played a chord. Silence fell in the hall and only Ania's clear voice could be heard, reciting the poem:

> Over the Vistula's waves now flying
> The Spring's cool wind does blow.
> It flies towards my land for miles,
> To the Tatra's peaks of snow.
> Wind! Over mountains, forests, spread
> My greeting call from here!
> Upon my birthplace greetings shed
> And on Dunai's current clear.
> All roadside acacias, forest firs,
> In gardens every flower,
> And all the meadows, greet and bless,
> And the folk in every bower.
> And to these snowclad rocks return,
> To plateaus, lakes, then stream
> And greet, for me, a thousand times
> All my mountainous country.

Loud applause came from all sides, and suddenly Ania found herself in the arms of her mother, who embraced and kissed her, her eyes moist.

'I want to go home,' Ania whispered, trembling all over.

'Why be in such a hurry?'

The teacher came up to them and patted Ania on the head. Ronia, Halinka, Cesia and Ada gathered around them.

'I want to go home', Ania repeated. 'Home, home.'

In May a small altar was put up in a corner of the classroom and for an entire month the Christian schoolgirls and their teacher would gather around the altar, kneeling and singing special religious songs of a kind that were only sung in the month of May. The five Jewish girls sat quietly and waited until the end of the prayer. Then too Ania wanted to get away, to go home, or anywhere else.

* * *

'I saw him! Today I saw him! He ran away from here like a thief!' Thus Izio greeted Ania one day on her return from school.

'What, didn't he go back into the closet?'

'No.' Izio was a bit bewildered.

'Who else saw him?'

'Only me.'

'What did he look like?' Izio shrugged. 'Ordinary ...'

'Quite, quite ordinary??'

'Maybe ... maybe I didn't see very clearly.'

The school year was almost over and the summer vacation was close. Reli stubbornly demanded to be allowed to go to the Hebrew school for the continuation of her studies. The parents gave in to her pressure and hired a private teacher, whose task was to prepare Reli for entrance examinations in Hebrew subjects.

Izio had stopped going to the *heder* because he had caught pediculosis there. Apart from which, the rabbi had little patience, and pulled his pupils' ears very hard. So they had hired another rabbi for him, who visited him at home twice a week and prepared him for his *bar-mitzvah*.[5]

Mother arranged the schedule and made sure that the music lessons didn't clash with the Hebrew lessons, and that Mademoiselle Gautier didn't clash with the rabbi.

14 Hebrew Gymnasium

Reli was a very special girl. As a little child she had been very pretty, then, in puberty, she had as it were gone into a cocoon, and then, suddenly, she became a beautiful butterfly.

In her childhood her parents had filled her life with as many occupations and studies as possible. The child was full of contradictions. She was afraid to ride a bicycle or to swim, but excelled at mountain climbing, ice-skated beautifully, and was a champion group-ball player. She was absent-minded and forgetful and Mother was often angry at her. Mother liked everything to be organized and thought-out and Reli scoffed at Mother and her pettiness. When Mother commented on how she hadn't folded her clothes nicely, she would reply in a gushing voice:

'I suppose you want me to be like you? To fold them like you fold your sheets and to tie them with pink ribbons?!'

Mother's innocent blue eyes would expand in anger and astonishment, and shouts and weeping would fill the air. There were a thousand-and-one reasons for the quarrels between them. And then Father would appear and always, always, without going into the matter, he would take Mother's side. When Father appeared in the arena, it was no longer possible to shout or be impudent, even the tears seemed to stop. Father would get angry at Reli because of her absent-mindedness, while forgetting how absent-minded he himself was. Once, when he was in Italy, he wrote letters to Mother without putting down the sender's address. Then in his letters he would complain sorely about the fact that Mother didn't reply and didn't keep him informed about what went on at home. And she, to her grief, wrote letters that remained at home because she didn't know where to send them. Did Father forget all these things when he got angry at Reli for being forgetful and negligent? Reli lived in a world of books and imagination.

Once, on a Sabbath Eve, they all sat at the festively set table. Five Sabbath candles burned in the large candlestick and two more in ordinary silver candlesticks, freshly browned *hala* loaves baked by Mother winked from a basket covered with a white napkin, their smell stimulating the palate. And then Father turned to Reli and asked her to bring fish to the table, for the first course. Father, who was dressed in his good suit, had gone with Izio to the *mikveh*, the ritual bath, earlier in the evening, and then the two of them had gone to the synagogue in Dluga Street, where Father had a permanent place, and they had returned from the synagogue with two strangers, young men visiting the city as guests of the community, whose families lived in one of the nearby villages. All sat at the table, which was immaculately set. Reli sat in her place, her thoughts floating in other worlds, when she suddenly heard Father's strange request that she bring the fish to the table.

'Where are the fish?' Reli asked, obediently.

'Well, where can fish be?' Father replied.

The two strangers chuckled. Izio and Ania became tense. Mother made a movement as if she wanted to get up and call Marynia to bring the fish (on Sabbaths they didn't ring the little bell beside the table), but Father stopped her. Aunt Hela made a sign to Reli, pointing towards the kitchen, but Reli didn't catch the movement, and asked automatically: 'Where?'

Father put on an amused expression and said: 'Reli, think a little, where can cooked fish be? Perhaps in the night-closet in the bedroom?'

To everyone's amazement, Reli got up without thinking and went to the night-closet in her parents' bedroom, came back empty-handed, and declared in all seriousness:

'No. Not there.'

Everyone burst out laughing and Reli blushed to the roots of her hair. Only then did she grasp that Father had 'pulled her leg', and that she, instead of thinking about practical things, had continued day-dreaming, and this was the outcome.

In the meantime, Marynia served the fish. Reli sat there ashamed, silent sobs stifling her throat. On top of this she had heard a whispered sigh from one of her parents: What will become of this child?

This same Reli, the absent-minded dreamer, who would have tantrums when she was disturbed, had become everyone's pride and joy. Her parents had become reconciled to her weaknesses, and they saw her future as most promising. She loved studying and her achievements were brilliant. It was evident that she had to continue at high school and pass her matriculation examinations and then go on to study at the university.

It was Reli who stubbornly requested to be allowed to go to the Hebrew high school, or gymnasium, as high schools in Poland were called. Her parents had hesitations. A Polish gymnasium could be cheaper, even free, for a talented pupil like Reli. On the other hand, she would be obliged to attend on Sabbaths and Jewish holy days too.

Reli was very attracted by the Hebrew gymnasium, but her parents had several grounds for hesitation. The co-education practiced there, boys and girls together, was something new, something they were not accustomed to. The Zionist education too worried them. Mother was a Zionist herself, and was very sorry that her family had not 'gone up' to the Land of Israel. But Reli alone? What would happen if the girl suddenly wanted to migrate to Palestine with a youth group as she herself had wanted to when she was young? Then the family would disintegrate? This had already happened in several families, which were not at all happy about their children's decision to 'go up'. Mother wanted to preserve the unity of the family, and so did Father. But Reli finally got what she wanted. She passed the entrance examinations, which included Hebrew studies at a high level, and was accepted into the gymnasium. And so a new chapter in her life began. The school was still located in its old building, while a new and modern building was being erected beside it. The pupils liked their old school building, and affectionately called it *buda*, which means a ruin. A kind of anthem had been composed – or had, it seemed, almost composed itself – in honor of the old *buda*.

Our *buda* is very good, say we/ Our *buda*'s where we like to be/ Here we've had our happiest hours/ Dearest *buda* of ours.

Reli found a different climate here to that which had reigned in the Polish school. Other winds blew here. About 1,000 children went to the elementary school and the gymnasium, and all of them knew each other. The classes were mostly mixed. In Reli's class there were several girls who, like her, had come to the gymnasium from other schools and had taken the entrance examinations in the Hebrew subjects, and had difficulties in these at the beginning. The teachers and the other pupils showed understanding towards the newcomers and helped them to catch up to the class's level.

Reli was intoxicated by the free atmosphere and was happy that she was making new friends. Before coming here she had had only restrained relations with grown-ups and children of her own age alike, and here she was immediately infected with feelings of identification, belonging, and brotherhood. In front of her sat Stefa and Esther. Esther, who was plump, was very friendly, and was always offering Reli delicacies that she brought from home. Reli always forgot books and other things, and it wasn't long before the whole class knew how absent-minded she was. Once, after a physical exercises lesson, she came home wearing a skirt that was not hers, one too that was short and wide for her, without even noticing.

'Take my book,' Esther would suggest to her. 'The teacher won't be angry at me. I can forget a book for once. You've already gone far beyond the limit.'

Reli would arrive at school at the last minute, huffing and puffing from having run so hard. Esther, in contrast, would arrive at the school gates even before dawn, and would wait in the freezing cold, stamping her feet in the snow, until the janitor deigned to let her into the heated building. The janitor was a very authoritative man, squat, red-cheeked, who proclaimed every morning in Esther's ears that 'The Headmaster does not permit pupils to run around in the building without the supervision of teachers.'

This janitor had risen in status the year before, when he had become the father of triplets, and had received the present of a triple perambulator from Marshal Pilsudski himself.

Esther would prepare her school-bag meticulously every evening, while Reli would carry all her books and exercise books with her every day, because she didn't remember the timetable. Once it even happened that she came into class at the last moment, and her school-bag remained outside, in front of the classroom door. The school-bag vanished: someone had taken it to the headmaster's office. The headmaster accused Reli of planning to play truant. That year Reli got a 'Satisfactory' in Conduct, instead of her usual 'Praiseworthy'. This was a great shame, but at home the incident was passed over lightly and Father laughed and said:

'Let her forget her school-bag. So long as she doesn't forget her head.'

Esther and Stefa stood by her loyally even in these difficult moments. The trio became a 'triumvirate', dedicated to each other and ready to go through fire and water for each other.

Other boys and girls in the class included: Irka and Berta, Pepka and Rutka, Janek and Fricek, Poldek and Beniek, Dola, Lidka. Each child had their own world, their own dreams. And they had teachers they were proud of. There was Professor Katz, who taught Hebrew subjects and classical languages – Latin and Greek. Apart from teaching at the gymnasium he was a lector at the Jagielonska University, and everyone knew that he could have had a distinguished career there. The pupils respected him highly, though this did not stop them from making jokes at his expense. The Professor's entrance into the classroom was a ritual in itself. The pupils stood to attention and he would scrutinize them closely over the spectacles he wore low on his nose, and then would march to the rostrum. Before mounting he would bend down and tie his shoelaces. Then he would motion to the pupils that they should sit. He would take off his spectacles, take a handkerchief out of his jacket and wipe them pedantically for a long while. He would replace the handkerchief in his jacket, and with a vigorous gesture stretch his arm to look at his wristwatch. Then he would sit down in his chair, and begin the lesson. From the moment he came into the classroom until he went out there was absolute silence in the classroom. Would he tie his shoelaces, wipe his spectacles, look at his wristwatch? The lesson itself would be enthralling. Katz's Latin was a living, dynamic language.

Other teachers in the gymnasium were good professors too, some of them great humanists. Once a month a concert was held. Famous artists from outside the school appeared, and young talents from within the school, of which there was no lack, were also given a chance to appear.

Reli came home late. She hurriedly took her place at the table. Only then did Father pronounce the blessing, and everyone began to eat. Reli did not know if Father was angry with her or not. After the meal, Aunt Hela invited her to her room. They sat down on the sofa that was covered with a striped blanket, and Reli felt heavy-hearted. Aunt Hela went to the cabinet, brought out a box of chocolates, offered it to Reli, and smiled. 'Life is hard, isn't it?' she said. Only then did Reli begin to think that her own troubles were not real ones, and if Aunt Hela said 'Life is hard', she was probably thinking of her own life. She was still beautiful, true, but no longer so young – 30, or maybe 35 – and she still didn't have a home of her own, or a child. Reli looked at the large cabinet and it seemed to her that something was moving inside it. Aunt Hela followed her gaze.

'What do you see there?'

Reli became embarrassed and blushed. 'You know, Aunt Hela, they say that in the other closet, the one behind this cabinet – they say that someone lives in there.'

'Someone lives in there?!' Aunt Hela became unusually upset. 'Who says such nonsense?'

Reli's embarrassment increased. It was obvious that everything that Izio and Ania imagined was stupid, but if she informed on them they would hate her. As it was they accused her of being snooty, of being against them and not with them. Why on earth had she started talking about the closet?

'Sometimes a guest comes to me,' Aunt Hela said suddenly, her voice hoarse and strange. 'Izio saw him once, this guest of mine. It was probably he who told you this nonsense about someone living in the closet.'

Reli nodded. She felt very close to her aunt. She wanted to tell her that at school too there were all kinds of tragedies that stemmed from relations between the sexes. The red-headed teacher, for example … but what was the use of talk. Those examples wouldn't make Aunt Hela feel better. How could she console her? They sat together in silence.

'When you're older, Reli, I'll tell you some time, maybe you'll understand me. Your father and mother don't want to understand.' Aunt Hela said this in a quavering voice, and Reli felt a twinge in her heart. She understood that her aunt was very lonely and had no-one to share her thoughts with. She apparently loved someone who could not give her what every woman wants – open friendship, honor, a home, a family. Reli almost said: 'So leave him, this man who comes to you, forbid him to come, try to forget him, he isn't worthy of you, don't let him ruin your life, make him decide, make him stop getting the best of both worlds.' But she didn't say anything. She was wise enough to understand that these were matters connected to the feelings of the people concerned, and that it was very difficult to get to the bottom of them. Reli understood that it was better for her to keep out of it. And Aunt Hela sat there, stooped, sunk in thoughts known to her alone. Suddenly she shook herself and said:

'What shall we buy your mother for her birthday?' Right away Reli forgot her troubles, the tension that existed between her and her mother, the anger she had felt at her parents today when they reacted to her coming late with such a distressing silence, and immediately responded, willing to cooperate in preparing a surprise for her mother's birthday. She would collect all her savings, and Izio's and Ania's too, and they would borrow the balance from Father. And they would buy a present for Mother, as they did every year. That always made her so happy.

Time passed quickly in Aunt Hela's room. They planned what they would buy, and when, until it was time for Aunt Hela to conclude her lunch break and return to her job at the institute. They parted warmly. The little secret had woven strands of mutual trust between them.

Life flowed on comfortably. So at least it seemed during those days. Something dreadful divides me from my memories. Great blows descended on everything, on memory too.

The world collapsed and was erased. Very slowly the days pass. They pass and shape our souls. They plow deep into our souls, to the very bottom of the soul and the heart. And then everything renews. Detail after detail, event after event, they return, and the sights reappear on the screen of the memory – the home, the family, the city.

Small worries and great ones – small joys – festivals and birthdays.

Mother lay in the wide bed in the fine bedroom that overlooked the monastery garden surrounded by a concrete wall. Under her head were two large pillows and an additional small cushion called a *jasiek*. When Mother was reading a book she put the *jasiek* under her head. She was wearing a night-gown with fine embroidered stripes, and was covered with a soft down blanket. She was pretending to be asleep. You could see that she was pretending, for her eyelids fluttered slightly and a faint smile hovered over her lips. The children too pretended not to be aware of this. They stood at the foot of the bed. On the wall opposite was a large mirror attached to a dressing-table, on which stood bottles and jars with pink water and fragrant blue creams. The bed, and Mother on it, were reflected in the mirror, so everything looked double: the room, the children, the flowers and the presents, and Father and Aunt Hela. Aunt Hela gave Reli a gentle push.

'Forward,' she said, in a tone of encouragement.

Reli had prepared a song in honor of Mother's birthday. Mother should live many many years, that was what Reli's verses said.

How many years do you still have to live, Mother? Who can prophecy? Mother opens her eyes. They are moist and gleaming at the corners. 'What a surprise!!' she says. 'How did you know it was today?'

Now she is no longer pretending, she is really embarrassed.

So it was every year.

Mother jumps out of bed and Father helps her put on her dressing-gown. Father and Mother kiss – a shy, restrained kiss. The children smile generously.

'Until a hundred and twenty,' they all sing.

Then they all hurry off, because they have to go to school and to work. Only Ania is still trying to make up her mind what to wear.

Mother is generous today, so Ania makes demands.

'Wear what you like, Aniusia.'

Sometimes they speak about politics at home. Recently there has been more and more mention of Hitler.

'The man is insane,' Father has ruled, more than once. It could be sensed that the grown-ups were very worried about this madman, and followed his speeches, writings, and actions with apprehension.

'In a state like Germany such a leader won't last long. True, many are getting enthusiastic and are swept along after him. Many have fallen into his net, but this wave will surely pass and everything will calm down.'

And then they would speak of the homeland of Schiller and Goethe, of men of culture and science, of civilization and of highly developed intellectual life.

15 'Jews – to Palestine!'

'The Germans have Hitler and we have Marshal Pilsudski.'
Irka said this to Ania, and explained that Hitler was insane while Pilsudski was a kind of good grandfather.

True, he ruled from above, but he cared about the citizens of the state. Even the anti-Semitic Endeks were afraid of Marshal Pilsudski and did not perpetrate violence against the Jews.

Everyone admired Marshal Pilsudski. In offices and schools his picture was everywhere. A broad-shouldered man in military uniform, with a thick mustache and eyebrows, his army jacket decorated with many medals.

Pilsudski's influence was everywhere in evidence. To many people he was the all-powerful leader of Poland. No decision on internal or external affairs could be made without his agreement. But he knew how to give the people the feeling that they were partners in the decisions. He would receive deputations of youth and children and minorities. And there was a feeling that there was an attentive ear and a guiding hand.

Then suddenly Jozef Pilsudski died, and Poland was frozen in by shock.

The whole country donned the black of mourning. Millions of schoolchildren wore black armbands, millions of black flags fluttered in the air, as if a black cloud was hiding the golden sun. The good and strong father of Poland's citizens had passed away.

Irka was very agitated. She stood in the doorway of her cousins' house, a black ribbon on the lapel of her coat and a black armband around her sleeve. Her school badge and class number, both made of gleaming metal and attached to her hat, were also covered with patches of black. Even on her plaits she wore black ribbons. Everyone looked at her in astonishment. Mother said that it was not a Jewish custom to tie black ribbons on one's hair, and Irka said that all the girls in her class did it and she was not going to be an exception.

The streets were thronged with people. Masses of people were streaming to Krakow from all over the country and from abroad. The radio played mournful melodies and Chopin's funeral march, and informed the public about arrangements for the funeral.

On the Marshal's last instructions, his heart was to be buried in Vilna, his birthplace, while his body, without the heart, was to be buried in the Wawel Palace in Krakow. In all the schools studies were suspended, and children were prepared for the funeral. Choirs of children sang:

It isn't true that you are dead
It isn't true that you're in your grave.
The whole land of Poland weeps for you
The whole land of Poland mourns today.

Irka said that the funeral procession would pass by their house.

Irka's parents had moved recently from their first small apartment on Topolowa Street to a spacious apartment of four large rooms in Zwierzyniecka Street. Now everyone hurried to Hania and Olek's apartment, to watch the funeral procession. By one wide window stood the children: Ania, Izio, Irka, Reli, Renia from Podgorze, and Izio's good friend Wlodek. At the other window the grown-ups were cramped together. From Podgorze, with Renia, had come Uncle Shlomo's nieces, Pani Regina and Pani Frania. The sons of these ladies were students at the *yeshiva* of the Rabbi from Bobowa, but their mothers, although they observed the precepts, were modern women in every way. Now both were wearing black clothes, black stockings and black shoes, black hats with black veils, black gloves and black handbags.

Below, the funeral procession advanced slowly. Distinguished visitors had come from far away – kings, presidents and heads of state. Companies of army and police, squads of cadets, representatives of churches and novices in the clergy, classes of pupils bearing large wreaths, and mounted cavalry. All streamed in exemplary order towards the famous Wawel Palace. The procession went on for many hours, until finally the street was quiet and was opened to ordinary traffic.

Regina and Frania shook hands with their weary hosts and returned to Podgorze with Renia.

A short while after the funeral, work began on the erection of a memorial mound to honor Jozef Pilsudski. One memorial mound had already stood in Krakow for many years, honoring the memory of the hero Kosciuszko. On a clear day, when there was no mist on the horizon, the Kosciuszko mound could be seen from all parts of the city. It was white in winter and green in summer. Weeds had grown on it, with long dense stalks, their heads swaying in the wind and their roots gripped firmly in the earth. Pilsudski's memorial mound would be bare for several years, until there too weeds would strike root, and rise up upon it with high stalks and even glorious flowers.

The memorial mound was built quickly.

Irka, who lived not far from there, visited the site every day, to load a wheelbarrow with rich earth and push it up the mound which grew from day to day, from hour to hour.

'It's a civic duty,' Irka explained to Ania. Men and women of all ages, soldiers and civilians, students and schoolchildren, stood in line for wheelbarrows, trying to take up at least one barrowful, to add some earth to the growing mound.

Izio and his friend Wlodek had already done four rounds. The nimble boys glanced contemptuously at the girls and without wasting any time went up with full barrows and came back with them empty. Wlodek's face was serious, concentrated on the work. At home he was called Wowek, in the street Wlodek. He would address Izio without calling him by name.

Irka and Ania did the same. They were cautious. Not everyone had to know.

The Jews of Kazimierz did not arrive to help in the raising of the mound.

271

'You see,' Irka said, 'Jews don't know how to do physical work.'

'Who told you that?'

Irka shrugged. 'It's a known fact.'

Ania got annoyed. 'Maybe those are just prejudices. See how Izio and Wlodek work like demons.'

Towards evening the four of them turned to go to their homes. The pyramid-like mound stood behind them and in its huge shadow they looked like little helpless ants.

Yesterday Izio had come home from school without his glasses. In a fight with his classmates he had received some blows and his glasses had got broken. The teacher told everyone to return to their places and called the class to order, but he didn't punish the guilty ones. Izio came home feeling insulted and degraded, and this hurt him more than the physical pain.

Mother tried to discover what had happened but he was unable to explain and just said:

'I was alone ... by myself. And they were many ...'

Mother washed his wounds and said to him in a pleading voice: 'I've told you not to provoke them. I've told you to get out of their way. You don't know them yet.'

When Mother moved off to change towels and bring bandages, Izio said with his teeth clenched:

'I don't want to! I don't want to! I don't want to!' His eyes looked strange without the glasses. First they were watery and helpless, and now they were aflame, shooting fire and arrows.

'They won't start with me again! They won't make up tales about me, I won't let them!'

Mother came back with the bandages. Reli and Ania stood to the side, holding hands.

Ania thought how good it was that girls weren't violent.

It's a good thing I don't wear glasses, she thought. Reli burst out:

'You should send him to the Hebrew school too, where he won't be the only Jew in his class!'

Tears came to Mother's eyes.

272

'I'll speak with Father,' she said in a faint voice.

In the afternoon, when Wlodek came to visit Izio, the two friends whispered together for a long time. They went to the bookcase, took out an encyclopedia and searched for something among its pages. Then they replaced the volume, returned to the front room, and started working out a defense plan.

'Most important, we have to have a communications instrument, a kind of telephone between our homes,' said Wlodek. They began working out a way to make such an instrument. 'The kids in Ditlowska Street and Kazimierz don't need a communications instrument, because they live near each other and there's lots of them. But here, in this area, there's only the two of us.'

'We have to inform each other immediately about any suspicious occurrence, and any approaching danger.'

One day a huge inscription appeared on the wall of the monastery opposite:

JEWS – OUT! JEWS – TO PALESTINE!

Izio and Wlodek sensed that they were too late.

Mother always said: 'It doesn't matter what the others do, you should be good children, and keep out of the others' way.' It was as if she had said: 'Shrink, become dwarfs, erase yourselves, vanish.'

It was an especially beautiful day. The sun shone with a warm radiance and a pleasant breeze caressed all things and spread the scents of spring. But the inscription on the wall kept the children inside their rooms. This inscription had lowered their spirits and they no longer felt happiness at the sight of the wall and the monastery garden outside their window.

Only when Passover came did their hearts expand and their spirits rise.

The large cabinet in Aunt Hela's room was moved and the way cleared to the closet that contained the various Passover dishes and utensils.

Reli, Izio, and Ania helped to carry the colored dishes and completely ignored the anonymous man who was supposedly hiding in the closet. They kept silent on this and even felt ashamed that they had uttered such childish and ridiculous suppositions.

On Seder night Father looked like a real king. Wearing a white shirt embroidered with gold, he reclined expansively on the sofa, which had been brought up to the table especially, and leaned back on a great cushion. Before him was the Passover bowl with all the requirements, and a silver goblet for the Prophet Elijah.

Izio asked the four questions with a pure Sephardi accent: *'Ma nishtanah halaylah hazeh mikol haleylot?'* ('Why is this night different from all other nights?')

Father was surprised and probably said to himself that it must have been Reli who had taught him to ask the questions in modern Hebrew pronunciation, as Hebrew was spoken in Palestine and as it was taught at the gymnasium.

The children stole the *afikoman* with the help of Aunt Hela, and bargained over the present they would return it for. Father ate the bitter herb without pity for himself. He cried bitterly as he ate the pungent herb. 'So we must do,' he said, 'in memory of the disasters that visited our people in Egypt.'

Father read the *Haggadah* loudly and emphatically in the holy tongue, and Mother and Aunt Hela took turns in translating what he read, about slavery, decrees, and about the exodus from Egypt.

'The boys at school said that we Jews drink the blood of Christian babies on Passover.'

Ania's eyes broadened, and the piece of *matzah* that was in her mouth stuck in her throat. Had she heard right?

Reli burst out laughing. Mother shuddered and Aunt Hela said: 'Don't spoil our celebration.'

'Why do they say that?'

Father coughed and the tears caused by the bitter herb streamed down his cheeks.

'They're jealous.'

'I asked you not to spoil our celebration,' said Aunt Hela. 'I wish that in the years to come we'll be able to sit down to a Passover table in Jerusalem.'

The word 'Jerusalem' sent a tingle down everyone's spine. All of them looked at Aunt Hela with admiration. Before Passover, Mother had told them that in the past Aunt Hela had had an internationalist and class-conscious world outlook. She had believed in an 'internationale' of working people: that working people from all over the world, regardless of race, religion, or nationality, would unite and build a new and better world. But Aunt Hela's socialist friends had, one by one, taken their position under the national banner, and then she too had begun to take an interest in the fate of the blue-and-white flag. Now she was a serious reader of the Jewish Zionist newspaper in Krakow, the *Nowy Dziennik* ('New Daily'), which was edited by an excellent journalist, Mr David Lazar.[1] For Passover, the newspaper had brought out a special supplement. And during the *Seder* Aunt Hela interspersed Father's reading with selected passages from this supplement.

Mother wanted to compensate Father for the bitterness of the bitter herb, and Izio for the blows he had received at school, and Aunt Hela for her disappointment with the 'Bund' movement. For the *Seder* dinner she had prepared gefillte fish, roast duck, and dumplings. The apartment was sparkling clean: all the corners that had been cleared of leaven had also been cleaned of dust. In the kitchen, during all the eight days of Passover, there stood a bowl full of hard-boiled eggs and a large pan of beetroot *borszcz*, into which Mother would put boiled potatoes. The potatoes absorbed the color of the beets and had a special taste, the taste of Passover, and the distinctive smells of Passover filled the house. In the afternoons, Father would crack large nuts. He would draw the soft fruit out of their shells and distribute them equally among his children.

The inscription had not disappeared from the monastery wall, but they had somehow got used to its existence.

The month of May came. The last of the snow thawed and the world appeared to be washed in radiance, blooming with flowers.

The city markets were flooded with lilacs and morning-glory and dozens of other kinds of flowers. The Planty filled with strollers, young mothers who showed each other their new babies, who had been born in the winter and had not yet seen the glory of a sunny world.

On the 3 May, Poland's Constitution Day, the traditional military parade, a very impressive affair – was held – even after Pilsudski's death. Most of the parade marched along the Blonia, the wide boulevard beside the Rudawa that led to the grove known as the 'Quiet Nooklet'. The children of Krakow, like all children, loved to watch the colorful demonstration. All the more because on the way one could get onto a carousel and enjoy the wild spinning, or mount a hired donkey, or even just lick one of the large Italian ice-creams that were sold in the streets.

To feel summer in the air. To dream of the approaching vacation.

One day, on her return from school, Ania found the apartment filled with guests she didn't know. She sneaked in. Beside the table in the children's room sat two women who were probably about Mother's age, but their clothes were old-fashioned and shapeless, and perhaps that was why they looked a lot older than her.

By the window stood a lad of about 17 years, wearing a black *capota*. From under the black hat on his head, sidecurls streamed. When she came into the room he turned his head towards her and she noticed that the sidecurls swayed with every move he made. He quickly turned his gaze away and, embarrassed, went back to looking out of the window.

On Reli's bed lay a young woman of about 20. She was very thin.

Ania had never seen such a thin person in her whole life. For dinner, the table in the dining-room was set for nine people, but only the two older women accepted the invitation. With slow, uncertain steps they approached the table and sat down. The thin young woman asked to be left alone, and not to be offered food or drink, while the lad with the sidecurls agreed to eat a hard-boiled egg and to drink a glass of water, and no more than that.

Father and Mother and Aunt Hela tried to be warm and friendly to the two strange women, and attempted to encourage them to talk. The children felt uncomfortable.

'They're not strangers,' Father said. 'They're relatives of ours, and for as long as they need to be in Krakow, our home is their home.'

Gradually more details became known. The lad with the sidecurls was called Meir, and the thin young woman was called Rela, like our Reli, after the same grandmother. Meir and Rela's father had been Menashe, Hesiek's brother, and he had died as an Austrian soldier during the First World War. One of the women – the shy one whose name was Haicia – was Uncle Menashe's widow, and her sister Mircia was her guardian.

Father gave instructions for all necessary arrangements to be made to make the guests feel at home.

'For many years Menashe and I shared the same bed. It's unthinkable that now, in my spacious home, we can't find room for his wife and children,' Father said.

Ania was moved into her parents' bedroom, and her bed was given to the thin Rela. Aunt Hela vacated her room for her sister-in-law Haicia and her sister Mircia, and moved into the children's room with Rela and Reli. Meir and Izio slept in the living-room. The whole apartment was turned upside-down.

Father and Meir spoke Yiddish with each other, and the children didn't understand a word of their conversations. Rela lay in bed most of the time, her face to the wall. It was because of her that they had all come to the city, to consult with their relatives and with doctors and specialists. For years they had held back, but recently things had become unendurable. Rela refused to go on living.

Stefa and Esther came to visit Reli. Today of all days, when the apartment was full of guests. They had come to set a time and a place for a meeting of their branch of the *Akiva* movement, a secular Zionist movement (not the *B'nei Akiva*) to which most of the pupils at the Hebrew gymnasium belonged.

Father didn't want to give his agreement to meetings of any kind. 'Not in our home,' he would say. 'That's not what you go to the gymnasium for. At school one should study, not get involved in politics.' In vain, Reli would explain that these meetings took place outside school hours and outside the school building, and therefore his agreement was needed if she wanted to invite members of the movement. Father was adamant: all this activity took time and energy which would be better spent on studies.

'Do you know anything about ostriches?' Reli asked Esther and Stefa. 'My parents are like ostriches – they don't see anything around them. They want to raise nice well-groomed children, polite and educated, but unprepared for life. My parents don't understand a thing about the need to get organized to struggle for something. My father doesn't know what a youth movement is, he was never a pupil, he was never young.'

The girls became grave.

'You're going too far in your criticism of your parents,' said Stefa. 'Your father's still young. And he's not a fool. He'll understand if we explain to him. I'll speak to him.'

'Let me speak with your mother,' Esther volunteered. 'You said yourself that when your mother was a girl she was in a Zionist movement.'

'Mother won't do anything without Father's agreement. That's what she's like. Apart from which, there's no point in talking to them now. The house is full of guests, we have some poor relatives staying with us.'

The word 'poor' had slipped from her mouth and she was immediately sorry she had said it. Fortunately for her, Stefa and Esther were involved in an important consultation and hadn't noticed her slip of the tongue. Reli accompanied her friends to the staircase and went downstairs with them. On the ground floor, to the right, there was a way out into the street through a large gate, while to the left several steps led to a small gate that opened on the courtyard. By the small gate stood a slender girl, about the same age as the three of them. Her hair was frizzy and she had freckles on her nose. She stood in the dimness of the staircase, in the shadiest corner, withdrawn, waiting. Reli stood with her back to her and spoke in a lively tone to her friends.

'So as I said, that it's impossible at our place this week.'

'That's not the end of the world. We'll find a place.' And they left.

The frizzy-haired girl stepped out of her hiding place and stood in front of Reli.

Oh, are you there? I didn't see you.'

'I'm here, and you saw me very well; you just pretended not to. You're ashamed of me when your rich friends come to see you.'

Reli did not try to deny this. A deep blush flooded her face.

'Why do you say that?' She didn't know what to say.

'I've noticed it. When you're bored, I'll do. You visit me, and you're glad when I visit you. But when they come to you, your pals from the gymnasium, I'm a nuisance.'

Reli was silent. It was all true, yet she didn't feel guilty of anything. It was true that she liked her friends from the gymnasium, and that in a different way she also liked Felka, her frizzy-haired neighbor. Everything had its place.

'That's not true,' Reli defended herself. 'I'm not ashamed of you. You can come and visit me anytime, even now. You see, I've sent them away, and you can come. Want to?'

The girl looked at Reli with a suspicious glance. Suddenly she smiled.

'What difference does it make, I was just talking nonsense. Come to my place.'

They went into the yard and from there to a small apartment on the ground floor. This was where Felka lived. Thanks to her, Reli knew something about poverty. Six souls lived here, cramped in one room and a kitchen. The kitchen also served as a work room: here they sewed gloves and socks on contract, for the few pennies that various manufacturers paid for this kind of work.

Felka's parents had arrived in Krakow from Eastern Poland, from a place that had belonged to Russia and which, until the end of the war, had been known as 'the Pale of

Settlement'. Her father had fled from there, but he used to say that the Russians of today were different from the Russians of those times. Jew-hating, cities of slaughter, pogroms, the Pale of Settlement – all these things belonged to the past. To a different time. Today, he used to say, today Russia is my ideal.

Felka told Reli that her Father was a zealous communist. In deep secrecy she confided that several times he had served prison sentences in Poland for forbidden political activity. The Polish regime persecuted him for being a communist. The Polish market persecuted him for being a Jew, or perhaps for both reasons. Thus most of the time he had no work. His wife, his sisters-in-law, and his children worked to support the family. They knew that anything he tried his hand at would fail. He had no luck.

'My father hates the rich Jews,' Felka confessed to Reli. 'He says that they are bringing disaster upon the world.'

Reli felt hurt.

'Only rich Jews? And those who are not Jews can't be rich?' Felka had no answer. It was too complicated and they preferred to talk about things closer to their hearts. About volleyball, for example, or about another ball game that was called 'war of nations', or about film stars. Movies starring Shirley Temple, the child prodigy whom all the world's children were crazy about, were not for them any more, the girls decided. They talked about Deanna Durbin, Greta Garbo, Jeanette Macdonald. And also about Polish movies such as 'The Leper Woman', 'The Deluge', and 'The Fir Princess'. There was no lack of topics for conversation.

Here they didn't eat buttered rolls. Here they would cook a hot gruel in a large pot and distribute portions to every member of the household in a deep plate, without ceremony.

Felka's mother liked Reli, and as usual gave her a broad smile. Reli was grateful to this good-hearted woman for not condemning her because her father was rich.

Despite the poverty, the atmosphere in Felka's meager, cramped apartment was full of human warmth, and this had a great influence on Reli. Here her eyes were opened to things that she did not see in her parents' home. She noticed the difference between the ways of life and levels of capacity of the two homes, from which perhaps stemmed the differences in world outlook, in scales of priorities and in attitudes to people. Here, in this small cramped apartment, the people were more realistic, and pretended less.

The two girls, Felka and Reli, walked lightly on the narrow bridge of friendship they had made for themselves, but whenever another person appeared on the horizon, that narrow bridge would collapse, and the abyss that existed between them would open.

A dark curtain was hung under the muslin curtain and blocked the rays of the May sun which tried to steal into the mauve room.

The room was dark and dismal now. The whole apartment had changed amazingly since the guests had come: in every corner strange objects lay; it was impossible to keep the apartment clean, and the cramped conditions were oppressive.

The first to leave was Meir. The relatives from Podgorze, the sons of Aunt Mania and Uncle Shlomo, who wore *capotas* and sidecurls and beards as he did, took him in. Izio said that Meir had not been happy to see them and had not wanted to go with them. He had hesitated and dallied, but had not said anything. He hardly ever spoke as it was. Only with Father, sometimes, in Yiddish, and then it was impossible to understand what they were talking about. But once when the two lads were preparing to go to sleep in the living-room, Meir had told Izio that he hated the religious. This was the first and only time he had allowed himself to speak freely. His Polish was quite good, only his accent was a bit strange.

Izio tried hard to comprehend. How could he hate the religious if he was religious himself? Meir told him that he was wrong if he thought he was religious. Izio pointed at his clothes and Meir was flustered and confused.

'I find lies and contradictions in everything,' he said. 'They feed us straw and lies, and hide the world and life from us. And the result is that Rela is slowly killing herself.'

'Killing herself?!'

'Don't you know? Can't you see?'

'I thought she was sick,' Izio stammered.

'They made her sick.'

'Why? How? Tell me!'

'How can I explain to you?' Meir said, and Izio sensed that Meir was unable to speak freely any more. What he had said, he had said – he would say no more. Izio exerted all his powers to try to understand. He fixed a solemn gaze on the older boy. For a brief moment another crack opened in Meir's silence, and he said in a broken voice:

'You're too young to understand.'

He didn't say another word. After that the *Hasidim* took him away, and he went with them like a condemned prisoner.

Aunt Hela's room was still occupied by the two women, who wore those strange shapeless and tasteless clothes, which had almost certainly been bought or sewn before the war.

The atmosphere of the great outside world had vanished from the room. The fresh breeze of the Champs Elysées and the reflections of the Muses, which only recently had rested and hidden here in every corner, had vanished with the coming of the two women, and in their place within the walls of the room there was a compressed and oppressive atmosphere, which seemed to be marching against time, in the opposite direction to progress. Other smells – wilting and moldering – came from the bundles of these women, whose hands and clothes smelled of laundry soap. At nights they would take the wigs off their heads and lay them on Aunt Hela's table, beside her books of poetry, her novels, and her professional journals. The delicate golden slippers had vanished, and in their place stood two pairs of check slippers made of cheap flannel.

The two women, the shy Haicia and the dominating Mircia, did their best not to be a burden, but since their arrival Aunt Hela had found no place for herself here, and had stopped coming home. 'Where does she go?' Mother asked in a worried tone. Rela, as usual, lay with her face to the wall. Since her arrival here no one had seen her face. One could see only the fragile back, a frame of bones covered only with thin skin and a thin dress. From day to day she became thinner;

she was fading away before their very eyes.

The shy Haicia paced to and fro in the room – a useless, desperate walking – from the window to the door and from the door to the window and back again.

Mircia was more balanced and optimistic. She sat by the white table in the mauve children's room, knitting. Reli, Irka and Ania stood around her and she demonstrated to them how she knitted, and allowed each of them, in turn, to knit a number of loops.

Mother looked in concern at the clock and again asked:

'Where can she be? Today she didn't appear at dinner, and also didn't come home to sleep.'

'Aunt Hela's sleeping at our place tonight, she said she'd spend a few days with us, said Irka, and Mother breathed freely again.

'Thank God! So everything's all right?'

The question was directed to Irka, but she didn't reply. How could she know if everything was all right? On the contrary, she was certain everything was not all right. But it was better not to go into details in front of so many people. To Ania alone she whispered:

'Aunt Hela told Mother and Father that she has nowhere to live again. My mother got a shock. She had no idea that the family from Chszanow was in town, or about how bad Rela's condition is.'

No one had ever taken an interest in the late Menashe's widow and children. Mania and Shlomo had gone to visit them once. Hesiek had visited them once too, to quiet his conscience. The widow hadn't complained and had never asked for a thing. Her relatives in the city had the feeling that she was not interested in their involvement. They all knew that she had a small pension from the Polish government (Poland had received global reparations from the Austrian government) as the widow of a soldier. No one knew exactly what was the amount of the pension given to a family of three who required food, clothes, shoes and other essential needs. Had anyone bothered to find out, it would have been discovered that, while they would not die of starvation on this pension, they certainly could not live properly on it either.

The widow's father and sister helped her, and dominated her. They gave money and demanded obedience. They insisted on a say in Meir's and Rela's education. The widow was dependent on them and did not have the strength or the courage to object. Thus Rela suffocated, more and more. They simply stifled her, they and the environment, until she reached her present condition. For weeks she had lived on water alone in an attempt to put an end to her life. Now, when her life was in danger, Mircia and Haicia had suddenly woken up (their father had died in the meantime), and had decided to try to find out what had caused her deterioration and to try to help her.

'My mother changed color several times when she heard the story,' Irka went on. 'She said that her brother Menashe would turn over in his grave if he knew what had been done to his children. Mother cried and after a couple of minutes she started quarreling with Father.'

Irka remembered only vaguely the period when Aunt Hela had lived with them in Topolowa. She had been a baby then, but she still remembered that Mother and Aunt Hela had cried a lot during that period. They had cried and laughed in turns and Father – Olek – had turned from one to the other, not knowing which of them to console or with which of them to rejoice. The three of them had sought refuge with Irka who was three or four years old at the time. They used to come to her, for consolation, or to find warmth and softness. Perhaps that had been an additional reason for the tension and the jealousy in the home at the time.

'Yesterday Aunt Hela asked my parents if she could live with us for a few days, as she had in Topolowa. My mother said immediately that now we have a big and spacious apartment and that we'll all be glad, but when my father said the same thing in slightly different words Mother got angry and said: 'Are you starting again?' And Topolowa came back to me all over again. It doesn't matter if the apartment is big or small, or if I'm three or ten, they – the three of them – just don't know how to live together.'

In the mauve children's room Aunt Mircia still sat knitting. Reli sat beside her, learning the craft. Absent-minded Reli liked to knit.

'It's pleasant work, it calms the nerves,' Reli would say, pleasing Mother.

Aunt Haicia was still pacing the floor of the room, wringing her hands in a gesture of despair. Father came into the room and said that he'd spoken with the doctor. Everyone looked at him inquiringly. He glanced at Reli, Irka, and Ania, and apparently decided not to let their presence matter.

'The doctor says she must be allowed to do what she wants!'

A silence fell upon the room, and then Mircia spoke.

'The whole problem is that she doesn't want anything.'

'But there must have been something that she wanted.'

Haicia and Mircia exchanged glances.

'We can't discuss such matters in front of the children,' said Mircia, and looked towards Reli's bed, on which the bundle of bones that was Rela was huddled up.

Several days later there was a change: Rela got up. Pale and fragile, neat and serious, she sat on a chair and tried to straighten her back. There was no knowing who had wrought the change. Someone had bought her an easel, paper and canvasses, paints and pencils, and she sat down to draw and paint, absorbed in her inner world, her eyes alert and her hands nimble and gifted.

When Mademoiselle Gautier came into the room she exclaimed in astonishment:

'But this is a great artist! A rare talent!'

Doctor Willi Mantel promised to speak to his colleagues at the Academy of Fine Arts about Rela.

Haicia and Mircia were embarrassed. An argument flared up about Rela's future – where she would live, and how. Her brother Meir arrived from Podgorze at the very height of the argument. It was only with great difficulty that he had managed to get away from his Hasidic relatives, who kept him confined on all sides. The young fellow, who had always been silent and reserved, promised to take care of his sister.

Everyone stared at him. A *yeshiva* student with side curls, with no secular education, no trade or profession, what would he be able to do?

In the end, Mircia imposed her authority on the two of them. Father's and Mother's attempts at persuasion were of no avail, and they all returned to the town of Chszanow. Aunt Hela left Olek's and Hania's and came back to her lovely room. Once again the scents changed, the delicate golden slippers appeared under the bed, and everything returned to normal.

After a short while, they heard of the death of Rela, who had wasted away longing for her easel.

16 A Visit From the Land of Palestine

Aunt Rozia wrote from Palestine to say that she would be spending the summer of 1937 in Poland:

> I have already arranged to get a long vacation from my job. For three years now I haven't taken a single day of rest or holiday, and I now have six weeks of paid leave coming. I'll take an extra two weeks of leave without pay, and so I'll have two months free. I've been saving all my money, and the idea of seeing you in the summer gives me strength. In the meantime my life turns around three hubs – myself, my family and my homeland. I've already bought tickets for the trip and I keep pinching myself to make sure I'm not dreaming. Everything else I'll tell you when I see you.

These letters from Palestine had a strange, almost mystic, power about them. The Eretz-Israel paper, the envelopes with the Mandate stamps and postmarks on them. Mother held them in trembling hands, and as she read her eyes filled with tears. Even Father, who had told the children often enough that Aunt Rozia was the black sheep of the family, was very glad that she was coming. Mother and Aunts Mania, Hania and Hela started making arrangements for the guest's arrival. They met almost every day, or spoke on the phone to discuss every detail. A new spirit invigorated the routine of their lives, and gave them all energy. The men were occupied with other things: business, politics and studies, whether sacred or secular.

Father was building a house.

'I too had a dream,' said Father. 'And my dream too is

coming true.'

He was very enthused by the idea. Night and day, he thought only about the new house that was being built. He himself was the architect and the engineer. With unwearying perseverance, he invested the best of his energies in the building. He himself supervised the work of the laborers, brought in the building materials, and took care of dealings with municipal institutions and with the banks. He bought himself some check sports shirts, and in the mornings, after prayers, he would deck himself out in his new clothes and dash off happily to the building site.

Mother was worried about the large amount of money invested in the building.

'Perhaps it'd be better to wait a while with this investment,' she said to Father. 'Rozia will come in the summer, and we'll be able to hear something from her about the possibilities of investing money in Palestine.'

Father protested. What would Rozia understand about such matters? How many years had she been away? She herself had written about her difficult situation. What did she have there, except hard work?. With no support from outside, the whole enterprise of Jewish settlement there just could not sustain itself. It was more important that we be here for them, so that we can support them.

Mother was sad.

And Father went on. 'I'm building a house,' he said. 'A house is something fixed and certain. It stands firm for generations. We will pass away and the house will go on standing there and will be a source of livelihood for our grandchildren.'

'Things might change,' Mother said. 'For the better, or, God forbid, for the worse.'

It was sad to see that at the same time as Father's dream was becoming a reality, Mother's dream was being buried.

Living conditions in Aunt Mania's home were getting very cramped. Two of her four children were already married.

Rela, Mania's eldest daughter, was already a mother of three – two boys and a sweet little baby girl. Her brother Jacob, who was married to the eldest and loveliest daughter of the Bidermans from the cloth store on Dluga Street, had had two children born to him one after the other: a boy, Muniu (Maurice), and a girl, Scheindl (Jeanette). Aunt Mania, still young and beautiful, enjoyed the position of matriarch of the family. Her husband, her sons, her daughters, her son-in-law, her daughter-in-law, and her grandchildren, all respected her and she, with her sweet and pleasant attitude, her smiles and quiet speech, put every one of them at ease.

Naftali, Shlomo's eldest son, who had been six when Mania married his father, was now 26, and decided to go to Australia.

'Only criminals go to Australia,' people said. 'Only people fleeing from law and judgment.'

'And from Hitler.'

'What Hitler? Where's Hitler? Here in Poland there's no Hitler.'

A silence ensued. People didn't look into each other's eyes. 'No,' someone said. 'To America, that one could still understand. But to Australia?'

Rela adjusted her wig and said:

'It would be good if we could go to Eretz-Israel. I've heard that there too there are religious settlements, in Tiberias, and in Jerusalem.'

'Meantime Eretz-Israel is coming to us!' Renia, Aunt Mania's younger daughter who was Reli's age, reminded everyone. 'Aunt Rozia, have you forgotten?'

Now everyone spoke only of Rozia. When would she arrive? How many years is it since we saw her? Why is she coming alone? Will we ever meet her husband? Who is he? Whom will Rozia stay with? There's a lot of room at Hania's and Olek's. Aunt Hela, too, has invited her to her room. And in the summer Bronka will be letting a large resort house in Zakopane and will invite all her sisters-in-law to come there.

At last! She was here! The naughty daughter, the black sheep of the family. Tanned, dark and handsome, tall and slender. What kind of a sun was it that tanned so deep? That dried and sucked the marrow of the bones? Aunt Rozia's face was wrinkled and her hands were rough. 'It's not the sun,' she said, after all the kisses and the embraces. 'Our sun is good. We have a good pleasant summer nine months of the year. It's not the sun, it's the hard work and the difficult life.'

Aunt Rozia opened her suitcases, which were full of presents. Exotic robes with Arab embroidery, tiny pieces of jewelry containing green stones set by craftsmen. Little ornamantal knick-knacks, mainly camels made of olive wood. She was brought to Aunt Hania's apartment, and it seemed that the winds of the desert and the scents of distant citrus orchards were entering there together with her.

The adults sat down at the table, gathered around the guest, and had coffee and cakes.

In the next room Irka said to Ania:

'My mother wants to go to a kibbutz, with me, without Father. I'm willing to go to a kibbutz, but I want Father to come too. My mother doesn't know what she wants. A week ago she went to some office and asked them to change her name in her identity certificate from "'Hannah" to "Anna". She said that if we're living in Poland, we should have Polish names. Father asked her what she had done it for and then they started quarreling and she said she'd go to a kibbutz with me, without him.'

Irka spoke seriously, and Ania didn't know how to respond to this news, which sparked many thoughts.

'I'll tell you something else. But this is a great secret. Swear that you won't tell anyone.'

'I won't tell anyone,' Ania promised.

Irka whispered in Ania's ear:

'My mother's pregnant, in her third month!'

The two girls hugged and kissed each other, and Irka scratched her head, and said, with a knowing expression:

'I know how babies come out of their mother's wombs. I also know how they get in there. What I find hard to understand is how Mother and Father did it when they quarrel so much.'

Ania creased her brow and sank into a pensive mood. This conversation had given her a lot to think about.

Wlodek and Izio were playing ping-pong on the large table in the dining-room. Mother was always miserable when they played ping-pong indoors, exploiting Father's absence.

Just then – when the dining-room had become a playing-field, a green ping-pong net had taken the place of the embroidered tablecloth, and a crystal vase with lilacs in it stood on the floor and not on the table — just then the guest appeared.

They had to stop their game, of course, and Marynia came in from the kitchen and helped to put the room in order. The chairs, the tablecloth and the vase returned to their places, and order was restored. Mother set the table for coffee herself. The two women sat down comfortably and Rozia told Mother everything she was able to tell. Other things she passed over in silence.

From the house they had rented in Zakopane, a breath-taking mountain view could be seen. The house itself was surrounded by soft fresh grass, and a few paces away the clear water of a brook streamed by, washing over thousands of colored pebbles. The house was comfortable. It had large rooms, and wide beds. The toilets were outside, country-style, and water had to be drawn in buckets from a well.

This was real happiness. Here one could run barefoot in the fields. Even washing was unnecessary. Izio was the sole representative of the 'stronger sex'. Father had remained at home as he usually did, this time busy with his house-building. On the other hand, Aunt Hela had also taken a vacation, and she and Aunt Rozia had taken Irka under their wings because her mother refused to travel in her condition.

The lawn surrounding the house was shared with the occupants of the house next door. These were His Honor Judge Doctor Rosenblatt and his wife Hanka, their maid Olga and their little son Leszek. His Honor the Judge would lie for hours in an easy-chair, with eyes closed, occasionally stretching his limbs. When little Leszek fell down, the Judge would call out loudly: 'Hanka! Olga! Leszek has fallen!'

And the two women, who looked a little alike, would come quickly and pick up the baby.

'See how that man indulges himself,' Mother said. 'And my Hesiek doesn't even know what a vacation is, and never allows himself to rest, except on the Sabbath.'

'What sort of comparison are you making?' said Aunt Hela. 'That's Doctor Rosenblatt, the only Jewish Judge in a high government position. He gets a good salary, and can afford to rest quietly on his vacations.'

A peasant girl, Kaska by name, was hired as a help. She went barefoot and spoke a local dialect that was difficult to understand. She could neither read nor write, but was very good at drawing water and hewing wood and also at walking in the mountains and valleys without losing her way. The children climbed with her to the tops of mountains and followed her down to the depths of valleys. They wounded their feet on the high precipices, when they pressed against the rocks that verged on chasms. Kaska didn't allow them to fall. They drew the mountain air deep into their lungs, shouted aloud, and a dull echo replied to them: 'heigh ho, heigh ho'. The sky darkened and a strong summer storm surprised them in this dangerous and distant place. Fire pierced the sky, lightning-bolt followed lightning-bolt. Thunder set the unstable and elusive earth atremble under their feet. Driving rain drenched the children's clothes and bodies; they thought that one of the mountains would collapse and bury them entirely, but Kaska saved them. Trembling and exhausted, they returned and announced their presence to a world that had quietened after the storm and that once more responded to them with dull echoes from all directions: 'heigh ho, heigh ho'.

One time they crossed the state border and trod on Czechoslovakian soil. The significance of the event stimulated their imaginations. In their minds they saw foreign patrols approaching, catching, and imprisoning them. From this danger too they were saved by Kaska, who could not read or write but who understood well the language of nature and all its secrets.

One day a stranger appeared at their country house. He stood in the doorway, polished and buttoned, holding a bouquet of flowers for Aunt Hela. The man was very embarrassed, and flushed often. He stammered: 'A friend gave me the lady's address ... Therefore I dare ... I'm here on vacation ...'

He was invited in, and accepted the offer of fresh blackberries, which had been picked in the forest just that morning, with sweet cream and a slice of country bread and butter. It was funny to see him using a knife and fork to eat the slice of bread in the country where it was customary to eat with a wooden spoon and one's hands.

Aunt Hela sat opposite him, looking bored, while Rozia smiled at him from her tanned face. When the man heard that she was from Palestine, the knife and fork dropped from his hands, and he told them that his grandfather's grandfather was from Safed.

When the man left Aunt Hela said angrily: 'Maybe once and for all you'll all leave me alone and stop these stupid matchmaking attempts!'

The children played in the cow-pen and the barn and slept on straw mattresses. Before going to sleep they fooled around, leaping on top of one another, tickling each other, rolling around laughing, screaming and screeching. Even the serious Reli took part in these games and pranks. There were also quieter moments, when Irka told Ania about the baby that was to be born.

'My mother said that when the baby's born we'll be a happy family, because the baby will bring us everything that's missing in our life.'

'I'd like us to have another baby too,' Ania confessed, 'but my mother said that I'm the last because I was born in a Caesarian operation and she can't and doesn't want to have any more children.'

'Can we have a bit of quiet?' Reli interrupted. 'I'm reading Dostoyevsky's *Crime and Punishment*, and you're carrying on with that nonsense of yours.'

Izio was exhausted by all the larking around. He tried to read a book by Karl Maj, but he fell asleep and the book dropped from his hands and fell to the floor beside his bed.

On Friday, Mother came into the kitchen and baked *hala* loaves. In the afternoon she laid the table. On it she placed small candlesticks, which she had brought from home, and put candles in them. Kaska said that this was the first time in her life that she was seeing how city folk prepare for the weekend. She told them about herself, and said that every Sunday she had a wash and washed her hair, combed her braids, put on clean clothes, took her shoes in her hands and walked to church. Only when she was next to the church did she put on the shoes, which hurt her feet. After Kaska had told these things about herself, Mother said to her that we were preparing for the Sabbath, not for Sunday. The girl did not understand.

On Friday afternoon Father arrived, and it was only then that Kaska realised that she was in a Jewish home.

'Jesus Maria!' she blurted out.

Mother said that Kaska had thought that Jews were monsters. She had thought they were black and dirty and had long noses and humps on their backs. There were zealots who used to spread such rumors among simple people, who – having no other source of information – used to add details as their imaginations allowed. When Kaska had seen Mother and the aunts and the children and had discovered that these affable people were Jews, she hadn't been able to believe her eyes.

Mother told them all this at the Sabbath Eve dinner, after Father had said *kiddush* and the blessing over the food.

Everyone became grave and Rozia said:

'It's ten years since I've heard a *kiddush*, even though I'm in Eretz-Israel. But when I hear things like this about Kaska and where she must have got those ideas from, I want to get back to the Land as quickly as possible and get away from here. All this good life you're living here is just an illusion. In fact it's a life of degradation, lacking any self-respect.'

Father rose from his seat.

'I wasn't wrong about you,' he said.

Everyone was upset and agitated. Mother cried again, harsh and unrestrained words were flung into the air. Rozia was of the opinion that Kaska should be dismissed at once. Father said that it wasn't because of Kaska that they were quarreling. 'It's ridiculous,' he said. 'She's an ignorant, illiterate girl. We don't have to take her seriously.'

'Don't you be a prophet of doom!' Father raised his voice.

'Your way hasn't been so moral and exemplary!'

Hesiek, enough!' Mother cried, and Aunt Hela made efforts to calm everybody down.

'I don't mind,' said Rozia, who had taken no offence at Father's remark. 'I'm leaving here, thank God, and you – your end will be bitter and bad.'

'She doesn't know what she's talking about,' said Aunt Hela, and tried to change the subject.

Mother whispered something into Father's ear. Perhaps she was reminding him that Rozia was a guest in this house.

Towards the end of the vacation everyone made peace with everyone else. Rozia was supposed to travel by a day train to Lwow and by a night-train to Konstanza. From there a ship would take her directly to Haifa. Her suitcases were crammed with all the good things the family had lavished upon her in provisions for the journey: good chocolate, some coffee and perhaps cocoa? And a new blouse and a new dress …

'You're forgetting that I'm going to the land that flows with milk and honey.'

'Every land devours its inhabitants,' someone said, and Mother added in a trembling voice:

'At any rate give our regards to the Land, and please don't forget us.'

Rozia mounted the train. Tall and slender, free in her behavior, and different from all the other passengers – as if she belonged to another world. At least, she didn't belong here.

17 Laughter and Tears

It was fall again.

The apartment gleamed after being whitewashed and painted. In the kitchen, large brown necklaces of strung mushrooms decorated the walls and the cupboard. In broad and low earthenware pots jams and jellies boiled – mixtures of forest fruits and cherries brewing in red syrup. Mother and Marynia stood there for hours, stirring the contents with wooden spoons, until the fruits were mashed and emitted a thick, sticky red liquid. Mother filled large jars with jams and jellies and hid them from Father and the children.

'I must find hiding places,' Mother said. 'My seventh sense warns me of danger.'

Father laughed and said:

'You still remember my sins? You remember how I finished off the jellies, jar after jar, when you were all in the country and I was in the apartment alone?'

Mother smiled and hid the jars away.

In the kitchen there was the smell of burnt sugar, and outside there were clouds and rain. School had started again, and once more the children went to study every day, through the parks and public gardens, where the summer colors had given way to fall colors, the yellow-green to the red-brown, A strong wind shook the branches of the trees and sent soft and lovely chestnuts plummeting down, flinging them from their mother shells into the cold. Masses of these chestnuts, in various sizes, shapes and colors, rolled about superfluous.

Occasionally a child, or a dreamer, would pick up a chestnut, stand amazed at its beauty, and then throw it away. Then there were others who thoughtlessly or maliciously trampled on the soft fruit, which shed its juicy inside quite uselessly.

The branches of the trees that only recently had flourished with rich blossoms now stood bare, and leaves rustled at their feet. Fall.

At home they had begun preparing for the High Holy Days. In the kitchen they cooked stuffed carp and roasted ducks. They kneaded dough and baked cakes and biscuits and sweet honey-buns with nuts and almonds. Mother carried heavy baskets from the market and Father got angry at her for this.

'Ask them to deliver. Pay a few more pence.'

'It's not a matter of money. It's hard today to find anyone who'll help.'

Father had Polish friends who owned beehives and a honey shop, and they occasionally sent various kinds of honey in jars and bottles. Mother felt grateful to them, and Father asked her to cook extra portions of gefillte fish for his new friends, who would surely like the dish.

Father's philosophy of life was not elaborate or consolidated, and rested mainly on religious conceptions. Since he was a vigorous and practical person, he understood that although everything was foreseen, 'permission was granted'. He worked hard, followed his impulses, and was aided by healthy instincts in protecting himself and developing his ego. At times he would be stricken with despair or dread that perhaps this way was distancing him from the God he believed in unreservedly. He held on to God out of desperation in the face of phenomena he could not understand and questions he could not answer.

Stubbornly, studying by himself, be obtained a good education. He would surprise his children with his knowledge of mathematics, especially of algebra and trigonometry, and would help them solve problems quickly and precisely. He had a good knowledge of local and general literature, and knew a lot about botany. At the same time he was not a great scholar, and despite his wealth he often felt himself a pauper. 'For there is no greater poverty than ignorance', as Ibn Ezra said. So he placed his hopes and expectations in his children, that they might achieve everything he had not been able to achieve himself. For this reason he invested a lot in their education.

He always used to return to what he saw as most important: the Torah of God, work and charity.

Charity too he divided into the good of the community, the good of the individual and secret giving.

Father's largest block of land was at the edge of the city, in the street of warehouses (Skladowa). It was close to the freight train lines. A private track of his own led to this lot and served for the loading and unloading of merchandise. Here there was a huge stock of building timber, plywood and floor-boards; and from here shipments went out to all over Poland and even beyond. This was the home of faithful old Antony, and of the white horse, Hirsch, the industrious four-legged friend. Other laborers and clerks worked here too, and the children would come out on summer days to play among the planks, to climb up and down, to hide, to ride in a cart drawn by the white horse and to look at the black trains traveling to distant places.

Father's second house, his new project, was the large and modern apartment building being built on his second block of land. Beside this structure, which was already rising, stood the splendid mansion of Professor Mazurski. On the remainder of the block, sunflowers grew in the summer and in the winter a down of snow covered the flowers and froze their roots. On winter days the children would come here to slide on sleds and to build snowmen.

The third house and block of land were the closest to Father's heart.

This was a old two-stoey apartment house on Krowoderska Street. On the ground floor of this house, in a three-room apartment, Father had an office. Three male clerks worked there, and one female clerk, and they used three telephones and two typewriters.

The house was old and the apartments were small. Poor people and petty artisans lived in them. They could not afford to pay the rent and they paid for their apartments with their work.

298

Here, on the first floor, lived a shoemaker, Pan Wajda, with his wife and a dozen cats. Pan Wajda's apartment was comprised of one unit in which stood a double bed and opposite it a cooking stove and a cupboard. Between the stove and the cupboard Pan Wajda had his 'workshop', which consisted of a stool and a wooden board, on which were some tools and nails. Here Father's shoes, and those of the other members of the household, were repaired. With the final accounting Father would pay Pan Wajda money too, because the repairing of soles and heels for the whole family was more expensive than the shoemaker's rent.

Next to the shoemaker lived a photographer, a bachelor who wore spectacles. Once, when Ania came out of the shoemaker's apartment carrying a pair of Father's shoes that had just been fixed, the photographer opened the door of his apartment and blocked her path: 'Just a minute, little girl, just a minute. I've taken the photograph, now you can go,' the strange man said, then folded up his camera and hurried down the wooden stairs of the house.

Ania went down after him, but he had vanished. She went into Father's office. The girl working there smiled sweetly at her and the three male clerks also smiled at her and spoke flatteringly to her. Father wasn't there.

'Maybe he's upstairs at the tailor's,' said Bernard, the trainee clerk.

Ania went upstairs again and knocked on the door of Mr Ledwon, the tailor. This was a 'large' apartment, consisting of one room and a kitchen. In the kitchen stood a tailor's dummy, a sewing-machine and an ironing-board, all the equipment a tailor needed.

'Is my father here?'

'No,' the tailor replied affably. 'You can tell your father he can come. His suit is ready for him to try on.'

Here too rent was paid by work.

'Do you want to play with Kazik a little?' the tailor's wife asked, and brought her one-year-old baby forward.

Ania refused politely. 'No, I have to find Father.'

The baby started crying and Ania went out. Outside she

bumped into the bespectacled photographer again. Again he nimbly pressed the button on his camera. He photographed the tailor's apartment with the tailor's dummy dressed in Father's suit, and vanished.

The girl ran through the streets without looking right or left.

All year long Father worked hard, but he never violated the sanctity of the Sabbath. On Holy Days he and Mother reserved seats in the synagogue in Dluga Street. This was a place of prayer for Jews who lived in the area and were not willing to become completely assimilated. A high-ranking officer, with the rank of colonel, would appear only on Rosh Hashanah and Yom Kippur to hear the blowing of the *shofar*[1] and the *Kol Nidrei*.[2] The cantor was a thin, weak man, and Father used to blow the *shofar* instead of him. The children stood in the synagogue yard and listened to the blasts.

At the end of the service, men wrapped in prayer shawls would come up to Father and express their appreciation of how cleanly he had blown the *shofar*. Father would breathe heavily after the effort, but his face showed satisfaction.

Suddenly the bespectacled photographer appeared among the congregation, aimed his camera and took a photograph: Father wrapped in his prayer shawl, surrounded by his admirers, and next to him the colonel in a uniform decorated with medals, and to the side women and children.

'Father, father, he's photographing you,' Ania said, but her father didn't hear her in the din, and the strange photographer disappeared again.

On Yom Kippur, Father used to walk to synagogue in sports shoes, and Mother walked beside him in soft shoes made of cloth.

Apart from Marynia and Ania, everyone at home fasted. Izio had been fasting since he was ten. Yom Kippur, Father used to say, is the day of judgment, the day for soul-searching. Fasting purifies the body and the soul. There had been no need to tell Izio this twice. He enjoyed putting his will-power to the test, and liked making himself strong, and believed that there was nothing that could stand against his will. How could he have known how untrue that was.

'Next year Izio will be *bar-mitzvah*,' said Father.

'Next year will be a year of celebrations,' said Mother.

'How so?'

'His thirteenth birthday is an important date in a boy's life. It can be a beacon to light his way in life. Father and I have great expectations for the boy. We have high hopes for him. He will lead us in the right direction. He will understand what we don't understand. Everyone thinks that he's a strong lad and only I know he isn't, he gets worn out like the rest of us. That's why we have to equip him well for the way, and give him a lot of love. Love is the most important thing to give him, without it one gets lost.'

'Mother, didn't you say celebrations? Why are you going on about such serious and obscure things?'

'Right. Yes I said celebrations. There'll be many next year: Izio's *bar-mitzvah*, Uncle Marek's wedding.'

'What, really!'

'Yes, he's finally engaged too. The girl's ten years younger than him, and very much in love with him. It'll be hard for Grandmother. The last of her sons, her favorite, will be leaving home. We'll have to look after her more, she'll be very lonely.'

Again she had digressed on to sad subjects without noticing it. Then she went on:

'We'll have three new cousins next year: Hania, Rachel and Adela are all pregnant. And we, well we won't have a new baby, but we'll have a new home. Father will finish the building next year and apart from that Itzik Herzig will finish his second degree in mathematics next year too. It hasn't been easy for him, all these years at the Jagielonski University. Only his love for his studies and his tireless perseverance have got him through all the difficulties to where he almost has his Master's degree. He'll have it next year. So you see it really will be a year of happy events. Itzik says he's become friends with an amateur photographer, who wanders around the campus taking photographs.'

'I've seen him!'

Mother smiled.

'You've probably seen "our" photographer. The one who

photographs us in return for his rent. Ah, mentioning the photographer reminds me of yet another celebration: Menashe, Fela, and their little Yossi will be migrating to Eretz-Israel next year. They've reached a final decision.'

'I don't understand – what's the connection between their going to Eretz-Israel and that strange photographer?'

'There is a connection. That same photographer walked through the entire city, and photographed a large number of inscriptions calling on the Jews to go to Palestine. He has so many photographs that we suspect he might have photographed one place several times. On the doors of the YMCA he photographed a sign that says: 'No Entry to Dogs and Jews.'

'That's awful. Why don't we leave here too?'

Mother bent her head down.

'I don't know. I really don't know.'

Outside it was raining. The sky was heavy as lead. Mother took up her knitting and sat down to knit. Beautiful classical music came from the radio, and Mother put on the earphones so as to get the maximum pleasure. The music charmed her. Gradually the creases vanished from her face and an expression of supreme delight spread over it.

During the early autumn Mother and Father used to go out one evening a week, to the cinema, the theater, or the opera. At the opera, when the singers sang at the top of their voices and the plot reached its climax, Father would usually take a short nap, but Mother would enjoy it, and that was enough for him.

On the weekends they used to invite people home. Their receptions became a byword in the family, on both sides. Those invited were all family, and there was a kind of unspoken agreement not to bring in 'outsiders' so as not to disrupt the family harmony. Mother would prepare piquant dishes: salt-herring and fine salads, and for dessert she would serve rich cakes and crispy biscuits made at home, with fresh and aromatic tea or coffee. In the hall Father and Marynia would help the ladies take off their fur coats, and open the door to the living-room for them.

The relatives would accuse Father of entering into too close relations with Poles.

'I work with them,' was his defense.

The prevalent view was that contact should be limited to the most essential matters, and no more. 'They're all Jew-haters.' Hania and Olek were of a different opinion, but they were in a minority together with Father, whose connections with Professor Mazurski's family and with the owners of the honey shop were unusual. Serious conversation did not develop in the living-room. The people sitting there preferred the trivial small talk that flowed easily around the table all the evening.

At times Marek would begin singing one of Jan Kiepura, the famous singer's songs. His mother on one side of him, and his fiancee, Balka, on the other, looked at him with pride. Everyone loved his singing. Aunt Herzig told jokes one after the other, until Father could not stand any more and asked Itzik to tell them something about what was going on at the university.

Itzik's stories would bring the conversation back to the subject of anti-Semitism, and Hitler. Hania would get hysterical, and was often on the verge of fainting when they talked about these things. For this reason they tried not to say too much about them.

Rachel had great success when she taught the ladies knitting or embroidering, or gave them a new recipe for a good cake.

The bespectacled photographer would appear from time to time to photographs the guests, instead of paying rent, and they were eternalized in his photographs, sated and at ease.

When the Feast of the Tabernacles approached, Father built a booth next to his office in Krowoderska Street. Reli, Izio and Anio prepared decorations for Father's booth. Wlodek, Irka, and Felka helped with ideas and in the work. They cut colored paper into strips, stuck rings through rings, and made a chain. They pierced eggs, making two little holes with a pin or a needle, sucked out the contents, and on the shell painted eyes, a nose, and a mouth, and had clown's heads to hang up in the booth. Father's booth had no roof, as the precept prescribed. It had fresh thatching on top of it, and the decorations were hung from that. The children used to set the table, and bring food from home. The booth was beautifully decorated, and was the only one in the area. Father was elegantly dressed, and alone. At times some acquaintances from the synagogue would join him.

Ania came up to him and placed her little hand in his.

'Father, can I call the photographer and ask him to photograph the booth and us?'

'Have you forgotten that it's a holy day today? On holy days photography is forbidden.' His hand stroked hers. He was jovial and happy, as he always was when he fulfilled the commandments, but the sensitive lens in his daughter's eye caught the shades of sorrow and anxiety in his eyes.

In the spring of 1938, all the Krakow newspapers published a special edition. Hitler's armies had invaded Austria and annexed it to Germany. This was a grave violation of the Versailles Treaty, which had now become a worthless scrap of paper. The news items were brief but terrifying. The once gay Vienna had become a hell for the Jews who lived there. Many committed suicide – single people, and entire families.

The Jews of Poland waited for Hitler to either be overthrown, or to resign. They did not believe that his rule could last very long.

'Mother, have we any relatives in Germany?'

A cloud passed over her face.

'Years ago some distant relatives of ours migrated to Germany – Marta and Arnold. When Marta was little her father died suddenly. Everyone used to call him "Red Joseph", because he had bright red hair and a red beard. Her mother was sickly and Paula and Stefa adopted her.' Mother continued. She said that the two sisters had adopted Marta and had sent her to school. Marta was a talented and introspective girl who read a lot of books. When she grew up she married Arnold, who was a law student at the time. They had felt cramped in Krakow. They had felt very European, very Western, and had gone to live in Germany. Marta had died during one of her deliveries, and Arnold, a lawyer by profession, had hired a governess to help him raise his daughter Rosemarie and his son Hans.

'What funny names, Rosemarie and Hans!'

'German names. As befitting people who live in Germany.'

'How old are Rosemarie and Hans?'

'The girl is the elder. She would be 16 now. And Hans is two years younger, about Reli's age. I've never seen those children. Their father cut all connections with his wife's family, and we don't know any more about them. Your father too had cousins in Berlin. Fortunately they managed to get away. By some miracle they got a visa to America.'

'Why did they have to run away? What are they doing to Jews in Germany?'

'Persecuting them. Persecuting them in the most disgraceful manner. They've deprived them of rights as citizens, and they've been left there completely defenseless. They confiscate their property and dismiss them from their jobs.'

'But why?'

Mother didn't answer. About a second later she uttered something like a curse: 'That madman Hitler!'

'Is he mad?'

Izio had been listening to the conversation. Now he interrupted.

'You say he's mad but at our school I heard that he's not mad at all. No one protests about what he does. On the contrary, people cheer him. The Austrians are glad that he has annexed them to Germany, because they're a small and unimportant nation, and now they're part of a great and important nation.'

'Who put that nonsense into your head?' Mother interrupted him in disgust. 'He's a criminal. And how come you children talk politics?'

'We're worried, Mother. We talk a lot with Wlodek and Irka. We're concerned about the fate of the world.'

Mother smiled sadly.

'God grant that you manage to mend it. There never has been real peace in the world. Conflicts of interests, struggles, wars, that's what goes on in the world in different ways.'

'And what are we doing for the Jews of Germany?'

Mother felt cornered.

'What can we do? Who hears us? We boycott German industry. What else can we do? Our situation isn't good either, because since Hitler's rise to power anti-Semitism has been increasing in force all over the world, like an epidemic. We also boycott those Polish industrialists who propound anti-Semitism. What else can we do?'

'It's because of the boycott that we've stopped buying "Wedel" chocolate, isn't it?'

'Yes. What else can I do?'

Mother and Father were now devoting a lot of their time to preparing the lists of guests to be invited to Izio's *bar-mitzvah* celebration, which was to take place in July 1938. A month after that, Marek's wedding was to be held. For this celebration a hall had already been reserved in the Royal Hotel, and a menu designed for two hundred guests.

'Maybe we too should hold our celebrations in a hall?' Mother said in a moment of weakness. 'Our family's so big, how will we get them all into the apartment?'

Father objected. A bar-mitzvah is not a wedding. There's no need to do things for show. We'll cut down on the number of guests, and invite only the closest. Brothers and sisters and their spouses, and first cousins.

The three new babies due to be added to the family would be born before June, so their mothers would be able to leave them with baby-sitters and come to the party.

The first to give birth was Rachel. Despite her pregnancy she had been more beautiful than ever, nimble and light, like a gazelle. Though her stomach was large she worked like a demon, starting her day with morning exercises, then quickly cleaning their modest two-room apartment in Starowislna Street, sending her six-year-old son Romek to *heder*, then going out with her husband Szajek to work in their wool shop in Dluga Street. At noon she would return home by streetcar, doing her shopping on the way. When she came home she cooked, baked, and helped her son with his secular studies, and in the evening, after she had bathed the boy and washed the dishes, she sat down to knit sweaters for her husband and her son, and after that even found the time to read books. During the summer, despite her pregnancy and her husband's orthodoxy, she would steal out to the banks of the Vistula, which ran near her home, find a quiet nook and, sheltered from strangers' eyes, would take off her clothes and in a bathing suit with a tunic to hide her stomach, would plunge in among the waves and swim.

The ninth month of her pregnancy passed and the child gave no sign of being born. Days passed, and the situation began to be unbearable. Without telling his wife, Szajek went to consult the rabbi.

Rachel herself called in a midwife. The woman examined her and said that a doctor had to be called. Only then did Szajek tell her that he had been to the rabbi's, but refused to say what the rabbi had said.

'What did he say to you?' Rachel urged him, 'Why is the birth late? What is it a sign of?'

Szajek evaded answering, and sought an excuse to change the subject.

'A lazy child,' she said and sighed. 'Or maybe a coward.'

Finally a soft, cute, pink and round baby boy was born – little Ahrale. The expression on the little face was innocent and slighly bemused, as if he wanted to ask: 'What do you want from me? Why all the fuss?'

Rachel lay weary and grieving, trying to hold back the tears that came to her eyes.

'Why are you crying, Rachel? Your child is healthy, praise God, healthy and beautiful.'

'I don't know,' she replied, in a tone of weakness mixed with dread.

Little Ahrale was an omen of things to come. Both Adela and Hania had difficulties giving birth. Their deliveries too occurred in the tenth month. It was as if all three new infants did not want to come into the world. Finally both Adela's Ella and Hania's Nina were born healthy, plump, and pretty. The babies brought their families much joy and many hopes.

The building of Father's new house was completed, and all
the apartments in it were let immediately.

'You see,' he said to Mother. 'You were afraid for no
reason. Now that the house will return everything we've
invested in it, we'll be able to live peacefully and quietly, with
no worries.'

Izio's bearded rabbi came every day to prepare the lad for
his *bar mitzvah*. Izio would 'go up' to the Torah reading in the
month of Av, which was the month of his birth. By then he
would know how to put on phylacteries, and would know
the musical notations for the reading of the scriptural
portions.

'Hear, O heavens, and give ear, O earth, for the Lord hath
spoken:

'I have nourished and brought up children, and they have
rebelled against me ...'

He recited the biblical passages, and they aroused an echo
in his soul. The rabbi did not interpret. His main effort was to
teach the boy to know the passages by heart. Izio felt the
power of the words, and trembled at God's rage, and at the
awful threat:

'Ah sinful nation ... they have forsaken the Lord, they have
provoked the Holy One of Israel unto anger ...'

What had made God so angry? The question tormented
the boy. He read on:

'Your country is desolate, your cities are burned with fire;
your land, strangers devour it in your presence, and it is
desolate, as overthrown by strangers.'

What had the children of Israel done to so arouse God's
wrath? Had they offended Zion and forgotten it? Could such
devastation actually happen? The boy became absorbed in the
text, getting confused between the Sephardi and Ashkenazi
pronunciations and trying to understand.

The rabbi read with his pupil and immediately translated
the words into Yiddish, verse by verse. The boy repeated
them after him in both languages, and with all the effort to
remember the words he found it difficult to concentrate on
their meaning. The hour dragged on and the boy was pleased

when the rabbi got up, kissed the *mezuzah*, and left the room. Then Izio returned to the book of Isaiah and tried to read the verses again, this time in the Sephardic pronunciation as taught at the Hebrew Gymnasium,

Father's two new suits were already hanging in the wardrobe in the parents' room. One was made of gray English cloth, and Father would wear it to the synagogue and at the party at home. At the wedding he would wear the black evening suit, to which he had already matched a white silk shirt, silver tie, gold cuff-links and an Anthony Eden hat.

'You'll be able to renew your new clothes for Reli's first performance at the Conservatorium,' Mother suggested.

For her, two new dresses had been ordered. One was long, with a low neckline. Mother would wear it with a pair of long satin gloves reaching to the elbows, and black silk shoes with very high heels.

In the winter Mother's fur coat had been stolen. The furrier, who was to change the cut of the coat to adapt it to the latest fashion, had been robbed, and had reacted to the robbery with a severe heart attack. When his wife had gone to the insurance company where they were insured, she was told that their policy was not valid. Their life was ruined. At home the family decided not to make any claims on the furrier. On the contrary, Father asked Mother to ask them if they could help them in any way.

'Buy yourself a new fur coat and forget the whole affair,' he said.

They also had to get suitable clothes for the children. The girls were taken to the 'salon' for young people's fashions run by the Koral Sisters, in Stradom Street, where they ordered beautiful and expensive dresses.

Reli was now in her full bloom. Her body had filled out with gracefuls feminine curves, and her new dress suited her perfectly.

Izio would probably be the first boy to ever 'go up' to the Torah in sports clothes. Mother insisted that he should be dressed in conformity with the fashion now prevalent in the world. Father yielded to her will.

'One can also serve God in clothes that suit the spirit of the time,' she ruled.

She bought some superior tweed and ordered trousers that closed with buckles below the knee, like riding pants. To this she added a short-sleeved pink shirt. On his head he would wear a small skullcap.

Izio looked good in his new clothes. The color of his shirt went well with his flushed and freckled complexion. He did not waste his time. Wherever he went and whatever he did, his lips kept rehearsing Isaiah's vision. The preparations at home were intensifying, and there was little time left. Two cooks had been hired, a man and a woman, and after they had made clear that their work would be only in the kitchen, so it became necessary to hire a waiter and a waitress. The preparations were reaching a climax.

'Perhaps we should postpone the party?' Mother said. She was so tired. 'After Izio goes up to the Torah we could all go away somewhere and rest?'

'Celebrations must not be postponed,' said Father.

So Mother had to take some tranquilizing pills.

About a month before the party all the old curtains had been taken down. They were worn, and had lost their original shape. Mother and Father decided to order new curtains without delay.

Two days before the party the curtains were not yet ready. Mother became anxious.

The big bath-tub had been filled with water, and in it swam about a dozen large carp. Ania stood beside the bath-tub, looking at the live fish swimming around in circles, and she felt sorry for them. The fish kept opening and closing their mouths. Water was all they needed to stay alive, and even that wouldn't be given to them. In this world whoever asks for only a little gets nothing. That was what Irka had said to her when they had talked together about life and the world. Fish don't disturb anyone. People even say that they bring good luck. Why, then, do they kill them?

'If they didn't kill them, they'd multiply and multiply and the whole world would be full of fish,' said Izio.

310

The cook had already sharpened his knives, and stood there rubbing his hands. His face was flushed and his eyes shone. He looked as though he was excited and delighted about the work awaiting him. Mother's nerves gave way. What about the curtains? The apartment looked bare.

In the morning Pani Doktor Stanowska came up.

'Might I perhaps weigh some flour and sugar for a cake?' she asked with an innocent smile. 'There's something wrong with my scales.'

Today of all days. When the apartment was so ugly and bare, without curtains, and the kitchen so full of activity.

Aunt Herzig, who was sewing the curtains, worked night and day, and when she finished Itzik brought them himself, apologizing for his father, who didn't feel secure about walking through the streets of the Polish city and was not accustomed to going beyond the Jewish quarter. Itzik nimbly hung the curtains, as his mother had taught him, and immediately turned to go.

'Stay and drink something,' Mother stopped him.

'I have no time,' the young man apologized. 'I have to finish my master's thesis today, or I won't be able to come to your party tomorrow. Mother insists on all of us coming to the party.'

'We insist on it too. Your mother raised me as she raised you. Did you know that?'

Itzik had already gone.

On the day of the party Father's sisters, Mother's brothers, all with their spouses and children, Mother's and Father's cousins – some of whom were setting foot in this apartment for the first time – all came. Willi Mantel the pianist presented his wife the violinist, and with them came the lovely Liz and the jolly Fredek. Dora the doctor introduced her husband who was a doctor too, and with them came Ila and Henia Carmel's parents, who Ania remembered well from the vacation at Kowaniec and the Hebrew Gymnasium. The other close cousins were already in Eretz Israel, and the more distant ones – even Mother herself didn't know how they were related to each other – hadn't been invited.

The apartment was lit with many lights. Grandma, Mother, Father, and Hela stood in a row in the doorway and greeted the guests as they arrived. Izio, Reli and Ania mingled among the guests and collected presents. In one of the rooms the religious men sat apart. In the living-room were elegantly dressed ladies and the secular men. In a third room the youngsters gathered around Reli and Ania, and in Aunt Hela's room the presents were piled up. The waiter and waitress started serving. Suddenly Mother became anxious: where were Itzik and his parents?

'Why don't you telephone them?'

'They don't have a telephone. Maybe something's happened?'

The party went on. The bespectacled photographer arrived too and photographed the assembled guests. Marek and his fiancée Balka laughed into the camera. Then they looked into each other's eyes and the photographer photographed them in profile.

'Now he'll be able to live a whole year without paying rent', someone quipped.

'Why haven't they come?' The expression on Mother's face was worried. 'Maybe Fela's sick? She works so hard.'

'She's healthy and strong,' said Grandma. 'And she hasn't complained about anything. I know that she sewed herself a new dress for the occasion. And Itzik said that he would stay up all night studying so as to be able to come to the party, They'll probably get here.'

Father returned to the room where the religious men were. There they prayed and spoke blessings, ate fish and drank wine. Towards the end small cups of coffee and chocolate canapés were served.

Some of the guests started to leave. Izio went to be with his presents. He was very happy.

The next day the dreadful news appeared in the newspaper. On the table lay the *New Daily*, the Polish-language Jewish paper, and Mother was holding the Polish newspaper, called the *Kurier* (*Courier*). Mother and Father were pale.

Israel Herzig, 48, was murdered in cold blood yesterday near the PKO Bank. At about 12 noon he came out of the bank after withdrawing a considerable sum from his wife's account. A group of Endek students accosted him and accused him of stealing the money. Herzig tried to escape from them, and was knocked down to the sidewalk. He tried to get up and was knocked down once more. The police were called, but arrived too late, after a doctor from among the passers-by had pronounced the victim dead.

(*New Daily*)

A deathly stillness fell upon the room. Hela took the other paper and read in a trembling voice:

An unfortunate incident occurred yesterday near the PKO Bank, when Israel Herzig, 48, came out of the bank. An eye-witness reports that the man's creditors were waiting for him outside the bank, and asked him to repay his debt. The Jew, who tried to escape, fell down, hit his head heavily on the ground, and died of the injury. The police arrived on the scene, dispersed the crowd, and opened an investigation. The investigation is proceeding.

(*Courier*)

Itzik did not complete his master's thesis, and refused to enter the university campus again. When the days of the *shiv'a* were over, he started helping his mother, cutting cloth, ironing curtains, doing errands and deliveries. At first they followed the 'investigation … proceeding', but finally they wearied of it and lost interest.

Izio was now a big boy. Having entered into the yoke of the *mitzvoth*, the responsibility of observing the precepts, he was assiduous about observing them. In the mornings he would stand beside Father, donning the phylacteries with an unpracticed hand. Father had a prayer shawl around his shoulders, his eyes were closed in sorrow under his deeply creased brow, and his mouth muttered the prayers. Izio watched Father's face with concentration, and it looked as though the secrets of the connection between a Jewish man and his God were passing from father to son.

Of all the presents Izio had received, the one he delighted in most was the bicycle. He affixed a bell and lights to it and rode it through the city streets, proudly and bravely.

Grandma hated the bike, and became more nervous about it from day to day. Ever since her youngest son had left home to start a home of his own she had been living alone, and she found it hard to adjust to the new situation. Reading the newspapers did not contribute to her health, and her children forbade her to read them. Even so, her nerves began giving way.

'How can you allow him to ride that bicycle in the city streets, among streetcars, automobiles, and horses? It's terribly dangerous!'

But Mother and Father were not moved by her. They knew that in the city streets one could get killed without a bicycle too. There was danger everywhere. If the boy enjoyed riding, let him ride to his heart's content. How many enjoyments did a human being have in his life?!

At Marek's and Balka's wedding, Mother and Father wore their elegant clothes, and looked like a bride and groom themselves.

Immediately after the wedding Mother fell ill. She had suffered a massive internal hemorrhage. The doctors instructed her to lie with her legs raised, with cold compresses around the pelvic region. Father believed that it had all come about from over-exertion, excitement and stress – the celebrations and the disaster had been enough to shake the health of a fragile creature like Mother.

Grandma would come in every day from Kazimierz to sit beside Mother, and Hela ran the house in her stead and gave Marynia her instructions. Father delegated additional responsibilities to the manager of his office, Mr Fuchs, and appointed his young mending clothes, as he had done many years ago. Mother looked on from her bed, and wasn't pleased with the crookedly sewn hems.

Grandma sat by Mother's bed and enumerated her own

troubles: she had palpitations, she couldn't sleep at nights, her hands and feet trembled, and her vision was blurred.

'Does she come here to take care of you or to look for help for herself?' Father asked.

Mother's eyes filled with tears.

'She can't cope with living alone. Please, don't say a thing.' In her weakness it seemed to Mother that her life was drawing to its end, and she was only 38.

Father looked at her in concern.

School had started again quite some time ago. Mother was still weak but her condition had improved. In the winter she would go to Zakopane, to convalesce. The children would go to Zakopane too, to a ski-camp. The time had come to learn to ski – and to get used to heights, to strive for goals, to overcome obstacles. It was important to be strong in mind and body.

Mother tried on her new fur coat, and looked at her face in the mirror. She had lost weight, and her body looked young. The skin on her face was smooth and there was no gray in her hair. Hela used to tease her, telling her that her world was as narrow as an ant's. Until her marriage she had looked after her three brothers, and since then, after her three children. 'I couldn't be satisfied with that,' said Hela, 'I at least have seen a bit of the world. I've traveled, I've met different people. Now I can get married and raise a family.'

'What did you say?' Mother grasped Hela's hand. Then she let go and took off her fur coat. She was sweating profusely.

'Are you very weak?'

'No, I just felt very hot. What did you say about getting married?'

'He's finally come to an arrangement with his wife. We still don't know how it'll work out, but Aleks has promised me that next year we'll go on our honeymoon.'

Mother's eyes grew moist again.

In October, everyone was talking about the new German decree, which forbade Jews of Polish origin to stay within the boundaries of the Reich. In the wake of the decree, 15,000 Jews with Polish citizenship, many of whom had lived in

Germany for many years, were evicted from their houses, loaded on trucks, and transported to the Polish border.

The newspaper fell from Mother's hands. She said that everything was turning over inside her. Her hemorrhages began again.

The Polish border authorities were not willing to admit such a great number of refugees. No clear directions had been issued regarding them, and so the people who had been thrown out of their homes stood around under the open sky, or huddled together in families, in canvas-covered carts, in the cold – hungry, thirsty, the roads closed before them. The way back was blocked, and the future was shrouded in mist. The Jews of Poland exerted pressure upon the authorities. How could they let these people stand around like this? After all, they were all Polish citizens. They had to be allowed to enter Poland. The authorities delayed their reply. The negotiations and the nightmare continued.

Reli started preparing for her matriculation examinations. 'This year is a fateful one for you,' Father said. 'With a matriculation certificate, the whole world will be open to you. You'll be able to choose whatever occupation you like. You have to get good grades.' And Reli was trying.

The newspaper said that many Jews had been expelled from Dresden. Didn't Arnold and his children live in Dresden? Right now they were most probably standing with the others in the no-man's land by the border. But Arnold was a lawyer, couldn't he do something?

Izio returned home with a high temperature. He had red blotches all over his face and stomach. In the afternoon inspectors from the health department came and announced an epidemic of scarlet fever. There were 40 cases in his class. He was taken to hospital and the apartment was closed for disinfection. For three days no one was allowed in or out.

Finally the Polish government permitted the entry of the refugees from Germany. The Jewish communities organized themselves to assist them, and action committees were set up everywhere. One of Reli's friends said:

'What's all the noise about? All that's happened is that the

Germans have given the Poles back their subjects. They like order.' Izio angrily told him to shut up.

Arnold, Rosemarie, and Hans arrived in Krakow, and the family joined together like one man to help them.

Paula and Stefa gave up their comfort and moved into one room of their two-room apartment, and gave the other room to the children of the late Marta. The children's father, Arnold, did not need help from his wife's family. A handsome young man who despite his Polish citizenship couldn't speak a word of Polish, he found a wife almost immediately after arriving in Krakow. She was not beautiful but she had American citizenship and a rich brother in America. The two soon married and started making preparations to leave Europe. When he saw his children being looked after by their mother's relatives, Arnold shook off the yoke he had born with responsibility and sacrifice for so many years. Everyone said that he was reclaiming his own life at the expense of the terrible national tragedy.

The children remained at the spinster sisters' home, and their father promised that as soon as he got organized in America he would send them the necessary papers so that they could join him.

Mother was weak, but went every day to Kazimierz, where the refugees from Germany were concentrated. She also took the opportunity to visit Grandma, who was suffering from many pains.

One day Mother came back from Kazimierz bringing Rosemarie and Hans with her.

At this time one of the refugees was staying with them as a kind of guest, a man who Father wanted to employ in his business. He was single, about 28, thin and quiet, and wore a ragged gray coat over a creased and worn suit, the only one he still possessed, and shoes with worn-down soles. The children were repelled by him, by the strange smells that still came from him. Father asked them to be polite to him and explained his situation to them. The man had worked in the editing room of one of the large newspapers in Germany, had studied in the evenings, and had dreamed of a career in

317

journalism. In the meantime Father was employing him as his German 'correspondent' even though business with Germany was decreasing.

Rosemarie was a clumsy, thick-bodied girl, pale of skin. She dressed tastelessly, dragged her right foot slightly as a result of an illness contracted in childhood, and spoke only German. Hans, two years younger than she, could already put several sentences together in Polish. He wore three-quarter-length pants held up by funny suspenders.

Mother insisted that Izio and Reli play with Hans and Rosemarie. 'What are you talking about, Mother?' Reli said angrily. 'Are they little children, that we should have to play with them? Hans is a year older than me, and Rosemarie is three years older. There's no need to entertain them.'

Hans and Rosemarie sat there, tense, and didn't know, or pretended they didn't know, that they were being talked about.

'They need special attention,' said Mother, and ordered Reli to take them to school with her.

That was all that Reli needed: she was horrified by the thought of appearing before her classmates with these strange relatives, who dressed in such a funny way and spoke only German.

In a couple of days Reli changed her attitude. A large section of the Hebrew Gymnasium had been turned into a hostel for refugees, and several of the younger refugees were warmly accepted by the pupils.

Most of them, Reli said, were nice, and intelligent, and had much to contribute to the society they had come to. From this time on Reli would go by Stefa and Paula's apartment every morning and pick up Hans on her way to school. Rosemarie didn't suit, she was too old. She would spend her time alone, more idly than ever, eating a lot, voraciously, so that her old clothes were already bursting at the seams.

'We must do something for the poor girl,' Mother said. The spinster aunts reported that they had tried to make her learn sewing or book-keeping, but the girl had shown in interest in neither and was continuing to idle her time away.

Just before Chanukah, Mother took Rosemarie and Hans to the Koral Sisters' Salon in Stradom Street and bought them new clothes.

'Instead of Chanukah gelt,' Mother said to them. They were quite assimilated and this was the first time they had heard of the miracle of Chanukah or of the tradition of giving gifts of money to children at this festival. Their father wrote from America that he would be sending them their papers soon.

High snows covered the Carpathians and Zakopane filled with vacationers and sportsmen. Father obtained a good place in one of the pensions for Mother, and she was pleased that the children would be learning to ski. According to the camp program, they would spend four hours a day at the sport.

'It's important,' Mother said, repeating her arguments. 'We mustn't rot away.'

Hela announced that she too would be spending a weekend at Zakopane together with Aleks, and everyone pretended not to have heard. At the last minute they decided to invite Hans and Rosemarie to come to the ski camp too. The proprietors of the camp had said that there were no more vacancies, but when they heard the story of Hans and Rosemarie, they agreed to add them to the list. Of the two, only Hans accepted the invitation.

'It really is hard to imagine her on skis,' Izio scoffed. 'She's so big and fat.'

Izio was good at sport, but Reli had a fear of heights and Ania got chilblains on her feet, and the instructor – who wore a colored woolen cap and thick mittens – gave up on them. In contrast, Aunt Hela, in ski-slacks and a Scandinavian sweater, would arrive at the camp on skis, merry and jovial. Behind her came Aleks, also on skis, laughing and joking and throwing snowballs at her back.

When they returned home they found out that Rosemarie was pregnant. The news was a great shock to the family. The old spinsters, Paula and Stefa felt helpless.

'Arnold left us in charge of her, what shall we tell him?'

The adults consulted together in whispers. They naïvely

believed that the children would not find out the secret. No one dared to speak to Rosemarie to discover how it happened and who the father was. She was already in her fifth month, and the father was in fact a youngster, one of the refugees from Germany. His father had got lost on the way – he had either fled or been killed – and his mother, also in shock and not knowing what to do, had forbidden him to meet the girl.

A doctor said that if they were considering abortion there was no time to be lost. In any case it was already very late to operate, and the operation, if decided on, would be very expensive.

'The money doesn't matter,' Father said.

'Such a sin,' said Grandma and all the aunts.

The girl became more and more depressed. It looked as though she didn't have the strength to cope with the situation without encouragement and support.

The spinsters were persuaded that an abortion had to be carried out. Other members of the family objected forcefully. The argument became heated, and was no longer kept hidden from the children, who had already noticed Rosemarie's swollen stomach, which she vainly tried to conceal under her folded hands.

The case of Rosemarie temporarily kept their minds off Hitler's atrocities. Everyone was ceaselessly busy with Rosemarie's future, though no one consulted her at all.

Finally it was she who found a solution. One day they found her in the attic of the house where Stefa and Paula lived. A loop of rope was tied around her throat, and her heavy body, with the unborn baby inside it, was swaying lifelessly from it.

On a note she had attached to her dress Rosemarie had written: 'Thank you for everything. It's a pity you didn't discuss things with me too. My blessings to my father ... and to Hitler.'

Father informed Rosemarie's father of the disaster, by cable.

Rosemarie's father sent back a hasty cable, but didn't arrive for the funeral. Everyone was at their wit's end. Father arranged everything with the Jewish burial society, the Chevrah Kadisha, who insisted that she be buried outside the fence. Father looked after Stefa and Paula — both of them had become hysterical. He instructed Hans to leave their apartment and financed his journey to Turkey. In Ankara a group of migrants to Palestine was being organized, and Father made contact with the group for Hans. Then Grandma announced that she was going to die and Father rushed to talk with the Professor, who calmed him and told him that all her pains were of a nervous origin. Father mediated among the brothers in the wool business with regard to the defining of authority and the division of profits in their mutual business. He advised Olek how to run his business during the days of boycott and how to look after Hania during the new crisis that had arisen in their family. He persuaded Itzik to cut down on his work in ironing curtains and to finish his studies. Father also helped Rachel, who was in financial difficulties, and made it possible for her son Romek to take up secular studies with a private teacher. And he spent hours talking with his sister Hela. He was the bulwark of the family.

'Everyone depends on you, and comes to you,' said Mother, who had long since given up talking about leaving Europe.

Sometimes there was the feeling that if he could, he would get up and run away from all these pressures, all these troubles, but the net had already closed in around him. It was already too late.

'All of us here need you,' Mother complimented him. There were signs of anaemia on her face.

'Reli will finish her matriculation examinations. Then we'll see,' he said.

18 The Last Beautiful Summer

When the civic year ended and 1939 began, everyone said that the new year would be easier than the last. Everyone wanted an easier year.

The spring came in all its glory. Young Hershl Grinspan made an attempt on the life of the advisor at the German Embassy in Paris, to avenge the degradation of his exiled parents, and in response to this act of desperation an unprecedented wave of pogroms broke out against the Jews in Germany. The rose tree blossomed more beautifully than in previous years; its flowers opened to the sun, unclouded by the shadow of the events. SA men fell upon Jewish homes and shops throughout Germany, plundering them, and still the almond-groves yielded fruit. Thousands of Jewish businesses had been destroyed and tens of thousands of Jews had been thrown into concentration camps, while clocks of birds circled in the pale blue skies. And the grain ripened in golden ears after all the Jews in Germany had been forced to pay a billion marks in 'compensation' to Hitler's government for all the damage caused during the pogroms. The fresh and glorious spring came to Europe at a time when Jewish children in Germany were forbidden to attend local schools, and while the Gestapo kept under direct surveillance the movements of all Jews and all who were married to Jews and all offspring of a Jewish father, mother, father's father, father's mother, mother's mother, or mother's father; the world looked on and was silent. The spring came, radiant with light, the fragrance of the fields excited young nostrils, all of nature opened up in all its beauty – and awaited a miracle.

Once more Mother felt ill, and had to go into hospital. She was taken into the operating room while everyone awaited

Britain's response to the German invasion of the Sudetenland. How would Great Britain react to this crude aggression against her ally Czechoslovakia, with which she was tied in a mutual defense pact? This was the question that hung in the air, the answer to which held explosive consequences. Mother fell asleep. The strong smell of ether overpowered her senses, a black abyss opened up and swallowed everything. Knives cut her living flesh and she did not budge. When she awoke, she felt a strong nausea. The smell of ether still blurred her consciousness. Father sat beside her and moistened her lips. She smiled faintly at him.

'I'm alive, I came through it safely, what did Chamberlain say?'

Father looked down to the floor. She waited for his reply, struggling against sleep.

'He gave in to the Germans, and Poland has confirmed her new border with Czechoslovakia, several kilometers by the Olza River.'

Mother closed her eyes. The bed turned with her.

'I'm falling … Maybe … Maybe it's best now …?'

The strong smell of ether also blurred Father's senses slightly. 'Chamberlain did give in to the Germans,' he added in a soothing tone, 'but he promised the world a hundred years of peace. It's a pity about the courageous and democratic Sudetens, but a price must be paid for 100 years of peace.'

'Maybe … it's best … now …' she said obscurely through the narcosis.

He sat beside her till she fell asleep.

When Mother came home Father forbade everyone to talk politics in her presence. She was too excitable and the wound might open. Reli too needed absolute quiet before her examinations. It was forbidden to turn on the radio at home. Noise and superfluous talk were forbidden too.

Aunt Hela was very busy. She had already informed the family that things between her and Aleks were about to work out, but now Aleks's wife suddenly changed her mind, refused to give him a divorce and chose to accept the 'status quo' until 'Aleks's sickness' passed.

Hela thought only of Aleks.

Spring came as a fulfillment of enchanted dreams. The city had not known such a beautiful spring for years. In a splendor of lilac blossoms and may-bells all was flooded with sunlight and awash with intoxicating scents.

There was a general sense of a need to run to the limits of one's breath, to dance to exhaustion and be gay. This spring their parents were very generous. They allowed Reli – who spent hours studying – to go out with boys and to come home late at night without having to give an account of her actions.

This spring she was lovely and glamorous, and young Milosz, her latest beau, would look at her through eyes misty with love and tormented with doubts, taking in her graceful form and hating his pimples.

This spring also, Izio was permitted to devote his time to soccer, even at the expense of his studies in Ashkenazi Hebrew and Yiddish, and he was allowed to build, with Wlodek, a spacecraft in which they planned to take off to other places, at the expense of his studies at the Gymnasium.

The spring dazzled people's senses and created many sweet and crisp illusions. Mother bought herself two new dresses. After her operation she was thin once more and could allow herself fashionable dresses. Father bought a new painting for the apartment. He was pleased with his purchases and said that an art work always preserved its value.

After school girls and boys burst out of the school buildings and rushed to the green parks, where they mingled with each other and with the nature that had given them their youth.

In May Father and Olek went to a wonderful place called Muszyna, to rent a resort house for the months of July and August. For this journey Father bought himself a green Tyrolese hat and Olek wore hunting clothes.

The summer of 1939 was a joyous one. Everyone waited eagerly for the vacations, and promised themselves compensation for the difficult year that had passed.

When school ended they started packing: clothes, pots, sheets, all went into a huge wicker basket; Mother's fine clothes into two suitcases; and books, utensils, and shoes were put into several sacks. Grandma came along too. Her doctors had told her that the country air would cure her aches.

Irka was outwardly gleeful, but serious and responsible with regard to everything to do with her mother and little sister. Hania no longer spoke about going to a kibbutz without Olek. Since Nina's birth there had been a change in her. She had become more dependent, less aggressive. Olek believed that looking after the baby had released her from the difficult tensions she had suffered from for no apparent reason, but Irka knew that the submission had come after a profound crisis.

The train moved off. Father and Olek stood on the platform, waving goodbye. The children stuck their faces against the small window-panes. The fathers became smaller and smaller until they disappeared from view. The outskirts of the city passed by as on a conveyor-belt and yellow-green fields filled the windows. Before them stretched a broad land of good and fertile earth, which was known as the granary of Europe. At the small stations on the way the train was met by aging conductors with little flags and whistles who signaled to the train until it slowed down and stopped.

Windowless stone houses appeared on the sides of roads. Who lived in those strange houses? In a field a peasant walked after a horse and a plow, both moving slowly with their heads bent to the ground. The train gathered speed once more. Barefoot children tried to run after it on muddy earth tracks. In a field they saw a herd of sheep moving as one, with small rapid steps, all in the same direction, like a body without a head. One little sheep strayed from the way, and rushed around frantically until it caught up with the herd. Only then did it calm down and walk with them all towards their shared destiny.

Cows at pasture chewed patiently, swishing their tails to chase away the worrisome flies that tried to settle on their backs. The wheels of the train turned rapidly and a sharp whistle pierced the air from time to time.

A train journey can be a delight when you're a child, and your mother is beside you, and she buys you orangeade and triangular chocolate-coated wafers made by Piszinger.

Izio had brought the Kodak camera he had received for his *bar-mitzvah* and took one photograph after another.

'Don't overdo it,' said Mother. 'Who'll have time to arrange all those photographs? I still haven't put the pictures of your party in an album.'

He took no notice and continued photographing. He also taught Ania to use the camera: 'The important thing is to catch the picture in the lens.' Ania practiced and photographed without cease.

The country house the fathers had rented was large, spacious, and contained no luxuries. Water was drawn from a nearby well, lighting was by means of paraffin lamps. Large flies, their wings changing colors in the sunlight, circled around inside like gliders, buzzing noisily. In the middle of each room Marynia hung a yellow strip covered with poisonous glue – the flies last resting-place.

Beside the house was a small enclosure where feathered creatures and mammals lived peacefully together, busy obtaining food and in procreation.

Reli was suddenly filled with feelings of compassion for animals. In the city, she always used to feed stray dogs and cats she met on her path. Once, a beggar dressed in rags, his teeth chattering, had approached her and Reli had taken off her sweater and given it to him as a present. Now the animals aroused her sympathy: they procreated, and man milked them, exploited them, made them work for him, and finally slaughtered them for food. This sad truth about mankind struck Izio, Irka, and Ania too. These creatures were so human. The chicks ran about so gracefully and with so much understanding as they searched for grains, and the calves pressed their bodies against their mother cows seeking warmth and security.

'They're almost like people,' Izio said. He tried to find a way to explain to the girls that evolution did not contradict the Torah's version of God's creation of the world.

The girls watched the animals, hypnotized by their responses. There were pigs here too, two big ones and one little one. The country people too aroused the children's curiosity.

They in turn stood around and looked at the city people who had come to their house, having paid money to live in it without doing anything. Marynia explained that during the summer the permanent occupants of the house would sleep on bundles of hay in the barn. She herself tried to talk to country girls of her own age but they just giggled and exposed their white teeth, which would probably soon turn black.

'It's impossible to talk to them,' she decided.

Reli, Izio, Irka and Ania stood beside her, opposite a group of country folk. 'My family's like them too,' Marynia confessed. 'They wanted me to return to the village. But I'm already a city person.'

The children gazed up at Marynia. They had always seen her as an object, part of the apartment. It had never occurred to them that Marynia actually belonged to a different world, which they knew nothing about. She was only a few years older than Reli. Sometimes she borrowed books from Reli. Reli had got to know her taste and supplied her with novels that would appeal to housemaids. When she read, Marynia's finger would travel along the lines. The children standing in front of them resembled the barefoot children who had come out of the windowless stone houses and had run after the train. They were handsome children, with fair hair and blue eyes. Flies sat stubbornly on different parts of their body, and their bare feet were black as the earth.

'In our village there is no electricity yet. No telephone either.'

'Newspapers?'

She burst out laughing. 'Who can read there? What would they need newspapers for? They're born and they die in the same place, and they don't know that anything else exists.'

One of the village girls, who must have been mad, left the group and went to the end of the yard, where she raised her skirt and squatted down. The urine she released sprayed onto her bare feet, which she later wiped with the edge of her skirt.

'She isn't wearing underpants,' said Irka in amazement, and Izio turned his head away.

On the other side of the hill the river flowed, its water washing the sleepy banks. Trains, full of people, arrived here one after the other. Multitudes of people were fleeing from the great cities, escaping civilization and noise, coming to the coolness of the forest and the clearness of the river, to breathe truly fresh air.

At one of the small hotels at the forest's edge, Marek and Balka had taken a room. They had not managed to take a honeymoon trip outside Poland as they had planned. Muszyna had enchanted them at first sight, they said, and they felt it had no less to offer than the mountains or the famous spas in Germany. 'They'll have a baby soon,' the children whispered, 'you can see it already.'

'Don't talk nonsense,' Marynia said. 'They'll have a baby when the stork brings them one.'

They burst out laughing.

In another 'pension' lived Hela, Aleks and his wife. The mothers took care not to speak about them in the children's presence. 'As if we care,' Irka said, calmly. 'Maybe I too won't be content with just one when I grow up. I can love many people. Maybe I'll have two men too.'

The children grew grave. Some people had more than they needed and some didn't have anything. In another rented room without conveniences lived Rachel and Adela and their children. Rachel behaved like a young girl, tripping about mischievously, laughing, letting her hair loose. The men in the resort looked at her with hungry eyes.

In another country house whose occupants had also moved into their barn, Wlodek was staying with his mother and sister. There too there was no water or electricity, and they too had fled from the newspapers and the telephone. Wlodek could not be relied on – his head and heart were muddled because of a red-haired girl aged 13. This summer Reli was in love with Milosz, Uncle Marek's young brother-in-law. Their love story was quite a serious one, for both of them were on the verge of maturity.

They spent the mornings on the banks of the Poprad River. Its water flowed in a mighty current towards the Dunaiec. The Poprad and the Dunaiec merged somewhere, increasing their force and together washing the banks of several lands on their way to the Vistula.

Izio and Irka, the two swimmers in the group, went to acquaint themselves with the water in the river. Their first meeting surprised them. The current was very strong. With hesitant steps they waded into the waves to reach the deeper water. Ania stumbled on the sharp stones on the bank of the river.

'Just a few more steps,' the swimmers called to her. 'In here the river bottom is as soft as down!'

They started swimming. The current took them up as if they were weightless feathers. They had an unfamiliar sensation of fear and helplessness, like tiny non-existent grains against the might of the elements. It was impossible to swim against the current. They had to learn how to resist it. If a storm arose or they entered a whirlpool, the waves would carry them off. But there was no storm. The sky was blue and clear.

The anxious mothers stood on the bank.

'This reminds me of the mother hen that hatched a batch of duck's eggs. Her duck chicks went swimming and the mother hen stood nervously clucking on the bank. Like our mothers.'

The swimmers came out of the water wet and gleaming, spraying drops of water around that glistened like pearls. Irka's little sister, a straw hat on her head, made mud-cakes. Two girls with fine figures, their skin the color of milk chocolate, passed by, riding on bicycles. These were the Krischer sisters, Paula and Celina. They rode without using their hands. Izio gazed at their suntanned skin and his glance met the proud and mischievous glance of the black-haired Celina. Irka suddenly became sad.

'I can ride like that too, it's no great feat.'

In the center of the esplanade there was a dance platform. Reli and Milosz spent many hours there, embraced in the tango. The dance floor was usually packed. Reli had many admirers. Whenever Milosz left her for a moment, young men presented themselves to her, sweating from the dance, and bowed, asking her to dance.

'She mustn't refuse, because that's insulting,' Izio explained to Irka, who lowered her eyes and said quietly: 'If you asked me to dance, I wouldn't refuse.'

'But I can't dance!'

'It's easy. Look,' she said, and took both his hands and led him to the dance platform.

'You hear the music, you move to the rhythm, and try not to step on other people's feet.'

Everyone danced. Until they became dizzy. Until they had no strength left.

In the afternoons Grandma joined them for the traditional walk along the tree-lined path that led to the forest on the other side of the river. Here the road was paved and at its end stood a modern house, the only one of its kind in the village. This was the 'Home for the Blind'. Its residents were people who had lost their sight in the First World War, which the mothers remembered so clearly. The house was surrounded by a cultivated garden with a row of benches in it, but the residents preferred to go outside the fence, with the aid of white walking sticks or seeing-eye dogs, and to walk in the tree-lined road among the vacationers. The blind men were mostly in their late 30s. When the war ended in 1918, they had been 20 years old at the most.

Izio rode his bicycle, taking care to move out of the way of the blind people, while trying to imitate the Krischer sisters' style of riding. Grandma would go out of her mind. 'Izio, don't upset Grandma,' Mother would say to him, her eyes not moving from the figures walking cautiously, in the radiant light of the path, as they groped their way through the thick and constant darkness in which they lived. Suddenly she said:

'Izio, ride somewhere and see if you can find me a newspaper, I have to know what's going on in the world.'

He turned around and rode off, and quickly vanished from sight.

Mother immediately regretted having sent him off on his own.

'How could you have sent him off on his own?' Grandma scolded her. A tremor ran through Mother's body. It was getting dark, and the blind men were groping their way back to the garden of their house. There were fewer vacationers on the path. Back at their house Marynia had lit the paraffin lamps in the rooms and Izio had not yet returned. Everyone went out onto the main road and stood watching tensely from the observation point on the hill. And then, on the purple horizon, two shadows riding on bicycles appeared, with the setting sun behind them. The pair of them, against the background of the huge red sunset, were holding hands. A freckled boy and a black-haired girl.

'Did you get a newspaper?' Mother asked.

'What?' He sounded abstracted. His gaze followed Celina as she rode off in the direction of the sunset.

'What? A newspaper? No. I didn't get one. There's none in the whole village.'

'It doesn't matter,' said Mother. 'The main thing is that you're back. You might have fallen off your bicycle, or worse.'

A troupe of gypsies arrived at the garden. Everyone surrounded them as they produced enchanting sounds from their violins. Sad sentimental songs reached the listeners' ears:

Gypsy, gypsy, who are you? Man without home, without country or land? Happy I am with my violin, my song and my melody ...

About ten minutes train journey away from here was the resort town Krynica. Glittering cafes, elegant people, five o'clock teas and dancing characterized this town. A place for people with a lot of money and time to spend, Father used to say. Grandma longed for a bit of luxury and glamor, and Mother sometimes took the afternoon train with her to Krynica, to meet acquaintances and to sit in cafés.

Reli and Milosz would walk from Muszyna to Krynica, through forests and valleys, with packs on their backs and hats on their heads. They would rest beside each other in the shade of pine trees, on a carpet of pine needles and learn to love.

One day they received a note about a parcel that had arrived from Krakow. Mother went to the post office, and the clerk brought her a large heavy crate, which she could not lift without help. She hired a cart and with the carter's help brought the crate into the house. Everyone gathered around in curiosity to see what was in the crate.

'Watermelon! Watermelon! Red and juicy!' And they quickly cut it into slices and the watery red juice poured down their faces.

'But the market here is full of watermelons. He would have done better to send us a newspaper.'

That day, towards the end of summer, Olek arrived for a brief holiday. He stole into Bronka's kitchen and asked for something to eat.

'Just don't give me watermelon, please, I need something more solid. Everyone at my place is on a diet, all they eat is cucumbers and carrots.'

'What, the little one too? Already!' Mother asked, and gave him buttered rolls and wild berries with sugar and cream.

'Can you imagine?' he replied, his mouth full of sweet cream. 'Hania's already worried about the baby's future and the fine figure she wants her to have.' And he laughed, with his mouth full.

'That's not funny at all,' Mother said, and gave him another bread roll.

One of the destinations on their walks was the oak forest, which spread across the broad ridge separating Muszyna from Krynica. One afternoon the group went out and climbed among the oak trees to the mountain top. At the head of the group was little Nina, like a tiny gazelle. After her came Irka and Izio, who exchanged a few words and a few restrained smiles. Then came Hania and Olek, silent, concentrating on how they stepped on the unstable earth beneath their feet, and attentive to the whisperings of the wind. At the end of the line came Ania, with the camera. At the top of the mountain, on a soft rustling carpet, they stopped to rest. Below, the river streamed. From the dance platform on the other side of it came sounds of waltz music. They stood on the plateau, and Olek bowed to his wife.

'May I have this dance, Madame?'

'Are you crazy?' A blush came to her cheeks, and there was hesitancy in her voice. But a moment later she began to dance with him. Above them the heavily-leafed branches formed a canopy, and a single bird accompanied the waltz music. Izio

smiled to Irka and made a clumsy gesture, as if he too wanted
to ask her to dance. She looked at him expectantly. Both of
them were very tense. And then little Nina pushed in
between them, and the tension dissipated. The three of them
looked on forgivingly as the parents danced gaily. Olek kept
stumbling and led Hania clumsily. 'Where's your responsibility?' Hania scolded him. 'We almost went over the side!' She
took the initiative and began to lead. The surface was full of
obstacles. Her skirt opened like a parachute.

Ania stood to the side and took photographs.

That evening the children went out into the yard to look at
the stars. Izio and Irka got into a deep conversation about life
and death. Is there life after death? How temporary our life in
the universe is, compared with eternity. We come to the world
like guests, for a short visit. And those stars above us, each star
might be a complete world, perhaps each of them is like our
earth, for the earth too is a star which together with other stars
revolves around the sun. What is this perpetual motion of
each star, around itself and around the sun! Can one star catch
up with another? Anyone who believes that it was God who
created all this, also believes in life after death. After we die
will we become stars? Are the body and the soul of equal
importance? Or is it the soul that is important, and will it be
released only at the moment of death?

A star fell.

'Did you see?' Irka cried. 'When a star falls, something
ends. Something finishes, ceases to be, vanishes ...'

'Think of a wish. Quickly!'

'I've thought of one,' she whispered. 'I want to go on living.'

'Me too,' the boy said.

They sat close to each other, trembling. They had already
planned their world to come and had nothing else to talk about.
Their conversation stopped. It was impossible to photograph,
because of the darkness. One could only register by sound his
gropings and her hesitations – fear and wonder. Ania slipped
into the house. A small flame inside a sooty glass flickered and
trembled, struggling for its existence. It was hard to fall asleep.

The next morning Marek arrived, running, with a newspaper in his hand. The first newspaper since they had come here. A special edition, bad news: a general mobilization of the Polish army had been announced. The Germans had massed huge concentrations of troops on Poland's western borders, ready to attack. Immediately a telegram came from Father: Come home.

They started packing hastily. Olek ran to the railway station to buy tickets. The tickets were all sold out. Masses of people crowded the place, long lines stretched from all the ticket-offices. The army had appropriated trains, and the station was full of soldiers. 'Soldiers travel first. They're going off to defend us.' No one objected. The trains left at irregular times. Everything was disorganized. Finally they managed to get on a train. The crush was terrible. The train was full of soldiers in four-cornered caps. Young men, almost children, with arms and equipment. Mother said that this was how all those blind men at Muszyna had looked 20 years ago.

Hela, pale and frightened, pushed her way through the crowd.

'Where's Aleks?' Mother asked, not thinking about the presence of the children.

'He left this morning. He got a draft notice.'

The train crawled. It stopped near army camps, to take more soldiers aboard. From the villages and the fields women, old and young, came out and waved their hands or their kerchiefs. Their long broad skirts danced as they ran.

'Come home safely!' a young woman shouted. She raised her apron and wiped her eyes. Barefoot children ran in groups after the train. A little girl with a long plait stumbled, fell, and burst out crying bitterly: 'Daddy, daddy.' The mountains cast dark shadows on the fields.

The train entered a long black tunnel. On the other side of the tunnel the sky was black. Night had descended early. The day was over. The last summer was over too.

Finally the train stopped. Father was standing on the platform. Tall and strong, a handsome man in the prime of his life.

'Thank God we're together again,' Mother said.

Only then did everyone notice how exhausted she was. Before the journey, Father had asked them to look after her. She's weak after the operation, he had said. And they had promised to do so, but they had forgotten. They had been busy with their own affairs and had forgotten the entire world. The time had been so short and everyone had thought only of himself, his own world, even about his own death, but not about another.

The children lowered their heads.

'Don't preach at them now,' Mother said. 'They were all right. And I feel fine.' She looked as if she was about to faint.

'There'll be a war,' Father said. 'If you want,' he looked at her, ignoring her paleness, 'we can get on another train now and cross the border. I've taken out enough money to get us to Palestine. That's the only place we'll be able to find refuge. Everything here is sinking.'

'I don't know you,' she interrupted him. 'I've never heard you speak like this.'

He ignored this and went on:

'If we reach the shores of the Land, whatever way we can, our people will not abandon us there. There they have a feeling of brotherhood and purpose. They won't allow us to be thrown into the sea, and we'll defend ourselves together. If we want to do it we'll have to give up luxuries we're used to, but we can become a part of the upbuilding of the Land.'

Mother was pale as chalk.

'When did you see the light?' she asked softly.

He didn't answer, but continued to press:

'Do you want to? Are you ready? Here, in that train that's standing over there.'

Mother was about to faint. The children had heard, and couldn't believe their ears. Why, in another two days school would be starting again, had Father forgotten? Mother was pale and Grandma's face was flushed. All her old pains were attacking her again.

'Do you want to run off and abandon me?'

Father made an impatient gesture.

'I can't,' said Mother.

'You come too', Father said to Grandma. 'Here's the train.'
'Now???!'

'Yes, now. As you are.'

'That's impossible. How can I? I have to get home first, arrange some things. And what about my sons, my daughters-in-law, and their children?'

Mother could barely stand on her feet.

'And our apartment?' she said to Father. 'And the new house you've built!'

The children were impatient. Six hours train journey through the tunnels and in the dreadful crush had wearied them completely. They wanted to get home. Home, to their lovely comfortable apartment. To their comfortable beds, with their clean sheets and blankets.

Olek and Hania came past, loaded with their belongings.

'Where are you going?' Father asked them.

'We're going home.'

They went on. Irka pulled her little sister, and vanished after her parents. Hela, her hands full of belongings, said she had to get home. Perhaps there'd be some news.

Marek and Balka were already sitting in a carriage. Rachel pulled the fat Adela and their five children and stopped beside Father.

'You decide,' she said to him, directly. 'I'm willing to get on this train right now.'

'You're out of your mind!' Adela shouted at her, and all the little children started crying.

'Our husbands are waiting for us at home.'

Father no longer stood as erect as before. On one side of him stood Rachel and on the other his wife and his children.

Someone passed by them and laughed:

'What's all the panic? There's no certainty that there'll be a war. France and England have already pronounced warnings, and so has America.'

Mother said weakly:

'In any case I don't have the strength to travel now. It's a pity that ...' She didn't finish the sentence.

Father left Rachel, and wound his arm around Mother. She

leaned on him and he supported her and helped her into the carriage.

'Soon you'll be able to rest,' he tried to soothe her as they sat in the upholstered carriage, under a black roof which closed them off on all sides. Outside, a terrible storm raged. Thunder and lightning blasted the world. The horses galloped through the streets of the panic-stricken city, whose inhabitants had started to prepare it against attacks from the air and the land. In the parks trenches had been dug; paper had been stuck on the windows and black screens closed out all the sources of light. The city was blacked out. Reli's head rested on her brother's shoulder and both of them fell asleep. Father and Mother sat tense, fear and weariness in their eyes. Father's self-confidence had vanished.

'I was wrong, I was wrong,' he whispered, over and over, and his words were swallowed up in the loud noise of the thunder. Mother covered her ears. The carriage reached their house and stopped. Marynia stepped down first, light-footed, not reaching out a hand to those coming after her, and moved off rapidly, vanishing in the darkness. There was a real deluge, and the others had difficulty getting out of the carriage.

'Perhaps we really should have got on to that train,' Mother said, in despair.

All the good trains had left the city. It was already too late.

Afterword

Other trains, not long after, transported this group of people to the extermination camps.

My story is the story of the calm before the storm.

All characters mentioned in this book are based on real people. Here and there names have been changed, and vague recollections have been given fictional embodiment. I wanted to paint these characters who died before my eyes in living colors, to distinguish them from the six million and to redeem my dear ones from anonymity and oblivion.

Only six remained of our family, and today we six have become 30. How many would all of us have numbered? Of the six survivors, only three live in the Land of Israel, and the other three live in other parts of the Western world. Still. That is the fate of our nation.

Of Grandfather Weinfeld, who arrived in Galicia towards the end of the last century and fathered three sons and five daughters there, no trace remains on that soil. The same is true of the family of my mother – Bronka, née Plessner.

Notes

A Death in the Family

1. Afternoon prayer.
2. A prayer for the dead.
3. The righteous.
4. A prayer.
5. Religious dress.
6. The required forum of ten Jewish men over the age of 13 for Jewish religious ceremony and public prayer.
7. Place of Jewish learning.
8. An ancient structure containing a commercial center and a museum.
9. Stones used for a game such as 'jacks'.

Bronka

1. Afternoon and evening prayers.

Gunpowder

1. Desciples.
2. Non-Jews.
3. A Polish patriot who concealed her womanhood and died in battle.

Happy is He Who Believes

1. A resort town in the Carpathians.

A Black Sheep and a Pair of Doves.

1. A common Polish proverb.
2. Agricultral training.

PART II

Man's Home is His Castle

1. A prayer said after Shabbat.

PART III

Children's Games

1. Trade School.

2. The one week mourning period.
3. Jewish education school for boys.
4. Leader of a rebellion against Poland's conquerors, in which Jewish volunteers under the command of Berek Joselewicz had found for Poland's freedom, some losing their lives.
5. A boy's thirteenth birthday.

'Jews – to Palestine'

1. Later to be one of the editors of the Tel Aviv evening paper *Ma'ariv*.

Laughter and Tears

1. Ram's horn.
2. Opening prayer for Yom Kippur.